The Dark Lake

The Realm of Light, Volume 2

Sunny R. Winstead

Published by Sunny Winstead, 2024.

THE DARK LAKE

First edition. May 16, 2024.

ISBN: 979-8224601776

Written by Sunny R. Winstead.

Also by Sunny R. Winstead

The Realm of Light
The Lady Guardian
The Dark Lake

To Michael, for supporting my writing, and for everything else.

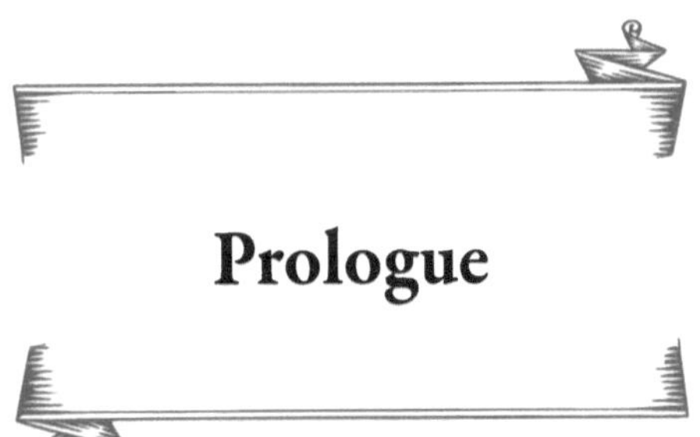

Prologue

Krale's hand shook as he held the bone to the light. The tan, roughened nub looked like a pebble or a piece of debris, but the mage knew it for what it was: a bone from the tip of a man's finger. A distal phalanx. He smiled to himself for remembering the scientific term. That was really no surprise though, he thought. He was a learned man after all, a man who had succeeded beyond his beginnings.

And yet this bone represented his failure. He wanted to believe it was anger that caused his hand to shake. But as he sat on the edge of the bed, with the leather pouch open and its contents splayed around him, Krale knew the emotion he felt was not anger, but shame. Shame that he had failed to do what the old man had done so easily. Shame that–despite all his education and training–he had not been able to master the magic that a mere Guardian had used on him years ago.

Krale set the bone fragment carefully on the bed and pulled back his left sleeve. The skin of his inner forearm was ridged and disfigured. It was the site of the failed blood-bind, and Krale's eyes were drawn to it no matter how often he told himself to ignore it.

Staring out the window, he stroked the ruined skin with the palm of his right hand, first slowly and gently, and then faster and with more pressure. Still not looking, he picked up the bone and began to roll it along the skin of his forearm. At first, he couldn't feel anything, but as he pushed harder, his forearm began to sting and then burn. When he allowed himself to look down, there was a trace of blood, bright red against the dark red of the scar.

He sighed and rolled his sleeve back into place. He put the bone fragment into his mouth and sucked it clean. Then he carefully patted it against the bed cover. Its color lightened as it dried, and he thought about the remnants of his blood being absorbed into the honeycombed depths of the bone. The thought made him queasy.

Tiburon had taken one of Krale's teeth, long ago. From the other boys, the old man had taken bone. Krale had tried both in his turn, but neither had worked.

Now he began to line the objects up on the bed cover. They must always be returned to the pouch in the same order, ending with the bone. With steady hands, Krale placed each item into the pouch, enjoying the suppleness of the leather as he pulled the cord to cinch the pouch closed. Straightening his cloak and smoothing his left sleeve several times, he then lifted the strap over his head and positioned the pouch at his waist.

Krale might have failed with the magic of the blood-bind. But that was far from his only option. The old man would be sorry for what he'd done all those years ago. And the world would recognize that Krale was right; it would recognize his power and the truth of his cause. He just needed the Sword. And someone to wield it. It was nearly time.

Chapter 1

Erritus and I examined the cake. It leaned to one side, and its surface was pocked with bits of cake that had stuck in the pan. I'd tried to match each piece to its corresponding hole, but the result could hardly be called a success. I looked at Erritus, and she met my gaze. Erritus–a charmingly efficient, elderly woman–had been the cook at the Peace guest house for decades, and while she didn't often bake desserts herself, she had high standards for everything that came out of her kitchen. I shifted the cake, optimistically centering it more precisely on the plate.

Erritus took a breath. "Well then," she said, in her chirpy, high-pitched voice. "I can see that the filling is a pretty color, and with a little dusting of sugar over the top...well then...yes, certainly..." she trailed off, nodding her head several times for emphasis.

I sighed and tucked a strand of hair behind my ear. "Thanks for your help, Erritus. I tried to follow your directions, but I'm kind of hopeless in the kitchen. Maybe I should've tried a simpler dish, but I really wanted to bring something special to the Wintertide supper." I sighed again and wiped my hands on a towel. Erritus began to clean the counter.

My sisters, Paislie and Bellina, and Bellina's husband Obrin, had invited me, Andris, and JenVie to a Wintertide supper in town. I appreciated the invitation, but I was anxious too. I was starting to reacquaint with my sisters, but I worried that I'd accidentally say or do the wrong thing. They were kind people, and I knew my worries were groundless, but still... Maybe it was just that I'd grown used to being solitary over the six years that I'd been the only female Guard at the Guardians' Peace. I'd become skilled in my work, but I still doubted myself when it came to the people I cared about.

The past months had brought so many changes though. I thought back to the autumn day in Associate Prefect Klinweh's office when I'd agreed to serve as a liaison to the three visiting scholars from Clanstin College. I remembered the morning in Matron's study when I'd agreed to help with her niece Linnia, a prickly adolescent devastated by tragedy. I thought of all the decisions I'd made since then, all the choices and actions and friendships that had led to now. *I've changed so much, so how can I still feel wrong-footed over a cake or a family supper? That doesn't make any sense.* I shook my head at my own foolishness.

I'd grown up in Clanstin, the oldest daughter of a tailor. My parents had owned a small house, and my father had rented–and later owned–a shop on the merchants' street. Bellina and Paislie ran Father's shop now, and they lived in the small apartment above. Bellina and Obrin were expecting their first child, and the three of them seemed content, even happy.

And yet when I saw them, I wrestled with guilt over leaving home when my sisters were still so young and my mother so numbed with grief. I couldn't stop thinking of all the things I hadn't done that an older sister should. All the ways in which I might have helped my family if I'd been at home instead of training or living at the Peace. I wasn't usually one to dwell on the past, but when it came to my sisters, my mind looped again and again to what might have been if I hadn't been so single-minded in pursuing my own goals.

"Marolaine?" Erritus asked tentatively, interrupting my thoughts, "would you like me to make a cake for you to bring tomorrow? I have plenty of ingredients for a nice butter cake, or maybe a lemon cake with raspberry filling? It would be no trouble at all, you know."

I looked into her wrinkled face. *She's being kind; maybe I should say yes. But I don't want to give up on this.* This cake would hardly fill the gap of years or make up for everything I'd missed. It certainly wouldn't impress anyone with my culinary skills. And yet it suddenly seemed important.

"No thanks, Erritus," I said with a grin and a shake of my head. "I know it doesn't look like much, but I think it'll taste good, and it's the best I can do right now. I'll take your advice about the dusting sugar, and hope for the best."

Erritus's eyes twinkled. "That's a girl," she said warmly, "And don't fret, Marolaine, many's the cake I made in my early years that wasn't perfect either. Everyone has to learn. It's thinking of your family that will be most important to them, I'm sure of it." She smiled and patted my arm. I couldn't imagine Erritus ever producing a cake like this, but I smiled back. *Maybe the dining room will be dark...*

The guest house's lobby door banged shut, and Erritus and I glanced at each other as we heard the sound of laughter and adolescent voices. *Oh no, not Linnia, not when I've just come to peace with this ridiculous cake.* I looked around for something to cover the cake, or alternately, someplace to hide myself.

Linnia and Wyst burst into the kitchen bringing with them the dry smell of winter air and hay. Their faces were flushed with cold, and by their clothes I guessed they'd just come up from the stables.

"You two, out of my clean kitchen with those mucky boots of yours!" Erritus pointed to their feet and wagged her finger, mock-stern, or perhaps fully serious. Linnia pulled off her woolen cap, releasing her brown hair in a cloud of static. Beside her, Wyst, shook her own curls and rubbed her hands together.

"I'm sorry, Erritus," Linnia said sweetly, tilting her head to the side, "it smelled so lovely that we just had to come and see what you were cooking." Wyst, the friendly girl who served as kitchen and house maid, bobbed her head in agreement with her friend as she unbuttoned her jacket.

"Oh yes," Wyst beamed, "we were hoping for some of your wonderful biscuits, Erritus, or maybe some soup to warm us up?"

Linnia's eyes moved quickly around the kitchen, and she spotted the cake, alone and defenseless on the counter.

"Oh my," she said, gulping down a giggle. "Marolaine, you didn't tell us you were baking today. Is that a cake?" she pointed.

"Indeed, it is," said Erritus curtly, "and seeing as how it's not for you girls, I'd kindly ask you not to tease Marolaine about it."

"Tease?" said Wyst, her brown eyes wide and innocent, "why would we possibly tease her?"

Both girls began to giggle then, and I shook my head. "I know, I know. I'm a terrible cook and everyone knows it. I just wanted to make something special to take to my sisters' supper tomorrow, and Erritus was nice enough to give me a lesson..." I trailed off. I could see the girls were trying to contain themselves. "Obviously it wasn't a complete success." I shrugged at this understatement and a splutter of laughter escaped Linnia.

"I hope the man you marry knows how to cook, Marolaine," she said, "otherwise..."

"Now you stop that, young lady," scolded Erritus. "Miss Marolaine is a long way from marriage, and even so, cooking's not the only talent that can win a man, not by a long ways." Erritus stopped, then blushed at her own comment. She brushed her small hands together briskly. "Now out, you two troublemakers. Go wash up and put on some proper lady-like clothes. Then, you can both come back and clean this mud off my floor." As she spoke, she pulled a plate of biscuits–golden brown and studded with dates–from a cupboard and slid them across to the girls with a wink. "Now off with you!"

WE PAUSED OUTSIDE THE shop on the merchants' street in Clanstin. Although my sisters ran it now, Father's sign still hung above the door, his name painted in plain black letters against the gray of the wood. Through the window, I could see the bolts of fabric neatly stacked, waiting to be turned into dresses and jackets and cloaks. Memories filled me.

Andris hesitated too. The young mathematics professor was neatly dressed, with his dark hair combed to the side and his beard trimmed very short. He'd been unusually quiet on our walk to town, and his handsome face was serious now as he looked at the front of the shop. *I wonder if Paislie has any idea how he feels about her?* I gave his arm a squeeze and he smiled, handing me the bulky cake holder that he'd insisted on carrying.

"Come on, you two," said JenVie, shaking her head and smiling at us like a fond but exasperated parent, "this is a family supper we're going to, not some dreaded committee meeting at the college. Let's go inside before everyone wonders what we're doing out here." JenVie was fair and petite, her pretty face framed by the fluffy pink hat that she often wore on cold days. It was hard to believe I'd met the two of them only four months ago when they first came to the Peace as visiting scholars from Clanstin College.

I thought of how jealous I'd been of Professor JenVie Twill on the first night we'd met, when she glided around the reception room in her blue silk gown, so friendly and self-assured. And to be honest, it hadn't been just that first night. JenVie's prettiness, social skills, intelligence, sweetness, flirtatiousness, even her lovely singing voice: all these things had annoyed me at one time or another over the past months. We all have feelings that do us no credit, and I was relieved to have put my envy in the past.

I smiled back at my friend, then stepped forward and knocked on the door.

PAISLIE, MY YOUNGER sister, greeted us at the outer door to the shop. Her cheeks were flushed pink, and she had an apron tied around her waist. But my eyes went immediately to her left shoulder, which was immobilized by a sling of white fabric.

"Paislie! What happened?" I asked.

She gave a shrug and a smile. "Oh, it's nothing to worry about. Come on in, you three!" Without waiting for our replies, she turned and led us upstairs to the small apartment above the shop, her light brown hair bouncing around her shoulders and wafting a faint herby smell.

In the years that Father had owned the shop, he'd rented the small upper apartment to a series of elderly couples. This was the first time I'd seen it since my sisters and Obrin had moved in, and I looked around with curiosity. My gaze took in the clean, neat space with its cheerful hand-stitched curtains, rag rugs, and hanging plants. It didn't look like much room for three people though, and I wondered how they would squeeze in the baby who was due to arrive in a few weeks. Bellina had told me that they hoped to eventually purchase a cottage and were putting money aside for this goal.

Bellina rose from the kitchen table and came to greet us, while her husband Obrin waved from the kitchen. He was a large, placid man. He worked as a groundsman at the College, but he also helped in the shop, and I knew from experience that he was talented with a needle. Apparently, he had culinary skills as well, because, like Paislie, he was wearing an apron, and I could see he was mashing turnips. He smiled at us without speaking, then returned to his task.

Bellina greeted me with a long embrace, and I felt the hard roundness of her stomach against me as she whispered, "I'm glad you came, Mari. You look lovely."

After a few minutes of greetings, JenVie had established herself in the kitchen, Andris was setting the table, and Bellina and I were at ease in the sitting area. This room was open to the kitchen, and so in fact all of us were very much in the same space.

"Paislie wouldn't say what happened to her arm," I said to Bellina. "Should I not ask, or should I be worried?"

Bellina shifted on the sofa, looking for that comfortable position that eludes women at the end of their pregnancies. "Well..." she started, ever the diplomat.

"I didn't say I wouldn't tell you," Paislie called cheerfully from the kitchen, where she and JenVie were arranging a platter of sliced chicken and roasted vegetables–my sister using only her right hand. "I just didn't want it to be the first thing we talked about when you walked in the door," she continued.

"Paislie never wants to cause any worry or trouble," said Bellina fondly.

"What happened?" asked JenVie.

Paislie patted her arm. "It's nothing to worry about, really. The truth is, I was injured by a man who came into the shop a few days ago."

I raised my eyebrows, and I saw Andris lower his. I was trained to be observant, and to listen before asking questions. It was a skill that Father had taught, and the Peace had reinforced, and it usually served me well. Still, there was a knot in my stomach as I kept my face calm.

"What did he do to you?" Andris's words were sharp. He stood at the table with a plate held in mid-air. Paislie turned in his direction as if surprised.

"Well, I'm alright," she said quickly, "which is the main thing. It was four days ago now, in the middle of the afternoon. A man came into the shop, but he didn't look like a customer. You know, he didn't look around, didn't seem interested in the shop. In fact, he immediately came over to the counter where I was standing. He...well, he asked about Linnia actually. He asked if I'd seen her recently, if she had any plans to come into the shop. He knew her full name, so at first, I assumed that he knew her. But when I said no, I hadn't seen her, he got more insistent, and then kind of angry. I knew by then that he obviously wasn't a friend, and so I asked him to please leave the shop unless there was something he wanted to buy. Truthfully, I was frightened..." Here she paused, and looked toward Bellina, who nodded slightly.

Paislie took a visible breath and continued. "He walked around to the side of the counter–which I didn't like at all–and his voice changed, and he said it might be worth my while to give him the information he wanted. I wasn't sure if that was a threat, or maybe an offer of a bribe, but in any case, I asked him again to leave the shop."

"I wish I'd been there," Obrin said quietly, adding salt to the turnips, his eyes down.

"Me too," said Bellina. "Obrin was at work at the College, and I'd gone upstairs to take a short nap since the shop was quiet. I didn't hear anything until Paislie came up." She shook her head. I had no doubt that my capable sister, even hugely pregnant, would be a match for almost any situation.

"What happened then?" asked JenVie. She was standing close to Paislie, and her voice was direct and comforting. I thought about what a good listener JenVie was, and how reliable, despite her sometimes-frivolous demeanor.

Paislie's voice was quieter, and a little hurried, as if she were anxious to get to the end of her story. "Well, he came behind the counter and grabbed my arm. I tried to pull away but there wasn't much space. I called out, but there was no one close to hear. So, I reached around behind me on the counter and grabbed a pair of scissors, and I stabbed them into the back of his hand." She sounded matter-of-fact, but her hand was clenched white around the serving spoon she held.

"You stabbed him?" JenVie repeated, her eyes wide.

"Yes," said Paislie, "I mean, I didn't know what else to do and he had me kind of trapped behind the counter."

"That was smart." Andris's voice was tight, but he forced a smile. "The women in this family know how to handle themselves, I've learned that much from Marolaine." Andris was usually light-hearted, but I could see that even this small joke was an effort. I felt the same anger that I read on his face.

Without thinking, I walked across the open space and put my arms around my younger sister. Her hair was soft against my cheek, and it smelled of fresh-baked bread and lavender. I felt her relax against me briefly, before taking a deep breath. I stepped back, and then I wasn't sure what to do next. Emotional interactions with my sisters–with anyone really–were new territory and I was always afraid of a misstep.

JenVie smiled at me, then stepped closer and squeezed my hand. Her hand was warm and soft, and I was glad for her support. She was one of those people who always knew the right thing to do or say, and I was glad she approved of my gesture. We both turned back toward Paislie.

"He was surprised by that I think." Paislie gave a half-smile and quirked her eyebrows, then continued. "He yelled out and shoved me back against the wall. He said something rude to me, and then he left the shop." She shrugged, as if this were a usual day in the life of a seamstress. There was silence, except for the rhythmic sound of Obrin chopping parsley.

"Did you recognize him?" I asked finally. "What did he look like?"

"I couldn't really tell. He wore a cloak with the hood up. He was taller than average, not old or young that I could tell, and his face was clean shaven. It's hard to remember, but I don't think I'd ever seen him before."

"I assume you contacted town security?"

"Oh yes," said Bellina. "Paislie woke me up after the man left, and once I made sure she was alright, that was the first thing we did."

"And?"

"They came right away," said Paislie. "But there wasn't much they could do. I gave what information I could, and they wrote it down. They said they'd increase their walking patrol along the street for a few days, and they suggested that I shouldn't work alone in the shop. I was a little vague about the man's threats at first, because honestly, I wasn't sure if I should involve Linnia. She's had so much trouble as it is..." Her voice trailed off.

Bellina added, "but I convinced her to tell all that had happened, including the man's questions about Linnia. The security officer said they'd talk to Linnia's guardian–Mrs. Rosevale–but be discreet about it."

JenVie squeezed Paislie's arm and said briskly, "It sounds like you did everything right, Paislie. It also sounds very frightening. I'm guessing you might want to talk more about it, but maybe not right now?"

Paislie looked gratefully at the pretty professor. "Thanks, JenVie, you're right. Now that everyone knows the story, let's get back to our supper." She smiled in a determined way, and we all smiled back. The least we could do was support her bravery by making small talk and eating the roast chicken and vegetables before they got cold.

AS WE WERE LEAVING, Bellina presented the small gifts that are traditionally given by the hosts at a Wintertide supper. For JenVie there was a bottle of rose water, for Andris a book of local maps, and for me a beaded bracelet with a silver clasp.

Remembering the dress I'd worn at the Solstice party, with its beautifully beaded bodice, I suspected that my bracelet was Obrin's work as well. He just smiled when I asked though, and said I should wear the bracelet for good fortune. It struck me to wonder if his beadwork might be a form of marveling. Marveling was a gift that some in the realm were born with, often a small talent or idiosyncrasy with little practical purpose. Unlike magic, which required rigorous training and study, marveling just *was*. I had none myself, and neither had my parents or sisters. In any case, the bracelet was truly exquisite, and I smiled as I tucked the jewelry box into the pocket of my jacket.

Andris had been reserved throughout the afternoon, almost tense. He was normally funny and boisterous, and I wasn't sure whether it was his nerves around my sister, or his anger over the story of her injury, that had led him to be a restrained version of himself. I'd been glad when he declined a second glass of wine, but other than that, the visit did not seem to have been a success for him.

The walk back to the Peace was quiet, despite JenVie's efforts at conversation. She commented on the delicious food, laughed kindly over my cake (which was surprisingly good), and complimented my family on their generosity. She reminded me a bit of Dr. Li's assistant, Orme, that gentle, patient man who'd had a knack for smoothing uncomfortable situations. My mind drifted briefly to Orme's death, but I pulled it back. "No need to add trouble to trouble," as Father used to say.

I have enough to worry about with Paislie and Bellina. I wonder if the man who threatened her was the same man who attacked Andris and I in town last fall? What if he comes back? Is there anything I can do? I know they reported it to the town's security forces, and I assume that the officers talked to Matron. But it seems like there should be something more...some other way to keep them safe...

I was preoccupied, and so we were almost through the gate leading back onto the grounds of the Peace before I realized that Manfrid and Laeglin were on duty. The Peace had two secure points of entry–the front gate and the gate at the Apprentices' Academy–and the rest of the perimeter was protected by spellwork. Those Guardians who served the Peace as soldiers took on a number of duties, including guarding the gates. Manfred and I often worked together, but it was less common to see Laeglin here, since his main duty had become serving as Prefect Tal's project manager and assistant.

As we passed the gatehouse, Manfrid waved cheerfully. Laeglin nodded to the three of us as a group but didn't meet my eyes. Part of me wanted to stop and talk to him, to pour out all the awkwardness and fear and uncertainty that I was feeling. But something in the stiffness of his stance prevented me. I greeted both men briefly, then hurried through the gate and back toward the guest house. It was a relief to return to the security of home.

Chapter 2

Most boys who hoped to become Guardians came to the Peace at age fifteen or sixteen to live, train, and attend classes at the Apprentice Academy. I came at eighteen, after training at home with Father and receiving a special dispensation to take the graduation exam. After passing the exam, I moved into a small suite of rooms in the guest house. There was no housing for female Guards (since there were no female Guards), and my father and the Master at the time thought it was best for me to have a woman as a chaperone. That's how I'd first been introduced to Matron.

As I looked around the dining room, I realized that the guest house had truly become home to me, especially over these past months. I now ate at least once a day in this room, sharing meals with Matron, Linnia, JenVie, Andris, and–occasionally–Erritus. My life had certainly changed when the three scholars arrived from Clanstin College, planning to stay for two terms as a kind of good-will exchange between the two institutions. And changed even further when Linnia came to stay, following the unexplained deaths of her mother and her sister, Prin. The guest house, which had been quiet for years, now hummed with activity.

I missed Dr. Li. True, he was intense and often abrupt. But I'd come to like the older professor, and I could relate to his reserve, his desire for independence. He'd returned to the College shortly after the funeral of his assistant, Orme, and I hadn't heard any news of him since. I hesitated to ask Matron. She seemed as capable and self-contained as ever, but I could only imagine that she missed her old friend. I glanced toward her office, which I could see from the dining room. She was working with the door closed.

"Where's Linnia this morning?" asked Andris. "I wanted to show her an interesting old mathematics text I found in the library. I thought it might be helpful for her studies."

JenVie laughed and shook her head. "Honestly, Andris? If it doesn't have something to do with horses, sword fighting, or a good-looking young stableman then I really don't think she'll be interested."

Andris gave a cheerful shrug as he speared a piece of his omelet. "I take it our young lady is still down at the stables?"

"Yes," I said, "Matron gave her permission to work later than usual. I think Cordyn and Fisk have a farrier coming this morning to trim the horses' hooves and Linnia wanted to watch."

"So, a classic mathematics text takes second place to horses' toenails?" joked Andris. "Tragic." He took another large bite of omelet, then contemplated the cloth napkin printed with purple daisies before bringing it to his lips. Matron was a no-nonsense housekeeper, so we all appreciated—but didn't remark on—her rare turns of fancy.

"Have you heard from Laeglin this morning?" JenVie asked me as she reached for the butter dish. "He said he might join us for breakfast if his meeting with Prefect Tal finished early."

I looked at the young history professor, with her heart-shaped face and ink-stained fingertips. Even spreading butter on toast, she looked pretty and refined.

"I'm not sure," I replied, "I honestly haven't been able to catch up with him much this week. We've both been so busy." It had been over a week since we kissed at the Wintertide supper, but I'd only seen Laeglin a few times, twice at sunrise training and once in a meeting with Tal and Klinweh, our respective supervisors. After the meeting,

I'd told Laeglin about Paislie's attacker. He'd been sympathetic, and we'd talked as we walked across the quad. Still, there'd seemed a distance between us, and I hadn't sought him out since, despite his offer.

I wasn't sure how Laeglin felt, but for me, it was confusing. Our budding romance had stumbled, and I wasn't sure why. I felt warm and fluttery when I thought about him, but somehow when I saw him, I never managed to do or say the right thing. I sighed.

"What's wrong?" asked JenVie.

"Oh, nothing," I said quickly, "I was just thinking about something else. Sorry." I sometimes forgot how observant she was.

We were finishing our tea and getting ready to clear our plates when Matron opened her office door and stepped out. She was a tall woman of middle age, with gray-brown hair pulled back in a bun and bright blue eyes behind glasses. She walked briskly across the dining room with a nod in our direction. A moment later she returned from the foyer and approached the table. She was smiling, and I could see she was carrying something in her hand.

"This just arrived from town with the early post," she said, handing me the letter. "It looks like it's from your sister." Andris and JenVie sat back down and watched intently as I opened the message. I felt nervous, whether because of their attention or my anticipation of the letter's contents, I couldn't say. I only realized I'd been expecting bad news when I felt the loosening in my chest. Relief.

I held the letter out to Andris once I finished reading. "It's from Paislie," I said to JenVie and Matron with a grin, "she's writing to say that Bellina and Obrin had their baby yesterday. It's a little boy, born sooner than they thought, but very healthy and doing fine."

JenVie's eyes filled with tears. "Oh, don't mind me," she laughed as she swiped her cheek with the back of her hand, "I'm just one of those people who cry when I'm happy." *Oh no, should I be crying too? Am I showing enough happiness? I'm Bellina's sister, after all. Ugh.*

Why am I even thinking about this? JenVie interrupted my thoughts by jumping to her feet. I stood too, and she hugged me tightly. "Congratulations, Marolaine! You're officially an auntie now."

JenVie turned to Matron and began speculating about the new baby's name, which wouldn't be announced until the ceremony in four weeks. Andris stood and embraced me. He patted my back, still holding the letter as if reluctant to give up the tenuous connection to Paislie. "They want you to take part in the naming ceremony," he said softly. "That's an honor, Marolaine. I'm really happy for you." He gave me a light kiss on the cheek.

And at that moment, Laeglin entered the dining room.

MATRON SAT IN THE CHAIR by the fireplace that afternoon. A square of knitting draped one knee, but she held the other needle still in her right hand. Usually she knitted during conversations, but it seemed I had her full attention. The room felt warm, and I fidgeted in my seat, pulling my uniform jacket down and adjusting a button.

I tried again. "I don't know, Fee..." I appreciated that Matron had suggested I call her by first name in private, but it still felt odd. I forced myself to push on, aware that I sounded like a cranky child. Matron's eyes were mild, and her face was calm.

"I really like him, but it's just that every time I see him, things seem to go wrong. I say the wrong thing, or he does the wrong thing. Or he gets the wrong impression..."

"About your friendship with Andris, for example?"

"Yes." She raised her brows fractionally. "But it's honestly just a friendship," I said, hearing the defensiveness in my voice. "Andris is interested in someone else, but we really get along well and we like spending time together. He's smart and funny and sociable..."

"And handsome?"

"Well, yes, but..."

"And so maybe Laeglin feels jealous? Or left out? Remember, this is new to him too, Marolaine. He looks like a man–he is a man, certainly–but in some ways he's a boy too. Like you, he's lived much of his life here at the Peace, without all the experiences of the outside world."

"I know that! But he still shouldn't feel jealous. That's what I'm trying to say. Andris and I are just friends, and besides, I have to spend time with him. It's part of my job as Klinweh's liaison to the College scholars. Laeglin knows that better than anyone, since he's working with Prefect Tal on the same project." Defensiveness was plunging headlong toward petulance.

"Relationships aren't easy, Marolaine, especially when you're new to them," said Matron firmly. She had a way of speaking that made her words sound final, immutable. Her hands began to move, and I heard the muffled click as the wooden needles began to cooperate to form stitches. Her hands agreed with her words.

"But," she continued, "they're no different from anything else that you care about: they require effort, and sometimes that effort is hard. If you want your friendship with Laeglin to grow, you may need to think about whether you're doing the work that's needed. It's not unlike your Guard training or your job duties."

"That's a pretty dull way to think about it."

She shrugged and I almost laughed because the gesture reminded me so much of Linnia. Was this serious older woman taking on the manners of her nonchalant adolescent niece? "Did you explain to Laeglin that you and Andris and JenVie were celebrating the birth of the new baby when he arrived?"

"I tried to," I said quietly, fiddling again with my buttons. "But maybe not enough. I guess I kind of expected him to just understand. Or I hoped he would. Oh Fee, I'm really terrible when it comes to hard conversations. Even easy ones for that matter. I just don't have the natural skills that JenVie and Paislie and Bellina all have..."

"You're a soldier, Marolaine. You serve and protect people, so you have different skills." She gave me a look that was nearly stern. *She's right. I'm just feeling sorry for myself.*

"You're right, Matron, and I'm sorry to complain. I really am excited for Bellina and Obrin, and it's an honor to be asked to join the baby's naming ceremony. I hadn't expected that though, and I suppose I feel a little overwhelmed with it all. Everything's happening so fast. Sometimes I think my life was better when it was simpler: just training, work, teaching at the Academy, then back to my room. I was good at all that...I always knew what to do and say." I sighed. Matron stood to poke the fire and to humor me with a pat on the shoulder. I smiled up at her.

As she sat down and resumed knitting, Matron asked about the Wintertide supper. She told me she knew about the incident with Paislie. A town security officer had come to talk to her, and Matron–in turn–had shared the news with Captain Matteo. I assured Matron that Paislie was fine, and our conversation shifted to family in general. Matron said that Linnia seemed to have adjusted well in the month since Orme's death, but she was still worried about her niece. Master Bowden was recovering from his injuries, but it wasn't clear when he'd be able to resume Linnia's training. In the meantime, Laeglin and Dele had taken over. Matron appreciated the Guards' willingness to help, but she knew the girl missed the old Master.

LEAVING MATRON'S SITTING room, I decided to walk across the grounds to the guard house and see if I could find Captain Matteo. The guard house was a large brick building that had once been a storage annex, in the days when the Guardians' Peace was an off-site library complex associated with Clanstin College. For generations though, the Peace had been separate, a self-contained community that existed to protect the Lightkeep, as well as to preserve the collection of books and artifacts now housed in the main library and its archives.

The leadership of the Peace was shared by a committee composed of Captain Matteo, Master Bowden, Prefect Tal–who directed scholarly affairs and overall operations–, Associate Prefect Klinweh, and Head Scholar Ang, who represented those Guardians who chose to specialize as scholars. Captain Matteo was the head of the Guards, and as such he was my supervisor and mentor. A visit to his office always had a calming effect on me, and I knew I wasn't the only Guard who felt that way.

A DEEP VOICE ACKNOWLEDGED my knock, and I entered the office of the man we soldiers knew as both gentle and fierce, confident and reserved. Captain Matteo was a large, quiet man with an unmistakable air of command. I would trust him with any problem, and I'd confided in him right away about Paislie's injury and the threats of the tall man.

"Hello, sir," I said. I took the seat in front of his desk, shaking my head to decline his silent offer of tea. I leaned forward slightly. "I'm sorry to interrupt, but I wanted to see if there was any news from town security. About my sisters' report?"

"No apology needed, Marolaine. You know my door is always open to my men." He said this last word with no self-consciousness. Although I'd sometimes felt distanced from my fellow soldiers by my gender, the Captain never seemed to notice. I was grateful for this, and I knew it was one of the reasons I felt comfortable in his presence.

"I wish I had better news," he continued. "I went into town this morning and talked with the commander of the local unit myself, and also with the lead security administrator at the College. His name is Urbandon and he oversees all the town-based units. Neither man had any further information. They both confirmed that the report had been filed, but without a better description or more information there isn't much more they can do. They suggested the usual steps: not working alone, talking with nearby shop owners, even carrying a weapon. I understand they talked with your sisters about those options too?"

"Yes, they did." I tried to imagine Paislie carrying a knife and failed. Now Bellina perhaps..."I just wish there was something I could do," I added. "I'm worried about my sisters, and Linnia too. Paislie said the man asked about Linnia when he first came into the shop."

"Yes," said Captain Matteo, "Matron and I have spoken about providing some extra security for Linnia."

"Here? Or when she goes to town?"

"Both. I know the girl may not like it, but we need to take the steps we can take. Until we know more. Matron agrees."

He steepled his large hands together on the surface of the desk and leaned forward. "Marolaine, unfortunately we seem to be back where we were last fall, when you and Professor Kinsilver were attacked in town. I know that one man from that attack died at the Stones, but the man Paislie confronted in the shop might be the second man. Or someone entirely different. We don't know. More information might help us identify him, and then we might be able to better understand what's behind it all."

I THOUGHT ABOUT THE Captain's words as I lay in bed that night. *I need information. The men who attacked Andris and I had something to do with the dark mage who killed Linnia's family and later caused Orme's death. Paislie's assailant might not be the same as mine, but there seems to be a reasonable chance that he is. After all, he asked Paislie about Linnia. That has to mean there's a connection,*

right? So maybe I should go back to Nod and see if he'll tell me more. That was a terrible day and Nod was a pretty terrible man, but if he has information that could identify the mage...or maybe he knows something about the tall man himself...but would he be willing to tell me?

Laeglin had gone with me the first time I'd met Nod, the owner of a curio shop in a run-down part of Clanstin. I remembered how Laeglin had blushed that day, when he saw me in a dress instead of my unusual training clothes or uniform. We'd been friends then, but other feelings had been taking shape beneath the surface, for both of us.

I also remembered how Laeglin had trusted me to make the decisions that day, even though it meant he was kicked, searched, and pushed around by Nod's sons, before being further insulted by the old man himself. In the end we hadn't learned much about the mage. Nod had taken my silver coin, but seemed afraid–or just unwilling?—to talk candidly. He'd advised us to stop our search for information and to not come back. The question was: What else might he know, and how could I get him to tell me?

Before falling asleep I decided on another visit to Nod's shop. If there was a chance of gaining information that could keep my family and Linnia safe, it was worth the risk. *Should I ask Laeglin to come? He'll probably try to talk me out of it, and if he does come, he'll think he needs to protect me...so no, I think it's better if I just handle this on my own. But I'll only go to the shop. That should be safe enough.*

Chapter 3

I stopped when I heard the commotion overhead. Dark shapes dotted the tree branches, and an amiable cawing filled the morning air. Crows always reminded me of Laeglin. He enjoyed watching birds, and crows were among his favorites, smart and social and long-lived as they were. He sometimes told me stories about their antics or showed me places around the Peace where they roosted at night or congregated by day. He even had a small pair of field glasses that he sometimes carried on his walks with Old Brown, the Peace's resident dog.

The route into town was becoming familiar, although I'd only been to the back district once before, and that was with Laeglin. I knew exactly where Nod's curio shop was located though, and I made my way directly there, ignoring the impulse to browse the merchants' shops or stop for a pastry as I passed through the prosperous part of town. I wanted to get this over with and get back to the Peace. Hopefully with information I could take to Captain Matteo.

As on my previous visit, Nod, the shop owner, was sitting behind the dusty counter and the shop was otherwise empty. He was a heavyset man of late middle years, with graying hair in need of a cut and a wash. I'd wondered if he would recognize me, and he obviously did because he dropped the sandwich he'd been eating onto the counter and pointed a crooked finger at me as I approached.

"Yer the lady Guardian, come back to see me now, have ya? And where's yer young fella? That nice looking soldier boy as was with ya before. I don't think he liked my sons any too much, now did he?" Nod chuckled to himself at the memory, and a large blob of saliva-soft bread shot from his open mouth and landed on the counter near the partial sandwich.

"I'm hoping we can have another conversation," I said mildly.

Nod's right eye roamed down and up my figure in a way that felt appraising but not sexual. His left eye stared straight ahead, and I remembered that it was glass.

"I don't recall we had much of a conversation the first time, Lady," he said. "I told ya to stop asking questions and let it go. No good comes of a young lady asking too many questions about dark doings and all." He folded his hands across his paunch and looked smug. Nod was a man who liked to proclaim.

"I appreciated your advice at the time," I said, hoping to sound sincere, "but new circumstances have arisen, and I need information that I think you can help me with."

"Hmmm...now why would I help you?"

"Because you understand that it's important to look out for your family."

"Is that right now?"

"Yes. I remember how you looked out for your sons, and how they respected you and cared about your safety in return." Laeglin might not agree with my characterization of our last interaction with the old man and his rough sons, but I hoped Nod would be flattered. I had many polite techniques for getting reluctant people to talk to me.

"Well, aye, that's true enough, all yer saying about my boys. But still, I'm not thinking that there's anything more I can help ya with. I told enough."

"My family's been threatened, and I think the dark mage is behind it...the man we spoke about before Solstice, the man who marks his servants with the tattoo I showed you."

"Ahhh...yes, I do remember that you showed me a drawing of a mark, a black bar with a black circle above and below."

"You told us it was the mark of a dark mage, a dangerous man. You wouldn't tell me who he was, but I'm hoping you might reconsider. You know the history of this mage, and I think you know a lot about Clanstin College and the Peace as well. I don't know anyone else who has that knowledge."

"Perhaps I do know some things..."

"Do you have any books of history here in the shop?" I looked around with curiosity, suddenly wondering how Nod came by his knowledge. His one functioning eye followed the path of my gaze.

"I've read many a book about history, but I only keep a few here in the shop. And they're not fer sale, if that's what yer wonderin' about."

I decided to try more flattery. I took a step closer to the counter and smiled. A different man would have offered me a seat, but Nod merely shifted his position and looked suspicious.

"Ya carrying a knife today, Lady? Maybe in yer boot or strapped there around yer arm?"

"Well, yes, I am," I said. "Both. That can't be a surprise to you though?"

"Naw." Nod gave me a half smile that showed his discolored teeth. "Ya got to look after yourself, same as anyone else, I reckon." We looked at each other in silence. Then Nod picked up the sandwich and took another large bite.

"There must be so much to know about the history of this area," I said, returning to my previous tactic. "I'm impressed that you can remember it all. You must have quite a memory for what you read and hear. Or maybe you have a system for recording notes, the way the scholars from the College do?"

"Ah then!" Nod exclaimed, slapping his hip with his left hand and laughing loudly. He choked on the food in his mouth, coughing into his sleeve until his eyes were red and watery. I glanced away, waiting for him to regain his composure. He was beginning to sound like a man who was enjoying himself.

"What I think yer really meaning, if I may guess, is that yer surprised someone like me could be a learned man of history. A man as could read and write. Well, Lady, I can't blame ya fer that. No, I can't blame ya at all. Ya shoulda seen my mother and pa." He paused and shook his head, then crammed the last piece of sandwich into his mouth. I waited while he chewed and swallowed. *He really is a man who likes to be the center of attention. I need to stay patient and keep him talking.*

"I grew up in a house with no learning at all. None. No books, no papers, nothing. My mother and pa, couldn't neither of them read nor write, and they saw no need for it. Same for my older sisters. But me, well, I was a different story, so to speak." He chuckled at his pun, and I smiled politely.

"How did you learn to read?" I asked.

"It's my marveling ya see. I was born with a marvel for reading. Even when I was only a baby, I'm told I could read a newspaper or any bit of writing that made its way in front of me. My sisters started bringing me things to read. They thought my marveling was funny. They thought it was a hoot to see a tiny scrap like me reading words from a paper, proper as any schoolboy. In the middle of that dirty old place, I'd just sit and read, all that they could bring me. And then, see, I could remember my readings real well too. Just had a way with it, and that's how it all started."

Nod's story seemed sad to me, but he was smiling, stroking his whiskered face with one hand. He looked pleased, and so I smiled back. "That's a remarkable story," I said.

"Right so it is, Lady. Right so it is." He nodded slowly, his eyes nearly closed as he gazed back into the past.

I decided it was time for a more direct approach. I'd established as much rapport with Nod as I was likely to. "Nod, I'd like to know about the dark mage. His name, or where he lives, or how I can find him. I'm also interested in a man who works for him, a tall man who wears a cloak and has been seen here in town." Nod's eyes were fixed on me now, and he frowned. Before he could reply, I reached into my pocket and pulled out a silver coin. I placed it flat on the counter, avoiding the glutenous blob of bread.

"I don't want yer coin," Nod said sharply, swiping his hand through the air as if clearing a bad smell. He looked around the shop, which was still empty. The nostalgia that had softened his voice was gone when he spoke again. "If ya want information from me, Lady, then you'll be needing to give me something in return. Something I want more than silver." My face must have hinted at disgust, because Nod scowled and shook his head. "I'll be wanting something of value, something as was took from me by that scoundrel."

"Scoundrel?"

"Don't pretend with me, Lady. I'm talking about the brother of that fella of yours."

"Laeglin's brother? What does he have to do with this?"

"He stole something from me, and he hurt my boy in the process of doing it. I want my property back, and if I get the chance to return the hurt to that no-good, all's the better."

I knew Nod was talking about Laeglin's older brother, Hollon. The first time we met Nod, the old man had mistaken Laeglin for his brother. I'd gotten the impression that Hollon had known one of Nod's sons well, but this was the first I'd heard about Hollon hurting someone.

"What did Hollon steal from you?"

"A little white bird, made of glass like, very lovely and very powerful." I immediately pictured Linnia's white ceramic bird. It was a dyad token, an object shared by two sisters of a dyad. Linnia had shared it with her sister Prin, until Prin was killed by a mental attack that I now believed came from the dark mage. *Did Linnia somehow end up with Nod's ceramic bird?*

"When was your bird stolen?"

"About two years ago, when that weasel Hollon was coming around, pretending to be friends-like with my son Darro." *It must be a different bird then. Linnia said she'd had hers since she was a young child. Can it just be a weird coincidence?*

"Do you have a picture of the bird, or maybe a drawing?" This seemed unlikely.

"Well now…" Nod grunted and heaved himself off his stool. He took a few steps to the side, squatted down, and rummaged under the counter out of my sight. When he emerged, he placed an old book on the counter, then wiped his face with a dirty handkerchief. "Here," he said, placing his hand on the book's faded cover. "Here's where I can find a picture."

After a few minutes, Nod slid the open book toward me, tapping lightly with a thick index finger. "This is my bird."

The drawing showed a goblet of some sort, with ceramic birds like Linnia's perched on the top of each arch of a double handle. The two birds faced each other, wings slightly open, as if they'd just alighted. I looked more closely and tried to read the surrounding text, but Nod pulled the book away and closed it.

"It's a special object," he said slowly. "Called a chalice, I believe. Very old and supposed to bring knowledge of the Light to whichever of those who drank from it. It needs both birds to have its powers, or so I read."

"Do you have the chalice? And what do you mean by knowledge of the Light?" I was intrigued.

"Naw, I never had the chalice, and I don't know who does, if anyone. I just had one of the birds, had it for many years. Such a pretty thing it was, there was just something about it…can't really explain it to ya, but ya'd know yerself if ya held it." In fact, I had held Linnia's ceramic bird, and I had some sense of what he meant.

I tried to refocus. "So, Nod, you're saying that if I find your bird and return it to you, you'll tell me the name of the dark mage and the tall man who works for him, and where to find them?"

"That's what I'm saying, Lady. Aye."

"But there must be some other payment you'll accept," I said. "Finding a ceramic bird for you just seems too...improbable."

"I don't much care how it seems to ya, that's what I want." Nod's voice was stubborn and for a moment we stared at each other across the counter.

"I'm not saying I'll do it," I said finally, "but if I wanted to, do you know how I could find Hollon? If he stole the bird two years ago, it seems like finding him is the first step toward getting it back. I imagine he would know what he did with it. Or maybe he even still has it. In fact, I wonder if you've tried to find him yourself?"

Nod mumbled cagily, something I couldn't understand. His good eye looked down, then evasively off to the side, avoiding my face. The glass eye stared straight ahead, as if hoping I wouldn't accept its challenge. "If yer looking for him, ya might start at the Hail Tavern in East Clanstin. I've heard that's a regular place for him. If ya go there, ya should mind yer safety though, especially at night."

"Thanks for your concern," I said, and I had the pleasure of seeing his right eye narrow slightly at the sarcasm.

"Gladly," he replied blandly.

"But are you sure there isn't anything else you can tell me?" I continued. "After all, if you haven't been able to find the bird, I'm at a disadvantage two years later." No harm in appealing to his sense of fairness, and I knew without doubt he was holding back information.

As I spoke, Nod got down from the stool, picked up a walking cane, and began to stump around the shop. His back was to me, and he appeared to be looking randomly at objects on the shelves, picking up one then another, only to put them back carefully within their dusty rings. *Is he looking for something in particular, or just avoiding my questions?* Silence lapped around us, and I noticed the buzz of a fly bumbling dully against the windowpane.

"Nod? Did you hear me? I feel there must be something else you can tell me, something that would help me find Hollon, or your bird, or the mage? Please."

"The Battle of the Peace." His back was still to me.

"What?"

"How much do ya know about the Battle?"

Laeglin and I had heard a street fabler talking about the Battle a few months ago. That had been on our way home after our encounter with Nod and his sons before Solstice. Other than that, I knew very little.

"What does the Battle of the Peace have to do with all this?" I asked, following Nod to where he stood near a table covered with assorted bottles and jars, some marked with words I didn't recognize. He ran a fingertip around the rim of a grimy bottle. I suddenly felt tired and frustrated. *What have I really learned today? And what have I gotten myself into? Trying to find a ceramic bird that Laeglin's brother stole...or might have stolen, if I believe Nod, which I'm not sure I do? And then exchanging that bird for the name of the mage and his underling? I should have known this wouldn't be easy or sensible. Ugh.*

"That's all I'm telling ya," said Nod grumpily. Maybe he was tired too. I noticed the sweat on his upper lip. He continued to stroke the bottle; I couldn't see his eyes.

"But I have your word that if I bring you the bird, you'll accept it as payment for the information I need?" I asked. "If I decide to try," I added.

"Ya have my word on that, Lady." He turned toward me, looking up. Challenge crept across his face as he spit forcefully into his palm.

Oh Lights, this is too much. I steeled myself, spit lightly into my own hand, and shook.

OUTSIDE THE CURIO SHOP, I ignored the wind, the stray cat dragging a half-chewed mouse, and the man leaning against the wall who called out a rude compliment as I passed. I hadn't gotten the information I'd hoped for, but there was now another action I could take. An action that might bring safety to my family, if I was successful in finding Nod's bird. *But what are the chances of that? Even if I can find Hollon, why would he tell me where the bird is? Even if he knows, he'd have no reason to help me, and he might actually be dangerous. After all, Nod said Hollon hurt his son. Then again, how far can I believe Nod?*

Father used to say, "You don't have to take all the steps, just the next one." As much as it made me anxious, I knew that talking to Laeglin was my next step.

Chapter 4

The dining hall in the guard house was a large interior room, and the lack of windows made it cozy in the winter but sometimes oppressive in the summer. It had dark walnut tables and chairs, closely spaced, that migrated around the room in response to the nightly cleaning. It had a soot-stained fireplace with two old sofas drawn close, inviting men to linger if they had the time. It was their space.

The Guards were entirely responsible for the dining hall; there were no servers or professional kitchen staff. Junior Guards were assigned to regular shifts for planning, cooking, and cleaning. Senior Guards were required to work at least once a month, but most did more than that. Laeglin—a new Senior Guard, like me—liked to cook and was good at it. He volunteered in the kitchen often, and always seemed at ease when I saw him there. I knew he was on duty tonight, and I hoped the comfort of the kitchen might smooth the awkwardness between us.

The room was mostly empty when I entered, although the fire was still blazing for the late-night diners. These days, I ate most of my meals at the guest house. But I always worked at least two shifts a month here, and I made a point to occasionally join my fellow soldiers for supper when I wasn't working. At full swing, the room was crowded and noisy, and the conversations sometimes crude. In truth, I preferred the less-male atmosphere of Matron's supper table.

But I was a soldier, and I knew that eating and drinking together built comradery and strengthened friendships.

I joined the table where Dele, Farron, and Ladogan were finishing their beef and barley stew. Dele–smaller than most Guards, amiable and brave–had become a friend, and he immediately included me in their conversation. A Junior Guard named Volund was on clean-up duty, and he joked with the three men at my table as he worked around us. I smiled at the appropriate times, but my mind was elsewhere.

There was a large pass-through window at one end of the room, where diners could pick up their food and return their dishes. Through the window I could see the two hulking ranges, the worn countertops, the open-front supply cabinets, and the ice chest. I couldn't see the washing area, but I knew from experience that it was around the corner: a deep metal sink with ceiling-high racks on either side. Being a terrible cook, I usually volunteered for cleaning duty; I was well familiar with the sink.

My anticipation—and my apprehension, if I were honest—increased, hearing sounds from the washing area but not being able to see Laeglin. Finally, Dele and his friends finished the last of their beers and left, teasing me good naturedly about why I was waiting around. Volund had finished cleaning the tables, and he walked back into the kitchen with me to say goodnight to Laeglin.

"Ho!" called Volund to Laeglin's back, "do you need any help finishing up here, Lae?"

Laeglin turned his head, keeping his wet arms and hands over the sink. My heart beat faster, like it always did when I saw him. He was a few inches taller than me, slim and well-built, with dark eyes and short-cut dark hair. His gaze met mine, and for a moment he was still. I couldn't tell if he was happy to see me, or surprised, or something else. I waved my hand in his direction, then immediately wished I could take back the silly motion.

"Hi." He smiled.

Then Laeglin's gaze shifted away from me, and he grinned at the junior Guard. "I'm almost done, but thanks," he said to Volund. "You can take off once you're done with the book; I'll close up."

It took forever for Volund to put away the cleaning supplies and fill out the logbook that hung on the wall near the storage room. I sat on a stool and waited, while Laeglin returned to washing pots. I distracted myself by flipping through tomorrow's recipe cards, rather than staring at Laeglin's back or letting my mind wander to the muscles in his bare forearms. Finally, the two men said goodnight, clapped each other on the shoulders, and then Laeglin and I were alone in the kitchen.

As the door closed behind Volund, Laeglin turned from the sink. Wiping soap suds on his apron, he walked to where I sat at the counter. He gave me a slow smile, and I smiled back. He cupped his still-damp hands around the back of my head and leaned down to kiss me. His usual smell of wintergreen was overlaid with oil and smoke. His lips were warm and firm against mine, and I felt the tensions of my day leave me.

"There's my girl," he said softly, "I wasn't expecting to see you tonight."

I felt a twinge of guilt, knowing I'd come partly for a reason of my own, to get information about his brother. And also to explain about Andris. I did want to see him though, and I smiled as I stood up, wrapping my arms around his waist and leaning my head against his shoulder. "Mmmm. I'm glad to see you too."

He was handsome, but what really attracted me was something else. Laeglin could be as physical and as masculine as any of the soldiers. But he was also gentle, caring, and funny. Not funny in the exuberant, joking way of Andris, but in his own way: wry and charming. He knew how to be patient, how to listen and wait. I knew he had his own struggles, of course: insecurities about his past, a need to prove himself. Still, he was my best friend at the Peace, and he made me feel safe. I wasn't sure if I loved him, but it felt close to that.

A few minutes later we were sitting at the counter, chatting about our days. Laeglin poured two glasses of fruit water and I knew it was time. *Ugh. I wish I didn't have to change this evening.* I turned my stool to face him; our knees touched.

"So, Laeglin?"

"Yeah?"

"I've been wanting to talk to you about something, but I guess I've kind of been avoiding it." I thought of Matron's words and pulled together my resolve. *She said this was no different from work or training.*

"What's that?" he said. *Is it my imagination, or does he sound wary? Does he dread these kinds of conversations as much as I do?*

"Well...it's hard to know where to start...I guess I just wanted to talk to you about Andris."

"Andris?" Laeglin shifted back on his stool, increasing the distance between us.

"Well, not really Andris," I hastened, and I could feel my cheeks getting warm, "I mean, it relates to him but it's not about him..." *Oh Lights, I'm saying everything wrong...* "It seems like you may have gotten the wrong idea about our friendship, and I just wanted to talk to you about it, now that..." *What did Matron say I should do? I can't even remember.*

"I don't really want to talk about your friendship with Andris tonight." Our knees were no longer touching, and I could hear the tightness in his voice. "I thought you stopped by so we could spend some time together. We haven't seen each other in days."

"I did. I know. But I also wanted to tell you that when you came in the other day—at the guest house—we were all celebrating because I'd gotten a letter saying that Bellina and Obrin's baby was born. We were all hugging, and that's why Andris hugged me...to congratulate me, it was nothing more than that." I trailed off, feeling resigned to failure.

Laeglin shook his head. "I'm happy about the baby, Marolaine, but I just don't understand why you spend so much time with him." He held up a hand to stop my protest. "I know you're the liaison for the scholars, and I realize that means spending time with them. So, I guess it's not only about the time. It's also that you always seem, I don't know, different when you're with him."

"Different? I don't understand." I tried to reach for his hand, like I'd seen Obrin do with my sister. But Laeglin pulled his hand back.

"I shouldn't have to tell you this." He shook his head again.

"Tell me what? How am I different, Laeglin? You know I'm an idiot about things like this." I smiled weakly.

"It's just that, when you're with him, you seem happier. You laugh more, you joke around, you talk about things other than work and training." He shrugged, but I could see the hurt on his face. I felt terrible. *The worst part is, I think I know what he means. But am I really happier with Andris than with Laeglin, just because we talk more openly, laugh, gossip? Because how can that be? Laeglin is the one I have romantic feelings for, not Andris...should I tell Laeglin he's wrong? Or is it better to be honest and hope he'll understand? Oh Lights, what a mess.*

"It's just different with Andris," I said, knowing as I said them that these words were probably not helping. "I got to know him because of my job, but now he's a friend, that's all I can say. It doesn't change the way I feel about you, but you have to accept my friendship, because there's no reason I should give it up." I felt indignant, and I knew it was in my voice.

"I'm sorry, Laeglin," I continued when he didn't reply, "I really am. I wanted to explain things, but it just seems like now they're worse." I reached for his hand again, and this time he let me squeeze it.

"I'm sorry too," he said, rubbing his thumb in circles over the back of my hand. "We're not very good at this, are we?" He smiled ruefully, then leaned forward and kissed my forehead. "Well anyway, Mar, I'm happy that you're going to be an aunt. Have you heard anything more from your sister?" After a few minutes of safe conversation about my family, I decided to plunge into my second objective.

"There's something else, Laeglin. I hope you won't take offense, but I wondered if you knew anything about where your brother might be living, or how I can contact him."

"Hollon?"

"Yes."

"Why would you want to find Hollon?" His voice was wary.

"It's a long story." *Is there any chance I can avoid telling him? Probably not. Ugh.* I was annoyed with myself for hesitating. *Why should I worry about what he'll say? I have every right to do anything I want, including whatever I can do to protect my family. He'll understand that.*

He raised his eyebrows and took a sip of his fruit water. I couldn't help watching his mouth, and the way his fingers held the glass. I took a breath.

"I went to see Nod again yesterday. I wanted information about the mage and the tall man. I think the man who threatened Paislie might be one of the two men who attacked Andris and I on the street last autumn...you remember how Nod told us about the dark mage and the tattoo? Well, I thought he might know more, and I wanted to find the identity of the tall man. So I could report him to town security and to Captain Matteo, and try to protect my sisters and Linnia from anything worse." I hurried to get it all out. *There. Done.*

There was silence, and then Laeglin asked, "What does all that have to do with my brother?" His voice was quiet.

"Nod wouldn't accept coin this time. He said he'd only give me the information if I helped him get back an object that was stolen from him. A ceramic bird, like the one Linnia has, only this one might be more powerful. Anyway, he said that Hollon stole it two years ago." I skipped the part about Hollon hurting Darro.

"And you believed him?" Laeglin's expression was hard to read. "That seems like a pretty weird request. And as I remember it, Nod isn't exactly a trustworthy guy."

"It is weird, I agree. And no, I don't know if he was telling me the truth or not. I'm sorry, Laeglin, I know Hollon is your brother, but you've never said much about him. Nod might be lying, for some reason of his own, but is it possible that he's right?"

"Do you mean, is it possible that Hollon stole something from him?" asked Laeglin. I nodded. "Well, yeah, that's possible. But even if he did, why would Nod ask *you* to get it back?"

"I'm not sure. Maybe it was just a whim, or maybe he said it because he knew it was impossible and he just wanted to put me off. Or maybe he thinks I'll be able to do it for some reason; I really don't know. I did ask if he had tried to find it himself–since the bird seemed really important to him–but he wouldn't give me a straight answer."

"That's no surprise, is it?" Laeglin sounded bitter and I assumed he was thinking of his rough treatment at the hands of Nod's sons. There was another uncomfortable silence.

"No, I guess not."

"So, you've already decided? You're going to find Hollon and try to get this bird back?"

"I wanted to talk to you before I made a final decision."

"It sounds like you don't need my advice. Or my help. As usual."

"That's not fair, Laeglin."

"I would have come with you to Nod's," he said, looking down at his hands. *This is about trust again. I've hurt his feelings by not asking for his help. Like the fight at the Stones. How can I explain that I do trust him, but I also like to make my own decisions?*

"I know you would have, I just..." I shook my head, overwhelmed by doubt and confusion.

"Yeah." Laeglin rose from his stool without looking at me. "Anyway," he said, walking back toward the sink, "I'd better finish the washing before the water gets cold. And I'm sorry, Marolaine, but I don't know where to find Hollon. I haven't seen him in the last few years. I think he traveled for awhile, but last I heard he was back around Clanstin."

"Alright," I said, forcing a smile in the direction of his back. My chest felt tight. "Maybe we can talk more about it another day." *Oh, please, let's not.*

"Sure, I guess. But, by the way, I might be busy for a while," Laeglin said, plunging his hands back into the soapy water. His voice sounded normal, but I could see the tension in the muscles of his shoulders. "Prefect Tal has asked me to take an assignment at Clanstin College, doing some administrative work to prepare for scholars from the Peace to spend some time at the College next term. You know how enthusiastic he is about this new exchange program." *And here we go again, back to talking about work.*

LAEGLIN WASN'T AT SUNRISE training the next morning, although that wasn't unusual since Prefect Tal favored early meetings. I went from training directly to the Apprentice Academy, where I spent the morning instructing boys in stick fighting, and the early afternoon meeting with Master Bowden, the head of the Academy, to finalize plans for the upcoming graduation exam. Master Bowden still had a sling on his right arm, and I knew that his injured shoulder was taking longer to heal than he'd hoped. He suggested bringing in another Senior Guard to help with the physical aspects of the testing, and I agreed. I rounded out my afternoon with individual advising meetings for several of the boys who'd been cleared for testing. Normally I enjoyed these mentorship sessions, but today I found it hard to focus. I knew I needed to find Laeglin and try again.

"IT SOUNDS LIKE YOU had a long day," said Matron, as we sat down in her study after dinner that evening. "Would you like some tea?" I accepted, and she poured. The scent of chamomile filled the air, reminding me of summer flowers and the color yellow.

"I asked you to stop by because I have a letter for you, and I thought you might prefer not to open it in the middle of the dining room." She handed me a letter, and I recognized Laeglin's writing on the outer cover. "And you certainly don't need to open it right now," she added, though I was already tearing the flap.

I turned to Matron after skimming the words. "It's from Laeglin." She nodded and stirred honey into her tea. "He says he's going to be away for a few days or maybe a week. The Prefect is sending him to Clanstin College to make arrangements for our scholars to visit next term." My next words escaped unbidden: "I don't understand, Matron. He didn't even say goodbye to me." I sounded like a jilted schoolgirl, and I was embarrassed to hear the wobble in my voice. I quickly stood and walked to the fireplace. I stared vacantly at the flames.

I heard Matron's spoon clink on the china of her cup, but she was silent until I returned to my chair. "Did you know he was going?" she asked quietly.

"He mentioned it the last time I saw him, but he didn't say that it would be so soon." Matron nodded and blew on her tea. Mechanically, I did the same.

"That's difficult, Marolaine. I'm sorry." Silence and more clinking.

"But, you know," I said suddenly, not knowing if my enthusiasm was real or contrived, "I'm planning to go to Clanstin for a week or so myself, assuming Captain Matteo agrees. I'll probably see Laeglin while I'm there." I realized that sometime between leaving Nod's shop and waking this morning, I'd made my decision. I would take the next step: I'd try to find Hollon and ask him if he knew where the ceramic bird was.

"Oh?"

I gave her a smoothed-out version of my second meeting with Nod, downplaying any unpleasantness or potential danger. I doubted that she was fooled, but she listened quietly, nodding occasionally and sipping her tea.

"Your loyalty to your family is admirable, Marolaine, and I know how you feel. Still, I urge you to be careful. Nod is not a reliable man. He's actually quite brilliant in his own way, but certainly not reliable or safe. I'd suggest you be very cautious about any venture that he engages you in."

I nodded and she continued. "And while I know you can take care of yourself, I'd still feel better if you took someone with you. With everything that's been happening. Someone familiar with Clanstin perhaps."

"Laeglin might help..."

"I'm sure he would, but it's not certain where he'll be or when. You might want to consider traveling with someone from the Peace."

"Andris was talking about returning to the College for a few days to do some research for his upcoming seminar."

Matron looked thoughtful and I knew she felt my hesitation. "That's definitely a possibility then. Andris knows the town and the college, which would be useful. And he's a man—and let's face it, sometimes that's useful as well." Her eyes twinkled, an unexpected reaction that made me smile.

"I could ask Dele or Manfrid," I said, "but I'm not sure how Captain Matteo will feel about giving me a week off, let alone them. I wouldn't want to put them in an awkward position." I paused. "Let me think about it, Matron. It's good advice, I'm just not sure about Andris."

She nodded and silence returned as we sipped our tea and watched the fire. I sensed that Matron had something else on her mind, and I stayed quiet, giving her thoughts a chance to assemble themselves. I looked up when I heard the rustle of fabric as she shifted in her chair.

"Marolaine?"

"Yes?"

"I have a favor to ask, a personal favor."

"Of course, Matron, what is it?"

"If you have the opportunity, while you're in town, to check in on Dr. Li, I would be grateful." Her eyes were uncharacteristically downcast.

"Have you heard from him since he left the Peace?"

"No." I heard the strain in her voice.

"I'd be happy to," I said quickly.

She stood and walked to her desk, where she wrote something on paper and handed it to me. "Here's the address," she said. "It's a boarding house for unmarried members of the College faculty." I nodded and put the paper in my pocket.

"Is there anything you'd like me to…" I trailed off, avoiding her eyes. Matron and Dr. Li had been romantically involved many years ago. I'd never gotten the full story, but I gathered that they'd been friends during her brief and unhappy marriage, and that perhaps their friendship had ended in misfortune.

Dr. Li had spent the fall term at the Peace, along with his fellow professors Andris and JenVie, and I'd secretly hoped that Matron and Dr. Li would renew their friendship. He was an intense man, private and proud; but he was compassionate too, and I was sorry when he'd returned to the College after the death of his friend Orme. *I won't embarrass Matron with any more questions. Because, really, why has he not been in touch with her, unless it's that he doesn't want to be?* "People do what they want to do," as Father used to say.

Chapter 5

Two days later, I stood with Andris in front of a small cottage in the College district of Clanstin. Prior to coming to the Peace, JenVie rented a bedroom here, and she'd arranged with the cottage's owner–Belva Ka-Sasritty–for me to stay as long as necessary. My trunk would be sent the next day by cart, but Andris and I had walked the short distance to town carrying travel bags. He planned to stay with friends at the College, but I'd told him the basics of my plan and he had promised to help me in any way he could. Captain Matteo had granted me a one-week leave, but I was optimistic that I'd be back at the Peace sooner than that. *Locate Hollon and find out where the bird is, learn something about the Battle of the Peace, and–hopefully–find Laeglin and clear up our latest misunderstanding.*

The cottage was set back from the street. Though neat and trim like those around it, it had several unique features. The first thing we noticed were the exuberant shutters. While most houses in the neighborhood had shutters of sedate gray, brown, or white, those on Belva's cottage were a vivid purple. I liked them, although I couldn't imagine choosing that color myself.

"I wonder what that addition on the side of the house is for?" Andris asked, as we stood on the street admiring the shutters. He pointed. Beside one of the windows, a box-like enclosure jutted about four feet out from the cottage's siding. It was built of small-gauge wire around a wooden frame, and it added an asymmetrical element to the front of the dwelling.

"I'm sure we'll find out soon enough," I said with a smile. JenVie had warned us that her roommate was eccentric, and apparently that extended beyond the shutters to the front walkway. The path that led to the cottage's front door was lined with piles of flat, round stones. Most were dull gray–like today's sky–but here and there we saw stones that had been painted in bright colors: pinks and yellows and apple greens. The effect was almost like flowers lining a pathway, except that it was late winter, when flowers were long dead of the cold.

"Well, let's go meet your hostess," said Andris cheerfully. He took a step forward and stopped. Looking past him, I saw that a squat stone toad blocked the start of the walkway. There was no way to know if it had been intentionally placed to block the way, or if there was some less obvious explanation for its location. In either case, it was a large statue, and I didn't want to step on it. Andris must have had the same thought, because he cleared the figure with a high step. I followed, careful that my bag didn't disturb the stolid sentinel as I passed.

It was several minutes before Belva answered our knock, and I had begun to fear that she wasn't home, or that she didn't know we were arriving. When the door opened, we saw a middle-aged woman of my height, with wide hips and a heavy bosom. She had tightly curling hair, tied with a magenta scarf, and her ears were lined with gold studs. She beamed at us in apparent delight, throwing up her arms and causing gold and silver bangles to cascade toward her plump elbows.

"You're here! And aren't you lovely! I've heard about both of you from my little JenVie, of course, and it's so nice to finally meet you!" As she spoke, she reached forward and grabbed Andris by the shoulders, pulling him against her in an awkwardly intimate embrace. After a shake of her shoulders and a sigh, Belva released the embarrassed professor with a pat on his cheek. He took an unsteady step back and I could see that his face above his beard was flushed. Wanting to avoid a similar greeting, I quickly thrust my hands forward. Belva grasped them in both of hers and shook them with enthusiasm. I liked her immediately.

"Welcome, Andris and Marolaine," she exclaimed, "please come in and..."

"What...?" Andris and I looked up at the same moment. A dark shadow, as fast as night and chattering angrily, was approaching along the wall of the room just inside the door. It appeared to be running along a narrow track about four feet off the floor. Andris had no time to finish his question before a small creature jumped onto Belva's shoulder, and then nimbly launched itself through the air toward Andris with an angry hiss.

Andris, already disconcerted by Belva's embrace, let out a cry of surprise and pain as the creature struck his face and then continued on, scampering down his back and off into the yard. I was momentarily stunned, but quickly turned toward my friend. He was holding his ear, and blood was running between his fingers.

"Andris, are you alright?" I asked.

"What in the realm *was* that thing?" Andris demanded of Belva.

Belva was clearly distracted, glancing with concern between Andris and the yard. "Andris? I see you have a bit of a scratch there. Oh dear...I'm so sorry about that. He's not used to company I suppose, although he was always perfectly happy with our little JenVie. I can't understand it. Oh dear...whatever could have caused him to..."

I pulled a handkerchief from my pocket. "Here," I said to Andris, "let me take a look." He removed his hand, and I could see that he had a scratch on his neck, and what appeared to be a bite—bleeding quite heavily—on his right earlobe. I wrapped the handkerchief as best I could around the wound, then pressed his fingers into place. "We'll need to clean those cuts, but for now, let's get the bleeding stopped. Do you want to sit down?" I gestured toward a chair on the porch, and Andris flopped into it.

I turned to Belva. I could see that her attention was now fully on the yard. She was casting her eyes around while rubbing her hands along her forearms. "Is that a...?" I couldn't even make a guess.

"He's a ferret," said Belva distractedly. "His name is Jay and he's been with me for almost four years. And I can promise you, he's never bitten anyone before. I can't think what came over him."

"I guess he thought I looked suspicious," said Andris with a rueful smile, "it's happened to me before." I smiled back at him, glad that he was regaining his sense of humor.

I turned to Belva. "I'm not sure where he's gone, but it can't be far. Should we see if we can find him?" She nodded gratefully. "It might be helpful if we had something to put him in when we find him," I added, "and maybe you should put on a jacket?"

Belva seemed glad for my suggestions. She disappeared inside, returning with a coat, a wicker basket with a hinged lid, and a scrap of chicken. "He's never tried to leave the house before, not once," she said, glancing at Andris. "He must be very upset." I winked at Andris before following Belva down the steps and into the yard.

As we searched, Belva told me about her pet. Jay was apparently a domestic black sable ferret. He looked like a weasel to me, and I had a negative feeling for weasels because of the friendly red chickens who scratched around the grounds of the Peace. The Peace's gardener, Joste, would have no sympathy for someone who kept a chicken killer as a pet. Naturally, I kept these thoughts to myself.

Belva said that–like most ferrets–Jay was fearless. He liked to climb, but she discouraged him from jumping, because he could get injured that way. She'd built a ramp that allowed him to get safely off and on the wooden track that ran around the living room. She'd also built the extension we'd seen, which allowed Jay to go safely outside into the fresh air by pushing through a flap in the living room wall.

Since ferrets like cold weather, he used this outdoor enclosure even now, in the winter.

I thought about Associate Prefect Klinweh and his pet cavy, but I couldn't think of anything to say to Belva that would connect the two animals. *Except that both their owners seem crazily fond of them, but I certainly can't say that.*

We eventually found Jay, wedged into a drainpipe, and Belva enticed him into the basket. I wanted to check on Andris, but Belva continued to stand under a tree, looking up through its bare branches. "The sky is so beautiful," she said wistfully. "But you know, I rarely spend time outside, especially by myself. My neighbor meets me each morning so we can walk to work together, and other than that, my life is inside. I imagine you find that hard to believe–as a woman of the world yourself–but my life is really quite limited."

I wasn't sure how to respond to this unexpected confidence. "I understand from JenVie that you work at the college?" That seemed safe. I rubbed my hands together. I'd taken off my mittens when we arrived, and my hands were cold.

"Oh, yes, my dear. I've worked in the Records Department for many years. I'm a rotating supervisor there."

I glanced at Andris, who gave me a wave but didn't seem inclined to leave the safety of the porch. I wondered if he was cold. "A rotating supervisor?" I asked politely.

"Oh, you know the College bureaucracy," Belva said with a grin. "In order to avoid any one supervisor becoming too powerful or being subject to the temptations of corruption or laziness, the College has three of us. We all do basically the same job, but on a rotating basis."

"Is that...efficient?" I asked, genuinely curious.

"Oh no, certainly not!" Belva chuckled, shaking her head so that her curls bounced, the wistfulness gone from her voice. "It's dreadfully confusing when decisions need to be made, and it creates lots of extra paperwork. But that's the nature of bureaucracy, I suppose...the more paperwork, the more the bureaucrats like it. It keeps us all busy and employed!" She laughed again and began to walk back toward the house. "It's a good job and no complaints, but still, sometimes I think that I'm ready for a change. I used to believe that interesting things would naturally happen to me as life went along, but lately I'm not so sure..."

ANDRIS HAD GONE TO his friend's house, assuring me that he'd clean his wounds once he got there. He was reluctant to come inside, and I didn't blame him. Even in the basket, Jay had hissed when Belva walked past Andris. Who could know what was in the mind of the vengeful ferret?

I'd put away my few items in the small second bedroom. The cottage's interior was warm and smelled of lilac perfume tangled with ferret musk. The combination was—of course—unpleasant, but I assumed I'd get used to it. *And hopefully I won't be here that often or that long anyway.*

My bedroom was spare, but the rest of the cottage was cluttered with paintings, ceramic figurines, wall hangings, plants, colorful cushions and lap blankets, crystals, a lute with a broken string, several large bowls of marbles, and a second stone toad that appeared to be the twin of the outdoor sentinel. This indoor frog squatted in the front corner of the sitting room, and in the light from the window I could see that it had a faint iridescence, as if morning dew shimmered on its bumpy skin.

The windowsills of the sitting room were lined and stacked with more of the flat stones I'd seen outside, and I asked Belva about them as we sat together. She had served me an odd drink, thick and sweet, and strongly flavored with herbs. I sipped it tentatively. In the back corner of the room, Jay was sleeping in a nest box; I could hear his faint, whistling snore.

"They're from Lakelands, the district north of here. I grew up there, and over the years I collected many stones from the lake shores. Have you ever been there?"

"No, I've never seen a lake, or a river or an ocean either, for that matter."

"Oh really? I thought you would be a person who traveled." Belva seemed surprised to learn of my limited scope, and I wondered why she'd expected more.

"I haven't had much chance, I guess," I said with a smile. "I grew up here in town, then moved to the Peace when I was eighteen. I've been there since. I'd like to see the lakes someday though. I've heard they're beautiful."

"Oh, yes. When I was a child, I loved to just sit and look at the water, noticing how different it looked each day. And the seagulls of course–I loved the seagulls. Have you ever seen them? We don't get them here in town, and I always miss them."

"No, I haven't."

"Well, some people–people lacking in imagination I always say–think seagulls are just flying pests. It's true that they have clamorous voices, and some can be a bit bossy, but it's fascinating to watch their behavior. Because they have different personalities, you know. Some muscular and arrogant, others shy, others fast and sneaky. Just wonderful." She sighed loudly causing her bosom to rise and fall dramatically.

"I have a friend who knows about birds," I said, thinking of Laeglin. "I'll have to ask him about seagulls."

"You won't be disappointed, my dear, certainly not! Maybe you and your friend will take a trip to Lakelands one day, I hope so." *A trip with Laeglin, alone and away from the Peace....* I blinked rapidly and shifted the subject.

"I noticed that some of the stones are painted," I said, "here and outside...is that your artwork?"

"Oh, yes! Thank you! Those are my marvel stones and they're most special to me. I try to capture the colors in paint, to remind me of my visions." She nodded emphatically several times.

"Your visions?" I asked.

"Well, yes, I've had visions of color ever since I can remember. It's my marveling, you know, although I used to think that perhaps it was the beginning of something else. Some special sense or ability. It may sound silly, but I thought I might become a spiritualist of sorts, and so I took my visions very seriously. But of course, that was long ago, before my job at the College."

She paused and peered at me, and I noticed for the first time that her eyes were slightly different colors: one brown and the other hazel. "You look confused, my dear. Let me try again. My marveling gift is that I sometimes see ordinary objects in extraordinary colors. So far it's only been the lake stones actually. Ever since I was little, I would walk the shores of the lakes near home, and sometimes a stone would appear to me in brilliant color, instead of its usual gray. I collected those stones, and when I got older, I got the idea to paint them as I saw them—although, I should say that it's been impossible to really capture the shades of my visions. Anyway, that's why some are painted but others aren't." She paused and gave a half-smile. "It's not a very useful marvel, but it gave me hope for a more exciting life."

We chatted about other marvelings we had heard of, including my mother's story about a man who could whistle two tunes at once. This made Belva laugh, and I was glad to help restore her good spirits. She asked my plans then, and I told her that Andris would come back that evening to escort me to a restaurant where we hoped to meet an acquaintance. That seemed preferable to admitting we'd be visiting a tavern where we hoped to meet a thief.

SOMETIMES IT'S TEMPTING to believe that because you're in a different place, other things will be different as well. That's the best explanation I can give for why I offered to make Belva tea and toast while she rested on the couch later that afternoon. I was at loose ends, waiting for Andris, and truly, I thought, how hard could it be to make toast?

The kitchen was small and crowded, but I recognized the range and found the tea kettle easily enough. While the water heated, I sliced the bread, managing to produce two slices not dissimilar in thickness. The broiler stymied me for a while, but I'd seen Laeglin operate the range in the guard house kitchen, and that helped. In minutes, the bread was broiling, and the water was heating, and I was feeling quite smug. *Not so hard after all!*

The kettle's steaming screech startled me, and I realized I hadn't yet found tea or cups. I turned the range top off and began to search the cupboards. *I really should have gathered all the supplies first, like Erritus told me when I baked the cake. I wonder if Belva likes cream or sugar?*

"How's the toast coming, my dear?" Belva called from the other room. "I think I'm getting a teensy smell of it." From the kitchen I could hear Jay racing along his wall track and making a clucking sound that Belva described as his "happy voice."

"Everything's fine," I called back. *Who smells toast anyway?* I was beginning to feel flustered as I placed two cups in matching saucers and continued hunting for sugar or honey.

"Marolaine..." There was a note of warning in her voice.

Oh no, I smell it too...it smells like something's burning. The bread's only been in the oven for a few minutes, though. Maybe I should have turned it over by now? Or not put it so close to the flame?

There was no doubt now: smoke was beginning to seep around the edges of the oven door. I grabbed for a towel to pull out the hot rack, but as I spun back toward the range, the towel caught one of the cups and it crashed to the floor. Avoiding the shattered glass, I opened the oven with my toweled hand and pulled the rack partially out. Smoke poured forth, and I had just a glimpse of the shriveled, blackened bread before it burst into flames.

Belva came running. She reached my side, but as she did, she stepped on a shard of porcelain and squealed in pain. Standing on one foot, she dumped a canister of salt over the toast and extinguished the flames. I reached toward the lumps, obeying some vague urge to clean up the mess I'd created.

"Wait!" said Belva sharply, "hand me a fork–the toast is hot, and I don't want you to burn your fingers." Wordlessly I did as Belva said, and she tossed the crumbling black bits into the sink where they smoldered accusingly while we looked around.

The kitchen floor was covered with broken porcelain, salt, and bloody footprints. Smoke hung in the air, along with a sharp burnt smell. Jay stood on his back legs in the doorway, chattering loudly, as if we might not already be aware of the calamitous state of the kitchen. I could feel the sweat prickling along my hairline. *Oh Lights.*

We looked at each other, and to my amazement, Belva's mouth twitched.

"Nothing like a restful cup of tea in the afternoon, I always say." Then she burst out laughing and put her arm around me. I felt the solidness of her body and let out a sigh of relief as the ferret continued to chide me.

Chapter 6

Andris nearly choked with laughter when I told him the story of my afternoon. It was early evening, and we were walking toward the Hail Tavern, which Andris knew by name but swore he'd never entered. The night was cold, and we were both dressed conservatively, me in a brown dress covered by a woolen jacket with wide cuffs. I was used to wearing my Guard uniform or training clothes most of the time, but I knew Andris was right: the less we stood out tonight the better. My hair was pulled back in a bun at the base of my neck, and my only weapon was the knife in my boot.

"So basically," said Andris, taking my arm and trying for a straight face, "in the four hours since you arrived, you've scared away her cherished pet, nearly burnt down her kitchen, broken her dishes, and caused her a painful bleeding toe injury. You're quite the houseguest, Marolaine, I must say." His brown eyes sparkled and his hair was tousled by the breeze, giving him a rakish look that matched his tone.

"No fair!" I said, pushing against his shoulder with mine. "You're the one who scared her pet away, not me. You heard what she said, four years and Jay has never bitten anyone before."

"Well, twenty-six years and I've never been attacked by a badger. So there's that in my favor." Andris tried to look self-righteous, and I laughed.

"A ferret."

"What?"

"Not a badger, Andris, a ferret."

THE WALK TO THE TAVERN was longer than I'd expected, and it was dusk by the time we arrived. I remembered Nod's warning about the place as I observed the dirty windows and broken stonework and heard loud voices from within. At the Peace I was confident in my skills and knowledge, but here in town it felt different. I found myself glad for Andris's company, and at the same time annoyed with my own insecurity. *I'm a Guardian of the Peace, for the realm's sake. It shouldn't matter where I am or whom I'm with!*

It was hard to gauge Andris's feelings about our mission, and I didn't ask. He tended to use humor to mask tension, so I wasn't surprised to hear him say, "cometh the moment, cometh the man," as he reached for the handle of the heavy door and pulled it open.

It took us a moment to adjust to the dimness and the noise. Smoke clouded the air, and the smell of beer and sweat was strong. Men of all ages sat at closely spaced tables or leaned against the walls. There was an imposing fireplace at one side of the room, and several pairs of boots steamed on its sooty hearth. A gray dog was curled up close to the flames, the rope attached to his collar trailing free on the bricks as if his owner had forgotten him, or maybe just trusted him to stay put.

Across the room a low wooden platform was crowded into a corner. The platform held a single chair, and the chair barely held the bulk of a man playing a harmonica, his hat pulled low so that it obscured the upper half of his face. The tune he played was both mournful and lively, its notes just audible above the din. From time to time, he stopped to wipe sweat from his face with a crumpled handkerchief, or to take a long drink from the mug on the floor by his feet.

I surveyed the crowded room and saw no other women. Long-practiced techniques calmed my breathing as I stepped ahead of Andris and walked toward the battered oak bar that spanned the back of the tavern. Its placement meant that anyone entering had to walk the full length of the room to reach either the bartender or the alcohol. I was aware of dropped conversations as I passed, men's eyes on my back. Andris was close at my side though, and while I kept my eyes forward, he dispensed a greeting or two, prepared to make friends here rather than enemies.

Two men worked the bar. One was thin and furtive, moving quickly and whistling tunelessly as he drew mugs of beer from a large barrel. The second man was clearly in charge. He was short, with a thick build, not unlike a barrel himself. His nose was crooked, as if it had been broken and never reset. He watched us approach with a calculating look, and I was glad for the cloak that covered my dress. When we reached the bar, he grinned and wiped his hands against the sides of his trousers in a preparatory way.

"Evenin' there, folks. What can I do for you?" Something in his tone made me uncomfortable, but I drew a quiet breath and reminded myself of my purpose.

"Good evening," I said. "We're actually hoping for some information. We're looking for someone and we're told he may be a regular customer here." Andris stood near me but kept his friendly attention on the room. He would let me take the lead.

"'Tis *customary* to order a drink when you come into a tavern," said the bartender, drawing out his words. "But I'll assume that—being a lady and all—you might not be conversant-like with what's *customary* in a place like this. So, I won't hold it against you none." His words were genial enough, but I heard the bully underneath. *That was a mistake. I should have known not to be so direct.*

"That's decent of you," said Andris affably, turning toward the bar and stepping fractionally closer to my side. "It's a welcoming place you have here, especially on a cold night. I'll take a beer, and the lady will have some cider if you have it." His voice was easy, his posture relaxed. Again, I felt both grateful to Andris and annoyed with myself for needing his intervention.

"Alright then, mate, I'll get those drinks right to you." The bartender turned and spoke roughly under his breath to the thin man, who moved down the bar toward the barrels, avoiding eye contact with his boss. Turning back to us, the bartender said, "I'm the owner of this establishment. Name's Creedling."

I had no idea how a woman should acknowledge an introduction in a place like this, but Andris gave a nod and said, "I appreciate making your acquaintance, Creedling, I'm Andris."

Creedling's eyes were on me again. "Pretty lady gotta name?" *I should've thought about this before we came in, should have planned it with Andris. Do I give my own name here? I'd rather not, but I can't be rude or we won't get information about Hollon.* Andris's gaze met mine briefly.

"This is Miss Kinsilver," he said. I was relieved that he hadn't told Creedling my real name, but at the same time discomfited by his decision to give me his own second name.

"Well, Miss, here's your cider, with my compliments." I received another wolfish smile as he handed me the glass. His calloused fingers fumbled against mine as I took it. "Now, perhaps we can have that conversation that you were wanting to have earlier. You were sayin' that you're looking for someone?"

"We're hoping to find a man named Hollon," I said. *Keep it simple, no explanations if we can avoid them.*

"Ahhh...Hollon." His eyes darted around the room, and I wondered if Hollon might actually be here.

"You know him then?" asked Andris, taking a long sip of his beer and sounding nonchalant.

"Well, I do and I don't, if you take my meaning, mate. It might depend on why you're wanting him, see." He turned to me. "This Hollon a *friend* of yours, Miss?" He raised his eyebrows, and the implication was clear.

"No," I said coolly, "I've never met him before. But we'd appreciate it, Mr. Creedling—if you should see him–if you'd let Hollon know that he can contact us..." here I paused. I hadn't thought about how to have Hollon get in touch with us. I suppose I'd imagined–naively I could see now–that we'd just find him here and talk with him. I couldn't give Creedling my address at Belva's, and certainly not at my sisters' shop...

"He can leave a note here, and we'll arrange to meet him," said Andris, placing a card on the counter. Upside down, I read enough to realize it was his own address at the College. *He's really helping me tonight.* "And thanks," Andris added, sliding a silver coin across the counter so it came to rest next to the card. He took a final sip of his drink.

"Anything for the lady," said Creedling with a wink in my direction that I ignored. "She's welcome in my establishment any time. I could use a bit of the feminine touch." He smirked.

WE WERE ALMOST TO THE door when I saw him. Alone at a corner table, sitting in his rolling chair, was Dr. San Li, Clanstin College professor and expert in dyad medicine, and recent visiting scholar at the Peace. Andris saw him too and looked at me. I nodded and we began to make our way through the crowd.

"Dr. Li!" I called as we approached the table. Dr. Li looked up and I was startled by the change in his appearance. His hair–usually glossy black and neatly secured with a leather band–hung limply. His shirt was wrinkled. The lines around his eyes and mouth were deeply carved, pulling his face down. A half-empty bottle and a smudged glass sat on the table in front of him, along with a greasy square of paper that might have held fried potatoes. In a room swirling with raucous conversation, he sat isolated in an island of silence.

I had a moment of fearing he wouldn't recognize us. But then he slowly raised a hand from the table, a half greeting, unclear in its meaning.

"Can we join you for a few minutes?" Andris asked, as if this was a normal meeting with a colleague. Dr. Li nodded slowly, and we sat. I was surprised to see a small dog lying on the floor to the far side of Dr. Li's rolling chair, away from the flow of people. It raised its head as I sat down, fixing me with soft eyes under a dirty tangle of fur.

"Want some?" Dr. Li gestured to the bottle. Andris and I shook our heads.

"Dr. Li," I said, "is that your dog?"

He glanced down and I caught the hint of a smile. "No. I think she's a stray. She's been following me around for the past few days though."

"She looks like a sweet-tempered little thing," said Andris warmly. "What's her name?"

"She doesn't have one, not that I know."

"Well, I think she should," Andris said with a smile, "a nice dog like that." He thought for a moment. "How about Min?"

"Where did that name come from?" I asked, curious.

"Oh, I don't know, it just seems to suit her. What do you think, San?" Andris paused, but Dr. Li was silent. Andris continued, undeterred. "And maybe I'll check in with you before I leave town. I'd like to see your place anyway, and if you still have her, I'll give Min a proper bath and brushing. I like dogs and it'd be no trouble."

Dr. Li looked at Andris without speaking, his expression inscrutable. I knew Dr. Li didn't like to acknowledge his need for physical help, and I worried that Andris had offended his friend by suggesting he couldn't groom his own dog. But then the professor reached forward and placed his hand on the younger man's forearm, and I knew that I'd misread the situation.

The conversation was slow to start, but Andris and I did our best. After a few minutes we'd learned that Dr. Li was on leave from teaching, although it was unclear whether this was by his choice. He was living alone, having not found a new assistant since Orme died. I guessed, by the ropy forearm muscles beneath his rolled sleeves, that he was propelling his own rolling chair wherever he needed to go. I wondered about the steps we had climbed to enter the tavern. *How in the realm is he managing? Matron and Linnia would be sad to see him like this.*

As sometimes happens when two people are silent together, our thoughts seemed to run parallel, finally snagging a common thread. "How is Linnia?" Dr. Li asked suddenly.

"Oh! She's doing well." I felt awkward with his question and not sure how to respond. *How much does he really want to know? Does he want to talk about Orme and how Linnia is coping with that?*

I glanced at Andris, but he had turned his chair toward the musician. As the harmonica wailed, Andris tapped his foot and looked around the room, whether in genuine interest or to give Dr. Li and I privacy, I couldn't tell. Dr. Li began to fold the greasy paper into smaller and smaller squares while I watched.

Finally, I fumbled on, "She wanted to come to town with us actually, but Matron said she needed to stay for her schoolwork and her training. I know she misses you though. Linnia, that is." There had been an unlikely camaraderie between the two, and Dr. Li had provided treatment and counsel in the early days after Linnia lost her family.

"I thought I saw her father in town a few days ago," said Dr. Li abruptly.

"Linnia's father?" I repeated. "I didn't know that you knew him. Or that he lived in Clanstin."

Dr. Li pinched the square of paper between his left thumb and index finger, then flicked the corner with his other hand, spinning the square one turn at a time. I wasn't sure he'd heard me, but after a minute he looked up.

"As you know, I was a friend of Mrs. Rosevale, your Matron, many years ago. At that time, her sister was still married, and I saw Linnia and Prin's father occasionally." I knew he and Matron were friends–or more–but now I remembered Matron telling me that her sister had consulted with Dr. Li when the girls were young, in his capacity as a local expert in dyad medicine.

"Matron–Mrs. Rosevale–told me once that Linnia's father was no good."

"That's true enough. Although I myself found him–in the early days–to be mostly weak of character, unsure of himself and unsure how to be a father and a husband. Only later did he begin staying out at night, getting paranoid and unpredictable, accusing his wife of all manner of things."

"He eventually left them?" I asked, "while the girls were still young?"

"Yes. I never knew the details, but it seemed he got entangled with some unsavory people. I heard he left the area, but that was years ago."

"But you saw him here in town just a few days ago?"

"Maybe. It's hard to be sure of anything these days." Dr. Li sounded like a man who no longer trusted himself. I wanted to offer him some comfort, but I wasn't sure how.

Andris broke the silence by turning his chair back to the table and asking if we wanted anything from the bar. The mood brightened as the two men jokingly debated the relative merits of the fried potatoes and the fried beef strips. I decided to ask Matron about Linnia's father when I returned to the Peace. If anyone, she'd know if the man was living in Clanstin.

Dr. Li surprised me when he changed the subject and asked about the sword. He didn't say 'the Sword of Light,' but I knew what he meant and I wondered why he would mention it in front of Andris. *Does Dr. Li think Andris knows about the Sword already? I've never had any indication that Andris knows, but who can say. I know he helped Dr. Li decipher some of the coded text, so maybe he knows we found it in the library archives?*

I trusted Andris, but I still wanted to be circumspect. "The sword's been put in a safe place," I said, hoping this would be enough to reassure Dr. Li.

"Racindalyn was furious." He stared at his glass, although he hadn't taken a sip since we sat down.

"Who's Racindalyn?" I asked.

"Chancellor Axelle," said Dr. Li with a sigh. "She wanted that sword, as you know, Marolaine. And when I returned to the College without it, she was beside herself. It's definitely safer if I don't know where it is."

"Did you ever find out why she wanted it so badly?" Like Dr. Li, I was dropping caution. Andris listened but didn't ask questions.

"In our last conversation," replied Dr. Li, "she lost some of her usual reserve, her self-control." He paused, as if remembering. I could smell the alcohol on his breath, but he was less drunk than I'd thought at first. Drunk enough to be more open than usual, but not so drunk as to be incoherent. I wondered how long he's been sitting alone at this table. "She was angry, but also upset. In fact, I'd use the word 'devastated' if I didn't know her better."

I nodded. I'd met Chancellor Axelle only once, and I recalled an elegant, alarmingly self-possessed older woman. As Chancellor, she held power over the entire Clanstin college-state, college and town. I'd heard that she was a brilliant administrator and a ruthless enemy to those who opposed her. It was hard to imagine any situation that would devastate her.

Dr. Li continued. "And so I thought it must be personal. She must have wanted the sword for some personal reason, although it's hard to imagine what that might be."

"Did you ask her?" After everything Dr. Li had been through to find the Sword of Light, it seemed fair for him to know why.

"She said she intended to send the sword to Lakelands, to a man she hated but couldn't refuse. I had the feeling the man was someone from her past, maybe someone she'd known when she was young. She regretted telling me that much though and refused to say anything more."

"Did she...I'm sorry, Dr. Li, but did she remove you from your position at the college?"

Dr. Li raised his shoulder wearily. "Not in so many words, no. She ordered me to find the sword again and bring it to her. I could tell she was desperate, but I said I couldn't. I wouldn't. She threatened me with something from my past. A form of blackmail I suppose. Either I brought her the sword or she would ruin my career, my reputation."

"What did she have over you?" Andris asked, his brows lowered in anger for his friend.

"Something from the past, Andris, something I did that I regret. She threatened to tell the Board of Directors, but worse, she said she'd tell Fee." *Fee. Matron. Oh.*

"That's terrible!" Andris was indignant. "There must be something you can do?"

"I did it already," said Dr. Li quietly. He dropped his left hand over the side of his chair. Min rose onto her haunches and nudged against his dangling hand until he absently scratched her head. "I resigned from my position at the college," he continued. "So, she can't hurt my career. I'm not sure what to do about the other half of her threat though. I just know that I won't bring Fee into this again, I won't let anything hurt her again." Something in his voice made me uneasy.

OVER OATMEAL THE NEXT morning, I talked to Belva. I was still vexed by my social incompetence at the tavern, but at least I'd woken with some new ideas. It had occurred to me that the man the Chancellor hated–the man from Lakelands–might work for the college or might have done so in the past. It would also be interesting to confirm that the Chancellor herself was from Lakelands, and if so, what area. I didn't know for certain that the man the Chancellor had planned to give the Sword to–according to Dr. Li–was the same man who had killed Linnia's family and threatened mine. But it made sense to learn what I could.

"Well," Belva replied, "basic information about employees of the college is public record. That means that it can be accessed by request, and the person doesn't need to give their permission for the Records Department to release it." She was wearing a flowing morning robe, patterned with pink owls. A sequined scarf covered her hair. Her feet were bare, and she flicked them absentmindedly as we talked, thwarting Jay's attempts to bite her toes. Having observed this ferret game previously, I was wearing slippers.

"So I could make a request to find out which staff members–current and past–are from Lakelands?"

"Yes, that should be open information in most cases."

"How do I make a request?"

Belva smiled wryly and my optimism stumbled. "There are forms, my dear. Forms to be completed by you, approved by a Records Department supervisor, and–if you're unlucky–reviewed by the Requests and Requisitions Committee. That can take a while."

She stirred her oatmeal. "Bureaucracy, you know." She shrugged one shoulder.

"Is there any way you could help speed the process?" I asked hopefully. "I have limited time in town, but this information might be valuable." Belva didn't know my true purpose, only a vague story about researching a friend of the family.

"I don't see why not," replied Belva, "as long as the information you want is public record. You could complete the forms today. I'm the rotating supervisor on duty for two more days this week, so as long as you turn the forms in to me during that time, I can approve them myself and make sure they stay out of committee review. I'll forward them directly to one of our clerks and you should get your report within a few days."

I thanked Belva and agreed to walk with her to the College to pick up the necessary forms. *Then afterwards, I'll try to find Laeglin. If he's still here.*

Chapter 7

Some wonderful person at the Toe in Boot Tea Shop had invented a new black tea blend, flavored with orange rind and spices. It was delicious, and Andris and I ordered a second pot after Paislie left. The chairs in the shop were unusually comfortable, and I settled back with a sigh. Andris appeared relieved too, loosening his collar and running a hand through his wavy hair. He looked especially handsome this morning, and I knew how much he'd been looking forward to seeing my sister.

Bellina and the new baby would stay secluded for four weeks, with Bellina's husband Obrin their only companion. That left more work for Paislie in the shop, but also more opportunities for Andris and I to entice her to socialize on her own. Today the three of us had met for tea just down the street from Father's shop.

Paislie had worn a becoming green dress with a floral overlay, but it was a dress I'd seen her wear before. I suspected JenVie would say that a young woman wishing to impress a young man would choose a new dress. But who knew? Paislie might have other priorities; as a seamstress, perhaps dresses were merely business to her. I'd looked for other signs of romantic interest, but she seemed equally animated and friendly to both of us. It was hard to know if there was anything more, although I hoped so, for Andris's sake.

As always with my sisters, the interaction—though pleasant—felt a bit effortful. I truly liked Paislie, but seeing her reminded me that there was more I should have done for her over the years. Ways in which I, as the older sister, could have compensated for Mother's disinterest, rather than turning to my own ambitions. Paislie was a lovely person, but that was regardless of me, not in any way because of me.

"So, what do you think?" asked Andris, after I thanked the server and poured our tea.

"About what?" I asked innocently.

"Stop it, you know about what!" He took the cup that I slid across the table and inhaled its spicy scent. Then his shoulders slumped. "I don't know, Marolaine. When I see her, I just feel so...kind of stupid. Like I don't know what to say or where to put my hands. I have the feeling I'm not making much of an impression. Or at least not a very good one."

I smiled. Andris was usually open and demonstrative, but he was right: with Paislie he was reserved, his hands restrained at his sides, as if on their best behavior like the rest of him. In some ways I thought he was too old for my sister, yet when they were together, it was he who seemed unsure, inexperienced.

"You are a little more subdued when we're with her," I admitted, "but I'm sure she notices that you're also brilliant, and funny, and handsome...how could she not?"

"I guess I do have a *few* redeeming qualities, now that you mention them," he said with a smile.

"Although you're not much good with ferrets." I kept a straight face.

"You're very funny, Marolaine, did anyone ever tell you that? Hilarious."

We sipped for a moment, and I thought about how relaxing it was to be with Andris. *He's a good friend. It's easy to be myself around him.*

"So," he said, "speaking of unrequited love," *Oh no...* "have you been able to get in touch with Laeglin? I know you said you'd try to find him when you went to the College this morning. Any success?"

I shook my head. "I spent most of the morning going to different offices and waiting in lines to fill out paperwork, trying to get some more information about staff from Lakelands. Thank goodness for Belva, although if that was an expedited process, I'd hate to see the *usual* process. But no, I couldn't find Laeglin. I went to the Chancellor's office after I finished my paperwork, but the receptionist said she didn't know where he was, or even if he was still at the College. She said she'd follow up and let me know through Belva."

"So, that might never happen?"

"Right."

"Sorry, Mar, I know you hoped to see him."

"That's alright. He might already be back at the Peace. I really don't know how long he was planning to be here." I smiled brightly and gave a shrug.

Andris kindly changed the subject as we finished our tea. "I'm going to stop by San's boarding house, then I'm heading back to the College for a meeting with Professor Podge. And yes, before you ask, he is as dull as his name sounds." He grinned.

"I'm glad you're going to see Dr. Li. I'm worried about him after last night."

"Yeah, me too. I'll see what I can do."

"I'm hoping," I said, "to find out more about the Battle of the Peace this afternoon. Nod mentioned it...he asked what I knew about it and suggested that the history of that battle might have something to do with the mage. Or at least that's what I thought he meant. He's not the realm's easiest man to communicate with."

"Are you heading back to the library then?"

"Maybe later. But first I'm hoping to find a fable teller. Laeglin and I heard one telling stories about the Battle of the Peace when we first met Nod, before Solstice. I thought that if I could find that fabler–or one like him–that would be a good start."

"Where does one find a fabler these days?"

"No idea."

AS IT TURNED OUT, WANDERING the streets looking for a fable teller was not an efficient strategy. I was walking back toward Belva's cottage, when I saw two men arguing on the street near a cart piled high with cabbages. It was unusual to see fresh produce this time of year. I didn't particularly like cabbage, but I knew that it stored well. Probably some enterprising merchant had saved his fall harvest, hoping late-winter shoppers would pay a premium for something green.

One of the men near the cart–short and stocky, bare-headed in the cold–caught my attention, and I realized it was Nod's second son. The son who'd been asked to confirm Laeglin's identity that day in the abandoned warehouse. The son who had, apparently, known Hollon well. And if Nod was to be believed, the son who'd been hurt by Hollon.

As I drew near, the man saw me too and his expression grew alert, then wary. *What was his name? That's right, Darro, I think. I didn't expect him to recognize me, but then, I suppose I'm not the only one who's observant.* I shifted the bag I carried over my shoulder and pulled my scarf tighter against the wind. The argument ended abruptly, as the other man pulled his hat down and hurried away, and Darro turned to face me.

"Miss," he said, touching his chest lightly, in the gesture of greeting between acquaintances who were not friendly enough to clasp forearms or embrace. I returned the politeness.

"I believe you're Darro?" I asked.

"That's right."

"Did your father tell you I might be coming to town?"

Darro's face grew even more cautious, and he rubbed his stubbled cheek with one finger. His hands were chapped by cold or outdoor work. "I heard ya might be lookin' for Hollon, is that right?"

"That's right, although I haven't found him yet."

"Been to the Hail?"

"Yes, and I talked to the owner, a Mr. Creedling."

Darro's lip curled. *At least we have that in common. I wonder why Darro dislikes Creedling? I know my own reasons.*

I continued. "Do you know where Hollon is, by chance?"

Darro rubbed his arms; his worn coat was too thin for comfort in the wind. "Nope. He makes himself hard to find, does Hollon. If I coulda found him..." he trailed off, kicking at the ground with one toe and dropping his gaze.

"Can you tell me what he looks like?" I asked, "that might help me recognize him." I assumed Hollon looked something like his brother, Laeglin, but Darro's description might be helpful. It was always interesting to learn what one person considered noteworthy about another person.

Darro was silent and I thought he wouldn't answer. But finally, he said, "Hollon's a little taller than you. He's got medium skin, dark hair, dark eyes...and he's mostly friendly-like, but then sometimes not, like he's got troubles inside." He shrugged and looked embarrassed.

"I'm also looking for a fable teller," I said, not wanting to prod a sore spot.

Darro looked up and raised his eyebrows. "What for, Miss?"

"I want to hear some of the old stories about the Peace."

"Rill Uldon's the best fabler in Clanstin," said Darro. "I've heard his tales many a time. He's got a fine speaking voice, carries something wonderful on the street."

"Do you know where he lives? Or where he'll be speaking next?"

"As to where he'll be fabling next for the crowds, no I don't. The fablers appear where they want to and tell the stories they want to tell. But for business on private matters, like, ya might find old Rill down at Fountain Park."

AS A CHILD I'D COME occasionally to the park with my mother and sisters, but it looked different now, with the trees grown taller and an expanse of new stone pavers creating an area where artists and musicians could gather in the warm weather. The park's main attraction was still the large pool, the only body of water I ever saw as a child. With adult eyes, I estimated it to be about two or three parrens in size, with straight-edged banks that showed it had been dug by men, rather than naturally formed.

The pool was encircled by a walking path and rimmed by a knee-high stone wall that doubled as a bench for families and visitors. At the pool's center–even in chilly winter–rose the sparkling plumes of water that had fascinated me as a child. I knew now that it was a gravity fountain, with a raised reservoir creating the pressure needed to force the water skyward in the lower part of the pool.

The elevated section of the pool was smaller than the main section and was less used. It bordered a dense copse of satinwood trees–now naked of leaves–and was the preferred destination for the flocks of ducks and geese that passed through on their way to other places.

There were only six geese floating on the upper reservoir today. Five were gray, with black necks and heads, and white eye masks. The sixth goose was white with an orange bill. She was lovely but alone, part of the flock, yet not, and I wondered why she was there. *Laeglin would know. He'd probably look at her with his field glasses, tell me her scientific name, and maybe write a note in that little book he sometimes carries. Lights, I miss him.*

Even though the day was brisk, several families were enjoying the park, and I stopped to watch two young girls–sisters I assumed–sitting on the stone bench. They were perched sideways, facing each other, and they'd removed their mittens to play a hand clapping game. Despite the complexity of its rhythms and sequences, I noticed that their eyes were intent on each other. Their lips moved, but at my distance the words of their chant were lost to the wind and the spray of the fountain behind them.

The small plaza was nearly deserted. On one side, an older woman–bundled in a shapeless jacket that reached below her knees–was selling apple cones. These were rounds of yeast bread, wrapped to form a cone and then filled with sweet apple filling scooped from a kettle over a portable fire. The smell of cinnamon and cloves filled the air as steam from the kettle whipped in all directions, a cyclone of scent. Next to her, a second older woman–perhaps a sister or a partner—had established a tiny tea stand and was selling hot tea in thick paper cups, complete with cream and honey.

Across from the vendors there was a small portable pavilion: a canvas roof and side flaps suspended on folding wooden supports. The hanging canvas had been staked to the ground, but a front corner had broken free and flapped in the wind. Under this canopy was a flimsy folding table and three straight-backed chairs. Through the pavilion's open front, I could see that one chair was occupied by a man, and the other by a boy; the third was empty.

Seeing no sign or other clues, I approached the structure and greeted the man from a few paces away. He confirmed that he was Rill Uldon and invited me to come inside.

I stepped into the dim space under the canopy, inching around the boy to reach the empty chair. The canvas blocked the wind, creating a welcome–if musty–warmth. Although I'd never been in a camping tent before, I imagined that this was how it would smell.

Up close, the man's face was dark and deeply lined. It was impossible to guess his age. The boy appeared to be about ten or twelve, very thin and wearing a coat that was much too large for him. His hands were bare, and he clutched a worn leather notebook to his chest. He didn't meet my eyes when I smiled and said hello.

"What can I do for you, Lady Guardian?" asked Rill once I was seated. His voice was low and graceful, and I remembered how powerful it had been when Laeglin and I heard him on the street.

"You know who I am?" I asked in surprise. I was again wearing a plain dress, with my heavy cloak and woolen hat; I didn't look like a Guardian.

"Tana told me as you approached," the man said, looking at the skinny boy. "Tana is my scribe, but he also gathers information for me. A fable teller must know the comings and goings of the town, as you might imagine." His tone was friendly, but he didn't smile. I decided not to press; how Tana had known my identity wasn't important, I supposed.

"I've never had the opportunity to talk with a fable teller before," I said. "I'm not sure where to start."

"It's quite easy," replied Rill. "The first question is, are you here to gather or to give?"

"I'm not sure I understand."

"Most people seek me privately either to gather stories–stories which I have, and they wish to buy–or to give me one of their own stories. In the second case, I use my gift to receive the person's story from their memory, and Tana writes down the words as I tell them."

"How do you receive the story? Do you mean they tell you?"

"I find that a story is received more truly and completely when I see the memories for myself, then put them into a story that Tana can record. I take images, visual memories, from the person's mind and turn them into words. That is one of the fable tellers' gifts. I do this by placing my hand against the person's head, and of course exchanging the phrases that allow memories to be given."

I thought about this but was still confused. I knew very little about fable tellers, other than that they had a gift for remembering and re-telling stories. I had assumed it was like a kind of marveling, but I'd never known that they could retrieve stories from people's memories. That seemed an astonishing power and I found the idea unsettling.

"Why would someone come to give you their stories?" I asked.

"Many reasons. Most often they want their memories recorded, and they trust me to do so more accurately than they can do themselves. We all know that our memories—as we think we know them—are very often fallible, vulnerable to so many influences, including time itself."

I nodded, thinking of how vague my childhood memories had already become.

"Some of my customers," continued Rill, "cannot read and write, so they value the services of my scribe." He inclined his head toward Tana, who remained still and silent. "Others, although they can write, believe that my words will be superior to their own. I try to be worthy of that trust." He stopped, and I sensed that his explanation was at an end.

"Thank you for helping me understand," I said. "I can say that I'm here to gather."

"I'll be happy to provide what I can," said Rill. There was a pause. "Although," he continued, and I heard caution in his voice, "I sense that you may also have an interesting story to give. Please remember my services if you should ever be so inclined."

"How do you know that I have a story?"

"It's part of the fable teller's gift. He can sense the presence of stories. Don't worry, it doesn't mean I can see your memories. That would require an agreement between us. But still..."

"Do you retell the stories that you're given?" I asked, suddenly wondering where a fable teller got his material.

"Only when that's part of the agreement," Rill replied. "Many people are quite glad to give permission for their stories to be used in a careful way. It makes them feel important, to feel that their stories might live on through my tellings. And certainly, the stories of individuals can be a valuable addition to the stories that fable tellers get from books, or documents, or our own oral traditions."

"Interesting." I meant it.

"Yes. But I'm sorry to have interrupted your request, Lady. What stories would you like to gather today?"

I told Rill that I hoped to learn about the Battle of the Peace, and we agreed on a price. He asked if Tana could stay, and when I agreed, Tana wordlessly left the table and curled up on a cushion in the shadowy corner of the pavilion. Still holding his notebook, the boy drew a faded blanket around his shoulders and appeared to fall asleep.

Rill's voice became even more melodic as he began to tell of the Battle of the Peace. I settled back to listen, wishing briefly that I'd thought to purchase a cup of tea from the woman across the plaza. I learned first of the Lightkeep, those mystical beings who had established an enclave at the Guardians' Peace generations ago in order to protect the books and artifacts that were crucial to the preservation of Light within the human realm. In establishing the Peace, the Lightkeep also created a sanctuary for themselves, a mostly-closed community defended by those humans—like me—who took the oath of the Guardian.

Rill described the Lightkeeps' purpose as maintaining balance in the world we know. Without their oversight, human affairs could easily be overwhelmed by darkness and despair. The Lightkeep prevented that from happening, by their own efforts as well as by their guidance of human agents. But of course, humans don't agree on the most desirable state for their world, and from time to time, groups of humans arise who wish to destroy the Lightkeep completely, or steal their powers, or both.

One such group arose at the Peace about a hundred years ago, when Tiburon, an influential Senior Guard, began gathering followers. They called themselves Realm Defenders, but history remembers them as the Dark Guards, for their goal was to eliminate the Lightkeep and take control of the artifacts of the Light for their own purposes. The Battle of the Peace pitted these Dark Guards against the Lightkeep and their protectors.

Despite their ephemeral nature, Lightkeep can both kill and be killed. The Battle resulted in many deaths, but in the end the Dark Guards were defeated. Most died, but several–including Tiburon himself–escaped and disappeared.

When Rill's story ended, we sat in silence, listening to Tana's faint whistling snores and the snapping of the loose canvas flap.

Could Tiburon be the mage who killed Linnia's family and controlled Orme's mind? No, that doesn't make sense. The Battle was a hundred years ago. Still, Nod suggested this story might be important. Maybe because Nod's bird is an artifact of the Light? If the bird was stolen–or the entire Knowledge Chalice–during the Battle, that might help explain how the ceramic birds came, eventually, into the hands of two young girls and an old curio collector...

I was opening my purse for Rill's payment when a young man entered the pavilion. His hair was long and windswept, and his coat hung open to reveal a red leather vest, soft and scuffed from wear. He stared at me, placing his palms flat on the table and leaning toward me. I half expected the rickety table to collapse, but it held his weight.

"Who are you?" he demanded, without a greeting or any other niceties. His eyes were fixed on me, his pupils wide and intense in the shade of the canopy.

"Irrin, what is the meaning of this? You're interrupting." Rill sounded stern, but the young man ignored him. Tana rustled in the corner, but I didn't turn.

"Your story, you must give it to me. I can feel it in you." The young man was breathing fast; I could see the rise and fall of his chest, bare under the red vest. His cheeks were flushed and there was a sheen of sweat on his upper lip, despite the cold.

"Irrin, stop this," said Rill. "You're not yourself. This woman is a customer, a gatherer. Step out of the tent so you and I can talk."

Irrin took an awkward step to the side, as if to move around the table. *What in the realm is he planning to do?* I stood up and stepped back from my chair, trying to create some space. Rill stood also. He reached for the young man's arm, but Irrin shook off the fable teller's hand.

With another stride, Irrin was close enough to grab my upper arm with his left hand.

"I must have it." His voice was a growl, and I felt the warmth of his breath on my face.

"Irrin, no!"

Irrin reached toward my face with his right hand, but I blocked his hand away with my forearm. I turned into his body, using my weight to move him off balance. When he stepped back, I struck his throat sharply with the side of my hand, then pushed him away as he dropped his grip. He fell to one knee, gasping for breath, and I moved around him and out of the pavilion.

I debated leaving to look for a security officer, but Irrin was now sitting on the ground, looking dazed and upset. He ran his hands through his hair, and I saw that they were shaking. Rill knelt beside him, talking quietly. A moment later, Rill came out of the pavilion.

"I deeply apologize for my apprentice," he said. "Irrin is experiencing a difficult stage in the life of a fable teller, a time when a young man senses stories very strongly. This can cause feelings that are hard to control. We have a name for this time, and all fable tellers must pass through it, must learn to control and respect their gift if they are to join the brotherhood of our calling. It's never permissible to gather a story by force or coercion, and the penalties for doing so are steep."

"Why did Irrin want my story so much?" I asked, feeling puzzled. "I don't think my life's been very interesting at all."

"I do not know, Lady. Something in your story drew him. I cannot say more, other than to assure you that this loss of control is very unusual for Irrin. He has never reacted like this before. Again, I apologize."

"What will happen to him now?"

Rill avoided this question and the one that I sent to follow it. Taking the cue, I paid for my story and left the plaza.

Chapter 8: Linnia and Laeglin

Laeglin had come to the Peace as a nervous fifteen-year-old. He'd been proud to be accepted into the Apprentices' Academy and also relieved to leave the home he shared with his father. He wouldn't miss the shabby house, with its peeling paint, drafty rooms, and bare cupboards. He wouldn't miss the joyless evenings, the lack of books, or artwork, or friends. And he wouldn't miss the sometimes-violent, broken man he called "Sir." Knowing his father had his own reasons, his own troubles, didn't make it any more tolerable for Laeglin.

His brother Hollon had left home two years before Laeglin, without even a job or an apprenticeship to set him on a path forward. Laeglin didn't blame him for escaping, but he missed his brother and often wished that Hollon had stayed until they were both of an age to make their way together. His anger toward Hollon had only come later, and mostly for a different reason.

Laeglin pushed his hands through his hair. This was a mannerism only, since his hair was cut too short to make any difference. He looked at the girl. Frustration must have shown on his face, because Linnia's chin jutted forward, and she scowled at him.

"I don't want to learn it without him." Her voice, though still girlish at fifteen, was stubborn.

Laeglin sighed. They faced each other in the small training room in the guard house. It was the room where Linnia had first begun her training with Master Bowden more than half a year ago. She had been a terrified, angry child then, but the older man—with his patience and insight–had been a match for her. He had ignored her lashes of temper, ignored the self-consciousness with which she shielded her body, ignored her rude questions and occasional tears. And in the end, they had become unlikely friends.

But now, still recovering from his fight with the dark mage, Master Bowden was unable to carry out the physical duties of the Master Supervisor of the Apprentices' Academy. Laeglin wasn't sure the Master ever would return to training and fighting, although he would never say this out loud and felt bad even for thinking of it. Master Bowden had given him a second chance, had shown him an acceptance and faith that Laeglin would never forget. Laeglin would always owe him a debt.

Laeglin took a breath.

"I know you want to continue with Master Bowden, Linnia. He's great and I understand, I really do. But you know he's still in recovery. I don't know how long that will take, but I do know that he wants you to continue your training in the meantime."

They had started today's session with basic warm-up exercises, then familiar knife drills–how to disarm an attacker with a knife, how to use your own knife as a distraction. Sometimes Dele attended these sessions too, but today it was only Laeglin. He'd decided that the girl was ready to move on to offensive stick drills, but that's where he'd met resistance. Apparently, this was a skill she'd planned to learn from Master Bowden, a precursor to sword skills, which she yearned to master.

Laeglin reminded himself that the girl liked him. She had formed a tentative friendship with him when she first arrived at the Peace to live with her aunt. They'd shared an attachment to the dog, Old Brown, and a comfort with silences. Later, he'd taught her to recognize common bird calls, and she'd tried to spark his interest in horses.

They'd trained together since Master Bowden's injury, and she had grown comfortable not only with his instructional style, but also with the necessity for physical contact with a new training partner. Laeglin thought she trusted him as much as she trusted anyone. With the obvious exception of Master Bowden, her champion.

What would Marolaine do in his position? Try to talk the girl into moving forward with the next step in her training, even if that meant learning from someone other than Bowden? Give in to her obstinacy? Something else? Laeglin wished he could talk to her about it. In his opinion, Marolaine didn't give herself enough credit for her insights on Linnia.

"So, what do you want to do?" Laeglin asked finally. "Your training needs to be guided, Linnia, and not just by your own whims. Is there someone else you'd rather work with?"

"No, I want to work with you. I'm sorry, Laeglin." She dropped her scowl and gave him what he knew was an intentionally endearing smile. It worked anyway and he smiled back.

"Let's find a time to talk to Master Bowden about it, then," he suggested. "Maybe he'll be able to come to some of our sessions, even if he's not ready for the physical parts of the training. That might be a compromise."

Linnia shrugged and he could tell she was ready to move on. "Sounds good," she said. "Can we take a water break now?"

"Sure."

The thin girl with the brown hair, the plain face, and the bright blue eyes slid down against the wall, facing the young soldier with the kind eyes and the quiet hands. They drank in silence, then Linnia changed the subject.

"So, when will Marolaine be back, anyway?"

Laeglin felt a slight increase in his heart rate.

"I'm not really sure," he said. "I just got back from the College myself, but I think she'll be there for a few more days at least."

"I wonder if she'll see Dr. Li while she's there. I wish he hadn't gone back to the College after Orme died, but I guess I can understand why he did. I think Auntie is really worried about him, though. I suggested that we could go together to visit him, see if he needed anything, maybe try to cheer him up, but she didn't seem to want to." Linnia began to re-braid her hair, which had come loose during their exercises.

"It's probably complicated for her," said Laeglin. "She might not want to intrude. We all know what a private man Dr. Li is, and how sad he was after his friend died. Hopefully Marolaine will have a chance to see him while she's there though, see how he's doing."

"With Andris, right? She'll probably visit Dr. Li with Andris, since they were friends too."

"I don't know. They traveled together, but I don't imagine they're spending too much time together in town–they're both busy, I'm sure." Laeglin wouldn't let the girl rattle him. Sometimes she just liked to cause trouble. Then again, she might have some other reason for saying this. Who knew?

"I bet you miss her–Marolaine," said Linnia. "She's a good person, not to mention pretty. I miss her too. I'm planning to teach her how to ride a horse this spring, if Fisk says it's alright. And I wish I hadn't teased her about her cake; I know she tried her best with it, and I know she wants to please her family. Did you ever hear whether her sisters liked it?"

Laeglin was used to topic changes when he talked to Linnia. "You know," he said, "I never asked her about the cake." In truth, he'd been too busy feeling jealous of the time she'd spent with Andris. Andris, who'd been included in a family supper with Marolaine's sisters. Andris, who was there to congratulate her when her nephew was born. Andris, who was not only a good-looking guy, but funny, intellectual, and obviously good company. Andris...

"You probably should have asked her about the cake," said Linnia seriously, squinting her eyes at him.

"Yeah, you're probably right," said Laeglin with a sigh.

Chapter 9

One might imagine the office of a professor would be intriguingly cluttered with books and papers, esoteric decorative items, or mysterious inventions and scientific equipment. But Andris Kinsilver's office looked entirely nondescript to me. It was a small, windowless room on the lower level of the Hall of Science and Mathematics, and it looked as if the desk, bookshelf, table, and chairs had simply been dragged in and then abandoned, misfits with no idea what to do or where to go. If Andris had made any attempt at office decor, it didn't show.

The only personal item on view was a battered sepak ball, rolled into a corner. This made me smile. I knew how much my friend enjoyed the challenging sport, in which two teams of men passed and kicked a ball across a chest-high net, without using their hands. Andris had convinced me to officiate a few games last fall, and I well-remembered the shouting and camaraderie.

The office was uncomfortably warm, and I unbuttoned the top of my jacket as I sat in the chair in front of Andris's desk. I was back in uniform today, and it was a relief to feel like a Guard again after several days in dresses.

"Sorry about the heat," said Andris, who had his jacket off and his sleeves rolled back, "this office is just above the building's furnace room. The rooms on the other side of the Hall are freezing, though–that's where the Realm Science professors have their offices–so I guess it could be worse?" Andris was a professor of mathematics, with a particular interest in how probability could be used to understand human decision making. I knew he already had an impressive reputation in his field, despite his youth.

I'd given Andris a summary of my meetings with Nod's son Darro, and with Rill, the fable teller. Andris hadn't known about story-giving either, and we spent some time discussing the implications of being able to read a fellow human's memories. I didn't mention my unsettling encounter with Irrin, the apprentice fable teller.

"So, what's next?" asked Andris, leaning back dangerously far in his chair and placing one foot on the desk.

"I learned a lot about the Lightkeep and the Battle of the Peace," I said, "but I'm not much closer to finding Hollon. Although," I added, "Darro's description could help. It sounds like Hollon looks something like Laeglin, which I guess I could have anticipated, since they're brothers."

"But you're here at the College to see the Chancellor?"

"Yes. It's strange, but she sent a messenger to Belva's house, asking me to meet with her this morning in her office. Belva didn't know what it was about, but she looked nervous."

"Chancellor Axelle has that effect on people," said Andris wryly.

"Anyway," I continued, "I'll find out soon enough. Although knowing how she's treated Dr. Li, I'm not exactly looking forward to spending time with her. And I don't intend to tell her any more than I have to, whatever it is she wants from me."

"Well, be cautious," said Andris, "she's a powerful person, and very persuasive. I have meetings this morning and then a sepak match this afternoon, but maybe we could meet for supper, and you can give me an update. I could come to Belva's if you think she'd be willing to put the wolverine in some kind of cage."

"Ferret."

"If you say so."

We both laughed, and Andris lowered his foot to the floor and stood to go.

"That sounds nice," I said, also standing. "Jay has a little house where he sleeps, so I'm sure Belva won't mind. I'll ask her though. After this meeting with the Chancellor, I'm planning to stop back at Belva's, and then visit Dr. Li's boarding house to see if I can talk to him. You didn't find him yesterday?"

"No. I went by, but he wasn't there. Min either."

THE CHANCELLOR'S OFFICE made Andris's seem cozy. Where his was merely neglected, hers was actively austere: large and impersonal and chilly. A fireplace at one end was unlit, as if someone eschewed the comfort it might provide to either the room's occupant or its visitors. The room was furnished in heavy oak, with fitted bookshelves covering an entire wall. I couldn't discern the titles, but the books themselves were placed so neatly that their spines formed an unbroken front, like a phalanx of literary soldiers in formation.

I passed an oval wall mirror as I entered. Its edges were fogged and spotted with age, but the glass showed what I knew myself to be: an attractive young woman, with brown eyes under straight brows, rounded lips, and dark hair pulled back in a bun at the base of my neck. The mirror was hung high enough to show only my face and upper body, but it was enough for me to see my red uniform jacket, with its stiff collar, gold buttons, and reinforced seams. *I'm so used to thinking of myself this way, but who would I be without this uniform? Am I any different than the Chancellor, creating a persona for others to know me by?*

The owner of the office sat behind a polished desk outfitted with a matching desk set: blotter, leather correspondence folders, a fountain pen, and a lethally ornate letter opener. Everything was organized and dust-free, and there were no stray papers on the desk to betray her recent activities. It could only be intentional, this impression of cold efficiency. *Is this who she needs to be to maintain her power? Or who she thinks she needs to be? Either way, I wonder if she's right.*

Chancellor Axelle was a trim, upright woman in her mid-sixties, her gray hair pulled back in a twist to reveal jeweled earlobes. She wore the dark green robes of her office, heavy velvet falling to her wrists and skimming the floor beside her chair. *Maybe that's why she doesn't light the fire—those robes look hot. I wonder if she has a personal seamstress...I'll have to ask Bellina about it sometime.*

The Chancellor hadn't risen when I entered her office, but she'd been courteous as she directed me to sit and offered tea or ginger water. I was still mystified about why she'd asked to meet with me. But I knew that Dase, the head of the Lightkeep at the Peace, didn't trust her. I knew that she'd manipulated Dr. Li into locating the Sword at the Peace. I knew that she was now desperate to obtain the Sword, and that she'd blackmailed Dr. Li over something in his past, forcing him to resign. *In fairness, much of what I know against her is hearsay, but still...*

"Thank you for coming in, Guardian Marolaine." Her voice was low and measured.

"Of course, Chancellor Axelle." *It's strange knowing that her given name is Racindalyn. It's a lovely name, but so whimsical, it seems out of keeping.*

We talked inconsequentially for several minutes before the Chancellor shifted in her seat and straightened her shoulders. I read these movements as a signal that she was ready to reveal the purpose of the meeting, and I was right.

"If we may move to business?" she asked. "I imagine you have a full day, as do I."

I nodded and waited for her to continue.

"I am aware that you recently submitted several written requests to the Office of Records," she said smoothly. "Requests that indicate your interest in those here at the College–faculty or staff–who may have connections to the Lakelands district. As one of those persons myself, I'd like to understand your interest in the matter."

This is unexpected. I wonder how she came to know of my requests. There's no way that she has time to oversee such minor College activities. Perhaps someone told her, but why would they?

I decided to say as little as possible until I better understood her motives. "I believe I followed the proper procedures," I said carefully, "but if I've made an error, I will certainly try to correct it."

"No, the forms were all correctly completed, and the information you requested falls within College guidelines for acceptable use and release."

I admired her economy of speech and her eye contact. I was a trained observer, but the Chancellor had none of the movements and mannerisms that so often betray underlying emotions. I waited, knowing that powerful people are sometimes impatient, and hoping my silence would encourage her to elaborate. I was overmatched however, and after several minutes under her cool regard, I spoke.

"Was there a problem with the approval?" I asked, thinking of how Belva had offered to circumvent the Requests and Requisitions Committee.

Chancellor Axelle smiled slightly, and I wondered if she was aware that she had out-maneuvered me. *Probably.* "No. The approvals granted by Supervisor Ka-Sastritty were according to procedure. In fact, I met with Belva briefly to ask her about them." *Oh no, I hope Belva isn't in any trouble for helping me. I wonder why she didn't mention meeting with the Chancellor though?*

"I'll be blunt," the Chancellor continued. "I'd like you to tell me why you're interested in faculty and staff from Lakelands."

I took a sip of my ginger water–unusually spicy–to give myself time to think. "I'm looking for information on someone who may have grown up there." I preferred some of the truth to an outright lie.

"Forgive my bluntness, Guardian, but I feel you're being evasive."

At that moment, we both heard noises from the hallway, and turned toward the office's closed door. It opened, and a man strode into the room. Behind him, the Chancellor's personal assistant–a thin, elderly man wearing large glasses on a silver chain–was gesticulating.

"You absolutely cannot enter without permission–" the assistant protested in a high voice.

Without looking back, the tall man interrupted. "I'm already here, Mister Sparks, and I intend to speak to the Chancellor before I leave."

Chancellor Axelle had paled, but her voice was steady as she spoke to her assistant. "Thank you, Mister Sparks, but I'll allow this interruption."

"I'm so sorry, Madame." His hands dropped to his sides, but his eyes burrowed resentfully into the tall man's back.

"Yes. Now please close the door, Mister Sparks."

The intruder approached the desk with a humorless smile. His face was clean shaven, but craggy and lined, his dark eyes hooded, his hair so black it must have been dyed. He was wearing a black cloak over a sharply tailored black suit and carrying a leather satchel, which he dropped on an empty chair as if it had no value to him. A small, gathered pouch hung at his hip, secured by a narrow strap across his chest.

"Hello Racindalyn, you're looking well as always." His voice was deep, and something about it seemed vaguely familiar. The Chancellor made no reply, her gaze hard.

"And who is this?" the man asked, gesturing at me dismissively but keeping his focus on the Chancellor. "One of your faculty members? They do get younger with each passing year, don't they?" He made a noise that might have been a laugh, had it not been entirely lacking in humor or warmth.

"This is a person with an appointment to see me," the Chancellor said pointedly. "What do you want, Krale?"

I sat frozen, wondering if I should offer to leave, or perhaps just leave without offering. But neither the Chancellor nor her visitor were paying me any attention, so I stayed.

"I was in town, just for the day. I'll be traveling to Jarradell College, perhaps for an extended stay, so I thought I'd take this opportunity to visit you and see if you had any information for me. I grow impatient, Racindalyn, although it pains me to say it. I'm a cultured man, a tolerant man–as you know–but eventually even our shared past may not be enough to ensure my goodwill."

I could see that the Chancellor's hands were clenched tightly in her lap, and I was surprised by this show of emotion. *He must be someone she dislikes but doesn't have power over. Otherwise, she'd simply throw him out of her office, or call security. I wonder...is there any chance this could be the man Dr. Li referred to? The man the Chancellor hated but couldn't refuse, the man she was planning to give the Sword to? If so, I might be looking at the mage who was behind Orme's death and the threats to my family. But wait...no, that doesn't make sense. This man–Krale—doesn't recognize me, and he would if he'd been the creature in Captain Matteo's office the night that Orme died, the mage who took control of Orme's body and fought with Master Bowden for the Sword. He must be someone else, but who?*

"I have no information for you." The Chancellor's lips showed white around their edges. I thought of the expression "pursed lips," and it occurred to me for the first time that this referred to lips drawn tight like the gathering of a purse when its string is cinched.

"That's unfortunate," said the man, raising his hands in a gesture I didn't recognize. I saw both of his wrists though, and neither was marked with the tattoo I'd seen on the men who'd attacked me and Andris in town last fall.

He continued. "Perhaps there's some message you'd like me to give to your son then, Racindalyn, should I see him. Some final thoughts–" His voice was mocking, and he moved closer to the desk, still standing but now leaning over the Chancellor. His long fingers gripped the pouch that hung at his side.

"Don't you dare threaten him!" Chancellor Axelle's interruption was nearly a shriek, and she jumped to her feet, her poise shattered.

The man moved so quickly that I heard the sharp crack almost before my mind processed his motion. He had struck the Chancellor across the face. She stumbled back in shock, breathing heavily and holding a hand to her cheek.

I leapt to my feet. I had no authority outside the Peace, but I certainly wasn't going to stand by as this man assaulted the Chancellor, no matter what my feelings for her might be. I called, "Mister Sparks!" planning to direct the assistant to summon the College's security team while I moved to subdue the uninvited visitor.

The words were barely out of my mouth, however, when the man cupped his hands together in front of himself, then slowly drew them apart as he turned in my direction. He stared at me, and I had to look away. I saw a black sphere rotating within the cage of his hands, and then, in an instant, I was thrown back against the wall.

The man had cast the sphere toward me, and it hovered now, in front of my chest where I sprawled on the floor. It looked like a ball of swirling black smoke, its center very dark and its edges gauzy. There was a sharp, metallic smell in the air. I couldn't move to stand, or to draw a weapon. It was as if I had no control of my muscles at all, although I longed to move away from the sphere. Something told me that as bad as I felt now, it would be unimaginably worse if the sphere were to touch me.

I could barely see or think with the pain in my head, but I tried to force my brain down a channel of logical thought. *The sphere isn't going to touch me, in fact it looks like it's fading. I just need to stay calm. Did I strike the wall when he forced me back? Or is this headache somehow related to magic?*

For there was no doubt now that this man was a mage, even if he wasn't the same mage who had attacked Linnia and caused the death of Orme.

He took a step toward me, and his voice was threatening. Arrogant. "I don't know who you are, but I strongly suggest you stay out of my affairs." *There's really not much I can do, paralyzed here on the floor, now is there?* Being powerless made me angry. And also afraid of what this man might do next. The Chancellor was still standing behind her desk, but I didn't trust her actions either—she wasn't the kind of person who would be intimidated for long.

With tremendous relief I heard booted footfalls in the hallway. Mister Sparks must have heard the commotion and called for help. Seconds later, the office door was flung open and four uniformed men entered, weapons drawn. Mister Sparks stood behind them, wiping his forehead with a handkerchief and looking defiant.

I expected the worst—an armed confrontation in a small space, with innocent people at risk. But instead, the man the Chancellor had called Krale picked up his satchel and walked unhurriedly toward the security unit. He waved a hand in their direction, and like me, they were forced backward, falling to the ground and creating a path for him to walk through unmolested.

As he passed the mirror, Krale glanced at it. Without warning, the mirror exploded, sending a waterfall of glass shards cascading down the wall, where they pooled on the floor below. A shard struck the nearest officer, slicing his face before falling at his feet. Blood trickled down his cheek, but he did not move.

Mister Sparks sidestepped the glass and glared angrily at Krale. Of everyone in the room, only Mister Sparks seemed unaffected by the power of the mage. As Krale passed him, the elderly assistant pulled a bound notebook from his jacket pocket and threw it at Krale's retreating back. The book struck true with a solid smack, but Krale kept walking, striding down the hall and out of sight.

AFTER THE CHANCELLOR had given her report, and the security captain had assured her that his men would search the campus until they found Krale (which I doubted), I was once again alone with the formidable woman. I had a headache, and I could feel a bruise on my hip where I'd struck the wall, but otherwise the physical effects of Krale's spellwork had been temporary. I settled back in my chair.

After overseeing the removal of the shattered mirror, Mister Sparks had insisted on making fresh tea. He had also brought the Chancellor a blanket. It was a pink knitted blanket with tasseled fringe, more like something one would give a new baby than the leader of the Clanstin college-state. Still, the Chancellor had accepted it with gratitude, and it now draped her knees. It made me like her a little more.

She was still shaken, and I empathized. I knew what it felt like to feel both angry and afraid in the aftermath of violence. Especially when one is unaccustomed to violence. *And after all, who expects to be attacked in her own office on a random day at work?*

"Are you sure you wouldn't like me to walk with you back to your house?" I asked for the second time. "It might be good for you to lie down, or just have a little time away to regain your equilibrium."

"Thank you, but I'm fine. I'm not hurt, and I'm relieved that neither you nor Mister Sparks are either." *Each person deals with stress in her own way. I know that for myself, and I'm sure it's true for the Chancellor too. Maybe she'll want to talk about it instead.*

"So, you obviously knew that man, Krale?" I asked exploratorily. Cinnamon steam scented the air, rising from the floral-patterned teapot on her desk and adding a note of domesticity to the chilly office.

She took a sip of the tea, then adjusted the blanket on her knees. "Yes. We knew each other growing up, years ago in Lakelands."

"Krale was a friend?"

"No, not a friend of mine. He was close with my older brother, Faris, though, so I saw him often."

Memories drifted across her eyes like clouds, and she continued. "They spent so much time together back then, always talking about science and how the world works, coming up with theories and new ideas. Faris wanted to move to the coast and be a professor, and Krale wanted to be a scholar at the Peace." She paused and I waited. I had shifted my chair, so my body was at a slight angle. It was less threatening than facing her square-on across the desk, and I hoped to encourage conversation.

"But even as a girl," she said finally, "I knew there was a lacking in Krale. He was brash and outspoken, and yet it always seemed that his bravado covered some fundamental fear." She raised the teacup, inhaling the steam but not drinking. Her gaze was unfixed.

"Fear?"

"Fear that he wasn't smart enough. Fear that people didn't like him or esteem him in the way he demanded. Fear that he would fail. I'm not sure, really. But after the Peace turned him away, he was angry and resentful. Faris tried to convince him to return to university, but Krale wouldn't listen. He began to make other choices...choices that led him in a darker direction." She shook her head, as if trying to clear unwanted thoughts.

"And your brother? Did he become a professor?"

Her eyes snapped up, meeting mine briefly. I saw her pain. Then she looked down at the desk and I strained to hear her reply. "My brother's dead. He died a long time ago."

I offered my sympathy, but she seemed not to hear. We sat in silence.

After several minutes, I ventured gently, "Chancellor, do you know where Krale's living now?"

"I'm sorry, but I don't have that information," the woman said stiffly. *She's trying to get back on professional ground, which I understand. She's probably lying when she says she doesn't know where Krale is, but it won't help me to pressure her about it right now.*

"Do you know when I might expect to get the results of my requests for information through the Records Department?"

"The Requests and Requisitions Committee usually has a six to eight week turn-around." *Oh great, she's going to put my requests into the hands of the college bureaucracy. That means I might conceivably never get a response.*

"But Marolaine?" she added, surprising me with the use of my name and the tone of her voice, "I suggest that you don't try to pursue this request any further. Krale is not a man who allows his privacy to be invaded without a cost. He could pose a danger to you." *Interesting that she's choosing to warn me. I'm sure she's right, and it sounds like Krale probably isn't the man I'm looking for anyway. But still...could it really be just a coincidence that I encountered him here?*

"Thank you for your advice," I said politely. Then, deciding on a change of strategy, "Did you know what he meant when he asked you for information?"

She stared at me, her face tightening. "Yes, and I think that you did too. I know you've spoken to San Li, so let's give each other the respect of honesty." *So Krale is almost certainly the man who wanted the Sword. The man she couldn't refuse. That doesn't mean he's the man I'm looking for though, especially since he didn't appear to recognize me today, even in my Guard uniform. And unlike the attackers in town, he had no marking on his wrist. This is all so confusing. I need to talk to Captain Matteo. And Laeglin.*

"What did he mean about your son, if I may—"

"He's taken my son," she interrupted, spitting the words at me so vehemently that I pulled back. Tea sloshed from her cup, splashing the desk.

She put her fist to her mouth then and turned away with a muffled sob. *Whatever is happening with her son, it must be terrible to cause this reaction. She'll regret what she's said to me; she's not the kind of woman who forgives herself for lapses in self-control.*

My instincts were correct. Whatever Chancellor Axelle might know or think or feel, she was now determined to say nothing more. I tried to offer comfort, but she turned it away. So, I thanked her for her time, asked if there was anything else I could do for her, and left her sitting at her desk. As rigid as an arrow and as lost as a child.

Chapter 10

It was that time of year when a cold, blustery day could be immediately followed by a fair one. I left the Chancellor's office and began to walk through the streets around the college campus. It was a residential neighborhood of small houses and cottages, neatly kept, and I passed several optimistic homeowners tilling soil in preparation for spring gardens, clearing dead leaves, or raking their gravel pathways.

As I walked, my headache subsided. Sunshine warmed the top of my head, and I intentionally slowed my pace, taking in deep breaths of early spring air. My thoughts, which had swirled chaotically for the last hour, began to settle. I knew that Krale was involved in the quest for the Sword of Light. It seemed clear that he was the reason Dr. Li had been sent to the Peace last fall, and the reason that Chancellor Axelle was so desperate to obtain the Sword that she had sunk to blackmailing Dr. Li. The Chancellor's son was a new and unknown element.

Is her son a child? Probably not, given her age. Could her son have actually been abducted? Or is it possible that her words were not meant literally, but rather that Krale has some hold over her son? Or even that her son is willingly associating with Krale in some way?

I nodded to a friendly woman walking a dog, then continued trying to order my thoughts. *I've learned more about the Battle of the Peace, but I don't understand how Tiburon and the Dark Guards fit into my current problem. If they do at all. I've learned that Chancellor*

Axelle is being forced to give the Sword to Krale. I've learned that she threatened Dr. Li with some kind of exposure, but he won't tell her where the Sword is, in part because he doesn't know. It's possible that there are many unrelated threads here: the past deaths of Linnia's family, the recent death of Orme, the mystery surrounding the Sword of Light, and the threats to my family by a man who may–or may not–be the tall man with the wrist tattoo who attacked Andris and I last fall.

My father used to say, 'You can't sew a straight line with tangled thread.' Was I tangling too many threads? I needed to decide on my next action. It now seemed likely that my attempt to follow official channels–requesting information from the Records Department–would be suffocated by the College's bureaucracy. The one source of information I hadn't yet explored was Laeglin's brother, Hollon.

If I could find Hollon, he might identify the man he'd stolen Nod's bird for. I might still be able to approach this man and buy back the bird. And in exchange for the bird, Nod would hopefully give me the identity of the mage who threatened my family.

I'll make one last attempt to find Hollon. I'm sure Andris will be willing to go with me again to the Hail Tavern, perhaps after supper tonight. After that–either way–I'll return to the Peace and talk this through with Captain Matteo and Laeglin. I thought of Laeglin–reliable, smart, and caring. I suddenly longed to be close to him, to smell his clean wintergreen scent, to know there was someone who would always see the best in me. *I don't like being away. I miss Laeglin and I miss the Peace.*

WRAPPED IN A VOLUMINOUS caftan that nearly matched her home's purple shutters, Belva was reclined in a chair on the porch when I returned. A book was splayed open on her ample bosom and her eyes were closed. Sunlight illuminated her body from the shoulders down, leaving her face in shadow. About eight feet away, Jay the ferret paced in the outdoor cage that jutted from the front of the cottage. Every so often he paused, rose onto his back legs, and used his small front feet to prop himself against the wire of the enclosure. In this position he stared at Belva, emitting a low, agitated chatter that his mistress seemed to be ignoring.

I stepped over the large statuary toad and walked slowly up the path. I didn't want to startle my host. With my approach, however, Jay began to chatter more loudly, fluffing up his tail and running from side to side in his enclosure. Belva opened her eyes. She grinned when she saw me.

"Well, hello there!" she called, sitting up and adjusting her caftan, a second too late for modesty.

"Hello, Belva. I'm surprised to see you outside, although it is a beautiful day. It almost feels like spring."

"Well, yes, I don't usually venture out on my own, as you know. Still, something felt different today. I felt different, I'm not sure how to explain it, but I didn't want to be inside." She shook her head and the large hoops in her ears swayed and glinted, tugging her earlobes down with their weight.

I sat beside her on the porch and told her briefly about my morning, leaving out my encounter with Krale. I trusted Belva, but I didn't want to worry her and there seemed no way to share just the reassuring parts of a story that included threats to the Chancellor and a magical attack on myself and a security detail. Belva was already concerned that she had inadvertently caused trouble for me by talking to Chancellor Axelle about my information requests. *If only she knew.*

"Oh! And I nearly forgot," said Belva, rummaging in the folds of her caftan, "this letter was delivered for you earlier. The carrier was friendly, we talked for several minutes. It seems strange that in all these years we'd only ever waved to one another through the window glass. It was wonderful to have a conversation out here in the fresh air and sunshine." She handed me the letter and I could see that it was marked with the insignia of the Peace. My heartbeat quickened. *I hope there's nothing wrong.*

Instead, it was a note from Laeglin, handwritten in his careful script. I knew that he'd worked hard to improve his writing since coming to the Peace, trying to make up for his lack of formal education as a boy. I imagined Laeglin sitting at the small desk in the room he shared with three other soldiers. His long fingers holding the pen. Concentration wrinkling the smooth skin around his eyes. His head tilted, exposing the muscles along the sides of his neck. I imagined running my finger over the scar on his temple, along his cheekbone, down to his lips...*Hold on, Belva is going to wonder why I'm sitting here blushing before I've even opened the letter.*

The note was brief. Laeglin was sorry we hadn't had a chance to talk before he left for the College. He'd had a successful trip. The arrangements hadn't taken long. He was back at the Peace. He missed me. When did I plan to return?

It was not the letter I'd hoped for. I knew that. But any fantasies I had about flowery prose and declarations of love were just that: fantasies. Something from a novel, perhaps. Something a bit embarrassing for a twenty-four-year-old soldier, no matter how inexperienced she might be. Laeglin rarely wrote personal letters, and for that matter, neither did I. This had been a genuine effort and I accepted it in that spirit. In fact, I wished I'd thought to write to him, rather than hoping the Lights would grace me with an accidental meeting here in Clanstin.

"What is it, dear?" asked Belva.

"Oh, just a note from a...friend."

"Speaking of," said Belva with a wink, "when is that tempting Andris coming back? I certainly hope he hasn't been scared off by my sweet Jay." She sent a loving look toward her ferret, who now managed to look like he was pouting, puddled dejectedly on the floor of the wire enclosure. Clearly, he wasn't happy about being separated from his mistress.

We talked about plans for supper, and Belva said she'd be delighted to cook something for the three of us. I told her I planned to wash, have a quick lunch, and then go visit a friend. Laeglin's letter had firmed my decision: I would visit Dr. Li this afternoon, hope to find Hollon this evening with Andris, and then return tomorrow to the Peace.

"I DON'T KNOW WHERE he is," the woman said sullenly. "Why would I?" Her hair was pulled back severely, and a worn, full-length apron covered her dress. She squinted suspiciously into the weak afternoon sun, its light unkind to the dry patches of redness on her cheeks and forehead. If one imagined the cheerful, plump, motherly landlady of fiction, and then reversed every particular, one might come close to describing the woman who stood blocking the entrance to Dr. Li's boarding house. I didn't know her name, and she hadn't offered it.

"I'm sorry to interrupt your work," I said politely, trying again. "I'm a friend of Dr. Li and I was hoping to visit with him this afternoon." I was still in my Guard's uniform, and the landlady eyed me now with open distaste.

"I'm certain we've never had any lady visitors of your type before." She made 'your type' sound infectious. "It seems to me that a friend—as you claim the professor is—would be here to greet you upon your arrival. If he was expecting you. And if he wanted to see you." She placed her hands on her narrow hips. Her meaning was clear, and I knew I was defeated.

"Is it possible you know where he's gone this afternoon?" I asked.

"Is it my job to keep track of all the gentlemen who live here, now would you say?" I started to reply, but she turned and pulled the door firmly closed behind her, leaving me alone on the front step with an awkward smile still clinging to my lips.

I felt wrong-footed. At the Peace, where I'd lived for the past six years, my uniform was recognized and respected. I was recognized and respected. Here in town though, I felt unsure of myself. It was like I was a Junior Guard all over again, trying to find my place in an unfamiliar world. I thought about my poor attempt to communicate with Creedling at the Hail Tavern, my inability to take faster action when Chancellor Axelle was attacked by Krale, and now my failure to have even a simple conversation with Dr. Li's landlady.

Am I even less capable than I realized? Have I let my isolation at the Peace shield me from the rest of the realm and what it demands? I'm certainly not like Andris and JenVie, able to move easily between communities, able to adjust to different people and situations. Is that why I miss the Peace—because I'm afraid I can't adapt anywhere else?

I didn't like feeling sorry for myself, so I decided to take what action I could. Dr. Li apparently spent much of his time at the tavern; it was only mid-afternoon, certainly a safe time for me to go there to look for him. And who knew? I might find Hollon as well. That would save Andris another trip to the tavern and give me a chance to prove to myself that I could handle a simple interaction on my own.

I HADN'T KNOWN THAT so many men drank in the afternoon. The Hail Tavern was less crowded than three nights ago, but far from empty. I forced myself to keep my head up, meeting the curious gaze of strangers as I entered the dim, over-warm space. *Maybe I should have changed back into a dress. Although I'm not sure I'd have been*

any less conspicuous that way. And perhaps the uniform will discourage Creedling. Ugh, he's seen me.

I nodded curtly to the tavern's owner, but turned to my right, toward the table in the corner where Dr. Li had been sitting last time. To my relief, he was there. I realized suddenly that I'd had no plan for what to do if he hadn't been. This was the second time I'd entered this tavern without being prepared. *Not smart. What would Captain Matteo say, after all my training?*

Instead of a bottle, Dr. Li sat facing a silver tankard, its surface dull and smudged. He looked up as I approached and nodded briefly. Min, lying on the floor beside his rolling chair, thumped her tail softly in greeting. I reached down and ruffled her ears. As I did, I thought fondly of Old Brown, the dog who had saved the life of the Lightkeep Kies many years before, and now spent his time walking the grounds with Laeglin and sleeping on the porch of the guard house.

Dr. Li was unshaven, and I could smell alcohol, as if it radiated from his skin. He looked even thinner than I remembered. I was uncomfortable, aware that I had seated myself with my back to the room; Dr. Li already had the position I would have preferred. Between us, we were not at our best, and–after a brief discussion about Min–the conversation faltered.

I was startled when Creedling appeared beside me, standing too close and holding a foaming glass of cider. I shifted my chair to create some space, not caring if this appeared rude.

"Ho there, pretty lady, it's a pleasure to have you here in my establishment again. Let me offer you something cold." His smile was ingratiating, and as he put the glass down, he brushed against my upper arm. I pulled away, forcing an unconvincing smile in return. Dr. Li growled something under his breath and Creedling fixed him with a stare before turning back to me.

"Sooooo." He stretched the word out as he eyed my uniform. "I didn't realize you were a Guardian. Not often my establishment has the pleasure." He paused, but I stayed silent. Dr. Li rubbed his thumb in circles on the side of his tankard.

"Perhaps you'd like to join me for a private drink, since you're here alone and all. I have a nice room in the back for my personal guests." He smiled and wiped his hands against the sides of his apron. I honestly couldn't tell if this was a sincere invitation or innuendo. Either way, I was hardly tempted. My face must have shown it, because he stepped back and his eyes hardened. "Or maybe a lady like you is too good to have a drink with a man like me."

There was no mistaking his tone now, and I didn't bother with an apology. The tavern owner opened his mouth as if to continue, then closed it. His beefy hands clenched at his side as he turned his back on us and walked back to the bar.

A SHORT TIME AFTER Creedling left the table, another man approached. Like the proprietor, he was short and stocky, and I wondered if they might be related. Two men stood behind him, a few steps back and looking off to the side, as if reluctant to fully associate themselves with the man in front. Heightened alertness tensed my muscles, and I brought my hand to my hip reflexively, feeling the handle of the knife at my belt and the reliable heft of my Lightstick. Dr. Li continued to stare at the table.

"Well now, this is a sorry lot," the short man said thickly, thrusting his chin toward us. His stained shirt was tight across his belly and his eyes were red. "Last I knew this was a reputable tavern, but here I'm seeing a woman, a cripple, and a mangy dog. Now, what's a man supposed to think about that, huh fellas?" He turned to the men behind him and laughed, inviting them to share the joke.

Dr. Li dropped his hand beside his rolling chair, and Min nuzzled his palm. I kept my expression neutral. Sometimes a fight could be avoided simply by refusing to be drawn in.

"Can we help you with something?" I asked, my voice mild but firm. I didn't wait for a reply. "If not, I'd ask that you let us enjoy our drinks, like everyone else." *How am I going to get Dr. Li and Min out of here safely? Our path to the exit is blocked. I don't think the two men in the back want to fight, but the man in front looks drunk, unpredictable. I wonder if he's really related to Creedling. Would Creedling cause trouble for us just because I hurt his pride? Probably.*

"Well there, 'Miss Lady Guardian'—" he emphasized the title in a nasty way–"it seems to me that you're *not* like everyone else, you think you're a fair sight better. Too good for the likes of us." He snorted in appreciation of his own humor, then glanced at the bar for approval. Creedling was watching the exchange while he idly wiped the bar top with a rag.

"And I don't think we need any dirty mutts in here either," the short man said, turning his attention toward Min. The dog pushed herself up against Dr. Li's chair, her eyes wide.

The troublemaker moved faster than I'd expected, reaching down and snatching Min by the scruff. She hung helplessly in his grip, whimpering and looking smaller than before.

The man turned toward his friends then, preparing some humorous remark. He had just opened his mouth, when Dr. Li reached behind his back, grasped one of his long, metal forearm crutches, and swung it hard.

Dr. Li used a rolling chair most of the time, but I knew that his spinal injury wasn't complete; he could walk short distances using the forearm crutches. He kept these crutches attached to the back of his chair, ready to access if needed. And the professor had a strong upper body, more so now that he no longer had a personal assistant.

The crutch struck the short man on his exposed left side. When the metal thudded against his ribs, the man grunted and dropped Min to the floor. The dog scampered to the corner, where she cowered under an empty chair, her anxious eyes fixed on Dr. Li.

"You stupid crippled bastard!" the man shouted, spraying saliva. I was on my feet, but before I could restrain him, the short man grabbed the side of Dr. Li's rolling chair and tipped it viciously, dumping Dr. Li to the floor. The chair fell on top of him, and Dr. Li swore softly. From the corner, Min whined.

I grabbed the short man's wrist to stop whatever he might contemplate next. I twisted his arm up behind his back, while grasping his opposite shoulder with my other hand to keep him turned away from me. My goal was to force him away from Dr. Li, and I nudged the back of his knee to move him forward. I glanced over my shoulder. The professor was already pushing himself into a sitting position. He met my eyes and nodded. Given a few minutes, he could maneuver his chair upright, and then use his arms to pull himself back into his rolling chair. Everything depended on time though. The short man swore under his breath as he worked to break my grip.

I need to control this situation, to give Dr. Li time to get up and back into his chair. This is no place to use a Guard weapon, but I shouldn't need to, as long as this fight doesn't escalate beyond one drunk idiot. Maybe Creedling will finally step in...

I looked toward the bar, but the tavern owner had disappeared. The patrons scattered around the room seemed disinclined to help, avoiding my eyes as I searched for a friendly–or at least reasonable–face amongst them.

"Stop it!" I shouted at the short man, who continued to struggle and swear as his friends looked on. Then I lowered my voice and leaned closer to his ear. *No need to embarrass him. He might see reason on his own.*

"This doesn't have to get any worse. Let's just move away and calm down. We don't want any trouble."

The short man rejected this offer by slamming his head backwards into my face, striking the bridge of my nose. The sharp spear of pain filled my eyes with involuntary tears, and I felt the blood flow at once. I loosened my hold, and the man pulled away. Turning to his friends–who still hung back–he sneered, "No woman's gonna tell me what to do. Come on, you lot, let's show these two that we mean what we say."

I stepped back, holding my sleeve to my face to stanch the blood. In the meantime, Dr. Li had righted his chair, and was pulling himself into it, the muscles in his forearms straining. His hair hung loose over his face, but I could see the tension around his mouth. He was angry, and I was too.

I was also smart enough to realize that getting out of the tavern needed to be our priority. Things could easily get worse, and I needed to protect Dr. Li and the dog. I leaned toward Dr. Li. "Get Min–we need to go now," I said in a low voice. He turned and whistled, a thin reedy sound that caught Min's attention. She crawled out from under the chair and jumped onto Dr. Li's lap. The tension in his face eased slightly, and he placed his hand on her back.

I put my hand on the grip of my Lightstick but didn't draw it from my belt. "Stand back," I said to the three men, "we just want to leave."

With a yell, the short man charged me like a bull, his arms out, head aimed for my chest. I had no desire to hurt anyone, and–I knew from experience–the Lightstick could be a deadly weapon just as much as my sword or knives. But I had to get us out.

I dropped my center of gravity, grabbed his shoulder and arm, shifted my hip into his, and flipped him onto the floor. His own momentum carried him to a hard landing against the leg of an empty table. He groaned and lay still.

Chaos erupted then, as the two men who'd been watching decided to join the fight, and casual drinkers–who now seemed to be filling the tavern–drew closer to laugh and shout encouragement. The men's punches were clumsy, but they were both strong and reasonably sober. Once engaged, one of the two seemed to find real enthusiasm for the cause, swearing and yelling, even spitting as we grappled among the tables and chairs. *Where in the realm is Creedling? Surely he won't allow his tavern to be wrecked simply because I hurt his feelings? And how do I get myself into these situations, anyway?*

I was in a close-contact struggle with the younger of my two adversaries. I smelled the sweat of his body and the alcohol on his breath, as I blocked a punch and pushed him back. I registered the presence of the shorter man–still down–and the second man–engaged, but still holding back. I wanted to know what Dr. Li was doing, but I couldn't afford to divert my attention. I fervently hoped the professor would leave the tavern with his dog. I still preferred not to draw a weapon, and once Dr. Li was safe, I thought I could probably run to the door.

Then suddenly there was a crash–barely audible above the din–and beer splashed onto my face. The younger man slumped to the floor, leaving his friend staring in surprise. I wiped my face to clear my vision and felt the sharp sting of splintered glass.

The man I'd been fighting now lay at my feet, apparently unconscious. A curved handle lay near his head, all that remained of a heavy glass mug that had come down on the back of his head. I looked to see who had helped me. I had time for only an impression because at that moment the short man who had started all this roused himself from the floor. He and his second friend launched themselves back into the brawl.

Someone called my name. My new ally was grappling with the shorter man, so I stepped back and briefly scanned the room. Dr.

Li had taken advantage of the confusion to move toward the door, adroitly propelling his rolling chair with Min balanced on his lap. He said something I couldn't hear, and I shouted at him to get out. He needed to move his chair; he had no hands free for fighting. There was regret on his face, but I shouted again, and he made his way to the door.

Full-effort fights can seem endless to the combatants. But they're so exhausting that they usually last only minutes. I could tell that the two men who remained were tiring rapidly: sweating and breathing hard and moving unsteadily. The man who had come to my aid was clearly no fighter, but he was resourceful, and he still had some energy. Seeing the success of the smashed beer mug, he picked up a chair, turned it legs-up, and swung it into the back of the shorter man. It struck with a thud, and the man fell to his knees.

It was a turning point. The man who was still standing pulled his friend up. Apparently, the shorter man had finally had enough. He took one unsteady step, then caught his balance on a table and closed his eyes to–I assumed–stop his head from spinning. When he opened them, he looked toward the bar and then muttered something to his friend. With a parting insult to me that seemed half-hearted, they moved away into the crowd, leaving their friend still groggy on the floor.

I dragged my sleeve across my face to clear some of the blood and sweat. Out of habit, I pushed my hair behind my ears and straightened my uniform. The man by my side had his hands on his knees, and I wasn't sure if he was leaning over to catch his breath or to vomit.

He pushed himself upright and our eyes locked, each of us assessing the other while deciding our next move. The man looked a few years older than me, slim but fit. His eyes and hair were dark, and his jawline was shadowed with stubble. A cut above his brow was leaking a trail of blood down the side of his face.

We hadn't spoken during the fight, and we didn't speak now. A crooked smile twitched his lips.

I was about to suggest we get out of the tavern, and fast, when Creedling reappeared. The tavern owner surveyed the room, which was a mess. He scowled at me, then turned to beckon to two men who had entered the tavern and were standing behind him. I drew a breath and my hopes faded. They were armed security officers, wearing the uniforms of the town's force. And they were between us and the door. *So much for our fast exit. At least Dr. Li and Min are safely out. But things have just gotten worse for me and my anonymous friend.*

"I want these two arrested immediately," Creedling said sharply, pointing at me and the man beside me. "I want them charged with assaulting my decent, paying customers, who were just trying to enjoy a drink at a respectable establishment. And I want them held accountable for all the damage they did." He turned his back on the officers and smirked at me. Vengeance was in his eyes.

Chapter 11

We had attempted to plead our case, but the short man said we had taunted and attacked him without provocation, and none of the tavern's regular patrons seemed to have seen anything different. Creedling insisted on our detention, and so we had been taken to the district security office.

The security office was an annex to a larger building on the outskirts of the College grounds. On the outside, it was low and non-descript, more like office space for junior faculty than a detention center. And inside, we were treated more like inept employees who had made an annoying administrative error than serious criminals. I kept waiting for someone to step in and say it was all a joke. Or at least a misunderstanding.

The woman at the desk was short and heavyset, with shining black hair that foamed away from her head in swirls and mounds. She wore half-spectacles, which allowed her to peer at us with exasperation, while simultaneously referencing the documents on her desk. One of the officers who had escorted us to the office sat slouched in a chair near the doorway, sucking on a sugar straw. The other was gone. My weapons had been taken, but otherwise there seemed little concern that we might escape or pose any danger.

I had argued–unsuccessfully–that we had only defended ourselves and were not in violation of any security codes. My ally had been quiet, other than asking if he could have a snack. His request was half-heartedly declined by the officer. The woman behind the desk had stared at him as if he were insane, shaking her head and writing notes on one of the forms in front of her with a pen that scratched.

"It's after 5:00," she now said flatly, gesturing to a timepiece mounted beside her desk.

"Yes?" I wasn't sure of the significance of the time. I stood up straight. I had already done my best to tidy my uniform–which was understandably dirty from scuffling on a tavern floor–and to scrape the dried blood from my face. I wanted to look reasonable and professional, but judging by the woman's expression, I wasn't succeeding.

"Well after 5:00," she said pointedly.

I nodded, then nudged the man beside me until he nodded too.

"And there are a multitude of forms to be completed, reviewed, approved, processed, and filed. Along with a strict procedural protocol for establishing your identity, taking inventory of your belongings, documenting your statements of action, and so forth." This sounded like a rehearsed speech.

Feeling foolish, I nodded again. My new friend simply hummed under his breath, apparently no longer motivated to make a good impression, if he ever had been. I noticed he was chewing something. *Did he somehow manage to get a snack after all? That's impossible, he's been right here beside me...I'm hungry too, but he didn't offer me anything...*

"Are you listening to me?" The woman's tone was peppery, and I snapped my gaze back to her face. "I said that, being as it's after 5:00, the office staff is limited to myself and an assistant." She stared at me, implacable, reminding me of the toad statues at Belva's cottage. Then, in an explosion of movement like a tongue snaring an insect, her hand shot out and smacked a bell positioned on the corner of her desk. It made a jangling sound, and a thin elderly woman appeared, carrying a large box filled with mittens and gloves.

"Miss Kenestrel."

"Yes, Night Coordinator?"

"Are the holding rooms ready?"

"Room A is ready. Room B is not."

"Very well. Please lower the divider in Room A and prepare for two detainees. Bring a pitcher of warm water and towels so that the Guardian can clean her wounds."

"Yes, Night Coordinator." The elderly woman turned and left, the box still in her arms.

There was a long silence, broken only by the tuneless humming. Regardless of his previous help at the tavern, I now wanted to smack the man at my side to stop his humming. Didn't he care that we were falling into the maw of a slow and nonsensical justice process, when we had, in fact, done nothing wrong?

"Do you really mean to keep us here?" I asked, my voice pitched higher than usual.

"There is no way that I and Miss Kenestrel can possibly implement all the required procedures and protocols tonight. You will stay here until morning, when the full staff will be available to efficiently and fairly process your case."

"But that's ridiculous," I said sharply. The Night Coordinator glared at me. Then she nodded at the slouched officer, who stood, stretched his back, and approached us.

"This way," he said amiably, pointing through a doorway next to a large potted plant with dusty leaves.

"But–"

"Better not to resist, friend, who knows what the protocol is for that?" my ally said in a slow, ironic voice that sounded contrived. *Lights, it's almost as if he's enjoying this.*

We stood in the entrance to Room A as Miss Kenestrel used a flat key to open a panel on the wall. The panel door swung out to reveal a series of labeled buttons. I couldn't read the script, but the assistant poked a bony finger at the middle button. A shimmering screen began to lower from the ceiling. From our vantage point, it looked like a curtain made of wavery air. But when it reached the floor, it clicked into place with a sound like a sheet snapping on a clothesline. The room was now divided in two.

Each half of the room was the same, each resembling nothing so much as a vacant office after its tenant had moved out: dingy, impersonal, dispirited. The floor was wood plank, the walls white, and the furniture limited to a desk, a chair, and a table. Each table held a pitcher and two hand towels. Lamps were set into the walls, each behind a wire screen. Miss Kenestrel used her key again and drew back part of the divider so that I could step into my half of the space.

Refusing to answer any of my questions, Miss Kenestrel locked the outer door, and we were left alone. I flopped down in my chair and pulled off my boots with a disgruntled sigh. I scowled at the man across from me. He had dragged his chair closer to the divider, and we might have been simply two people waiting for a meeting to begin. If not for the locked door.

There was no cup, but the man walked to the table and raised the pitcher to his lips with both hands, taking a long sip.

"Isn't the water warm?" I asked peevishly.

"Yes, but I'm thirsty," he said, adding cheerfully, "You look awful." He dipped a hand into the pitcher, then used his wet fingers to clean some of the blood from the cut above his eye.

I scowled harder, knowing that dried blood tracked from my nose to my chin, and tiny cuts speckled my face where the glass shards had lodged. My hair had come out of its bun and tangled around my face. Not to mention the state of my uniform. I was tired and aggravated, and I knew I was taking it out on my ally because there was no one else.

I stalked to the table, turned my back on the man, and began slowly washing my face, wincing when I found a sliver of glass still embedded in my cheek. I hesitated before using the towels, not wanting to stain them. Finally, with a sigh, I patted my face dry, noting the specks of red on the white fabric. I combed my hair with my fingers, then gathered it into a twist with my remaining hair pins. I suspected the man watched me, but I ignored him.

I sat back down and looked at my cell mate, trying to regain my poise. His face was angular, his body thin but strong. He was a good-looking man, though his eyes held a wariness, a hardness, that put me on my guard. Something about him felt familiar.

As if hearing my thoughts, he leaned forward. "You know who I am, don't you?"

I shook my head slightly, at the same time raising my shoulders. *I have a pretty good guess, though.*

He gave me an appraising look, then his lips twitched again, like they had just before the security officers arrived back at the tavern. "I know you're Marolaine, a Guardian of the Peace. And quite a fighter, by the way. You looked like you were about to win that fight all by yourself. You and your friend, the professor."

I nodded but remained quiet, waiting to have my suspicion confirmed.

"Well, Marolaine, my name is Hollon."

THE DAY HAD STARTED with me being thrown against a wall by a dark mage, and ended with me fighting three men in a disreputable tavern. I was tired, dirty, and sore from many bruises and scrapes. And I was sitting within feet of Hollon, the man I'd sought for over a week. So much had happened, it was almost hard to remember why I'd wanted to find him in the first place. Looking at him–the guarded expression, the calloused hands–I could well believe he was a man with secrets. I just wasn't sure he'd tell me the ones I needed to know.

Laeglin's brother was like him, but not. The men shared a similarity of appearance, although Hollon was a few years older and a little shorter and thinner. They had the same skin tone, and dark eyes with long lashes, but Hollon's hair was longer, curling around his neck and ears. And while Laeglin's face was open, Hollon's was wary, as if there were things he didn't want to reveal. I remembered Nod's son Darro saying that Hollon was like a man with troubles inside. I understood what Darro meant, and I wondered how honest I should be.

We spoke cautiously at first: Hollon's tone humorous and lightly sarcastic, mine polite and superficial. We were interrupted by the appearance of Miss Kenestrel, who entered–without knocking, although that shouldn't have surprised me, given our situation–carrying a tray with a mound of vegetable turnovers, two apples, and a pot of tea.

While the door was open, there came the sound of voices from the lobby. My spirits lifted as I heard the deep, easy voice of Andris. And was that–? Yes, I could also hear Belva, her voice rising and falling as if she were filling in the cracks between Andris's words. I turned to Miss Kenestrel.

"It sounds like my friends are here." I gestured toward the open doorway. "Can you tell us what's happening? Are we being released?" It would be wonderful to go back to the cottage, bathe, put on clean clothes, and drink tea with Belva and Andris. I even felt nostalgic about seeing the maniacal ferret, Jay.

"That's really for the Night Coordinator to tell you, Miss," replied Miss Kenestrel in a hurried voice. She put the tray down on the table. She was on Hollon's side of the space, and she glanced at the divider.

"May I open the divider?" she asked, "or do you prefer to be separated?" *Hmmm. If I let her open it, Hollon might consider that a sign of trust and be more open with me. On the other hand, I really don't know anything about him...*

"Probably best to keep it closed," drawled Hollon from his chair. I noticed he hadn't risen to help Miss Kenestrel with the tray. "I wouldn't want to put the Guardian in any awkward situation–unmarried man and woman sharing the same room and all that." *Well, alright then.*

Miss Kenestrel began to separate the food, but I was still focused on the voices in the lobby.

"Will the Night Coordinator come in to tell me what's happening?" I pressed.

"No, I'd say that's quite unlikely," said Miss Kenestrel.

"Then–?"

She sighed, in the way of some elderly ladies. As if the sigh encompassed much more than the present circumstances, and she wanted me to know that. "I can say that your friends are asking for you to be released. But they're not likely to be successful, not with the Night Coordinator. Once she's made a decision..." Miss Kenestrel trailed off. She opened the divider, entered my space, and deposited three turnovers, one apple, and a large mug of steaming tea on the table.

"Honey in your tea, Miss?"

I nodded and she spooned a generous portion from a small pot. When the door closed behind her, it shut out the voices. I settled down to eat, resigned and famished.

THERE'S A GREAT SATISFACTION in being full after being truly hungry. Hollon and I had eaten every morsel, then pulled our chairs close together, separated only by the shimmer of the divider. I had covered myself with a blanket. The room had no beds, so if either of us were to sleep tonight, it would be in these chairs.

We discussed our predicament. We were both resigned to a night in bureaucratic detention, but assumed we'd be released tomorrow morning. It was a relief to me that Andris knew where I was, although I was sorry for the stress he must be feeling after his extended conversation with the Night Coordinator. Andris was a charming man, but I suspected he'd been over-matched.

Hollon revealed that he knew about my relationship with Laeglin, at least in general terms. This surprised me. I knew–from Laeglin–that the brothers had once been close, but that Hollon had left home early, leaving a young Laeglin to contend with their father for those years before he became an apprentice at the Peace. Laeglin had never been forthcoming about his childhood, and I hadn't pressed. I knew what it was like to have ambiguous feelings about one's family.

I wanted to ask Hollon how he knew about his brother's life, but this seemed intrusive. I was finding that Hollon shared what he wanted to share, and only that. If I allowed him to talk, he would. But if I asked too many questions he would retreat into sarcasm or silence. Still, I knew I needed to broach my purpose in searching for Hollon in the first place.

"So," I said, rubbing my eyes. It was after midnight, and I was exhausted. I also wanted to avoid looking at Hollon directly, and my gesture was intended to soften the significance of what I needed to discuss. He raised his eyebrows, and I noted the slight tightening of the skin around his eyes.

"I guess you knew who I was then," I said, "last night in the tavern?"

"You don't think that I always come to the aid of pretty warriors who defend stray dogs from drunken idiots?"

I surprised myself by giggling. "Does that happen often?"

"You'd be surprised. I have a pretty strange life." He shrugged and gave me his lopsided grin.

"But–?"

"Yeah, I knew who you were. I was in the tavern the first night you came in. With a handsome fellow who wasn't my brother, I might mention. You, that is, not me."

I hurried to explain my friendship with Andris, feeling oddly like I was repeating my recent conversation with Laeglin. Hollon nodded; his face was much less expressive than Laeglin's and it was impossible to tell whether he'd accepted my explanation or not.

"So why were you looking for me?"

"This may sound crazy," I began, then went on to relay the gist of my conversation with Nod. How the old man claimed a ceramic bird had been stolen from his curio shop, and how he'd said that bird was the price I must pay for further information about the mage who was threatening my family.

Hollon had begun to smile as I talked. Finally, he broke in, "That old bastard told you I stole the bird, didn't he?"

"Well, yes, he did."

"I'll bet he said some other unpleasant things about me too, am I right?"

I nodded and gave a small shrug of my own. *'Least said, soonest mended,' as Father used to say. An appropriate expression for a tailor.*

"Well, I can't say he's wrong, although that man is a menace in his own right. Him and those sons of his, I don't know which is worse." Hollon paused and I waited for him to continue. "Anyway. So old Nod thought I could help you find the bird. Then you'd give him back the bird and in exchange he'd tell you what you want to know. Is that about it?"

"I know it sounds convoluted, but yes, that's right. Although I don't know how fully I can trust him. He's–"

"You can't trust Nod at all," Hollon interrupted. "Like I said, the man's a menace. But I'm willing to tell you what I know about the bird. Then maybe you and I can help each other."

Caution rose in me. "What do you mean?"

"You'd like to get the bird back, and I'd...well, honestly, I'd like to see my brother again." His voice had gotten quiet, and he looked away. *Of course I can help him see Laeglin! I could easily...only, wait. Is it possible Laeglin doesn't want to see him? Laeglin told me in the past that his brother has acted dishonestly, maybe been involved with something criminal. And Hollon just now basically admitted to stealing from Nod. I need to slow down. I'm exhausted, but I need to think.*

"Do you know where the bird is?"

"I, uh, acquired the bird for a wealthy client. A few years back. But I didn't deal with the client directly. Everything was handled by this fellow who worked for him. Not the brightest guy, but not too bad either. I could talk with him, find out who the client was. Then we could talk about getting the bird back."

"And why would the man tell you who the client was now, if you weren't supposed to know back then?"

"You're right, he probably won't. Unless I bribe him or threaten him. Which do you prefer?" *Is he serious?*

"Bribe?" I smiled, as if this were a joke. Hollon just nodded.

"You have money then?"

"Some." Suddenly I didn't want to be too specific. I changed the subject. "And how would we get the bird back? Are you thinking the wealthy man might sell it to me?"

Hollon gazed at me for a minute without replying. "You're quite lovely," he said, "and very sincere. I can see why my brother likes you." He paused. "And yeah, it's possible the client might sell you the bird, if you use your charms or just get lucky. Maybe he'll be in a charitable mood, who knows? But more than likely, it'll need to be re-acquired."

"Stolen back?"

Hollon shrugged. *How far am I really willing to go to get the bird back? This has all gotten so complicated, and this conversation...it feels...uncomfortable? Unsafe?*

"I'm not suggesting anything," he said, the wariness returning to his voice. "Remember, you're the one who came looking for me. I was minding my own business."

"You're right. Should we–"

"I think we should both try to get some sleep. We'll see what the morning brings."

A NOISE ROUSED ME FROM a restless sleep. All the lights but one were out, and the room was dim and cool. I pulled the thin blanket more snugly around my shoulders. Hollon and I were still in our chairs, but an instinct told me he wasn't asleep. His voice was hoarse when he spoke, as if he too had been nudged awake and was reluctant to acknowledge it.

"Does he ever talk about me? My brother?"

"Sometimes," I said quietly, "but not very much."

"Has he told you...what I did..." he trailed off, then started again. "Is he angry with me?"

"I don't know, Hollon. But I don't think so."

"Will you help me? I'd really like to see him again. Try to make things right."

"I will, as long as he wants me to."

"Fair enough."

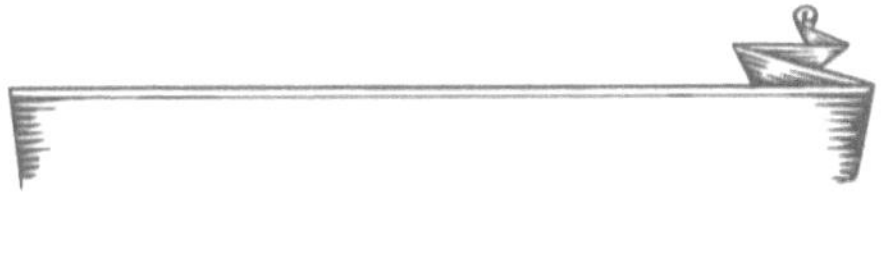

Chapter 12

Hollon and I parted mid-morning, after philosophically enduring the promised paperwork. Andris and Belva had returned and planted themselves in the front lobby, where we saw them when we were led out of Room A to have our cases "processed." Belva had even threatened to get a letter from Chancellor Axelle. The Day Coordinator was unimpressed, and secretly, I wasn't so sure the Chancellor would be on my side. But I was touched by Belva's loyalty, especially knowing first-hand how intimidating the Chancellor was.

Hollon and I were asked to wait back in Room A while the final forms were signed and filed. The divider had been raised, and we sat in our respective chairs with nothing to separate us. The door was open, and I could hear the hum of voices in the lobby and nearby offices. I'd convinced Andris and Belva to return to the cottage, promising to join them for lunch as soon as I was released.

"Well, that was certainly one of the stranger nights I've spent with a beautiful woman," said Hollon, giving me the half-smile that was becoming familiar. When he smiled, he looked more like Laeglin, and my heart ached a bit. Partly because I missed Laeglin, and partly because I was sad to think of the rift between two brothers who had no other family.

"Thank you for helping me, Hollon, back at the tavern. It seems like that was a thousand years ago, but I appreciate what you did for me and Dr. Li."

"Well, I hope he's alright. I've seen him at the Hail before, and frankly, he looks like a man who doesn't need more trouble than he's already got."

"I'm sure he'll be fine," I said. "I asked Andris to stop by his boarding house to check on him this morning."

"And the dog too. She was a cute little thing."

"Yes," I smiled, "Min."

"And I'll plan to meet you tomorrow morning so we can travel back to the Peace together. Assuming my brother will see me. In the meantime, I'll do my best to get the name of that wealthy client you were asking about."

"I'll send Laeglin a letter today to let him know our plans. He might want to come with me–us?—if we decide to meet with this client. I still hope I'll be able to buy back the bird."

"Well, if we have any further problems that need to be resolved with hand-to-hand fighting, I'd be glad to have you by my side." He gave me a long look. His dark eyes were flecked with gold, like his younger brother.

I smiled again, feeling reluctant to end the conversation, even though we were mostly repeating decisions we'd already made and discussed. When the assistant–not Miss Kenestrel, but another elderly woman quite similar in appearance–arrived to escort us back to the lobby, I impulsively stepped closer to Hollon and gave him a quick kiss on the cheek. I felt him draw back, but I was still glad I did it.

WHEN I OPENED THE DOOR, Jay immediately flew off his running rail and landed on the floor in front of me. With a clucking chirp, he nipped at my foot and then ran across the room, clearly inviting me to chase him. When I didn't, he spun around and came hopping back to me, his head high and his tail wagging like a dog.

From her bedroom Belva laughed and called out, "Just look at that sweet boy! He's so excited to see you!"

"Belva, are you packing?"

"Why yes, dear, I am!"

"I didn't know you were planning a trip."

"I wasn't, but the most wonderful thing happened this morning, on the way back from the security office. You see, Andris offered to walk with me, but I knew he wanted to visit his friend Dr. Li, so I said I'd be fine on my own." She came out of her room, several colorful caftans draped over her arm and her cheeks pink with excitement.

"Now, I know," she continued, bending down to let Jay climb onto her shoulder, where he burrowed into her hair with a contented purr, "that I don't usually like to be away from home on my own. But I've been thinking–since you came to stay and I've heard about all your adventures–that my life has gotten too narrow. Well, today I got the proof."

"The proof? What happened?"

"Just look!" she said gleefully, pulling two flat stones from the pocket of her voluminous skirt.

"I'm not sure–"

"My gift is back!" she interrupted. "On the walk home, these two stones appeared to me in beautiful colors, just like the lake stones I saw all those years ago when I was a child. I'm sure it's a sign, Marolaine, a sign that my marveling has been stifled by the predictability of my life here. So, I've decided to make a change."

I was still tired from the night spent in Room A with Hollon, and I felt a bit overwhelmed by my effusive host. I wanted to say the right thing though; this was clearly important to Belva. I focused my eyes on her beaming face and smiled back.

"That's wonderful news, Belva. I'm happy for you. Where do you plan to go?"

"Well, for now I'm traveling across town to stay with my sister. But after that, I really don't know. I'll be back once I make my plans. I'll need to pack up the cottage and find a home for all my lakestones. Do you know, I think I'll use them to build toad houses in the back garden...that would be perfect!" She laughed at this. "I've always liked toads, and I read once that if you build houses out of stones, with loose, bare soil inside, the toads will come. They like a cool spot in the summer, and they'll settle into the shady soil. Then in the winter, they'll dig themselves into the ground and sleep, protected from the worst of the weather by the stones. Doesn't that sound lovely?" Her eyes gleamed with pleasure.

"Oh, absolutely!" I said with as much enthusiasm as I could.

Belva nodded and looked pleased. Sparkling earrings shaped like birds and decorated with sequins swung almost to her shoulders. "But in the meantime, dear," she said, "you're welcome to stay as long as you like."

"I assume you're taking Jay?" I didn't relish the idea of staying alone in the cottage with the ferret. I still wasn't sure what he ate, and I didn't really want to find out.

"Well, of course! He'll be my adventure companion. For now, I'm just packing some clothes, Jay's supplies, and these two stones. Which reminds me..." Belva paused, walked to my side, and put both her large hands on my shoulders. We stood face to face and eye to eye.

"You have so much ahead of you," she continued, "and I want you to choose something of mine to take with you on your journeys...I'd like you to have one of my lake stones. I think you're the right person for that."

"Well thank you, Belva, I know how special they are to you." I felt a tightening in my throat. "Which one should I take?"

"Oh, that's not for me to say, dear. They're all filled with marveling to me, but I'll wager there's at least one that speaks to your heart. Just walk around and look at them, I think you'll see what I mean."

Doubtfully, I began a slow circuit of the room, looking closely at the lakestones that lined the windowsills and other flat surfaces. I knew that the painted stones were the most special; they were the stones that Belva's marveling had allowed her to see in brilliant color. *Which one should I pick? I don't want to disappoint her, but I don't want to accidentally choose a stone that's too precious to her either. Should I choose a painted stone, or maybe just a plain one?*

I've never considered myself a fanciful person, but at that moment I was struck by a strange sensation. My arms and hands tingled, and when I looked down, I saw a gray stone shaped like an irregular heart. It wasn't painted, but it had veins of white quartz running through it. I felt a strong desire to touch it, to trace the veins with my fingertips.

"Ah," said Belva quietly, her eyes following me from across the room where she still stood with Jay. "I see that I was right. Pick it up, child, it's yours."

LUNCH WITH ANDRIS AND Belva was animated. Andris made self-deprecating jokes about his feud with Jay, and Belva laughed with delight at everything Andris said. She seemed to find him even more charming than usual, and I had to agree. *I wish Paislie could see this side of him. But somehow, she doesn't bring out the best in him. It's strange, because they're both attractive and smart and warm; and yet, they just don't seem to be a match. I wonder if Andris is starting to realize that?*

Andris assured me that Dr. Li and Min were both fine. I didn't kid myself though. Dr. Li had a problem with alcohol, and a serious problem with Chancellor Axelle. I wasn't at all sure what I'd say to Matron when I returned to the Peace. *Well, at least there are no ill effects from last night. I imagine he won't be drinking at the Hail Tavern any time soon. Personally, I'd be happy never to see the place–or its owner, Creedling–again.*

"When are you leaving for your sister's, Belva?" asked Andris as we cleared the table.

"This afternoon, the sooner the better!"

"Would you like me to walk with you? Or do you plan to take a carriage?"

"Yes indeed, young man, I'm splurging on a carriage. Jay's never ridden in one before and he's very excited." She grinned. "Unless you'd like to carry him across town yourself?" She laughed and clapped Andris fondly and heavily on the shoulder.

"And you, Marolaine?" Andris asked, turning to me. "What are your plans?"

"It's getting late," I said. "I think I'll stay here tonight, then leave in the morning for the walk back to the Peace. Hollon wants to join me, although I'm waiting to hear back from Laeglin before I decide about that."

"I don't know," said Andris, shaking his head with mock seriousness. "First you invite this Hollon fellow to join you in a tavern brawl, then he spends the night with you in detention, and now he plans to walk with you back to the Peace. I'm getting a little jealous of this guy–sounds like he's trying to take my place."

I nudged his shoulder. "You don't need to worry. He's nowhere near as charming as you."

"Few are." He winked and Belva giggled, returning from the kitchen with a rag to wipe the table.

"Speaking of unknown men," she said, "I almost forgot to tell you that a man came to the cottage this morning. He was looking for you, Marolaine."

"Who was he?"

"Oh, don't worry dear, I didn't tell him that you'd been arrested or that you were in detention, I just said you weren't available but that you'd be back later."

Andris caught my eye and I sensed that he knew it wasn't a sullied reputation that had me worried.

"Did he say who he was?"

"No, I don't recall that he did, although to be perfectly honest I was a bit flustered since I'd just found my marveled stones and all. But no, I think he just asked to speak to you, and when I said you weren't here, he thanked me and went away. No message or anything. It was a bit strange, now that I think about it." She looked thoughtful, or as thoughtful as one can look with a ferret dangling upside down from one's shoulder.

"What did he look like?" asked Andris.

"Short, older but not too old. Nothing remarkable, except I noticed he was missing a finger...well, not the entire finger, but about half. And–I hate to be rude, but it did strike me at the time–he seemed polite but not overly bright. As if he were carrying out a task without knowing its purpose. Maybe that's what struck me as odd. He was almost like a merchant's helper, delivering something–like groceries or milk or firewood–except that he wasn't that."

"Well," Andris said cheerfully, "I'm sure it was nothing." He was looking at Belva, but as he spoke, he leaned closer and put his hand briefly over mine.

THE COTTAGE FELT DIFFERENT after Belva left. Her possessions were still there, but somehow her essence had gone, and the space felt empty. Or maybe it was the absence of Jay. His musky animal smell definitely lingered, but I had to admit I missed his chirping, clucking, chattering, and his antics–biting my toes, stealing small objects to hide in his sleeping box, splashing in his water bowl.

I wondered idly what Belva's sister would think about sharing her home with the mercurial little ferret.

Andris had offered to spend the night with me, making one of his jokes about serving as my protector. We both knew I could protect myself though, and sleeping alone in a house with a single man—friend or not—seemed a little too intimate. I could picture Matron, pursing her lips and making a disapproving "tsk" noise at the very suggestion. I'd thanked Andris but said I would be fine. I was planning to do some packing and cleaning, and perhaps write letters to my sisters Bellina and Paislie.

In truth, I also wanted time alone to think. Now that I'd met Hollon, I had decisions to make. Would I continue to pursue Nod's ceramic bird? If so, how? What would I do with the information I'd learned about Chancellor Axelle and the Sword of Light? What would I tell Matron about her friend Dr. Li? And—perhaps trickiest of all—would I choose to involve myself in trying to reunite Laeglin with his older brother?

In the time we spent together, I'd come to like Hollon. But I wasn't sure I trusted him. He'd been evasive about himself, seeming to acknowledge some unorthodox behavior in the past—theft for example—but not willing to tell me honestly how he made his living now. I didn't even know where he lived, or if he was married. With these doubts in mind, I wasn't sure I wanted to be the one to bring him back into Laeglin's life. So much could go wrong.

The restless night in the detention building was catching up with me, and I changed into my sleeping gown after a supper of cheese, carrots, and a hard-cooked egg. Yawning, I picked up the heart stone from the top of my dresser and dropped it into the side pocket of my gown. It fit perfectly against my palm, and I stroked it with my thumb as the stone grew warm against my skin.

I had planned to write letters, but instead I cleaned my teeth, washed my face, and got into bed. I hadn't taken the time to braid my hair, and it splayed around me on the pillow. *I'll be sorry for that in the morning when I deal with all the tangles.* It wasn't yet fully dark, and I expected to lie awake, thinking about Hollon, and Laeglin, and Dr. Li, and Andris, and my sisters. But instead, I fell deeply and quickly asleep, my hand still wrapped around the heart stone in my pocket.

OFTEN, WE DON'T KNOW the reason when we wake unexpectedly in the night. But I knew immediately when I opened my eyes and saw the silhouette of a man approaching my bed, his shape a darker dark in the unlit room.

I had only a moment to sweep my arm across the bedside table, knocking my hairbrush to the floor and breaking the mug that held the dregs of my evening tea.

Then I was pushed down against the mattress and a hand clamped against my face. In the instant before oblivion, my eyes and nostrils burned with a stinging cold. My mind made one last attempt to send a message to my muscles–sit up! fight back!—but it was too late.

Chapter 13

The first thing I noticed was the smell. There was a cold breeze against my face, and a raw, fresh smell that was unfamiliar. I knew I was no longer in Belva's cottage, no longer in the town, but beyond that I couldn't tell because my eyes were covered. Whatever was tied around my face was thin though, and light showed faintly through. *So it's daylight. But where am I and what's happening to me?*

My head ached and my reason struggled to surface, pushed down by whatever substance had been used to ambush my mind. I tried to move my lips–perhaps with some instinct to cry out for help–but no sound came out. I sensed that I was on a horse, and that there was someone behind me. I was half-seated, with both legs awkwardly dangling to one side. *But I don't know how to ride a horse. And why can't I feel my legs? Is it because of the drug he gave me?*

I shifted uncomfortably and tried to move my hands. They wouldn't move either. *Are they tied down? But why would someone tie my hands and put me on a horse?*

"Stop moving or I'll put this blade in your heart." It was a man's voice, low and cold and right beside my face. I turned instinctively away, then felt a sharp pressure against my left side, blunted by my jacket. Sluggishly, I registered that this might be a knife against my ribs. I stilled.

Observation and planning were two skills that made me a good Guard, two skills that Father had emphasized, and later Master Bowden. "You won't always be able to overpower people with strength," Father had said, "so you need to be smarter, to use skills that others may not have developed."

But now, with my brain fogged with poison, my hands tied, my eyes covered, and a knife in the hands of the man who rode behind me, I was terrified. My eyes stung with tears, but I somehow mustered enough sense to keep my breathing even. *It won't help if I lose control of myself.* Some distant part of my brain knew that I needed to stay still and calm until the drug wore off and I could think again, move again. *But how long will that take? My wits are as useful to me right now as a wet sock—how in the realm will I possibly escape?*

I tried to focus on what I could observe. I'd used this exercise many times in training, and I hoped it would hasten the return of clear thinking. What can I see? *Not much, just faint light through the fabric of the blindfold.* What can I hear? *The horse's breath. The horse's footfalls. A crunching sound, as if the horse is moving over stones or gravel? A squawking sound overhead. Some kind of bird?* What can I feel? *The body of the man behind me. The rope cutting into my wrists. The breeze against my face.* What can I smell? *The horse. It reminds me of the stables at the Peace. Leather...that's probably the saddle. The man. The air. It smells fresh, like the country only not. Could we be near water?*

I thought about the pool at Fountain Park. It wasn't large, certainly not like a lake or an ocean. But it did smell something like this. I felt a stir of excitement, daring to hope that my addled brain was beginning to work again. *This could be useful. I think we might be riding near water, possibly a lake. And that would explain the sounds overhead too...Belva told me about seagulls. Could this mean we're in the Lakelands district, somewhere north of Clanstin?*

I had no idea how long I'd been on the horse, or how long it had been since I'd been abducted from my bed. My joints were sore, but since I'd never ridden a horse, this was no indicator. I knew it was light, but I couldn't tell the time of day. Lakelands was a large district, but its southern sections were only an hour or two's ride from Clanstin. *Ugh. There's just too much I don't know.* The excitement ebbed. I focused on remaining as still as possible and giving the man behind me no indication of my clearing thoughts.

Better not to reveal your assets until you have to, Master Bowden had instructed, back when I was a Junior Guard learning to manage unpredictable situations with a minimum of force. I was afraid my mind might be my only asset when we reached our destination, since my hands and feet were numb, and I had no weapons. *I don't even know if I can stand, let alone run or fight.*

Looking down without moving my head, I could see that I was wearing my heavy cloak over my sleeping gown. My feet were in boots, but my legs were bare. I cringed to think of this man touching my unconscious body, even just to shove my feet into boots.

WHEN THE HORSE FINALLY stopped, I listened intently, hoping for any clues about our destination that might help me escape. I heard nothing. The breeze had stilled, and I no longer heard the quarreling seagulls overhead. I still smelled the scent I associated with water, but it seemed less fresh, less organic, different in a way I couldn't explain. I shivered.

The man shifted behind me, and I felt his movement as he dismounted from the saddle. His feet struck the ground and he sighed. I was just wondering if I should dismount too, when my body made its own decision. Without the man behind me, my muscles couldn't hold me, and my legs and hips slid over the horse's side of their own accord. My wrists twisted painfully, still tied tight to the saddle's horn. I thought my feet must be on the ground, but I really couldn't tell.

I lay my cheek against the horse's side, willing myself to be calm. Her hide was warm and damp with sweat, and she smelled sweet and alive. I took a deep breath, then turned my head, rubbing against her until I had partially dislodged the fabric over one of my eyes. Looking down I saw granite paving stones, tightly fitted and hand cut to form a geometric pattern. I saw the horse's flank and leg, ending in a white stocking and a shod hoof.

Then I saw the tip of a man's boot, and within seconds a knife had cut the ropes that bound my wrists. I collapsed to the ground on my useless legs. I had just enough control to keep my head from striking the stones. The man laughed.

"Now don't go anywhere, Lady, I need to tie the horse before I take you inside." He spoke the word 'Lady' like an insult, and as he turned to lead the horse away, he kicked me sharply in the ribs.

BY THE TIME THE MAN returned, I had worked off my blindfold. I stared up at him from the ground, where I'd managed to pull myself into an unconvincing seated position. My legs were still not cooperating, and I was cold. The grass beyond the stones was crispy with frost.

My captor looked down at me, and I hoped he wouldn't kick me again; it felt terrible to be so vulnerable. He sneered, making his handsome face ugly.

I recognized him as the man who had followed me last fall when I first went to town to have Linnia's ceramic bird–her dyad token, although I hadn't known it then–repaired. He had also been there when Andris and I were assaulted a few days later. He was the taller of the two men, the one who had punched Andris in the stomach while I grappled with his partner. I tried not to think of the shorter man, the man I'd fought and killed on the night Dase led the Lightkeep through the Stones to another realm.

I wondered if my abductor was the same tall man who had threatened Paislie in the shop. It seemed likely.

"Get up," he ordered.

Behind him stood a darkly imposing building, at least three stories high. It was built of weathered blocks of granite, with a sweeping front porch supported by pillars that reminded me of the twisted breadsticks Erritus baked back at the Peace. A small sound escaped my throat. The man glared down at me, and I dropped my gaze.

"Get up," he repeated.

I shifted on the ground and looked back toward the mansion, wondering if we were alone here. Stone statues flanked the front steps: a horse on the left and a bear–its front legs raised off the ground to expose its claws–on the right. Both statues were softened with a skim of green moss, and the horse's ears had crumbled to nubs.

I'd never seen any home so large and grand, although it was badly neglected. Dry leaves had matted into the edges and corners of the porch. There were cracks in the impressive steps, and tiny bits of greenery poked through, awaiting the chance to launch outward and claim the stones once spring returned. Water stains streaked downward from a broken gutter. The windowpanes were dulled with grime.

Looking beyond the building, I could see the lake. In the morning light it was flat and dark. Its surface looked impenetrable, and I imagined trying to poke a finger through and meeting only rubbery resistance. I was disappointed not to see or hear any seagulls. Everything seemed still and deserted. Unnerving.

I decided to risk speaking. "Where are we?"

Without replying, the man reached down and grabbed my upper arm. His grip was strong, and he yanked me to my feet. I winced as his fingers dug into my biceps, even through the cloak.

My legs were able to support some of my weight, but I sagged at the knees. The man jerked me roughly, then half-walked, half-dragged me up the steps to the front doors. I knew my chances of escape were best here in the open, but there was no way I could run or fight. I'd have to make another plan once my mind and muscles were functioning again. So far there'd been no sign of anyone else, but I dared to hope there might be someone on the other side of these doors I could reason with.

At the doors, my captor pulled back his sleeve, exposing a narrow band of metal. It encircled his wrist like a bracelet, but it appeared to be embedded in his skin. He held it close to the door, and I felt a wave of pressure that briefly hurt my ears and then was gone. The door opened. *The house is secured by magic. That will make it harder to get out.*

We stood in a wide, chilly entryway. An arched ceiling rose high overhead, with decorative plaster moldings and an ornate chandelier. Faded silk tapestries covered one wall, and the floor was spangled with rose, blue, and green where light prismed through a stained-glass window set high in the wall. Despite its beauty, the overwhelming impression was of neglect. I shivered and pulled my cloak tighter around me.

I had only a moment to glance around before the man began to drag me unceremoniously up the broad central staircase. There was still no sign of anyone else.

"Where are we?" I asked again. I was glad to hear my voice sounding firmer.

"You're a guest in the home of Excellency Krale," he said sarcastically. "We don't get many visitors here, lady, but I have a hunch you might be staying a while." He gave a bark of laughter at his own joke.

"Why have I been brought here?"

"How am I to know that? I'm just the man who does things. I don't make the decisions."

"Then Krale ordered you to bring me here. And you abducted me from the cottage." These were statements, not questions, and he didn't bother to reply.

He gave my arm another jerk, pulling me to the left at the top of the stairs. I could see that the hallway extended in both directions, but to the right the way was blocked by an ornate portcullis. Beyond it I could barely make out another corridor, fading into dust and shadow.

To the left was a shorter hallway, with closed doors: two on the left and two on the right. A lamp was mounted to the wall, casting a dull glow onto the floorboards. There was a small sitting area at the end of the hall, where two chairs faced a drape-framed window. I tried to observe and remember all the details I could, but there was little to see.

We stopped in front of the first room on the right. The man again held up his wrist, and the door opened with a slight puff of pressure.

"Here you are, Lady," he sneered, "your room awaits." He shoved me hard, so that my wobbly legs gave way, and I sprawled on the floor.

"Wait–"

But he was gone, and the door closed behind him.

THE ROOM WAS LARGE, and it had been recently swept. Broom straw tracks showed in the corners, and dust specks hung in the air, caught by the light that slanted through the single window. There was a bed against one wall–its sagging center visible through the spread that covered it– along with a wardrobe, and a table with two chairs. The furniture was huddled together at one side of the space, as if hiding from something. Or–more likely–as if someone had pushed it aside to sweep and hadn't bothered moving it back. The plaster walls had once been stained blue, but the color had faded until it was barely perceptible, adding to the room's washed-out, hopeless feel.

It matched my mood perfectly.

After my captor left, I lay on the floor where I'd fallen, overwhelmed and uncaring. There had been no sign of other people when we entered, and as I lay with my ear to the floor, I still heard nothing. The thought of meeting Krale here–especially in my weakened state–was terrible. Then too, so was the thought of being alone in the house with the man who had threatened me with a knife and kicked me in the ribs.

I sighed and eased myself into a seated position. I was sore but not seriously hurt. I got to my feet slowly, feeling my muscles quiver in protest. I knew I should explore my surroundings, take inventory for possible weapons, look for means of escape. But my mind–usually a soldier's mind–felt oddly dulled. I wondered if I was still feeling the effects of the drug that had stupefied me. I didn't think so though, because my mind had begun to feel clearer when we'd arrived in the courtyard. I considered the magic locks on the doors. *Maybe there's something else about this place that's affecting my thoughts.*

I walked haltingly around the room, drawn to the window. My view was down a slope of overgrown lawn–the grass brown and scraggly, not yet touched by spring re-growth–to the stone beach that shouldered the lake.

From my second-floor vantage point, the lake stretched out of sight, long and narrow, bordered on one side by forest, and on the other by low trees and patchy open areas. There were no dwellings or evidence of other people. I could see a path along the open side though, and I surmised that this was how we'd arrived.

The lake's surface still looked dark, although the sky overhead was clear. I thought idly about the reflection of blue sky on the fountain pool in the park and wondered why this section of the lake seemed to be obeying different physical laws. I couldn't tell about distant parts of the lake, but here, close to the mansion, it looked lifeless and forbidding.

I moved listlessly to the bed, where I lay down on top of the blanket without removing my cloak or boots. *I should be preparing myself, finding some way to escape or at least defend myself. Why am I just lying here? Why don't I care about anything?*

I stared up at the ceiling, with its fine webbing of cracks. There was a spider in one corner. I'd never liked spiders, although I was tolerant of the thin, industrious house spiders who confined themselves to corners. The air felt heavy, substantial, making it an effort just to breathe. Everything was quiet, as if I was the only living thing in the entire mansion. I lay still until finally I slept.

Chapter 14

I awoke a few hours later, disoriented as one often is when waking up in unfamiliar surroundings. My head ached and I was stiff and sore. My wrists stung from the chafing of the rope that had bound me. My throat was dry. As I slept, my body had migrated to the center of the bed, settling into the depression of other, unknown, bodies who had lain there before me. I felt only resignation, as if I'd fallen into a deep hole and would now lie there indefinitely.

I wiggled my toes, which were cramped and sticky in my boots. The room felt warm, and I was sweating beneath my cloak. I tried to focus my mind. I'd hoped that sleep would cure my malaise, but the indifference lingered. *Why am I still so sluggish? I need to focus my mind and take some control of this situation. What would Captain Matteo think of me, lying here like this?*

Time passed without form as I continued to lie on my back and gaze at the ceiling.

Finally—minutes, days, hours?—the pressure in my bladder forced me to roll to my side and sit up. I stumbled across the room to the small bathroom, where I found a toilet and a sink rimmed with iron stains like the stump rings of an ancient tree. I shrugged off my cloak and let it fall in a heap on the floor. I drank from my cupped hands, not caring that water ran down my chin and dampened the front of my nightdress.

When I returned to the bedroom, I dragged a chair to the window and sat, staring down at the lake. The surface remained dark and impenetrable, although the sky overhead was now the deep blue of late afternoon.

I leaned forward until my forehead pressed the cool, dirty glass. I wondered what Laeglin was doing. I tried to picture his face but failed, conjuring only brown eyes and long eyelashes. I wasn't sure if I was remembering Laeglin or Hollon or a stranger.

Thinking about Hollon brought a flicker of anger. Had he told Krale's man where to find me? Had he sold my location–my safety, maybe even my life—for money? I tried to follow this train of thought, to force my mind into the disciplined patterns of problem solving that had always been a part of me. Anger would be better than nothing, far better.

But I couldn't make the anger stay; it dribbled away, and I stared vacantly at the lake again.

Some time later, I decided–if a decision can be made without intention–to open the window. The sash was swollen with moisture and age, and my first attempt was unsuccessful. I looked around the room for something to wedge under the bottom rail, something to use as a pry bar. Briefly, my mind engaged, as if pushing forward through fog or a thick mass of cotton. *If only I had my knife...*

Finding nothing as useful as a chisel or a flat metal bar–and certainly no knife–I took off my boot and used the heel to pound against the window. My focus was slipping again, and I thought only hazily that the pounding might somehow loosen something: jar wood loose from wood.

When I tried again, now standing for better leverage, the wood groaned, and the window reluctantly opened to my efforts. I sat back with a sigh, breathing the cold, damp air that blew in from the waveless lake.

I braced my elbows on the sill and leaned my head forward and out the window. As I stared at the lake, I had a sudden strong desire to swim in its waters. *But I can't swim...*I longed to break through the surface, to feel the darkness enclose me, shelter me, contain me. *But I can't swim...* I wanted to taste the smoothness on my tongue, have the nothingness fill my eyes and ears and throat. *But I can't swim...*

I rose halfway from the chair so that I could fit more of my body out the window. My hands grasped the window frame from the outside now, as the sill pressed through my thin nightdress and into the flesh of my thighs. The air around me was peaceful, the sun bright, the ground far below. I contorted my body against the lower edge of the sash. I leaned closer to the water.

A distant part of my mind–my soldier's brain, pushed aside and barely conscious–registered the movement in the room behind me, just before I heard the scuff of a boot on wood.

I jerked backwards, striking the back of my skull sharply on the lower edge of the window sash. I yelped as I struggled to get my body back into the room. My foot tangled on the chair as I tried to spin to face my assailant. I stumbled, and the chair tipped on its side.

My eyes adjusted to the dimness of the room, and I realized I was not facing Krale's lackey after all, but a man I'd never seen before, a very large man. I had known a number of large men; several of my fellow soldiers at the Peace were either very tall or very broad or both. But the man who stood before me was truly a giant. He loomed over me, filling the room with his presence and a faint smell, something warm and vaguely familiar.

I took a slow breath. The giant was dressed in baggy pants and a homespun shirt, and his feet were shod in enormous black boots, clearly the source of the scuff that had altered me. His hair was past his shoulders, held back with a tie. His eyes were dark, overshadowed by heavy brows. His face was stubbled, and while this was dashing on Andris, it was menacing in the extreme on the huge man who faced me.

I took another breath, and a slight step forward. I didn't want to appear a threat (I almost laughed at this idea as it crossed my mind), but I also wanted my feet clear of the fallen chair in case I had the opportunity to run or the necessity to fight.

To my surprise, the man stepped back, awkwardly shifting his feet to the side. Muscles tensed along the sides of his neck, and his brows drew together. It dawned on me that he was holding a tray. A tray with a steaming bowl of vegetable soup, a rough loaf of brown bread, a pot of butter, a water pitcher, and a chipped mug. That was the familiar smell: soup and bread.

We stared at each other.

"Are you...?" I started. His eyes flitted to the table near the bed. A question.

I tried again. "Would you like to set the tray down?" I gestured to the table, assenting.

Without speaking, the huge man walked toward the table, his boot rasping as his left foot dragged the floor. He set the tray down gently, then reached into his pocket.

I tensed and automatically assumed a defensive posture. The body never admits that it's outmatched, even when the mind knows better. *I have nothing to fight with, and no hopes of overpowering him in a physical fight. I'll be far better served by diplomacy.*

I forced a smile as the man pulled something small from his pocket. He dropped his eyes to the floor and held out his hand, his head turned slightly away. His palm was thickly calloused, with a white track of scar along the length of his first finger. Curled in the cup of his hand lay the beaded bracelet that my sister and her husband had given me after Wintertide supper. My eyes widened in surprise. I searched his face, but he avoided my gaze.

"Where did you find this?" I asked finally. Had it fallen from my pocket as I was drag-walked into the house? Had I been wearing it? I honestly couldn't remember the last time I'd seen it, only Obrin's deep voice that night, telling me to wear it for good fortune.

Without meaning to, I snorted at this memory. *Not much good fortune for me at present, is there?*

The man looked up quickly, perhaps not expecting a snort from the groggy young woman in the dirty nightdress. He lifted his hand, indicating I should take the bracelet. I reached out slowly, and as I cupped my hand upward, his gaze snagged on the shimmer mark on my palm. This circular mark was given to me by Dase, the head of the Lightkeep at the Peace. Back in the fall it had allowed me to open and close a passage through the Stones, despite my lack of any magic or marveling. The mark had faded since then, and I rarely thought about it.

I closed my fingers over the bracelet, concealing the shimmer mark. The large man inclined his head, and I fastened the bracelet around my wrist with fumbling fingers.

The bracelet was instantly warm against my skin. The blue and amber beads seemed to gather light from the nearby window. They had been lovely when I first received them–so lovely that I'd wondered if Obrin's beadwork was marveling–but now they positively glowed.

It's hard to explain what happened when I put the bracelet on. Somehow, the air in the room became easier to breathe. A truss around my chest loosened. I found that I could think again too: I noticed details, I framed logical questions, I started to organize my thoughts. My brain was no longer a limp, wet sock.

Most amazing, my spirits lifted. The blanket of malaise that had weighed me down ever since I arrived was thrown back. And at the center of this transformation was a giant of a man who had released me from whatever darkness had gripped me. I gave him a genuine smile. His expression didn't change, but he nodded slightly before motioning to the food on the table.

AFTER THE GIANT LEFT and I devoured the soup and bread, I did what I should have done from the start. I made a thorough search of the room, and I began to formulate a plan.

I spent significant time examining the door. The door and the frame were solid oak, and I knew I'd have little chance of breaking them down, even if not for the spell that held the lock secure. I could feel a change in pressure when I placed my hand close to the handle, and when I tried to grasp it, my hand was pressed back as if a cushion of thick air surrounded the mechanism. *My abductor had a bracelet that unlocked the front door and my room. I wonder if the large man had one too–I didn't notice, but if he did, maybe I could steal it. Take him by surprise when he enters, or when he's distracted with the tray?*

I remembered that the metal band had appeared embedded in the skin of the man's wrist, but it still seemed the most obvious way to escape my room. *Will I see my abductor again? Maybe I should focus on the large man instead–he may come again with my meals.* But I balked at the idea of hurting the large man to steal his bracelet. After all, he had brought me Obrin's gift. That could make him an ally; or at least that was how I chose to think of him.

Turning to other options, I thought about the possibility of escaping through the window. After all, I had already opened it. The drop was too far though, and despite a search, I failed to find anything in the room to use as a rope or ladder.

Diplomacy? Persuasion? These had always been my strategies of choice as a Guardian. I wasn't sure if I would see the large man again, but if I did, perhaps I could convince him to let me out of the room. I had nothing of value to offer in return, but hadn't he already shown his good will by bringing me the beaded bracelet?

Taking a final circuit of the room–this time feeling the walls with my hands, hoping against hope for some kind of hidden door (and knowing this was a thin hope, childish really)—I decided that for now, my best strategy was to befriend the large man. Assuming he came back.

And if he didn't, or if the other man came instead, I needed to be ready. I hid the water pitcher under the bed and rolled the ceramic mug inside my jacket. I would have preferred better hiding places, but my options were limited in the sparse room. I hoped no one would wonder where the items were. I considered taking only the mug, but I needed any potential weapon I could find, and the water pitcher was heavy.

I saw no one else that evening. As the sky darkened, I sat on the floor and forced my tired mind and body through an extended series of breathing, stretching, and meditation exercises. It was hard to discipline my thoughts though, and they drifted to the people I knew. I thought about my sisters: were they safe? Would they hear that I was gone and be worried? I thought about Laeglin: he was my best friend, but did I love him? Did we have a future together? I knew how much the Peace meant to him; I couldn't imagine him anywhere else. I thought about Captain Matteo and Master Bowden, my mentors and training partners at the Peace. I thought about the past six years, the training, the friends, the work, the satisfaction.

And also, the sameness, the routine. I breathed deeply and considered this. For so long I'd been committed to becoming a Guardian, a female Guardian, against all odds and traditions. Once I'd achieved that goal, I'd been dedicated to proving myself worthy. I had gladly trained harder than most of my fellow soldiers, taken on extra duties, even agreed to become an assistant instructor when Master Bowden asked. But had my life become too safe, too narrow? Would I ever leave the Peace? And what would I do if I did?

I WENT TO BED EARLY. I felt the weight of the day: being drugged and captured, carried on horseback, kicked, dragged, enspelled, left alone and uncertain of my fate. But in some ways the physical effects of the day were easier to manage than the after-effects of my meditations. I felt unsettled by questions about my life and my future. Something about this place had caused me to wrestle with questions I normally avoided. Although I considered myself thoughtful, I knew I was ultimately a person of action. I could only hope that whatever lay ahead, there'd be an opportunity for me to take control, put some plan into effect, no matter how low my odds of success.

The bed tried to seize me at once, to roll me into its soft center and hold me there. But I resisted, grumpily pulling myself free and gripping the mattress's edge with one fisted hand as I fell asleep.

Chapter 15

My eyes snapped open. In the dim of early morning, I saw a figure standing within arm's reach of the bed where I lay. Instinctively, I reached toward the bedside table, but my knife was not there.

I rolled to my side, swinging my legs off the side of the bed and preparing to rise. The figure took a step closer. I registered it as a woman, although a strange one. In silence, she placed two fingers against my left shoulder. She didn't poke or push, and yet I immediately knew I should not try to get to my feet. I stilled and she withdrew her hand.

She was short, probably reaching only to my chest if I'd been allowed to stand. Her body was compact, and I could tell in the way she moved and stood that she was agile. She wore pants and a leather vest with laces. Across her chest was a leather bandolier with tiny pockets, apparently empty, although I couldn't be sure. The sleeves of her cotton shirt were rolled up, revealing muscled forearms.

At first—in the dim light—I thought she wore a scarf around her head. But as my eyes adjusted, I could see that her head was shaved and covered in darkly-inked tattoos. Her face was in shadow. It was impossible for me to guess her age.

"So. You're the one. Interesting."

If I had, briefly, been tempted to disregard her as a threat based on her stature, that temptation was now fully dispelled. Her voice was low and raspy, and there was authority behind the innocuous statement.

"I'm Marolaine. May I strike the lamp?"

I was surprised when she returned the introduction. "They call me Enestria." She jerked her head toward the lamp across the room, and light sprang forward. *What?! Does she have magic? Or is it the room itself, somehow?*

In the light I could see the intricate whorls and shapes that covered her head in tracings of blue and black ink, ending just above her dark brows like a cap. I could also see the line of ear clips that pierced both ears from bottom to top, and the stud that protruded from her full lower lip. A single inked vine grew down from the side of her head, curled along her neck, and disappeared into the collar of her shirt.

I felt at a distinct disadvantage, sitting on the side of the bed in just my two-days-worn nightdress, my teeth unbrushed and my long hair in disarray. I thought of the mug. Before bed last night, I'd broken it and stashed a ceramic shard under my pillow. Should I reach for it now? I shivered, certain, without knowing why, that this small, strange woman could–and might–kill me without difficulty or concern.

I forced a smile. "I didn't hear you come in." *Well that's stating the obvious.*

"I hear you're a warrior." I suspected she meant to suggest that I couldn't be much of a warrior, sleeping while a stranger entered my room. But who knew? *I won't assume. I need every potential ally I can find in this place, and I of all people should know better than to judge someone on appearance.*

"I'm a Guardian of the Peace," I said, not sure if this would mean anything to her. She held my gaze, but her expression gave me no clue. I continued. "I was abducted from Clanstin, where I was staying with a friend. Can you tell me where I am? Or why I've been brought here?"

"I can answer one question, aye. I can tell you this is the place Krale claims as his."

The man who abducted me had said I was in the home of Krale. Enestria's statement confirmed this, while at the same time casting doubt on Krale's legitimacy. I sensed her dislike for the mage in the way she said his name. *Well, that's something we have in common then.*

"And do you know why I'm here?" I repeated, leaning forward slightly to counteract the pull of the bed's soft center.

"Nay." For the first time since we'd met, she released me from her gaze. She turned slightly and gestured to a pile on the table. "Towels. Clothes. Elden will bring your food."

AS SOON AS THE DOOR closed behind her, I jumped from the bed, nearly shaking with suppressed energy. It was as if I had been physically restrained, prevented from action, and now my body sought release.

My first action was to check the door: still locked. I paced for several minutes before turning to examine the clothes Enestria had brought. I was glad to see they looked comfortable and functional: two pairs of pants and two long tunics, plus two sets of what I knew must be underclothes, though of a style so foreign I hardly recognized them. I could see that the pants would be too short, but they looked roomy and would certainly be an improvement over walking around in a nightdress.

I washed, dressed, then spent an hour on training practice. I was accustomed to morning sessions at the Peace, and my body fell easily into the familiar rhythm of stretching, movement drills, and strength exercises. I washed again–partly for something to do–then went to sit by the window.

The sun was up but still low in the sky. While I could see the glint of light on waves further away, the lake close to the mansion again appeared dark and flat, as if impervious to the effects of sun or wind. No birds in the air. No movement on the shore. I stared at the water. I still found it oddly mesmerizing, but thankfully–amber bracelet in place–I had no desire to climb out the window or to drown myself in its depths. I sighed heavily. Whatever this day might bring, I was anxious to get started.

I WAITED.

I paced the room and realized I was hungry. *Didn't that strange woman say that Elden would bring food? I wonder if he's the giant. Probably. I wonder what he'll bring. I wonder if I'll be able to talk to him...*

I was unused to being idle, and it made me restless. I looked out the window. I paced some more. I began to think about all the people who were probably worrying about me. My letter would have reached the Peace by now, and they would have expected me there yesterday.

I thought about the people who made up my life there: Matron, Captain Matteo, Master Bowden, Linnia, my friends in the Guard, JenVie, even Associate-Prefect Klinweh, whom I had worked with this past year as a liaison to the three scholars from Clanstin College.

Thinking of Klinweh reminded me of his pet cavy, and how strange it was that the prickly older man had such affection for the rodent with the swirling brown fur. I smiled to myself and thought about Belva's ferret, Jay. What would he be doing at Belva's sister's house? I could hardly imagine Jay as a welcome house guest, with his smells and his noises and his unexpected attacks. But who knew? Maybe Belva's sister was an animal enthusiast too.

I smiled again as my mind shifted to Andris. I remembered our first meeting with Belva and Jay. How the little animal had jumped on Andris and bitten his ear, and how my friend had kept his sense of humor.

Meeting Andris and JenVie had changed me. They had come to the Peace last fall, with Dr. Li, as visiting scholars from Clanstin College–part of a scheme between Prefect Tal of the Peace and Chancellor Axelle of the College to foster ties between the two institutions–and I had been assigned to work as their liaison. I'd doubted my abilities at the first, but I had quickly formed friendships with the two young professors. They were the first friends I'd had outside the Guards who were my daily companions in work and training.

Again, I felt doubt fluttering at the edges of my mind: had I isolated myself too much over the past six years? Since I was a girl, the Peace had been my dream, a dream I'd shared with my father. But was that dream too narrow? The dream of a child rather than the woman I was now? *And if the Peace is no longer enough for me, what about Laeglin?...*

Food arrived eventually, carried on a tray by the large man of the day before. He nodded when I asked if he was called Elden, but beyond that he answered no questions and offered no remarks. I wondered if he was angry that I'd stolen the mug and the water pitcher. He didn't look angry though, so I kept up my attempts at friendliness.

When he left, I ate as slowly as I could, virtuously saving the apple for later in the day.

I waited. The afternoon dragged on. Anticipation of an apple only goes so far.

I checked the locked door. I examined the window. I completed a second set of training exercises. I reorganized my scant personal items in the wardrobe. I combed and re-braided my hair. I measured the room in paces, with no particular end in mind. I considered a nap but decided against it, remembering how Enestria had surprised me this morning. I composed letters in my mind to Matron and Captain Matteo, telling them not to worry. I ate the apple, taking small bites and chewing thoroughly.

Up until now, thoughts of Hollon had just made me angry. I had assumed that Laeglin's brother was the reason for my captivity. I had convinced myself that his help in the tavern was only a ploy, a way to achieve some other goal. But now—with plenty of time and no occupation to fill it—I tried to order my thoughts objectively.

I was in the mansion of Krale. So, what did I know about Krale? First, he was a mage. He was—most likely—the dark mage who had killed Dr. Li's attendant, Orme, over the Sword of Light. He still wanted the Sword—now protected by the Lightkeep—and he had threatened Chancellor Axelle to get it. The Chancellor had said, "he has my son," although I still didn't know what that meant. The mansion had been quiet since I arrived, with only the occasional distant sound or voice. If another person was being held prisoner here, I had no evidence of it yet.

Less clear: Was Krale the mage controlling the men who had attacked Andris and I in town last fall? Was he directing the two men I'd battled at the Peace on the night the Lightkeep had made their escape through the Stones? Was he responsible for the man who had threatened Paislie? And how was the ceramic bird connected, if at all? Hollon had stolen the bird from Nod's curio shop. Hollon said he'd stolen it for a wealthy client but said he didn't know who the client was. Could I trust that that was true? And what was the bird anyway? Was it connected to Linnia's bird—the token she had shared with her dyad sister, Prin—or could the two ceramic birds be just a coincidence?

I'd been quick to assume that Hollon had revealed my identity and plans in exchange for money. That was certainly possible, but it wasn't the only possibility. I thought about other people I'd encountered in town who might have known–or guessed–parts of my story: the tavern owner Creedling, the fable teller and his apprentice, the unknown man who came to Belva's house.

Dr. Li? I was reluctant to include the professor on this list, but I had to admit that he knew more about the Sword than anyone else, and his livelihood and reputation had been threatened by the Chancellor. Worse, the Chancellor knew something that could threaten Matron's happiness, and I knew Dr. Li would do anything to protect his friend.

And finally, there was Krale himself. I had actually met the mage in the Chancellor's office just a few days ago. True, he had seemed not to recognize me, but maybe that had been deception. People lied all the time. I knew that well enough. If Krale had known who I was, it would have been easy for him to find out where I was staying. Which still left the question of why he would want to have me seized from Belva's home...

This was a puzzle with too many pieces. For now, I could be sure that Hollon's betrayal was not the only way I could have ended up here. It was possible that the man with the wary eyes and the half-smile, Laeglin's brother, might still be on my side.

WHEN ELDEN ARRIVED with the second tray of the day, the sun was nearly set, and I was exhausted. I'd never known that inactivity could be so tiring.

"Hello, Elden," I said, approaching the small table where he had placed the tray. "The stew smells delicious. Do you cook?"

The large man shrugged and shook his head, his right eyebrow tugging upward. I wasn't sure how to interpret this.

"I'm a terrible cook myself," I said, "although I have a friend who's been trying to teach me." I pushed on with a smile. "She's very patient."

This time it was the corner of Elen's mouth that twitched upward. Silently, he reached into the pocket of his smock and pulled something out. At first the object was shrouded in his large hand, but he released it to the corner of the tray, and I realized that it was a polished wooden sphere, created from the joining of many small pieces.

"What is it?"

He pointed, touching one finger gently to a segment of the ball. Looking closely, I saw that the segment he had touched was a lighter-colored wood than the rest.

"Is it...a puzzle?"

Elden nodded.

"Thank you," I said sincerely, "this will give me something to do while I wait."

He frowned slightly, then gathered the mid-day tray and turned toward the door, his left foot scuffing against the floorboards as he walked. I barely noticed the scent of magic as the door closed; I'd shifted my attention to the puzzle ball.

Chapter 16

When Elden entered my room the next morning, it took me a moment to register what was different. No puff of pressure, no metallic tang. Was the door unlocked? Excitement shot through me, but I sat at the small table and kept my gaze neutral, focused on the oatmeal that steamed from a bowl on the tray.

"Thanks, Elden. This looks good. Please tell Enestria I said thank you." This was a pure guess on my part, but Elden nodded, and I counted myself lucky.

I hurried on, hoping for information. "Is Krale here today?"

Eden's brows pulled together and he shook his head. He rubbed the stubble on his cheek, and I saw how short his fingernails were. He looked...I wasn't sure... Angry? Afraid?

"I'm sorry," I said, standing up but keeping a distance between us. "I don't mean to ask so many questions, it's just that I'm trying to understand why I'm here. Why I'm being held captive." I'd meant to sound plaintive–eliciting sympathy now might help me later–but the wobble in my voice was real. For the first time since we'd met, Elden held my gaze. I studied the deep lines around his eyes, and this time I thought he looked sad.

I forced myself to wait a few minutes after Elden left. Then I jumped to my feet, stashed the broken mug shard in the pocket of my tunic, and moved to the door. I reached out, testing the air around the knob. No pressure. I grasped the handle and turned. The door eased open, and I looked cautiously into the hallway.

I knew I was on the second floor. To my left was the top of the staircase leading down, and the portcullis blocking the unused hallway extending in the other direction. To my right, a poorly lit hallway with three closed doors beyond my own. I stepped out and began moving slowly along the hallway to my right. I had no plan, but the simple fact that I was out of my room and taking some small action made me feel better than I had since I arrived.

The first door I tried was locked. There was no pressure around the knob, so I guessed that it was a mechanical lock rather than magic. That might also mean I could force my way in. Something to consider for later.

The remaining two doors were also locked, and I moved toward the end of the hall. There was a window there, with two tall-backed chairs facing it. A narrow staircase led up from this landing, and I was just wondering whether to explore the third level when a man rose into view.

I nearly shrieked in surprise, and I definitely gasped. The man had been seated, blocked from my view by the tall chair back. Now, he faced me, not more than five feet away.

"Greetings," the man said with a slight frown. He was a few years older than me, of average height and build. He had a narrow face with a straight nose and strong chin. He wore a flat cap on his head.

I steadied my breathing and shifted my weight, prepared to dodge or run. Or even fight, although this was never my preference.

"Hello," I said. "You startled me. I didn't know anyone else was here on this level."

"I sit here in the mornings sometimes. But my room is on the third floor." He gestured toward the stairs. There was a pause. He glanced down at my figure. He continued, "I'm Stelan, by the way. I should have said that first thing."

"I'm Marolaine."

There was another pause.

"Would you like to sit?" He gestured toward the chair beside his.

His manner wasn't friendly, but it wasn't hostile either. Talking was a sensible step, although I didn't like the position of the second chair. I'd have to step around him to reach it in the cramped seating area.

I smiled politely. I'd need to make him change seats. I took a step forward, then inclined my head toward the second chair. "Do you mind?..." I raised my brows slightly in a question.

"Oh," he said abruptly. "Yes, of course." With that he moved into the seat by the wall, allowing me to take the seat he'd vacated.

I sat. I had an open route to the hallway now, but I still felt uncomfortable with this stranger.

"So..." We both spoke at the same time, then stopped. He looked at me then, and gave a stiff smile, the first since we met.

"Sorry," the man said. "This is a little awkward. I'm not tremendously good with new people." As I watched, he removed the cap from head, then rubbed his scalp with both hands until the hair in front stood up. Then he smoothed back his hair and replaced the cap.

"That's alright," I said, "you probably weren't expecting me either." I wanted to know who he was and why he was here, but I hoped not to have to ask directly. "Or maybe you knew I was here?..." I let the question linger.

"I knew someone was staying on the second floor, yes."

"I came two days ago, but not by choice or invitation."

He raised his eyebrows. "What do you mean?" Caution radiated from him.

I decided to be direct. "I was abducted from the home where I was staying and brought here. I still don't know why." I waited, folding my hands in my lap to still the urge to fiddle.

"I think we may have something in common then."

"What do you mean?"

"I told you my name was Stelan, but I suppose that wouldn't mean anything to you." He paused and shifted his cap, adjusting it with one hand. "I'm Racindalyn Axelle's son. She's the chancellor of Clanstin College."

"Really?" I couldn't hide my surprise. I leaned forward in my chair. "It's strange, but I do know your mother, slightly. I met with her just a few days ago, and in fact she mentioned something about Krale and her son, but I didn't realize she meant..." I trailed off. *Stop, Marolaine, go slow here until you know more.*

"Well, she was right." He reached for the mug of tea on the table between us. His response was unclear, but I stayed quiet, and he continued. "How is she, then? My mother."

I remembered Krale striking the Chancellor in the face. I remembered the anguish in her voice when she mentioned her son.

"I don't know her well," I replied carefully.

He shook his head and sipped slowly. He didn't speak.

"So, you were abducted as well?" I asked.

He nodded, his eyes still on his mug.

"Do you know why?"

He looked at me. "They took me to create an advantage with my mother. They want something from her, so they're threatening to kill me if they don't get it." His voice was flat. I had to resist the urge to make some pointless, placating comment.

"I'm sorry to hear that," I said, "although in a way I'm relieved too. That means that you and I share a common interest in getting out of this place. Maybe you can help me by telling me what you know about the people who are here in the mansion. I know it's the home of the mage Krale, but I haven't seen him."

"No, he's not here. I think he's away most of the time, meeting with people in other parts of the realm. I think he fancies himself the leader of some kind of society. I don't know much about it." He shrugged.

"I've met Elden and Enestria," I said, "I assume they're the caretakers, but I don't know who else lives here."

"I'm not sure about living, but there are at least two guards. Valek and Lorn. Valek is the tall one; Lorn is shorter, older, not overly bright."

"Are they both here now?"

"I know Valek is around. Lorn has been in town, but I think he returned last night."

"Do you know when Krale might return?"

"No. Although if they brought you here that would have been on Krale's orders. So, I'd assume he'd return soon to see you." Stelan spoke without emotion, but I felt a chill. I dreaded whatever confrontation with the mage was to come. I needed to gather as much information as I could before that time.

"Can we move freely around the house? The past few days my door was locked, but this morning it was open."

"Yeah, it was like that for me too. I don't know why. Now I can go anywhere I want, although a lot of the place is closed off. Unused, I guess. And of course I try to stay away from Valek. He can be vicious for no reason. Your room is the safest place to be when he's around."

"I can't just stay in my room," I said quickly, "I need to find some way out of here."

"Good luck. The place is warded with magic. You might be able to move around inside, but the outside doors don't open without Krale's direction."

"How does he manage that when he's not here?"

Stelan shrugged and returned to his tea, which I knew must be getting cold. *Maybe I've asked too many questions.*

"I think I'll..." I'm good at reading people's expressions, and I saw at once that Stelan was startled. I looked to my right. Halfway down the staircase that led to the third floor stood Enestria. The small woman with the tattooed scalp was wearing a floor-length dark coat and carrying a wooden box. The leather bandolier was strapped across her chest. *I wonder what she keeps in those tiny pockets?* She was frozen in place, glaring at Stelan.

I started to stand, then sat back down as she descended the final steps and stood before us on the landing. "Hello, Enestria," I said pleasantly. She ignored me but shifted her body suddenly in Stelan's direction. He flinched and an ugly smile creased her face.

She turned back to me and stared until I looked down. When I shifted my gaze back, she was halfway down the hallway.

"What in the realm was that about?" I asked Stelan.

"She hates me," he said stiffly. "I don't know why."

STELAN RETURNED TO his room on the third floor, and I advanced slowly down the stairs to the first floor. I wasn't sure what to make of Stelan. He was morose and wary, but that could easily be the result of being taken captive and held here in this oppressive place. I didn't exactly trust him, but I had to admit it was exciting to meet another person who was in my circumstance. That must mean we could eventually work together to escape, even if it took me a little time to earn his trust.

At the bottom of the staircase was the open foyer where I'd first entered the mansion with the tall guard, Valek. I remembered the chandelier, the stained-glass window, and the tapestries that covered the side wall. I moved quickly to the front door, raised the handle, and pushed. I hadn't expected it to open, but it was still disappointing to confirm that magic warded the house and prevented my escape.

Moving back along the tapestried wall, I stopped and looked more closely. The first thing I noticed was that the woven panels had an odd color gradient: faded at the top, then becoming saturated with color at the bottom. It was as if the color had run down and gathered in the weave at the bottom of the panels, like a piece of dyed fabric hung on the line to dry.

I was surprised to see that two of the tapestry panels showed familiar images. This was a depiction of the Battle of the Peace, a hundred years ago! The fabler in Fountain Park, Rill, had told me of how the Dark Guards tried to overthrow the Peace, kill the Lightkeep, and take possession of the artifacts the Lightkeep protected.

Except these panels told a different story. Or rather, the same story but from a different perspective. I marveled at how visual art could show meaning without words, for the meaning here was clear: the Dark Guards had been in the right. And leading their crusade, the artist celebrated an imposing figure holding a raised sword in one hand and a book in the other. Could this be the Dark Guards' leader then, Tiburon, whom the fabler had mentioned?

I pulled my attention away from the wall. *I can study the panels later.* Several rooms opened from the impressive foyer, as well as a hallway that led away to the right, parallel to the second floor where my own room was located. I cautiously opened doors to find a library, a sitting room, and a crowded storage space. I also observed the rounded footprint of a tower toward the back of the space, behind the staircase. The tower's wall was of rough stone, as if the mansion's interior had been built around this older structure. Set into the stone face was a wooden door with iron strap hinges. I was intrigued but didn't dare to explore further. *I'll come back another time, after I've studied the movements of the people who live here. I need time to look around when I won't be disturbed.*

To the other side of the foyer, I could hear and smell the kitchen. I assumed this was where Elden and Enestria worked, and I wondered if it might be useful to find Enestria and ask some additional questions.

At that moment though, I heard footsteps approaching along the hallway. I turned in that direction and saw the guard, Valek, striding toward me. He was tall, with sharp cheekbones and piercing eyes. His jacket had a military cut, but I could see that his pants were worn, and his boots scuffed. He had a knife holster strapped to his thigh and a wooden baton at his side. He sneered when he saw me.

"What then, lady, out of your room and exploring our little house?"

I breathed slowly and stood still: confident but not threatening, or at least that was my hope.

"I assume you're the guard called Valek?" I asked.

"Very smart, lady, very smart. It seems you've been talking to someone."

"Valek," I said, ignoring the sarcasm, "I'd like to know why I'm here, and I'd like to know when I can leave." I kept my voice steady, although my heart pounded, and I could feel the sweat prickling under my arms.

He made a barking sound that I took for a laugh. "I don't think you're going anywhere soon. At least not until Krale gets here."

"When will that be?"

"I told you already, I just take orders. I don't make the decisions. In fact, if I were in charge..." He paused, and then with a sudden lunge he covered the distance between us. He grabbed me by the collar of my shirt and brought his face close to mine. I remembered his smell from the ride on horseback. I pulled back as much as I could and instinctively brought my hands up between us to break his hold.

He was quick though, and he grabbed my chin with his free hand, squeezing hard. He held my gaze. "If I were in charge," he repeated slowly, "I would have tortured you right away for the information I wanted. So how about that, lady?"

He released me as quickly as he'd grabbed me, shoving me with one hand. I stumbled backward, hitting my hip on the edge of a table. Valek stepped closer as I quickly regained my balance and took a defensive position. I was prepared to be struck, but instead he laughed, standing with his hand on the baton that hung at his waist. The threat was clear.

I wanted to get back to the relative safety of my room. My jaw and hip throbbed, and I was afraid of what might happen next if I stayed. *I'm alone here though. Maybe someone will come to help me, but maybe not. I need to rely on myself, and that means I need information, even if it's from this bully.*

Ignoring the pain in my jaw, I stepped away from Valek and forced my voice and expression to convey calm. "Could we sit?"

I'd learned not to underestimate the element of surprise that can sometimes be gained through courtesy.

Valek's brows rose, and he laughed again, although this time it sounded more genuine than cruel. "You don't give up, eh, lady. Well, that's something, I suppose." He turned and walked with intentional casualness to the chair across from me. He sat, taking longer than necessary to adjust his weapons and smooth his jacket.

"So, Krale had me brought here so he could talk to me," I started.

"Maybe not just talk."

"What do you mean?" I asked.

"I reckon he could have done that in town, if he just wanted to talk to you. No, bringing you out here is for some other purpose. You can be sure of that." I heard the smugness in his voice.

"Some other purpose? I don't know what you mean." Some men felt important when asked their opinions. Flattery could make them more talkative than they'd otherwise be.

Valek settled back in his chair. Some of the tension was gone from his face when he replied. "From things I've heard, I think our brilliant Mr. Krale is hoping that you might lead him to something he wants much more than he wants you." *What? Did he mean the Sword of Light?*

"Do you..." I started. But he interrupted. "Like a certain little girl." He was smirking, obviously enjoying himself, at least for the moment. *Oh, he must mean Linnia, although I'm not sure how he knows about her. Krale did threaten Linnia, last fall when he killed Orme. Krale seemed to know about her powers, but I'd hate to think why he'd want to draw her here. If Valek is right...*

"Anyway," Valek continued, "that's just guesswork on my part. As I've said, I'm the one who does, not the one who decides. Lorn might know something too, but he's too stupid to see his own advantage. Too much a slave to Krale after all these years." He sneered in disgust.

"Who's Lorn?" I asked, picking up on the name Stelan had mentioned. *Stelan referred to Lorn as Krale's second guard.*

"Seems old Lorn ran into a thief in town, and that thief was asking about Krale. Krale's no dummy–he put the pieces together, I'd guess." I nodded. *Finally, something new.*

Valek scowled suddenly and started to rise; his enthusiasm for this conversation had run out. Or maybe he realized I'd led him to say more than he'd intended.

I heard a noise and we both turned to see Elden emerging from the kitchen with a steaming tray. The scent of fresh bread came with him. The large man glanced at us, and then quickly away, hurrying toward the door in the stone tower face that I'd noticed earlier. He raised his wrist and then ducked through as the door swung open. His relief was palpable in the set of his body as the door closed slowly behind him. After the last half-hour spent with Valek, I understood how Elden felt.

WHEN ELDEN BROUGHT my supper tray, I tried to ask him about the tower room. I'd considered talking to Stelan, but I hadn't seen him when I returned to the second level. Plus, I wasn't sure that I should ask him. After all, he hadn't mentioned the room–or its inhabitant–when he told me about the people living in the mansion. But then, maybe he just didn't know. I was troubled by my interaction with the Chancellor's moody son: I wanted to trust him (I badly needed an ally) but his manner had been odd. I decided to give myself time to think.

"Elden," I asked, as he moved toward the small table with a tray holding a vegetable casserole and a dish of stewed apples, "I saw the door in the tower wall today, when I was on the first level. Does someone live there?"

Elden looked alarmed. He set the tray down abruptly, causing tea to slosh over the rim of the cup. He turned and I could see that he planned to leave as quickly as he could.

"Elden! Please wait. I'm sorry for my question. Look." I stood and moved quickly to the wardrobe. I opened a small drawer and pulled out the wooden puzzle ball. I held it toward Elden and his eyes brightened. I gestured toward the table and the large man turned, slowly, as if reluctantly drawn.

Once we were sitting, I handed the ball to Elden. He turned it gently in his rough hand, then placed his finger on the light-colored segment and lifted his eyes to me in a question. I nodded and he pressed the wooden piece. The ball collapsed into a pile of wooden segments and Elden smiled shyly at me.

It took me several minutes to re-assemble the puzzle, and I had Elden's rapt attention the entire time. When the ball was restored to a gleaming sphere, he smiled again and sighed. I handed it to him and asked, "Would you like to try it?" He shook his head, but his eyes were still bright.

I had just picked up my fork in anticipation of the casserole when I remembered that I had planned to ask Elden about a second blanket for the bed. I stepped into the hallway, looking first right and then left.

Elden was not in sight, but at the top of the stairs leading down, Stelan was talking to Valek. I drew my head back but watched and listened, standing still and hoping I'd be hidden by the hall's shadows if they looked my way. They appeared to be arguing, but their voices were low, and I couldn't make out the words.

Chapter 17: Linnia and Laeglin

Linnia had been raised in town, and now–since her mother and sister died–she lived with her aunt within the nearly-closed community of the Guardians' Peace. Linnia loved her aunt, but the Peace was becoming too predictable. The prospect of a few days' travel–sleeping outside, cooking over a fire, and seeing a new part of the realm, all away from her aunt's supervision–had appealed to her. And of course she wanted to find Marolaine; she could help Laeglin and his brother with this task.

Linnia's only disappointment was that they were not traveling on horseback. Linnia loved horses, and the prospect of riding one through unknown countryside was tantalizing. Laeglin didn't ride though, so any gain in speed would be offset by inefficiency or worse. Linnia reluctantly agreed with the men's plan to go on foot, carrying as little as possible.

They had spent the past two days trudging along dirt roads, pushing through bare thickets, getting scratched by brambles, and freezing their feet in late-winter streams. The Lakelands district wasn't far from the Peace, but it was much larger than Linnia had realized, and more rural.

Both men were taller than Linnia, and they moved quickly, driven by their urgency to find Marolaine. It was a matter of pride for Linnia to keep up without complaint, and she did. Like the men–but for somewhat different reasons–she was worried.

Late in the second day they found the address Hollon was looking for. The house was abandoned though, and after some fruitless exploration they decided to spend the night beside a ramshackle, open-sided shed at the edge of the property. It was a secluded area with good visibility in all directions. After they ate, Hollon and Laeglin agreed to take turns staying awake and feeding the fire, while Linnia tried to find a comfortable place to sleep.

The shed was protected from the wind, but that was about all it had in its favor. The floor was no floor at all, just age-hardened dirt and stone, trampled by generations of men and animals. Linnia found a straw bale in the corner, but when she cut the twine, it popped open to reveal a nest of baby mice who ran in all directions.

Linnia had seen mice before, but she yelped anyway as the tiny pink creatures disappeared into the shadows. After a moment, she wrinkled her nose against the musty smell of mouse and the sharper smell of mouse urine and began to pull away the soiled straw. When she reached the bale's interior, she spread the cleaner straw as best she could to cushion her bedding.

After climbing into her bedroll, Linnia lay on her back, listening to unfamiliar noises and wishing there had been more to eat at supper. Laeglin was a good cook and he'd made stew in a tin pot, first soaking the dried meat until it was tender, then adding carrots and potatoes from his sack, plus some early mushrooms that Hollon found in the woods that looked like a stack of frilly, orange pancakes. Linnia rarely ate meat, but the stew had been thick and fragrant, and she'd swiped her bowl clean with a slab of bread for Erritus's kitchen. Thinking about supper, her stomach grumbled, and she shifted, trying to evade a stubborn stone beneath her shoulder.

"Everything alright?" It was Laeglin's voice. He was sitting by the fire with his socked feet extended for warmth, his hands deep in his pockets. His boots steamed nearby, lined up neatly beside hers and

Hollon's. They all fully expected to wear damp boots again the next day, but it wouldn't hurt to try.

Hollon slept rolled in a blanket on the ground, his back to the fire and his cap pulled low against the cold night. Linnia understood that the men had considered it polite–maybe even proper–to let her have the shed to herself. Still, she wished Hollon were sleeping inside with her. She appreciated his stories and his wry humor. She also liked his reserve. She didn't need to worry that he would pry into things she didn't want to talk about. As a wary person herself, she understood wariness in others.

Laeglin was more open than his brother. He sometimes talked about his own feelings, and he sometimes asked about hers. Linnia wondered if it was a trait of the younger sibling, this tendency to share, to offer oneself. Her younger sister, Prin, had been that way too: whispering girlish confidences into the dark of their bedroom, or catching Linnia's hand as they walked, or smiling when she gave Linnia something they both wanted.

Linnia liked Laeglin, even if he sometimes made her uncomfortable with his questions, and the way he listened to her answers like they mattered. He'd been her first friend at the Peace, and she thought Marolaine was crazy not to marry him right away.

Still, Linnia wasn't in the mood to talk tonight, so she called back, quietly, "Yeah, thanks, Laeglin. I'm fine."

"I know you're probably thinking about Marolaine," Laeglin replied. "I am too. But don't worry, we'll find her." He turned back toward the fire, and Linnia spent a few minutes silently observing his profile as he poked the fire with a stick.

THE NEXT DAY THEY EXPLORED the area further, looking for some sign of Marolaine. Linnia's damp feet had developed blisters: the left on the heel and the right on the side of her little toe where the leather rubbed. She didn't mention them, but she found herself wishing that her aunt was there to give her some advice, or to make a salve.

They had traveled roughly north of the original address, and in the late afternoon they came to the southern shore of a lake. There were many lakes in this district–hence its name–but Linnia thought this one was particularly charming, with the trailing branches of willows sweeping the water's edge and flat stones forming a beach. It would be even prettier in the spring and summer.

They had been walking along a twisting footpath, but here at the lake the path widened and became a road that could be traveled by horses or carts or cyclers. They saw several small cottages ahead, and Hollon speculated that they had come to the outskirts of a Lakelands village. He hadn't known its name, but he seemed more guarded than usual, and offered to set up the tent and gather firewood while Laeglin and Linnia walked to the town for food and information.

THE FIRST SHOP THEY entered was a bakery. Linnia nearly swooned–she'd read this expression in a novel, and it seemed to apply as well to encountering an amazing pastry as to encountering an amazing man–at the smell of vanilla, cinnamon, and ginger. Half of the shop was devoted to the repair of small household objects, such as clocks, lanterns, and shoes. But the more interesting half held a wooden rack with two open shelves, each draped with translucent white fabric that Linnia supposed kept the flies out in warmer weather.

Behind the fabric wall, the top shelf held loaves of fresh bread, including several studded with raisins and dripping with sticky icing. The bottom shelf held three trays: the first stacked with apple hand-pies, the second with wedge-shaped scones sprinkled with coarse brown sugar, and the third holding a single cinnamon-swirled bun.

The man behind the counter was small and thin, and old enough to be Linnia's grandfather, although she'd never heard that she had one of those.

"A good afternoon to you," he said, wiping his hands on a blue-striped apron that reached almost to the floor. "You'll be travelers, I'm expecting?" He tilted his head to one side. His scalp was pink and freckled, with sparse white hair that grew thicker around the edges than at the top.

"Yes," said Laeglin politely. He stepped forward, leaving Linnia to study the pastries. "We're from the Guardians' Peace, a way south of here."

"Ah! A bit out of your way, then, aren't you?" the man asked.

"Yes," Laeglin smiled. "We've been looking for a friend who we thought was visiting these parts, but so far we've had no luck in finding her."

"Where is she staying, this friend? And a pretty friend, I'm guessing?" The old man chuckled to himself and shook his head, as if enjoying a fond memory. "That's always the way with young men, always the way."

Laeglin looked embarrassed but continued. "We don't know exactly where she's staying. We had an address, but it turned out to be wrong, so now we're hoping that someone in the district might give us some information." He gave a brief description of Marolaine that Linnia thought was quite un-romantic.

"And we'd like to buy some bread and pastries," Linnia interjected, moving to Laeglin's side. She removed her mittens and slipped her arm through his—also something she'd read in a novel. "They look wonderful."

The old man beamed. "That they are, my girl. My wife is the baker, and none like her anywhere near, that's what I say." He pointed to the lower shelf. "She just brought out fresh scones and pies, but I'm afraid that's the last bun until tomorrow."

"I think we should try one of each," Linnia suggested to Laeglin, "including that last bun if we may." As the old man wrapped each pastry slowly in waxed paper, his attention returned to Laeglin.

"I wish I could help, young man, but I haven't seen anyone like you were describing, nor heard anything either. Not many strangers in this part of the district, so a woman like that–a Guardian–would likely be noticed if she came into town." He paused and looked at Laeglin. "That's assuming, as I am, that you mean your friend is a guest in this area."

Linnia held the parcel, feeling the warmth of the hand-pie seeping through the paper. It had taken the shopkeeper a long time to wrap each item, his fingers stiff and thickened with age and rheumatism. And yet, she reflected, he had taken the time to do so. He'd given each pastry its own package when he might just as easily have dumped all three into a single bag. Linnia was sometimes struck by the loveliness of the realm's details, of the small actions and choices that made each human life what it was.

She sighed and brought her mind back to the conversation.

She understood that Laeglin didn't want to say too much about Marolaine's situation. He'd always tried to respect Marolaine's privacy, plus–as a soldier–Laeglin was trained to be stingy with information. Linnia shifted and the shopkeeper turned his attention toward the young woman with the blue eyes.

"What if," Linnia said slowly, "our friend was not exactly a visitor. Are there places in this district where a stranger could stay without others taking notice?"

"Aye, young lady, I must admit as there are. To the worsement of our district, there are several unfriendly residents. Those as keep to themselves, or maybe even those as have reason for secrecy, especially as you move further north. In fact, the north end of this very lake is home to one of them. Or so I've heard. Mark, you won't find me traipsing around looking for trouble. No, no you won't. My wife wouldn't be keen on that, and right she is." He shook his head at this and closed his mouth as if he'd said more than he intended.

"Who lives at the north end of the lake?"

"It's quite a way from here, mind. Folks tell strange tales about the man who lives in the old mansion there, though as I say, I don't know anything for myself. Some folks say he's a powerful mage, and a collector of magical artifacts."

Linnia and Laeglin spoke at once: "How do we find him?"

The shopkeeper shook his head. "I don't know much about it, nor want to. I've been told that the north end of this lake is something of an unnatural place. The water is dark near the mansion, the fish don't swim, and the plants don't grow. Even the birds avoid the place." He shrugged his thin shoulders and began to wipe the counter with a rag. "At least that's what I've heard. I'm sure it's not a place your friend would visit. And nor should you, nice folks as you are."

Chapter 18

I spent that evening and the first half of the following day sneaking around, avoiding the guard, Valek, and trying to learn as much as I could about the routines of the people living in the mansion. Twice I heard the front door open, but by the time I reached the top of the stairs it had closed again. I'd hoped to talk to Enestria, the caretaker, but she was elusive. Elden brought me a new puzzle—a flat case with seven painted geometric shapes that fit together—but was otherwise uncommunicative. I didn't see the Chancellor's son, Stelan, or Lorn, the older guard.

The mansion felt forlorn and dispirited, despite the presence of chandeliers, paintings, woodwork, and furniture that must once have been beautiful. Enestria and Elden cleaned diligently, but the scent of lemon oil and vinegar wash wasn't enough to overcome the pervasive feeling of neglect. As I moved around, I thought what a shame it was that such a stately home was reduced to abandoned hallways and faded draperies.

Shortly before lunch, I heard Valek exit the front door and I ran to the window at the end of the hall where I had a partial view of the front of the mansion. A horse was saddled and waiting, and after a few minutes Valek rode away.

I might never have a better opportunity, and I didn't know how long the guard would be away. I crept down the main staircase and hid in the recess behind it, giving myself a clear view of the tower door. It was a heavy door, and I knew from observation that it swung slowly. I wouldn't have much time once Elden entered, but I had to hope that I could obstruct the door enough to deactivate the magic that usually secured it.

When Elden approached with the tray, I moved as close as I dared. I watched while he held up his wrist band and waited for the door to open. As he shuffled forward, carefully balancing the tray, I darted to the wall closest to the door and crouched down, gambling that Elden's attention would be to his front rather than his back.

I hadn't had much to work with in my quarters, but I'd decided to try a sliver of damp soap. I quickly pressed it to the door frame at floor level, hoping it would stick. As I worked, I had a glimpse of the room beyond the door.

The room was round and constructed of stones heavily chinked with plaster. I could see a large fireplace, and in front of the fireplace, the back of a man's head where he sat in a chair before the fire. My heart beat faster.

The door swung slowly closed behind Elden, ending my perusal of the tower room. I held my breath as the door came to rest against the frame. The sliver of soap remained in place, although I wouldn't know if it was enough to disrupt the warding until Elden left the room.

I moved back into the recess behind the staircase and waited. After several minutes Elden emerged. I took a final look around, then moved quietly to the tower door. I reached for the knob and felt nothing. I turned the knob and to my relief the door moved under my hand. I hadn't been at all sure this would work, and now I paused.

Should I just walk in without knocking? I have no idea who the man inside this room is. Will he be a threat to me? Does it matter? I need to find out who he is—maybe he's someone who can help me. I wish I had some weapon other than this ridiculous shard of pottery...

I took a breath and opened the door fully. The air inside the tower was cool and damp, and the smell hit me immediately. It was like stepping into a root cellar and knowing instantly that somewhere, in some dark bin, a potato or a turnip had started to soften and rot. I grimaced and nearly stepped back. *Ugh. Maybe this wasn't the best idea.*

I was prepared for the man to jump up, or to confront me, or to call for help, but none of these things happened. As I took several steps into the room, there was no movement at all from the man in the chair. *Could he be asleep? Or waiting to catch me off unaware?*

I looked around, making sure no one else was present. There was a bed and a washstand, an ancient wardrobe inlaid with brass embellishments, and several bookshelves. Other than the man before the fireplace, the room was empty.

"Hello?" I called, deciding I couldn't just sneak up on whomever this man was.

There was no reply and no movement from the chair.

"Hello? May I come in?"

I stepped to the side of the chair, keeping a distance but bringing the man into view. He was old, very old. His skin was deeply wrinkled and an unhealthy gray that matched his unkempt beard and hair. His eyes were partially opened, but unfocused.

His left hand had been amputated above the wrist, and the skin above the stump was puffy and irritated. As I watched, he scratched and picked idly with his right hand, sending flakes of skin drifting to the floor. He seemed not to notice what he was doing.

Sitting on the man's lap was an orange cat with a blocky head. It yawned widely as I approached, then jumped to the floor and made its way toward me. It was large and obviously old, with matted fur along its flanks and a hazy blur in its right eye. Still, it wound around my legs like any other cat, lending a welcome bit of normalcy to the unsettling scene.

I kept my eyes on the old man, although he appeared no threat at all.

"My name is Marolaine," I said more loudly. "I'm sorry to disturb you."

Slowly, as if he were pulling himself from a dream, the old man's gaze moved toward me, searching haphazardly before landing on my face.

"Beck." His voice was a croak.

"I'm sorry?"

"Beck."

"No, I'm Marolaine." *Maybe Beck is the cat?*

"Mare of the lane, many's the many of many a mare." His voice had a sing-song quality, and I had no idea what he meant. I shifted on my feet.

"Well, uh…" Was this all a waste of time? Was this man beyond reason? I didn't have much experience with old people, but I'd heard–of course–that sometimes age could steal one's sensibility.

I tried again. "Who are you, sir? Your name?"

The old man pulled his sleeve down to cover his amputated left arm. The orange tomcat jumped back into his lap, circled to get comfortable, and then began to knead the man's skinny thigh. When he spoke, I was surprised by a voice that was clear.

"This old cat's got the claws of a kitten. And the soul of a lion." The old man smiled and stroked the cat. "My name is Tiburon." *Tiburon! That was the name of the Guard from the fabler's story, the Guard who led a rebellion against the Lightkeep and the Peace. But that was 100 years ago…this can't possibly be the same man, can it?* I mentally compared the man in front of me to the hero depicted on the tapestry in the foyer. *I suppose it could be the same man, but it's hard to tell. Maybe the name is just a coincidence.*

"Is this your manor?" I asked.

His face darkened and he stopped patting the cat. He stared at the fire. I waited until he looked back at me.

"I'm nothing but a prisoner now." His voice was so quiet I strained to hear. "It's all come to nothing."

"Someone is holding you prisoner here? Krale?" I asked. Tiburon nodded.

"He's keeping you here by magic I assume, but why?"

"I used to control him, now he controls me. He has his revenge for my arrogance." A tear grew and hovered in his right eye, then spilled over and slid down his cheek, following the furrows in his skin. He stared at the fire. The cat nudged his hand, but Tiburon didn't respond.

"Isn't there some way you could leave?" I asked.

"I can't leave, never again. It's all nothing. And yet it's still something. Beck, my boy, oh Beck." His right hand slipped under his left sleeve, and I heard the rasp of nails on skin.

His mind was clearly drifting. I was powerless here myself, yet I felt compelled to ask, "Is there anything I can get for you? Some way I can help?"

If this really was the long-ago leader of the Dark Guards, I knew I should have no sympathy for him. He was an enemy of the Peace, and I was a sworn protector of the Peace and the Lightkeep who lived there. Yet it was impossible to look at this creature–confused and miserable and alone–and feel anything but pity.

"No, child," he replied softly, without looking up. "Not unless you have the rings. Not unless you can bring me death." He closed his eyes, and within seconds I could hear him snoring.

AS I SLIPPED FROM TIBURON'S room a few minutes later, I encountered Elden. The big man was simply standing near the door with his hands in his pockets. His eyes flickered to my jaw, and I knew he saw the bruises left by Valek's fingers. His mouth tightened. I smiled and tried to engage him in conversation, but he turned and walked back to the kitchen, leaving me alone in the foyer. *Had Elden known I was inside the tower room with Tiburon? If so, why hadn't he entered, or told someone? Did he want me to talk to Tiburon, and if so, why?*

AFTER MY MEETING WITH Tiburon in the tower, I went back to the second floor and sought Stelan, the Chancellor's son. I needed someone to talk to, and someone who might be an accomplice in escape. Although Tiburon's history was interesting, I couldn't see how his presence offered any help to me. I needed to leave this place so I could assure my friends and family that I was alright. I hated to imagine the anxiety that my unexplained absence must be causing.

I preferred to talk to Stelan in a public place, so I was relieved to find him in the sitting area at the end of the hallway. This time his head was bare, his hair was combed back from his face in a way that highlighted his strong features. He had a book open on his lap, but he was looking out the window. He turned when he saw me, and his frown shifted. I noticed that he was one of those people who smiled without showing their teeth. It was unconvincing.

"Are you watching for Valek to return?" I asked, sitting and smoothing my tunic.

"Not really. Although he left this morning on horseback."

"Yes, I saw him go. Do you have any idea where he went or when he'll be back?"

Stelan shook his head. "No, although Lorn mentioned that Krale has been delayed for some reason. The two things might be connected."

"It's hard having so little information about what's happening," I said. "It's frustrating."

"Yeah, I know what you mean. Although I'm hoping to get some news soon that might be useful."

"Really?" I asked, sitting straighter. "Like what?" *Does he have a plan after all?*

"Oh, nothing specific," Stelan said cautiously, "but I've been trying to arrange a few things since I've been here. Looking for a way out, as you've said. By the way, have you found anything interesting in your exploration of the house?"

I decided to allow this change of topic. Wary people often didn't respond well to pressure. "I found the library," I said. "Most of the books looked old and dull, but still, I plan to go back tonight when it's quiet and see if I can find something to read. It would be nice to have something to do in my room."

Stelan pointed to the book in his lap and the tension eased from his face. "Yeah, I know what you mean. It's not exactly a page-turner, but better than doing nothing."

"There's a storeroom, too," I continued. "Down on the first level near the library. I didn't have time to look around, but it's full of stuff. In fact, I was hoping you might come down with me this afternoon, while Valek's still away, and serve as a sentry while I take a look around."

"Are you looking for something in particular?"

Should I be honest? Should I tell him I'm looking for a weapon, and a map of this area, and a ceramic bird that might or might not be part of a magical chalice?

"Not really," I replied, "but who knows what might be in there. It can't hurt to take a look. If you're willing...?"

Stelan looked reluctant, but said, "Well, sure, I suppose I can come down and stand outside the room if you really want to take a look. Probably useless junk though."

"Probably," I said brightly, as I got to my feet.

AS PROMISED, STELAN stood outside the storage room while I went in. I'd brought a lamp, and I shone it around the windowless room. I might not have much time, but I proceeded cautiously. Who knew what magical objects the room might contain? Not to mention the spiders.

It wasn't a large space, but it was fitted with floor to ceiling shelves, and these were packed with items of all kinds. There were trunks and boxes, secured with locks, metal bands, or leather lashings. There were piles of books and manuscripts, in no particular order that I could discern. There were pieces of furniture and other household items, some draped in fabric, and all covered in dust. There were shelves of porcelain and glassware, some of which looked old and valuable, although I had little knowledge about heirlooms or collectibles.

It was on a shelf packed with dishes, bowls, pitchers, and statuettes that I noticed the white ceramic bird. It looked identical to Linnia's, and I immediately assumed it was the bird Nod had lost. Stolen from him by Hollon and given by Hollon to an associate on behalf of a rich client. The associate I now knew to be Lorn, and the client Krale. So, this was the bird that had once adorned the Chalice of Knowledge. Now, it rested on its side in a shallow bowl lined with a piece of folded, faded red velvet.

My mind swam with questions, but first in line was this: should I take the bird? It looked neglected, but who knew if its loss would be noticed. And if it was a powerful object, as Nod claimed, would it even be safe for me to touch it?

No, I decided, it was better to leave it here and come back for it once I was ready to leave. It no longer had the potential import it had had previously. I knew much more now, and there might be little Nod could add, even assuming he kept his bargain to accept the return of the bird in exchange for information. Still, I'd come this far, and it had all started with the story of this bird. When I left the mansion, I'd try to take the bird with me.

I moved away from the glassware, toward a cabinet on the back wall. It wasn't locked and I opened its front door to reveal a line of glass vials in a wooden holder. I stared, hands at my sides but curious. Then it suddenly struck me that each vial contained what looked like some human bit. I stepped back in disgust, then forced myself to look closely again, knowing my time in the storeroom was limited.

The vials–plain glass with glass stoppers–each contained a single sample, suspended in clear liquid. The vials were labeled, but in a language I could not read. Several held teeth. Several others held what appeared to be pieces of bone. In one, strands of hair poised motionless in a swirling drift of black threads. *Ugh. I don't even want to know what these are for.*

At that moment, Stelan whispered loudly from the doorway. "Marolaine! Quick, Valek is coming!"

THE FOYER WAS DIM AND quiet when I slipped down the stairs that night after supper. I knew both guards were somewhere in the mansion, but Stelan had told me they usually kept to themselves in the evening. In any case, I was willing to take the chance of meeting Valek or Lorn for the promise of finding a book. Even a dull one.

When I opened the door to the library, I was surprised to see a lamp burning at a small reading table near the window. The man who sat bent over a book was middle-aged and shorter than me, with gray-streaked hair thinning on top. Like Valek, he wore a military-cut jacket, and I assumed right away that he was the second guard, Lorn.

The man was startled by my appearance. He quickly removed his spectacles and shoved the book he was reading under the table, like a boy caught at something forbidden. Before he did though, I noticed that part of his little finger was missing. *Like the man who came to Belva's house.*

Stiffly, the man got to his feet, setting the book behind him on the chair, face-down. His hand rested on the butt of a hip knife, but he made no move to unfasten the strap. I held this as a good sign and decided to take the opportunity that had presented itself.

"I'm Marolaine" I said, turning my body slightly and loosening my hands.

"I know who you is, Miss." His voice was slow and slightly indistinct, as if he held something in his mouth and was forced to talk around it. More than one person had referred to Lorn's lack of intelligence, but I wasn't quick to make that assumption.

"And you must be Lorn."

"Aye, that's right." He sounded suspicious. "What's you doing down here at night?"

I softened my stance further and gave him my most non-threatening smile. "Oh nothing. Just looking for a book. Something to read before I go to sleep."

"I ain much of a reader."

"No?" I asked, giving a brief glance to the shelves that surrounded us. "Well, I can see that it's peaceful in here. I'm sorry to have disturbed you."

Lorn shrugged but some of the tension dropped from his face. His hand drifted off the knife's butt until it rested against the sheath, further down. I wondered if he had the tattoo that marked Krale's men: the black bar with circles on either side. I didn't know its symbolism, and it likely didn't matter now. Still, I found my habitual curiosity intact. *Maybe I'll ask Stelan about it.*

I didn't look at the knife, and he seemed to have forgotten that his hand rested on it. We continued to stand, facing each other across the reading table. The lamp cast a circle of light, but we were both a step outside its yellow warmth.

"Have you had a long day?" I hoped he would tell me something new about the routines of the house or its inhabitants.

He looked surprised by this question, and I thought he might not answer. But a social response is ingrained in most people, and Lorn was no exception.

"Normal-like, I'd say. Just the usual."

"I heard the door open and close several times," I ventured mildly.

"I look after the horses whenever I'm here. It's my job, and a job I like the doing of," he replied.

"I knew Valek had a horse," I said, shutting out the memory of the day I'd arrived on horseback with the tall guard. "But I didn't realize there were other horses here too. I guess a large estate like this would have stables though. That makes sense."

"Well, aye. Three altogether. Valek's big un, plus two others. A gentle old gray and a cart horse. Not as they get much use."

"Only Valek rides, then?"

Lorn peered at me. He rubbed a hand through his hair as if trying to figure out what to say. I couldn't blame him. This was a strange conversation for a mage's guard to be having with a mage's prisoner in a library in the middle of the night.

"I used ta ride more, when I was a younger man. Before my joints started painin' me as they do now. Still, I'll take the gray to town now and again. She's a nice old thing, sweet as the day is long." For the first time, the older guard smiled, showing a broken front tooth.

I nodded. "I can see you like horses," I said, searching my memory, without success, for any equine knowledge that might prolong this conversation.

"Aye," Lorn replied, sounding cautious again. He pulled a timepiece from his pocket and then glanced at the door.

I didn't think I would get more information, but I hoped I'd made a friendly impression that might pay advantage later. I quickly grabbed several books from the shelf while Lorn stood and watched.

I was almost to the door when his slow voice called me back.

"Miss?"

"Yes?"

"I'd be appreciative if you didn't mention this to Valek." I wasn't sure if he meant his hidden book, our conversation, his presence here, my presence here, or even the fact that he liked horses. Regardless, I fully agreed.

"No, Lorn, I won't say anything. Sorry again to bother you."

"Good night then, Miss."

Chapter 19

I bathed, cleaned my teeth, brushed and braided my hair, and put on my nightdress. I was trying to decide between the three equally dull books I'd taken from the library, when there was a knock at the door. I jumped. No one had ever knocked on my door before. Not for the first time, I wished for an interior lock, the old-fashioned kind that keeps out unwelcome visitors, even those with magic.

Stelan smiled awkwardly when I opened the door. He was again wearing the flat cap that he'd worn when we first met, and I wondered why he wore it indoors. He was holding a bottle of pink spirits and two unmatched glasses. I pulled my robe tighter and hoped he didn't see the color that came to my cheeks.

"Oh!" I said, "I wasn't expecting anyone so late."

"Sorry, I hope I'm not disturbing you." He glanced down at my robe and bare feet, then thrust the bottle forward. "I thought you might want a drink. Or if not, maybe we could talk a bit. I didn't get to properly hear what you found in the storeroom today."

I didn't really want to let him into my room. Matron would never have allowed an unsupervised man to enter a woman's bedroom at the guesthouse at the Peace, and I heard her voice in my head, urging me to say no. I was anxious to talk to Stelan though, and we could never be assured of privacy in other parts of the mansion. I hoped Matron would forgive a breach of etiquette in the interest of information gathering.

I took a breath and directed Stelan to the table. We each pulled out a chair. Our knees bumped under the small table, and I pulled mine back with a jerk. He poured two small glasses of the pink liquid, and we attempted conversation. He complimented my hair, which made matters even more awkward. I noticed blotchy redness was creeping up from the collar of his shirt. *It looks like he feels as uncomfortable as I do. I wonder why he's truly here.*

After a few minutes during which we failed to find any conversational ease, I looked out the window. I could feel the pull of the lake even though I could only see my own reflection against the darkness. It was a relief not to meet Stelan's eyes for a minute. He took another sip of his drink and cleared his throat.

"So," he said, "I've been thinking about what you said about a plan, and I thought maybe it's time we should exchange our secrets."

"Our secrets?" *Oh, Lights, where is this heading?*

"Like the game children play," he explained. "You tell me one of your secrets, and in exchange, I'll tell you one of mine. I think we both have things we haven't told each other, but since we're stuck here together maybe it's time to start." He raised his shoulders in a shrug that reminded me of Andris.

"Who goes first?" I didn't like the sound of this game.

"Well, it's not really a game. Just a conversation." He shrugged again, but it was less convincing this time. My gaze was drawn to the color that splotched his neck. "You asked about a plan earlier, and I wasn't fully honest with you. I do have a plan to escape this place, and I'm hoping it might come about soon. Before Krale returns."

"What's the plan?"

"I can tell you that it involves money."

"A bribe of some sort?"

"In a way. Truth is, I've been giving the guards small bribes ever since I arrived. Haven't you noticed that they treat me better than they treat you?"

"Yes, I had, now that you mention it." I brought my hand to my face, feeling a little surprised that Stelan hadn't mentioned my bruises.

"Have you considered it?" he asked.

"Considered bribing the guards?" I asked, confused. "How could I do that when I don't have any money? I certainly had no coins in my nightdress when I was abducted." *What an odd question.*

"That's true," Stelan said quickly. "I guess I just assumed that as a Guardian of the Peace you might have something of value that you could use to your advantage. Or maybe some magic or marveling that could help you. Although my own marveling doesn't work here, for some reason." He removed his cap, smoothed his hair, and put the cap back on.

"I didn't realize you knew I was a Guardian." *I'll have to ask him later about his marveling. I wonder, too, how he's coping with the depressing magic that I felt when I arrived. Does he have something similar to my amber bracelet to deflect spellwork?*

"Oh, well..." Stelan laughed uncomfortably. "Someone must have mentioned it to me, maybe Valek."

"Yes, I've seen the two of you talking."

"Nothing friendly, I can assure you," he said quickly. "Valek tolerates me because of the money, but that's as far as it goes. Anyway, since you're a Guardian, you probably know about the Sword of Light, too. I understand it was hidden there in one of the libraries at the Peace, although it seems no one knows where it is now."

How did he know this? I certainly didn't tell him, but maybe he knows that Krale is trying to get the Sword from his mother, the Chancellor. Either way, I wonder why he's asking me about it.

"So, your mother doesn't know where the Sword is?" I asked, deciding to take the initiative. This conversation was making me feel wrong-footed.

Stelan paused and took a sip of his drink. "You haven't had any," he said, gesturing toward my glass. I wondered if he was avoiding my question.

"It looks good, but I've already cleaned my teeth for the night." There was another pause, then I continued. "I'm curious about what your mother has said about the Sword, Stelan. Honestly, I'm a little surprised she mentioned it to you at all."

"I guess since it's at the bottom of this abduction and all of Krale's threats, she thought I should know."

"She communicated with you about the Sword once you were taken captive here? Or she'd already told you about the Sword before you were brought here?"

Stelan looked briefly confused. He reached out as if to touch my arm, but then pulled his hand back. "It's hard to remember exactly when she told me," he said finally. "Everything has been so difficult since I came here. I'm just not myself." He dropped his eyes and gave a small sigh.

"Does your plan involve the Chancellor? I understand that she has connections to Lakelands, and I assume that's where we are."

"You're preceptive, Marolaine, I'm impressed. Yes, this mansion is located somewhere in the mid-Lakelands. I haven't seen a map, so I'm not sure of specifics, but Lorn mentioned the location on the day I arrived. And yes, I'm waiting for my mother to send me money. Money that I plan to use to bribe Valek to let me go."

"Why in the realm would he do that?"

"I think Valek would do anything for enough money. Unlike Lorn, he has no personal loyalty to Krale. He sees Krale as nothing more than an employer. He doesn't respect him, and certainly doesn't like him. I think Krale has some hold over Lorn that he doesn't have with Valek. Something that keeps Lorn here, even though he's unhappy."

"So, you think Valek will take the money and let you leave the mansion?"

"Yeah, I do. In fact, I think he might even leave himself. He's been thinking about leaving for a while, and a full coin purse will make his decision that much easier."

"And you can trust him to let you go once he has the money?"

"Lights, no, I can't trust him at all. I'll have to come up with some plan to give him the money only after I'm out. Otherwise, you're right. He'd enjoy taking my mother's money and leaving me here to rot." Stelan shook his head ruefully and drained the rest of his glass.

He stood up and began to look around the room. I suddenly, fervently, wanted him out. I needed time to think. He hadn't mentioned my release as any part of his plan, and I hadn't asked. It struck me as odd that he was expecting to receive a personal letter here at the mansion. This seemed an unlikely privilege to be granted to a prisoner. And even if he did manage to receive money from the Chancellor or arrange for money to be sent to Valek, this wouldn't help me. *Why did he bother to tell me about his so-called plan? And why tonight?*

Stelan stopped near the bed. He reached down and picked up the tangram puzzle from where I'd left it on the bedside table.

"What's this?" he asked.

"Oh, just a puzzle to help pass the time," I said.

"I've seen Elden with puzzles like this. You know, the big guy who works in the kitchen, doesn't talk? I saw him spend the good part of an afternoon recently, sitting at the table in the foyer trying to figure out this round, wooden puzzle. It was in pieces, and I think he was trying to put them back together." *That sounds like the ball puzzle Elden gave me.*

"Anything to pass the time, I guess," I said lightly. "Although I guess he's busier now that you and I are here, plus the old man in the tower." I hoped for a reaction, but Stelan appeared not to have heard me. He put the puzzle back on the table and walked back toward me.

"Thanks for a nice evening," he said, as I stood and began walking with him toward the door. "It's late, but maybe we can talk again tomorrow evening. I'd still like to hear about the storeroom, and maybe we can talk more about your own options for getting out of here. Or maybe there's a way to convince Valek to let us both go." This last sounded like an afterthought, and an unconvincing one. Stelan turned toward me. He leaned forward. *Lights, is he trying to kiss me?*

I stepped back and, after a pause, he continued to the door. With his hand on the knob, he turned back to me. "Goodnight, Marolaine. And just a word of warning: I'd suggest you stay upstairs tomorrow. Valek is likely to be back, and it's not safe for you to be wandering around the house alone. Even if you are a Guardian."

Chapter 20

It was raining when I awoke the next morning. Watery rivulets squirmed down the window glass, obscuring my view of the dark, still lake. Although I wore the amber bracelet constantly, I found that at certain times of day–early morning and late evening in particular–the lake still had the power to draw my attention. I wondered then what it would be like to walk along its shores, to dip my fingers into its shallows, to break its surface.

Stelan's warning from last night was in my mind, but I had no intention of altering my plans for a return visit to Tiburon's tower. The old man had said that he used to control Krale. That might mean that Tiburon knew something that could help me when Krale returned to the mansion. Of course, he might or might not be clear minded enough to tell me, but it was a chance worth taking.

The foyer was quiet and somber as I descended the stairs to the first floor. I looked around, then moved cautiously into the recess behind the stairs, where I could watch the door to the tower room. From this distance, I couldn't tell whether my sliver of soap was still stuck to the lower jamb. If not, I planned to wait until Elden came with the tray and simply follow him in. After all, he'd known I was with Tiburon yesterday, and he hadn't seemed to mind.

I crept forward and bent to look for the soap.

The voice surprised me.

"Well, a goodly morning to you, Lady. Up early to sneak around, is it?"

Valek's foot struck the back of my knee, causing my leg to buckle under me. I turned as I fell and raised my right forearm to block the baton blow. Still, the wooden rod struck the outer bone of my forearm with a searing pain, and I cried out.

"Stop!" I said, "There's no need–"

Valek interrupted. "I would never normally strike a woman, of course. But Krale will understand that I had no choice, lady. Now I suggest you don't make this any worse." He raised the baton, and I took a defensive position as best I could with my arm numb. *I hope it's not broken.*

My back was to the tower wall, and I could feel the chill of the stones through my tunic. There was no obvious path of escape, and diplomacy seemed unlikely to succeed with Valek in his current state of mind. Still, I had limited options. *Without weapons, I'm overmatched in a fight, and even if I wasn't, I'm a prisoner here. Fighting with Valek doesn't help me. I might disarm him, but I can't leave as long as the doors are locked and warded.*

"I'd like to return to my room, Valek. I have no desire to fight."

Valek smirked. "What about what I desire?" he said nastily, smacking the baton against his open left palm and touching his upper lip with his tongue. "No one ever asks about that." I shifted and he threw himself forward. His body struck mine and the pain in my arm nearly made me faint. In an instant he had his baton across my throat, cutting off my breath and pressing me hard against the stones.

Our faces were close, and I could feel his breath, hot on my cheek. With a yell I stomped the top of his foot, then brought my knee up as hard as I could into his groin. He gasped and doubled over, but came up faster than any man I'd ever seen. His eyes were watering and he cursed as he swung his fist into my stomach. I collapsed to the floor, my vision blurring and my breath wheezing painfully.

As I tried to catch my breath, I heard footsteps moving fast down the stairs. Stelan came around the staircase, heading straight for Valek.

"Leave her alone!" Stelan yelled hoarsely, just before Valek punched him in the face. Stelan fell instantly, unconscious. Valek looked down and then–gingerly, I thought–kicked Stelan pointedly in the ribs. The Chancellor's son grunted softly but didn't open his eyes.

Valek returned his attention to me. "That was a pitiful rescue attempt, Lady, even you must agree with that." He nodded toward the sprawled form of Stelan. "A pitiful man altogether, if you ask me. Hardly worthy of you." He looked at Stelan with distaste, and for a moment I thought he might spit on the unconscious man. Instead, he drew two slip-knot loops from his belt, rolled Stelan over, and efficiently cinched the younger man's wrists together behind his back.

"Now for you–"

The sound clearly came from the front entrance. Valek and I turned simultaneously to see that something white was tapping against the wet glass of the sidelight that framed the heavy door. It looked like a bird fluttering against the glass, and I realized with a jolt that it was Linnia's white ceramic bird, her dyad token. *What in the realm is Linnia's bird doing here?*

This distraction was an opportunity for me to get up and away. I lashed out with my foot, attempting to sweep Valek's leg. I wasn't quite close enough to hook his ankle though, and my kick glanced off. He swore again as he pulled two more sets of loops from his belt and bound my hands and feet, all while keeping an eye on the door. The bird continued to flutter and tap, reminding me of Matron playing a tune on the pianoforte in her sitting room at the Peace.

"Stay," Valek growled at me. There wasn't much else I could do, so I watched as he approached the mansion's front door–still moving stiffly, I noticed with malicious pleasure. The bird had disappeared, but now I could hear that someone was knocking.

Valek looked around uncertainly. He clearly wasn't expecting anyone, and it occurred to me that while he might not respect Krale, he was still accustomed to acting on the mage's orders. I could almost read the question on his face: what should I do?

I heard a breath and glanced to my left, toward the kitchens. I was startled to see Enestria standing in the open doorway. Behind her I could see a counter with carrots and celery root half-chopped, and in her hand she held a kitchen knife. Her apron fell nearly to the floor, but somehow, she looked as intimidating as ever. Her eyes were fixed on the front door, and the vein that pulsed in her neck brought the inked vine to life. I thought about calling to her, then thought better of it.

Valek stood at the door. *I wonder if he's waiting for instructions from Krale?* Stelan said the mansion could only be exited if one had both the wrist key and the permission of the mage. I wished that I'd asked more questions about how this worked and whom it applied to.

After a moment, Valek held up his hand, exposing the embedded metal band. He reached for the doorknob and pulled the door inward, revealing an adolescent girl on the front veranda, wrapped in an over-large jacket and dripping with rain. As we stared, the girl lowered her hand and slipped a white ceramic bird into the pocket of her jacket. Linnia.

LINNIA PUSHED HER WET hair away from her forehead and looked around the foyer. If she was nervous it didn't show. Her thin face was the picture of nonchalance: her gaze was level, her movements were slow, and her expression was detached. She glanced down at me, where I lay bound on the floor beside Stelan. She raised her eyebrows and looked like she was trying to suppress some witty remark. Her blue eyes sparkled, even in the muted light. *I'm glad to see her, but Lights, how irritating she can be! I assume this is a rescue of some sort, but she looks like she's stepped into the mansion by accident and is amused by what she sees.*

"Stop where you are," said Valek sharply, as if trying to assert his authority even though Linnia had already halted just over the doorstep. "Who are you and why are you here?" His hand rested on his baton and his eyes gleamed in a way I didn't like.

"I'm Linnia, from the Guardians' Peace," she said briskly. "And I'm here to ask that you release Marolaine at once." She gestured vaguely to where I lay.

Valek laughed. "Well now, little lady, I don't think that's going to happen. And in fact, our esteemed Mister Krale would like you to stay until he arrives himself. It seems that you're just the girl he was hoping for." He glanced dismissively at her. "For some unknown reason."

Valek reached out to grab Linnia's upper arm, but she sidestepped. "Please don't touch me, whoever you are." Her words were mild, but her blue eyes flashed and Valek dropped his hand. Linnia looked at me and winked.

"So," she continued, "are you saying that you refuse to let Marolaine go?" She sounded like she was enjoying herself, like she was an actor playing out a scene. Or maybe a character in one of the society novels she liked to read.

"That's right," Valek said, his tone stubborn and suspicious, "No one's going anywhere until I say so. Or," he added, "until Mister Krale returns." He squinted his eyes as if he suspected he was being tricked or manipulated. With Linnia, either might be the case.

Linnia shook her head suddenly, her brown hair swinging in wet strands and releasing an arc of drips onto the wooden floor around her. Valek withdrew a step. Then Linnia straightened her borrowed jacket–it looked like it might have belonged to one of the smaller Guards but was still comically large on her slight frame–and wiped her hands against the sides of her trousers.

"Well," she said, "I really hoped that you'd be reasonable and just release Marolaine. That would be the best way for everyone, wouldn't you say?"

She raised her brows at Valek. The guard glared back.

"Well," said Linnia again, this time drawing out the word as if in resignation, "If you won't let us go, then I suppose you'd better find a room for me so I can dry off."

She turned back to me and added, "And I'm sure Marolaine wants to return to her room too. I assume she has one here in this gloomy place." She paused, then stared hard at Valek. "And I don't know what's happened here–" her voice dropped, "but you better not have hurt my friend."

Valek looked briefly startled, then he turned away from Linnia and shouted, "Lorn, come here!" The older guard did not appear, and after a short wait, Valek called to Elden instead. The big man emerged from the kitchen, walking more slowly than usual and keeping his eyes on the floor. As he passed Enestria, her small hand brushed his large one in fleeting support.

"Take these two back upstairs," said Valek, gesturing at me and Stelan. "And her,"—he pointed at Linnia but made no move to approach her–"well, we're going to have ourselves a little talk, then you can put her in the blue room. Oh, and secure all the doors." Elden nodded without looking up.

MY THROAT WAS BRUISED and sore, making it difficult to swallow. My right arm was no longer numb, and it throbbed with a bone-deep ache. My head hurt.

I had tried to stay in the foyer with Linnia, but Elden had apologetically escorted me to my room and locked me in. I'd begged him to make sure she was safe, but I couldn't read his expression. I could only hope and trust in Linnia's own resourcefulness. *She walked straight up to the door*, I reminded myself, *she must have a plan.*

I was lying down when Enestria knocked lightly and entered. I jumped to my feet, bracing my right arm across my chest.

"Where's Linnia? Is she alright?"

Enestria stared at me with her dark eyes. *Does she ever blink? Maybe that's why she looks so intimidating all the time...*

"Why are you friendly with the one who calls himself Stelan?" I hadn't expected this question, and it was my turn to stare.

"Ack," she continued in disgust, "Never mind that for now. I'm here to tend to your arm."

"What about Linnia? I don't want her left alone with Valek."

Enestria let out a strangled sound halfway between a jeer and a chortle. A grin split her face. "That stupid guard is no match for the girl, and he knows it. Oh, he might bluster in his stupid way, but mark my words, he won't set a finger on her."

"How can you be so sure?"

"Because I know power when I see it. And he does too. Plus, I wouldn't let him hurt a child in this house, and he knows that too." She stopped. There was color in her cheeks. She turned away and began laying out supplies.

I sat at the table while Enestria rolled up my sleeve and began to gently explore the bones of my forearm. I winced but stayed still as her cool fingers pressed and soothed. At one point she closed her eyes and made a faint humming sound. When she opened them, she stepped back and regarded me seriously.

"The bone's not broken, just deeply bruised. I'll make a sling so you can protect your arm from movement for a couple of days if you'd like. I also have a salve that you can rub in to help with pain and swelling." She handed me a small jar with a lid. I opened it and the strong herbal smell made my nose burn. She nodded as I dipped two fingers into the salve and began to massage it into the aching flesh of my forearm.

"And for your throat, I brought this." She held out a brown glass bottle. "Take a sip or two every so often for the rest of the day. It will help you breathe easier." I wanted to ask her if she'd seen everything that happened to me, and why she hadn't tried to help. But I didn't. She was helping me now, and she clearly had reasons for the things she did or didn't do.

"I'm really fine," I said, "but thank you." Enestria nodded. "How about Stelan?" I continued, as Enestria helped me secure the sling. "He had a cut along the side of his eye that was bleeding."

"I'll see to him after I finish here," Enestria said stiffly.

On impulse, I asked, "Enestria, it seems that you don't like Stelan, and I wondered if you would tell me why."

"How well do you know him?"

"I don't know him well at all. I just know that he's the Chancellor's son, and that he's being held captive here by Krale, like me."

Enestria sniffed. She began packing up her bag of supplies. I thought longingly of a bowl of hot soup. *Ugh. What's wrong with me? I can't ask for soup, not when she just took care of my injuries and promised to protect Linnia as well. I shouldn't even be thinking about food, not with everything that's happening.*

"All I can say," said Enestria, "is that you should be on your guard. Some things are not as they appear, and some people are not to be trusted." With that, the strange woman picked up the tangram puzzle from my bedside table.

"Elden gave this to you." Her voice was soft, and I looked at her closely.

"Yes. He gave me a ball puzzle too. He seems interested in puzzles."

"Oh, indeed. He's not very talented when it comes to them," she said wryly, "but he surely does enjoy them. He gets them from the old man, I think." She looked up sharply to see whether I understood. I nodded and she continued. "It looks that you, Guardian, have the talent Elden lacks."

"Well, yes," I said slowly, "I suppose I am good with puzzles. It's strange really, because I'm no good at all with most fine tasks. Things like sewing or knitting or papercraft–I'm hopeless." I laughed, but she didn't.

Chapter 21

When Elden came with my supper tray, he brought only the barest news of Linnia.

"Is she alright?" Nod.

"Have they taken her to her room?" Nod.

"Have you seen her?" Nod and smile.

"When can I see her?" Shrug.

I couldn't sleep, so I sat in bed and dutifully read one of the books from the library. It was as dull as I'd feared: an account of agricultural accounting practices in a distant part of the realm, including vitriolic commentary on the current system for calculating market prices for grain and produce, which at least provided a contrast to the tedious prose that made up the rest of the book. I longed for a new puzzle; I'd already spent hours with the tangram, arranging the seven pieces into hundreds of shapes.

I had mixed feelings when I heard the knock on the door. Stelan.

"Quite a day," he said once we were seated at the table, my knees carefully angled to avoid contact with his. I settled my right hand in my lap, adjusting the sling. My arm still ached from Valek's blow, but the salve and tonic that Enestria had brought had definitely helped. By tomorrow, I expected to be back to myself.

"How are you?" I asked, looking at the plasters covering the wound on the side of Stelan's face. Enestria might not like him, but she'd made a neat job of bandaging his injury.

Stelan touched his cheek gently and winced. "Well, not my finest hour. I remember running down the stairs when I heard the commotion, then not much else."

I smiled. "I appreciated the help."

"You're welcome," he said, "not that it was much." He shrugged and paused, and I thought he might ask about my injuries. He didn't.

"So say, Marolaine, I take it you know the girl who came to the door? I was surprised to open my eyes and see a girl standing there in Krale's foyer, bold as you please." *Yes, everything about Linnia is a surprise, that's the truth.*

"Yes, I know Linnia from the Peace." It seemed harmless to tell him that much, although I'd already decided to withhold anything specific, especially after Enestria's warning.

"Valek seemed to recognize her too," said Stelan, watching me closely. I'd poured us some tea left over from supper, and I used the excuse of sipping to avoid his eyes.

"Did you think so?" I asked noncommittally.

"Valek said she was the girl Krale was looking for. I wonder why. She must know something of value or have some ability that he prizes. I did hear Valek say once that Krale was always looking for followers. Although honestly, I can't see that girl as a willing follower of anyone. She has too much spirit. You know her, what do you think–why would Krale be interested in her?" His voice had become almost animated.

"I'm sorry, Stelan, but I'm not comfortable talking about this. She's a child after all, we need to think about protecting her, not gossiping about her."

"Gossiping, huh? Not sure I appreciate that." He scowled slightly, then forced a laugh and continued.

"Anyway, she didn't look like a child to me. Small maybe, but she must be 15 or 16 at least."

"Like I said, I think we should talk about something else."

"So now you're not willing to share what you know with me, is that it?" His voice was sharp, and he leaned forward. "And after everything I did to help you today. After I fought with Valek for you and told you about my plan. It seems pretty small-minded that you won't tell me about the girl." *Not much of a fight, really.*

"I'm sorry it seems that way to you, Stelan. I've had a long day and so have you. Maybe it's best if we both get some sleep." I pushed my chair back from the table. I was surprised by his tone, but I knew when it was time to end a conversation.

"I don't like being manipulated, Marolaine. I deserve better than that." *I want this man out of my bedroom. It seems he came in to find out what I know about Linnia, although I can't imagine why he'd care.* We both stood and I positioned my body to steer him toward the door while keeping a distance between us.

"Stelan, I'd like to get some rest. We can talk more–"

He grabbed my left forearm. "I'd like some answers tonight, if it's all the same to you. I'd like to know why this girl is here and what she knows. Or who she knows."

I stepped back, breaking his grip with a turn of my wrist, while protecting my right arm. "Get out, Stelan, and don't put your hands on me again." His face was dark, but he turned and left the room. It was only after he'd gone that I wondered how he'd entered in the first place; my door had been locked since Elden escorted me upstairs.

I SLEPT POORLY. I WAS worried about Linnia. My arm and jaw ached. I felt insecure, knowing that Stelan–and possibly others—could enter my room without warning. I missed Laeglin. I was disappointed in myself: I hadn't succeeded in freeing myself, and now I had Linnia's safety weighing on me as well. *Ugh. What I wouldn't give for a nice boring evening at the Peace. Maybe eating*

dinner with Laeglin, playing darts with Manfrid and Dele, having a late cup of tea with Matron...

"MAROLAINE, WAKE UP!"

A heavy weight struck the bed, and I opened my eyes to see the orange cat staring at me from his one good eye, his blocky head tilted to the side. Linnia stood just behind him, and I guessed that he had jumped from her arms. Linnia had a way with animals, and while she preferred horses, she was happy to befriend any creature she came across. She probably would have loved Belva's crazy ferret.

I smiled and sat up. "Oh, come here, Linnia, I'm so relieved to see you." She took a tentative step forward and I reached up and hugged her, wincing slightly as I raised my right arm. Embracing was not usual for us, but I held on–feeling her thinness and smelling the faint scent of campfire smoke in her clothes and hair–until she relaxed.

After I released her, Linnia stepped back and looked around. "There's nowhere to sit in this dreary room," she said, as if the lack of comfortable decor was my fault. I sighed, but still smiled at her. I was tremendously relieved. I knew she was powerful and confident in her own right, but still she was young and alone in this place with Valek. *Maybe I can convince someone to let her share this room with me.*

"I'm afraid it's the table or nothing," I said, pointing to the small table with its two straight-backed chairs. Linnia shrugged and sat down. I combed my fingers through my hair, pulled on my robe, and followed her, eager to learn about everything that had happened since I saw her last. I glanced at the sling on the bedside table as I passed, but decided I didn't need it.

"How in the realm did you get here? How did you find me?"

"I don't suppose you have any food?" Linnia was always hungry.

"Not much. Enestria left me a packet of biscuits, and I have a pitcher for water…" I trailed off, seeing the disappointment on Linnia's face. "But Elden should be here soon," I added, "and he brings a hot meal twice a day. Enestria's quite a good cook. Now tell me—"

"I wonder what his name is." The cat had found the soft middle of the bed and settled down for a nap. He wheezed lightly in his half-sleep, and Linnia watched him fondly.

I was exasperated by Linnia's diversions, but I opened the biscuits and poured cups of water. *If I want answers, I need to pretend I don't care so much. Otherwise, I'm just giving her a chance to be contrary. I somehow keep forgetting how irritating she can be.*

Linnia smiled sweetly, as if hearing my thoughts. "So, Marolaine, shall I tell you everything?" It was my turn to shrug, although it took all my effort not to lunge across the table and shake her.

"It started," she said, "when Hollon went to the house where you were staying–in Clanstin, you know–and you weren't there."

"Oh! Then, you've met Hollon. Is he here?" I caught myself. Too late. Linnia fixed me with a stare, her blue eyes unblinking.

"I guess," she continued pointedly, "you'd had plans to meet him there, so he was worried when he arrived and didn't find you. Plus, he said there was a broken mug and some other things on the floor by your bed, and this made him suspicious. He was reluctant to come to the Peace directly though, since you'd arranged to arrive together."

"Yes, I was waiting to hear from Laeglin," I said. "You know they're brothers?" Linnia nodded. "Hollon wanted to talk to Laeglin, but I didn't want to surprise Laeglin by arriving back at the Peace with his brother if he didn't want to see him." Linnia nodded again. "I expected to have a letter back, or a messenger, by that morning."

"Well," Linnia said, "Hollon waited a while, then decided to come along to the Peace without you the next day. He said he tried to contact your friend Andris first but couldn't get in touch with him. And he didn't know where the lady who owned the house had gone."

"Her name is Belva, and she'd gone to see her sister. The visit came about suddenly, so I didn't have time to let Hollon know she was leaving. Andris knew though, since he had lunch with us that last day."

"Yeah," said Linnia, "it seems that you told Andris lots of things you didn't tell anyone else." She shook her head slightly, reminding me of her aunt, Matron.

"I don't know what you mean by that," I said stiffly, "Andris is my friend, so of course we tell each other things." Linnia shrugged as if this were nothing to her. *Infuriating child.* "But you were saying that Hollon came to the Peace..."

"Yeah. I wasn't there when he arrived. I wish I'd seen it, but I was down at the stables with Fisk, taking care of the horses." Linnia's pale cheeks colored as she spoke the name of the Peace's younger stableman, really a boy of her own age. Seeing her youthful vulnerability banished my irritation, but I certainly didn't smile or acknowledge her emotions in any way. That would have been unwelcome.

She continued. "I heard that the Guards at the gate sent for Captain Matteo, since Hollon had no documentation, and they weren't expecting him. I don't know what happened next, but eventually the Captain and Auntie arranged for a meeting with Laeglin and Hollon at the guesthouse. Auntie was awfully closed-lipped about it all." Disappointment showed on her face and deepened her voice.

"I know how you feel," I said. "I'd hoped to be there myself when they met. Hollon told me that it's been years. I don't know what happened between them, but hopefully they can find a way to mend it." My thoughts went to my own sisters, Bellina and Paislie. With both my parents dead, they were all the family I had.

"No one knew where you were," said Linnia, "although Hollon had a partial address that he thought might be the place. I guess he got it from some disreputable acquaintance of his." She looked questioningly at me, but I just nodded. *That must have been Lorn. That story will need to wait until another time.*

"Of course, Laeglin wanted to head out immediately to look for you. But Hollon said they should wait. He seemed to think that you could fend for yourself, and that you might not want their interference." She smiled. "He has a high opinion of you."

"So, what happened?"

"Actually, it was weird, but that night I had a dream. I haven't been dreaming much lately–you remember how I had those night terrors a while back, after my mother and Prin died–" her voice trailed off and I tactfully stood to refill the water pitcher. When I returned, she picked up her telling.

"I dreamed," she said, "about a lake with black water, surrounded by rocks painted all colors of the rainbow. And when I told the dream to Auntie, she said it sounded like an image from the Lakelands district, north of Clanstin. I'd never been there, and apparently that convinced Hollon that we should go."

"We?"

"Well, naturally they didn't plan to take me at first." Linnia shrugged, raising her thin collarbones. "But I insisted. I used all my charm." Here she stopped, tilted her head, and gave me a hugely exaggerated smile and a flutter of eyelashes.

"How could that possibly fail?" I asked sarcastically.

"Right?"

"Who's with you now? Or are you alone?"

"Well, we tracked to the address that Hollon had, but it was abandoned. It took us half a day to get there, so that was disappointing. It was in the south Lakelands though, so we decided to scout around the area before returning to the Peace. It was just me and Hollon and Laeglin, although several of the other Guards wanted to come–your friends Manfrid and Dele, plus a couple of others. Auntie thought that was a great idea–safer for me–but Captain Matteo favored what he called a 'small party.' He thought we could travel faster and not be seen, then we could send someone back for reinforcements if we found you and needed more help. I think he kind of agreed with Hollon that you might be insulted by a big fuss, especially if you actually didn't need a rescue, like, if you were following your own plan."

"Nope," I said ruefully, "not exactly following a plan."

"Yeah, I see that." *Thanks, Linnia.*

"But obviously you found this place eventually?"

"We came upon it after another day or two of scouting. A man at a bakery said something that made us curious, and so we walked up here from where we were. It was honestly terrible, Marolaine, cold and boring and we didn't have much food. Plus, Laeglin and Hollon...well it was awkward. Sometimes they seemed fine, talking about their lives or just making plans for finding you. But other times, they'd be uncomfortable together, like they were mad or disappointed but didn't want to discuss things in front of me. You know how Laeglin is–you can read his face. But Hollon is the opposite: he kind of shuts down, goes silent and withdrawn as if he's miles away. Those two might need some help if they ever plan to be brothers again. Remember how Master Bowden helped me?"

I did remember. In addition to being the Master Supervisor of the Apprentices' Academy, Master Bowden also had experience working with troubled people. He'd helped Linnia in the early days of her training when she'd been so scared and angry that no one else could reach her. He'd also helped Laeglin and I after the night we'd killed two men at the Stones. My memories of that time were still painful, but I knew I owed my recovery to Master Bowden.

"Marolaine, are you listening to me?"

"Sorry. Yes, you were saying it was awkward..."

"Yeah. But then we found this place and Hollon recognized the tall guard, Valek, walking around outside. And I recognized the house too."

"You knew it from the dream you had."

"Yeah. Although that was honestly very strange to see it in real life. Have you ever had a dream like that? Something that became true?"

"No," I said, "I haven't." I suspected that Linnia had powers no one had guessed. She probably knew it too, I thought, and it made her uncomfortable. "I just have the normal, boring kind of dreams." I smiled. "What happened then?"

"Well," she continued, "when we first saw Valek, Laeglin pulled his weapons and wanted to rush him right away. He was crazy to get to you. But Hollon was less emotional about it. He held Laeglin back and eventually convinced him that it would be better to watch and see how Valek got inside. We saw that he had some kind of key that he held around his wrist."

"It's a metal band that they all have in their skin. But Krale controls the house, so the band alone isn't enough to open the doors."

"We found that too," said Linnia. "Hollon and Laeglin got close after dark that first night, and they realized the entire mansion was warded with magic. There was no way we could break in, even if we got Valek's key. So, I came up with this plan." She shrugged and smiled a half-smile that reminded me of Hollon. "It seemed like it would better if I was here inside with you. That way, we could make a plan together and find some way to either get out or get the men in. I told them to watch the mansion and be ready to go if the front door opened or we sent some kind of message."

"And Laeglin and Hollon agreed with this?" It didn't sound like much of a plan to me.

Linnia looked down, sheepish. "Well, no, I wouldn't say 'agreed,' exactly..."

"But they're out there now, in the woods nearby and watching the mansion?" I was excited.

"I assume so. I know they wouldn't have left once they saw me go inside yesterday."

I jumped from my chair with my hand already reaching for the window. Linnia stopped me. "It's no use, Marolaine, I checked all the windows this morning. All locked."

"But this window was unlocked when I arrived. I leaned out—"

"Sorry, but it's locked now," Linnia interrupted. "You can check if you like. I assume that when they brought you back to the room and locked the door, they also put extra wards on the windows. Krale that is. The guards don't have the magic to do that on their own."

I heard Linnia, and I nodded, but my mind stuck on one frustrating thought: Laeglin and Hollon were outside, maybe even within sight of my room, and we were inside with no way to communicate with them.

WE CONTINUED TO TALK until we were interrupted by Elden. The tray he carried held two breakfasts: oatmeal, toasted bread with butter, hard-cooked eggs, and two slightly shriveled yellow pears. Linnia was overjoyed and thanked Elden so effusively that he blushed.

"Elden, is the door still locked?" I asked as he prepared to leave. He nodded. *Then how in the realm did Linnia get in? I must be the only one here who obeys the rules of magic.*

"Is Krale here?" Elden gave a small negative jerk of his head, his expression wary.

As Elden left, balancing the tray and opening the door with his wrist, I stood close behind him and looked out. In the hall outside the room, a man stood on guard. I recognized the build and posture of Lorn, but his face and hair were different. I started to speak and then stopped. *He's disguised by magic.* I remembered the enveilment that Gyra Pellaqua, the Seer, had created when I needed to transport the Sword of Light without drawing attention. *But why would Lorn need a disguise? Is Valek disguised as well? Or am I wrong–could this be a new guard who simply shares Lorn's build and mannerisms?*

The cat had woken, and he wrapped around my feet as I walked back to the table, twining in the way of cats: underfoot but always just avoiding being stepped on. Linnia scooped him onto her lap and a deep rumble started in his throat even before he settled. She scratched his ears and fed him a scrap of egg she'd saved from breakfast.

We returned to our conversation, discussing the various members of the household and what I knew about each.

Abruptly, Linnia said, "So I wonder who the man in the hidden room behind the kitchen might be."

I was startled. "What man?"

"I don't know who he is, Marolaine, only that he's there. You didn't know, I see. Hmmm, well never mind, I'll ask Enestria about it."

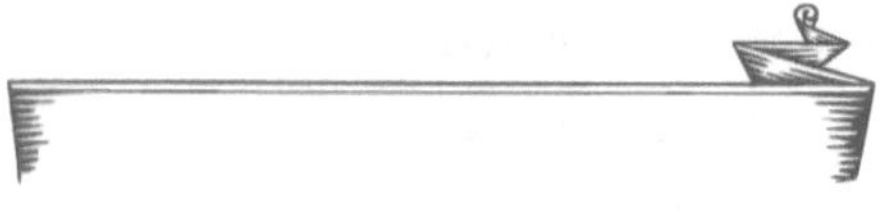

Chapter 22

Linnia returned in the afternoon, without the cat.

"We need to go visit the old man in the tower," she said upon entering.

I had described my visit with Tiburon during our morning conversation, including what I had surmised about who he was and what his history had been with the Peace.

"I told you: the soap is gone, and the door is locked. I don't know how you got in here, but I don't think it will work in the tower. Tiburon made it sound as if Krale had him under some particularly strong restraint."

"So?"

"What do you mean, 'so'? We can't visit him if we can't get into the tower. Honestly, Linnia, sometimes I don't know when you're serious and when you're just being a pain."

She stuck her tongue out at me.

"Well, anyway," she said, "Kies told me to remind you that you're the Lightholder. I talked to him and Dase before I left the Peace. They were worried about you, but they said I should remind you that you bear the mark of the Lightholder, and that gives you certain abilities."

She glanced at my hand, and I turned it palm-up. The shimmer mark that Dase had given me that night at the Stones—the mark that had allowed me to help the newer Lightkeep leave the Peace for safety elsewhere—was barely visible as a pale circle against my skin.

I stared at it now, wondering how I could possibly use it to open a magic-fused door.

On impulse, I placed my left palm over my right and spoke to the air: "Kies, I need you."

I was as surprised as anyone when Kies materialized in front of us. He looked as usual: a spherical being with an indistinct outline and a pulsing glow. Like all Lightkeep, Kies had the suggestion of a face and a human-like voice–although these may have been only my projections. Lightkeep had a place in the human world, but at the same time they were beyond our ability to understand or accurately perceive. I'd accepted this, and I'd come to like Kies as I knew him, with his grumpy manner and his unexpected loyalty to the dog, Old Brown.

"Kies! You came!"

"You called me." He sounded annoyed. "And I'll point out, Miss, that it was no easy task getting here."

I ignored his comment and moved a little closer. I hoped he would feel this as the greeting it was intended to be.

"Can you get us out of here?" I asked urgently.

"How would I do that?"

"I don't know," I said impatiently. "Opening the front door comes to mind."

Kies scowled. "I can't open the front door or any other door."

"I don't understand." Disappointment flooded through me.

"I can't do anything, because I'm not actually here."

"What?" Linnia and I spoke in unison.

"I came as called," explained Kies, "but this place is poisoned with darkness. I cannot enter it in my Lightkeep form. Not unless I'm prepared to battle its magic or its people. Which I am not."

"I don't understand," I repeated, feeling as I often did in conversations with the Lightkeep: one step behind and half a step to the side.

Kies sighed heavily. His raspy voice was slower when he spoke: "Miss Marolaine, I am not here. What you see is merely a reflection. A likeness. There are some things I can do in this form, and other things I can't. I can't open doors, even if I wanted to."

It was my turn to sigh as the hope of a quick escape slid away. "Well," I said finally, "Linnia said I might be able to use my Lightholder mark to gain entrance to the tower room, but I don't know how. If you can't release us from this place, can you at least help us get into the tower?"

"Please, Kies," added Linnia, "we need to talk to Tiburon. He's the old man locked in the tower. I'm sure you know who he was, though, don't you? Auntie and Dr. Li told me some of the story about the Battle. I know you might not want to help us with this, but we're hoping you could take us there." She raised her eyebrows sweetly, although I could have told her this would have no effect on Kies.

"I could," he said gruffly, "or you could do it yourself. Either way, you're right, I don't want to. I knew those who died in the Battle. I won't talk to that traitor, no matter how old he is."

"Tiburon is in pain, Kies. And he's dying. You know that. We have a role to play here. We have a role in bringing this chapter to a close for humans and Lightkeep alike."

The unexpected voice–warm but serious–came from behind me, and I looked around for the source. I saw that we had been joined by Dase, the leader of the Lightkeep at the Peace. She rotated until she was facing me.

"Marolaine, my dear girl! It's so wonderful to see you! I'd ask how you've been, but given the current circumstances, I'll assume it's been a trying time." She made a sympathetic clucking sound.

"Dase!" I exclaimed. "Are you really here? Kies said he was just a reflection."

"My friend is so poetic," Dase said with delight. "What a lovely way to describe it!"

"I didn't really understand," I admitted.

"Yes, certainly my dear, so many things are hard to understand," she said reassuringly. "It might help to think of a person standing on the edge of a clear pool. The person can move and talk and act as she chooses. But the reflection in the water–although it looks like the person–can have no impact upon the physical world. It is an image only, a trick of the eyes and light."

"So, you can't get us out of here either?" asked Linnia.

"No child. But then, you don't really need us to do that, now do you?"

With these enigmatic words, Dase shifted in such a way as to suggest she had clapped her hands together (although technically Lightkeep have no hands). "Very well!" she said brightly, "let's be on our way to this tower of yours. Kies and I can only stay briefly in this place, but we'll do what we can to help while we're here. Won't we, Kies?"

Kies grunted. Only the truest optimist could have taken the noise for assent, but Dase was already moving toward the door, and so Linnia and I followed. When we reached the door, Dase paused and shifted to the side, allowing Linnia to lead us through. The guard–Lorn–still stood in the hallway, but he paid no attention as we passed. I don't think he saw us.

THE SMELL IN THE TOWER was as bad as I remembered, and Linnia wrinkled her nose when we entered. As before, the old man sat in front of the fire with the orange cat asleep on his lap. This time though, Tiburon was alert, as if he'd known we were coming and had marshaled his strength.

I took the vacant chair in front of the fire, while Linnia sank to the floor and sat cross-legged on the hearth. Dase hovered to Tiburon's right, while Kies hung back, making it clear he was present under protest. No one spoke as we arrayed ourselves. I felt like I was preparing to view a theater performance, something I'd heard about from Andris but never experienced.

"Greetings, Guardian." Dase's voice was serious as she addressed Tiburon, unlike her usual motherly banter. She glanced at the dusty tea table and the lamp it held began to glow.

Tiburon straightened. The sleeve of his robe covered his amputated left hand, and his right hand rested on the cat. He had tried to straighten his robes, and there were finger-furrows in his unwashed hair. "You give me a name I don't deserve, Madam Light," he replied.

"You deserved it once," said Dase. Kies made a scoffing noise, but Dase continued. "We've come at the request of Miss Linnia and Guardian Marolaine. As you know, the Lightkeep endeavor to minimize our interactions with the human realms. Still, we have a role to play in maintaining the balance of light and dark, stability and chaos. Many years ago, Tiburon—nearly one hundred now—you challenged that role. Many years ago, you led the Dark Guardians in the Battle of the Peace. And many years ago, we lost both men and Lightkeep to your arrogance."

Tiburon's shoulders sagged. "Beck," he whispered.

"Yes," said Dase, more gently now, "and you lost your only son."

Some time passed, with only the popping fire and the cat's rusty purring to break the silence. Even Linnia was subdued.

Tiburon's right hand twitched toward his left arm, but he stilled it. "Why have you come, Madam?" he asked finally, "I cannot undo the past, want that I could."

"Ah, true," said Dase. "To humans, time is a river, flowing always in one direction. To the Lightkeep, it is more like an endless pool, with ripples that can move in any direction, crossing one another, magnifying, and diminishing."

"I don't understand," said the old man simply.

"It's not important that you do," Dase replied. "I only meant that we're here to help you look both back and forward."

"There is no forward for me."

"You want to leave the river. You want to rest on the shore."

"Yes, but I know it's more than I deserve. I caused so much damage. I thought I was right, back then, to challenge the Lightkeep and the Guardians. I thought I knew better, that I could lead my followers to a better future." He sighed. *It's amazing how clear-minded he is today. He's like a completely different person.*

"Many years after the Battle, you bound Krale to you with dark magic."

"Yes, Madam, in the early days of the Council I bound several young men to me. Krale, Ren Dalesin, Faris Axelle. They were just boys, no older than my Beck had been. I'm sorry to say that I wasn't satisfied with their allegiance; I needed to bind their wills." His shoulders began to shake, and tears rolled silently down his ravaged cheeks.

"A measure of your own cowardice," Kies spat. Dase gave him a reprimanding glance, but he continued to scowl as the old man wept.

"How did you bind them?" I asked quietly.

Tiburon glanced up, as though he'd forgotten I was there. The cat nudged his hand, and he resumed his stroking. In the glow of the lamp, bits of cat hair and dander rose gently into the air.

"I bound them with the blood of the body," said Tiburon. I must have looked confused, because he continued. "For many years after the Battle, I continued to study magic. In fact, it was through books that I originally came to know so much about the Lightkeep and their ways. But my later studies led me down dark paths. I began to crave power, not just to change the world, but to control those around me and to seek revenge." Tiburon glanced at Kies, but the Lightkeep had turned away.

"I believed that I could bind men to my bidding by trapping their blood within mine," Tiburon continued into the silence. "And it was true, at least for a time."

Here he stopped and pulled back his left sleeve to reveal the stump where his hand had once been. The skin was red and inflamed, and his urge to dig at it was palpable in the chill air.

"I embedded a piece of their bodies inside my own. I tried bits of flesh, bone, teeth...eventually I found the way to make it work. Along with the rings, it gave me control over their minds and actions, at least for a while." *How long will he be able to keep this up? Maybe the presence of the Lightkeep is stabilizing him, allowing him to think and talk clearly. And what does he mean about rings? He mentioned a ring the first time I came as well.*

"What happened?" Linnia asked from her seat on the floor.

Tiburon was quiet so long I wondered if he had fallen into some kind of state. Finally, he spoke. "Ren and Faris tried to break the bond by cutting off my arm where their teeth were embedded. They snuck into my bedroom while I slept and hacked through my arm with a knife."

I glanced at Linnia. The revulsion I felt inside flashed plainly across her face.

"Did they escape?"

Tiburon shook his head slowly. His face was still wet with tears, and several had struck the cat's back, dampening the matted fur.

"They died." His voice was so low I could barely hear it. "Krale found their bodies beside the lake."

Dase, who had been silent, now bustled forward, in the way she had of suggesting human movement with her inhuman form.

"Now then, that's enough," she said briskly. "Ren and Faris are gone, and Krale has managed to reverse the magic of the past. He's keeping Guardian Tiburon prisoner here. Krale is older than he appears, and he's learned much over the years. He's a danger that must be stopped."

"He won't let me die," said Tiburon. "And as long as I live, he lives. Please, Madam, will you help me? Will you end my life?" He had sunken lower in the chair, his voice blurring and his skin pale.

Kies snorted. "Why should we help a traitor like you? Even with death."

But Dase replied soothingly, "Tiburon, you're in great pain and imbalance. We have no wish to prolong your suffering, or to extend this unfortunate chapter in the history of humans and Lightkeep. However, it is not for Kies or I to give you death. We will do our part to release you so that you can seek your own peace, but only once Linnia and Marolaine are safe and the time is right. That's the most we can offer."

"Do you have the rings?" Tiburon asked Dase.

"No," the Lightkeep leader replied. "I suspect they are here in this house. I also suspect that I am not the one meant to find them for you." She gave me a meaningful look. *Oh, Lights.*

With an inward sigh, I turned to Tiburon. He looked exhausted and I wondered how long the presence of the Lightkeep could sustain his mind.

"Tiburon," I said, "you mentioned rings to me once before, but I didn't know what you meant. I still don't."

"They're here. He hid them in a book. The rings are in a book." His voice was weak.

This made no sense. I started to ask another question, but Dase interrupted by moving closer to Tiburon, commanding his attention.

"And now," she said, "I regret that we must leave you, Tiburon, although we will return if needed."

Dase and Kies began to pulse with light, their bodies dissolving slowly into the air around them. In the bright spot they left behind, there was an image: a very young man in Guard uniform, barely older than an apprentice. He was laughing as if caught in a joke. His image hung in the air like a treasured photograph whose edges have softened with time and handling.

We all stared. Tiburon began to rock slowly back and forth. As his son's face faded, the old magician fell forward with a cry, collapsing onto the floor like a pile of rags. The cat jumped from his lap just in time to avoid being unceremoniously spilled.

Even Linnia–usually full of the bravado of adolescence–looked horrified. She got to her feet. "What should we do with him? Is he dead?"

I was wishing fervently for the Lightkeep to return, when the door opened, and Elden entered. He walked directly to the old man, bent, and scooped him up like a baby. He walked slowly to the bed and laid Tiburon down, adjusting his robe and covering him with a blanket. The old man began to moan and twist. His words were gibberish, and I knew without a doubt that it had been only the Lightkeeps' presence that had given him such clarity over the past hour. Now, he was adrift.

Elden gave us a nod, and Linnia and I bolted from the room.

HALFWAY UP THE STAIRS, Linnia turned to me, her composure returned. "Oh, by the way, I found out who the man in the hidden room is. He's Chancellor's Axelle's son, Stelan."

Chapter 23

I knocked forcefully on Stelan's door. I had never been to the third floor, but after Linnia's announcement, I'd charged up the narrow staircase, determined to get the truth. I recognized the need to dispel the grimness of Tiburon's living death with action.

Stelan opened the door wearing rumpled clothes. He looked surprised. "I didn't expect to see you so soon, not after the way you spoke to me last night. Which I still don't appreciate."

"Can I come in, please? I need to talk to you, and I'd rather have some privacy."

Stelan raised his eyebrows, but if he was attempting to look suggestive, it failed. He stepped back and I entered.

His room was more comfortable than mine, with an upholstered sofa, two soft chairs facing a fireplace, and a sleeping area separated from the rest of the room by a screen. Still, it had the weary look that permeated the entire mansion. I walked to the sofa and sat. Stelan eyed the seat beside me, then chose the chair instead.

"I'm getting the feeling this isn't a social visit," he said. "But if you'd like–"

"Who are you?" I interrupted. "I know you're not Stelan Axelle, so who in the realm are you?"

"I'm Stelan Axelle–I don't know what you're–"

I interrupted again. "Oh, just stop. I know that there's a drugged man in a hidden room behind the kitchen, and I know that he's the real Chancellor's son."

"Well," he said sulkily, "if you know so much, why are you here?"

"Because I don't know who you are. And I can't decide what to do until I know." We stared at each other, each feeling hostile, but confined by the patterns of courtesy we'd developed over the past few days.

He sighed and broke the impasse. "Fine. Since you already know and I'm sick of pretending anyway. My name is Barret. I'm the son of Ren Dalesin." *That name is familiar.* He continued. "My father and Krale were friends, back when they were young, growing up here in the Lakelands. They got mixed up with Tiburon, and somehow ended up as part of his Realm Defenders Council. My father was older when I was born, close to 40, and he only told me a little bit about it."

Stelan paused and looked away, then continued. "He left us when I was fourteen. But before then, I'd gotten the idea that this place had been important to him. Maybe he was just feeling nostalgic for the past, but it affected me–I was only a boy you know, hoping for some excitement, something different." He shrugged.

"Wait," I said, "I thought your father died as a young man, trying to escape from Tiburon with the Chancellor's brother?"

"I don't know where you heard that, but my father was alive for many years after he left Tiburon. Obviously, since I'm here to tell the tale. I have no idea about any brother of the Chancellor." *Tiburon thought both young men had died, but maybe that wasn't true. After all, the old man said that Krale found his friends dead by the lake. Maybe Krale lied. Or maybe Tiburon lied to us when he told the story this morning. Either way, I can't sort that out now.*

"Why are you here now?" I asked.

"Well, I bounced around a lot over the years, after my father left us. Tried some different work–fishing, boat building, working on the docks. Got involved with some people I shouldn't have. Got into some trouble. Anyway, recently I was trying to figure out what to do with myself, and I thought about coming here. Maybe keep out of sight for a while, earn a little money. I'd never been here, but I guess my father's stories stuck with me all these years. I don't know." He shrugged again.

"And you saw a chance to fool me when I arrived." *Kind of clever. If it's true.*

"Yeah. Sorry about that. I actually like you, Marolaine, but I guess that's not mutual." He looked downcast, but I felt no sympathy. "I thought I could impress Krale by getting information out of you before he arrived. Valek had given me some particulars to go on, and he knew about my plan, so I was paying him to keep his mouth shut. I'm sorry I couldn't help you too."

Ignoring this, I asked, "And what do you plan to do when Krale arrives–become one of his guards, no better than Valek?"

"I could do worse, I suppose. But to be honest with you, Marolaine, now that I'm here, I'm not sure I even want to stay. It's so depressing, and I'm starting to wonder if Enestria will slit my throat with a kitchen knife some night when I'm sleeping. Or maybe poison my food. I know she hates me; everyone can see it. So maybe it's for the best that I can stop my charade and make plans to get out of here while I still can."

"Well, that's irony if I ever heard it," I said bitterly.

RETURNING TO MY ROOM, I found Linnia propped up on my bed flipping through a book about the history of men's footwear.

"Truly," she said as I entered, "who would write such a book?"

"And who would read it?" I agreed with a smile.

Sitting on the bed, I told her about my confrontation with Stelan–Barret, and she listened with interest. We agreed there was no advantage to be found in the information, at least not that we could immediately see. An aggrieved part of me wanted to tell someone, to reveal the man's dishonesty. But Valek already knew, and it was likely Enestria did too. So, it seemed I'd need to keep my grievance to myself.

I asked Linnia about the real Stelan, Chancellor Axelle's son, and Linnia said she'd only seen him briefly, but that he appeared to be enspelled, deeply asleep in a room beyond the kitchen.

"Did Enestria tell you anything more about how he came to be here?" I asked. "I'm assuming that he was abducted by Krale as a way of forcing the Chancellor to turn over the Sword. That part of the story still seems to be true."

"I guess," said Linnia. "Enestria didn't say much about it, and I didn't ask. I think she feels guilty about her role in all this." Linnia gave one of her shrugs and flipped another page of the book. "Oh, Marolaine!" she exclaimed suddenly, "Look! I've gotten to a section of shoe illustrations!" She giggled and turned the book so I could see.

"Should I go see him?" I asked, ignoring the drawings of footwear pushed close to me.

"What for?" Linnia replied, but not sharply or unkindly. She closed the book.

"Well..." I faltered. "I guess there's no reason. From what you've said, Enestria is caring for him, and there's nothing to be gained by seeing him. To be honest, I suppose I just want to do something. Plus, I'd kind of like to see the real Stelan, now that..."

Linnia poured me some water from the pitcher, and we sat silently. I assumed we were both thinking the same thing: now that we would need to think about Stelan's well-being. Now that we'd have an added responsibility that would complicate our own plans for escape.

Linnia reached over and placed her hand on my knee. Looking down, I realized that I'd been jiggling my foot up and down. It was a restless habit from my youth. It had been a habit of my mother's too, years ago. I could remember her sitting in a chair, doing something productive like sewing or shelling peas, while her foot moved up and down so fast it seemed disconnected from her conscious will.

My leg quieted under the pressure of Linnia's hand. *I wonder what Mother thought about, what made her restless. I wish I'd tried to ask, back when there was still time.*

"I wonder," said Linnia finally, changing the subject, "what the old man meant about the rings?"

"I'm not sure, but it sounded like they might be something important. Both times he mentioned them it was in connection with his own death."

"I'm not sure, Marolaine. Rings are usually a symbol of life, or promise, or something positive."

"I'm not sure either," I said, "but I'd like to learn more about them. And Dase–"

"She looked at you."

"You saw that too?"

"Yeah. And when a Lightkeep looks at you like that, it must mean something."

"I thought so too," I admitted. "And in fact, I have a plan."

Linnia's face brightened. "Oh good! Can I help?"

"Yes, you can."

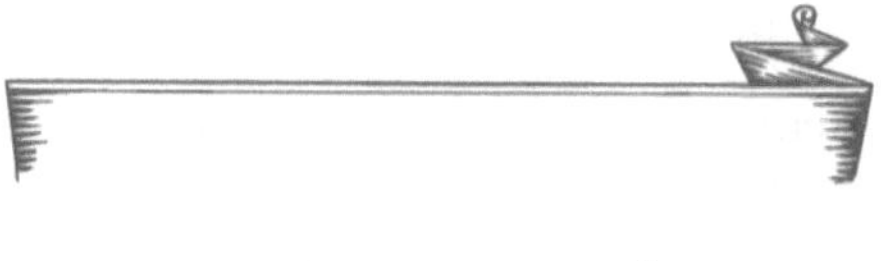

Chapter 24

In truth, I was happy to have something to do, even if Linnia said my plan reminded her of something from a novel. We were both frustrated by inaction, and I had the added weight of my recent conversation with Stelan, who–I reminded myself–I now knew to be Barret Dalesin.

I had no illusions. The plan I'd shared with Linnia was in no way guaranteed to work. In fact–like so many human plans–it would most likely fizzle out due to poor timing or logistics. It also had the potential to go badly wrong, although I minimized this possibility when Linnia expressed worry for my safety. Even an unlikely plan was better than no plan at all, and I think we both felt relief, even excitement, at the prospect of what we planned to do.

Linnia and I had agreed to eat in our own rooms, then meet on the second-floor landing if no one was around. There were, of course, no communal meals at the mansion. Linnia, Barret, and I were brought trays by Elden. The guards ate either in their rooms or sometimes from trays in the foyer. Elden and Enestria–I assumed–ate in the kitchen. Therefore, Linnia and I had good odds of being alone on the second floor after supper.

I had observed the rhythms of the household for almost a week, and I knew that after supper was cleared, the household quieted further. This was the time of day when the guards, Lorn and Valek, sometimes met in the foyer for a late drink. Not because they were in any way friends, but because they had a common occupation, and because some men like to have a drink in the evening with another man.

On a previous night, I'd observed from the head of the staircase while Lorn and Valek sat below, blocked from my view by the position of their chairs. I had heard their voices: the occasional comment about the horses, the weather, or some veiled reference to the next day's tasks. I assumed that they would also be able to hear a voice on the landing above.

Supper was a dense stew made with carrots, potatoes, and leeks and served with large, doughy dumplings. I was in the habit of stretching out my meals, but tonight I finished the stew quickly. I used the bathroom, checked the shard in my pocket—still my only weapon—and twisted my hair back into a bun at the base of my neck. I did a few quick stretches, followed by one of the breathing exercises we used at the Peace to calm our bodies and minds during training.

I was nervous. I vastly preferred direct action to the tact I would take tonight. I didn't like leaving so much to chance, and I didn't like knowingly putting myself in a poorly defended position. I would also have preferred not to involve Linnia, although I knew she was capable, and the plan required two people.

We met near the top of the staircase. The hall was empty and there was no sound from the foyer below. I gave Linnia's hand a squeeze, then whispered, "Please remember, Linnia, as soon as you're done, get back to your room and close the door. I don't think anyone would come up to check, but who knows?"

Linnia nodded. She looked excited rather than nervous, giving me a flash of envy for the assurance of youth.

Linnia tucked in close to the upper newel, and I began to move slowly down the stairs. If the foyer was empty, I'd proceed with my plan. If either of the guards were present, I'd simply turn and go back to my room. There was little risk in the first part of the plan.

The foyer was quiet. It had the forlorn look that it usually had. I moved quickly around the furniture and headed toward the library on the other side. Once inside, I allowed my eyes to adjust. The lamp on the reading table was out, leaving just a faded square of gray to mark the lone window.

I knew the layout though, and I walked quietly to the sitting area. This side of the room held the reading table and two chairs, where I'd seen Lorn two nights ago. I still wondered what he'd been reading and why he'd looked so guilty. *Some things are destined to remain unknown, as Father used to say.*

And there was the sofa, facing the unlit fireplace, with its back to the shelves of books that crowded the other half of the small room. The fabric was faded across the front and sides, but still a dark blue brocade on the back. It had once sat against the nearby wall.

Linnia and I had argued this part of the plan. I needed a place where I could hide, out of view, yet–hopefully–not trapped if I needed to fight or make an escape. The room's layout offered no good option, and so Linnia had suggested moving the couch. I'd protested that this would draw Valek's attention, but Linnia said she'd never seen Valek in the library and he therefore wouldn't notice a change to the furniture. If he even looked into the sitting area, which he might not.

I'd reluctantly agreed to take the risk, and so now I placed my hands under one end and began to turn it until the sofa stood against the wall, close to the corner of the room. I moved into the dark nook between the sofa and the corner and prepared to wait. Soldiers are trained to wait in ready relaxation, and I eased into that state. I had no idea how long I might be here. The library door stood open, so I'd hear if Valek entered the foyer. I wouldn't be able to hear Linnia though, so even if my reasoning was correct, I couldn't anticipate exactly when someone might enter the library.

Tiburon said, "He hid them in a book." That "book" could be anywhere, but the library is a logical place to start. And "he" could be anyone, but it seems most likely to be Valek. Assuming Krale didn't hide it himself, he'd need someone capable who would follow his orders. I'm making a lot of assumptions here...

After close to an hour, I heard voices from beyond the library door: Valek and Lorn. If fortune was on my side, the guards might be planning to have a drink together. If not, they might simply pass through on the way to their solitary evenings.

After several minutes, it sounded like the men were settling. *I need to be alert. Linnia will carry out her part as soon as she knows they're sitting. That means someone–Valek?–could enter the library at any point. Or, of course, Linnia's words might mean nothing to them at all. In that case, I'll be stuck in here until they leave.*

Linnia's role was to stand at the top of the staircase, out of sight but in earshot of the guards below, and simulate a conversation, as if she were talking to Elden or Enestria. She was to say that she'd heard Marolaine might have found the rings in the library. Or might be planning to look for them there. I'd suggested specific words. But I knew Linnia well enough to know she'd probably improvise, and her improvisation would be better than my script. She was a bright young woman, and very intuitive when deception was called for.

Just possibly, Linnia's words would spur Valek to check the library, where–just possibly–he knew the hiding place of the rings. If all these possibilities came to pass, Valek might do one of two things: check the location of the rings and leave them in place or locate the book that hid the rings and move them. Either way, I hoped–from my dark corner–to observe and learn something about the rings.

More time passed. Doubt, which had tiptoed lightly around my mind ever since I voiced this plan to Linnia, began to storm and stomp.

I stifled a yelp when the orange tom cat suddenly emerged from behind the sofa and brushed my leg. He must have come along the wall, behind the sofa and out of my view. Now, he twined around my legs, and I could hear the rumbling as it began in his chest. *Oh, Lights, of all the wrong times for a cat! How can I get him to leave without making any noise?*

I nudged the cat with my foot, but this didn't discourage him in the least. My heart pounded and sweat pricked my underarms as his purring roared through the room. *Everyone in the whole house must be hearing this. What in the realm should I do?*

After my initial response, I quickly calmed my thoughts. This had been a far-fetched plan from the start. It was therefore most likely that no one would enter the library tonight. No one would see or hear the cat. It wouldn't matter one way or the other whether he was here or elsewhere. *I'll just ignore him and hope he goes away. There's nothing else I can do.*

I was busy ignoring the cat and trying to relieve a cramp in my foot, when I heard shuffling and voices from the foyer. *Are they leaving? Will I be able to sneak back upstairs? I'm going to hate telling Linnia the plan failed, but at least we tried. And maybe this means I was wrong and Valek knows nothing about the rings. I suppose that's something...*

I had decided to wait five minutes after the men left the foyer before returning to my room. The time had nearly expired when I heard a footfall near the library door. *Someone's coming! Oh Lights, where's that cat?* I looked around, gripped with panic. But the cat had disappeared. Everything was quiet and still.

I crouched down. My view was obstructed, but I could see part of Valek's silhouette as he entered the library. There was a faint whiff of sweetness, like honey. Valek carried only a candle, which cast a small yellow circle on the floor ahead of him. I had gambled that–if anyone came at all–they would value stealth and wouldn't want to be seen. I slowed my breathing. I needed to see which part of the shelf Valek went to, since I couldn't see individual books from my hiding place.

Walking softly but with purpose, Valek moved between the first and second rows of bookshelves. The shelves were open-backed, and I was able to follow his shape by looking around the front edge of the sofa. The beeswax candle he carried cast a dim glow that showed between the books and the tops of the shelves. I held my breath as he stopped at the far end of the row, almost at the back wall. *Yes, it would be natural to hide something at the end of the row, rather than in the middle, although I wonder why.*

Valek was still, but I couldn't tell what he was doing. The circle of light shifted, as if he was scanning the shelf. Then it stopped and held steady. *Has he found the book? What will he do? If there really is something hidden, what would prevent him from simply taking it and hiding it elsewhere?*

I froze my inner chatter. Success tonight had been improbable from the start. I should count myself lucky to make it back to my room without being discovered.

In the front corner of the library, along the same wall as my hiding place and close to the door, a small folding step stool stood in the corner. It was the kind with locking hinges that snapped into place to hold it open, and unlocked when the stool was folded. It could be used to reach books on high shelves, although it had been dusty when I noticed it a few days ago. Unused, by all appearances.

Now, into the quiet of the dark library, into the still of the evening-hushed mansion, the step stool fell with a tremendous crash. It was all I could do not to cry out in surprise. Valek didn't restrain himself and let out a loud curse. I heard a fumbling sound but couldn't tell whether he'd replaced a book or taken one out. I pulled my head back and shrunk into the darkness as Valek strode toward the front of the library.

"Who's there?" His voice was harsh in the darkness. It carried a remnant of his surprise. Valek was not a man who liked to be surprised. "Who's there?" he repeated.

He reached the sprawled step stool just as the cat shot out of the corner, brushing Valek's pant leg as he sped to the door of the library.

"Damned cat," muttered Valek.

But he didn't return to the shelf, nor did he search the library. *Maybe he's afraid of being found here? Afraid that someone else might have heard the noise and might come to investigate?*

Valek blew out the candle and moved swiftly out of the library, leaving the door open. A curl of smoke and a sweet papery smell lingered. Part of me wanted to return to my room and its relative safety. But I knew I might not have another chance to look where Valek had been looking. It was just possible that the cat had scared away the tall guard at a strategic moment. It was just possible that there was a book on the shelf, near the back wall, halfway up, that held Tiburon's rings. *Whatever in the realm those rings are.*

This plan had seemed by turns exciting, improbable, impossible, and downright foolish. But I was determined to see it through, and who knew?

After waiting a minute to see that Valek wasn't returning, I left the corner and hurried to the place where Valek had stood. As expected for a library, there were many books on the shelf. I could estimate where he'd been and what area of the shelf he'd reached for, but I had no way to know which specific book he might have removed.

Valek had been in a hurry though, rattled by the cat's crashing step stool. One book projected forward from the others, breaking the smooth line of spines. I couldn't read its title, but I pulled it from the shelf and opened it.

As a girl, I had pressed flowers between the pages of books many times. This was much the same. Only instead of a daisy or a clutch of purple violets, the center pages of this book were bunched around four intertwined rings, spread like a fan so that they were nearly flat. I shoved the book into the pocket of my tunic and fled the library.

Chapter 25

I slept fitfully that night. After spending a few minutes looking at the rings, I'd hidden them before collapsing into bed. But as sometimes happens when we crave it most, sleep eluded me. I lay in bed for hours, thinking about the day: the meeting with Tiburon and the Lightkeep, my conversation with Stelan—now Barret, the hours spent hiding in the library, and the exhilaration of finding the rings. My mind swarmed with questions.

The rings were a mystery I couldn't solve on my own, and I spent time thinking about who might know something. Tiburon was the obvious answer, but I wasn't sure I could return to his room. And even if I did, without the Lightkeep to prop up his mind, I wasn't sure he'd tell me anything useful. I'd talk with Linnia about that in the morning.

My mind shifted to Barret and to the real Chancellor's son, Stelan. I was annoyed with myself for being gullible, and angry with Barret for being dishonest. I had badly wanted an ally in this place, but now I wished I had kept my own counsel. Had I told Barret anything that he could pass along to Valek or Krale? Anything that could be used to hurt me, or Linnia, or Stelan? I honestly couldn't be sure. I just remembered the relief I'd felt yesterday when I heard Stelan's—Barret's—feet on the stairs and had known I wouldn't have to face Valek alone.

But now we were alone. Linnia's safety was my responsibility, and Krale could return at any time. I wracked my brain for new ideas.

According to Linnia, Hollon and Laeglin were camped nearby, but I couldn't think how to get them in, or us out. Or even to let them know where we were. I'd already spent time trying to force or break the window, without success. *There's always another option. I just need to give myself time to find it.*

I finally fell asleep having decided that tomorrow morning I would search the storage room, find a weapon, overpower the guards–hopefully only Lorn, but both if necessary–and force one of them to deactivate the lock to open the front door.

I knew from Barret that the interior locks required both a key and the permission of Krale. But who knew, maybe Barret had lied about that too. I only knew that I had to try something. Sitting and waiting was driving me mad. What good was being a Guardian if I couldn't escape a derelict mansion protected by only two guards and some magic?

THE EARLY MORNING SKY was tightly packed with clouds, but the rain had stopped by the time I finished washing and dressing. My plan seemed feeble by the light of day, but it was what I had, and so I resolved myself to it. Moving to the table, I sat and looked out the window at the soggy grounds and the lake, letting my mind wander.

Once, when I was eight or nine, my mother had arranged a day outing into the countryside. In later years, it was Father who took on all the arrangements of life, but earlier–when my brother was still alive–my mother sometimes had these inspirations, often related to gardening and the outdoors. And when they struck, she was quick to act, energized by new experiences and always happy when we could explore together as a family. *I had forgotten that about her...*

On that day, she'd rented an open-top carriage to take all of us to the country to see the blooming of the early spring perennials. She had chosen a wooded area near a stream, and she hoped to see trillium, starflowers, violets, and bluebells. She called these flowers the "springtime ephemerals," because their season was so brief. And because–she explained–after they bloomed, their foliage died back, leaving almost no trace until the next spring. *She was so animated. I remember how her eyes sparkled as she explained to us four children how special these early flowers were. How hopeful to know that something so fragile could survive the harshness of winter and return each spring with new loveliness. Father had kissed her cheek and smiled at her...*

The carriage was a rare extravagance, and Mother was excited. She wore a dark green dress that day, under a practical canvas apron with large pockets. "You never know what you might discover in the spring woods," she had said with a laugh, "I like to be prepared." We'd clamored to know what we might find, and Mother had spoken of mushrooms, and water-smoothed stones, and insect larvae, and maybe even wild strawberries, with their tender seeds and juicy sweetness. She told us how these tiny jewels had stained her fingers and tongue red when she was a child herself, collecting them with her cousins.

The day had been a success, although the details were fuzzy to me now. I remembered my mother and father holding hands in the carriage. I remembered my sisters and I giggling when the horse passed wind, causing the driver to wink and make some joke. I remembered one of my sisters walking into the stream with her boots on, chasing a crayfish. I remembered my brother, Medin, finding us each a walking stick, breaking sticks over his knee to make sure each was the right height. I remembered that we were happy. *And Mother was beautiful and untroubled. I wonder why I don't more often think of her that way?*

"DIDN'T CATCH YOU ABED today, now did I? That's better."
Enestria gave a rusty chuckle as she opened the door to find me still
sitting at the table. My plan to search the storage room required me
to first leave my own room, and I'd decided to do this with Enestria's
help. Hopefully her willing help. But first I decided to see what she
might know about the rings. It couldn't hurt.

"Enestria," I started, "Tiburon mentioned some rings yesterday,
and I wondered if you might know what he meant?"

"Rings?" She sounded cagier than usual, but maybe that was my
imagination. She walked to the table, set down the stack of towels
and bed linens she was carrying, then turned slowly to face me. I
took a few steps back and sat on the edge of the bed. It didn't feel
polite to tower over the small woman.

"I don't know much about them," I continued once I was settled,
"but I had the feeling they might be important. And that they might
be hidden here in the mansion."

"You'll look for them, then?" she asked. "You'll try to find the
rings?" She remained standing, her legs spread slightly as if to brace
herself.

"I might."

There was a long pause, and then she seemed to make up her
mind. "Aye," she said with a nod. "Well, I don't think there's harm
in telling you, then. In fact, I suspect you might already know more
than you've said." She paused to give me her customary glare, but I
didn't flinch, and she continued. "There's a set of rings, four I believe,
although I've never seen them myself. They were forged fifty years
ago by Tiburon, when he first founded his crazy Council. They were
meant to symbolize the bonds between the original four: Tiburon
and the three young men."

"Were the rings magic?"

"I'm not sure. They may have had something to do with binding
the four together or holding the boys in Tiburon's power. I don't

know. But I do know that Tiburon began to use the rings to taunt Krale, to force Krale to recognize the control that Tiburon had over him. This was after the other two boys died, I suppose, and Tiburon was angry. Anyway, Krale hated it. He never could stand being subordinate to anyone. And so, years later, when Krale began to take power himself, he stole the rings from Tiburon."

"For what purpose?"

"Originally, maybe just to have them, to take something of value away from the old man out of spite. But eventually, as Krale gained more influence over his former master, Krale decided to use the rings for a new purpose. He enspelled them with magic of his own, and they took on a new meaning."

I was transfixed. I hadn't imagined that Enestria would know so much. *Although I wonder how she does? She seems to hate Krale, so it seems unlikely he would have told her any of this. Maybe she learned it from Tiburon? Or Elden...or maybe it isn't true at all, although I don't know why she'd lie to me when she could have simply said nothing.*

"What was the new meaning?"

"The new meaning had to do with Tiburon's imprisonment. The gold ring originally stood for Tiburon, and it still does. But now the other three–the rings that used to represent the young men–are symbols of the magic that traps Tiburon and always will: the magic of the tower, the mansion, and Krale himself. Three rings, like links in a binding chain. It gave Krale a perverted kind of pleasure to turn the rings from a symbol of Tiburon's power into the means of keeping the old man helpless."

"Why are the rings kept hidden now?"

"Krale hides them, or asks that idiot guard Valek to hide them, to keep them away from the old man. Like many men who crave power but are essentially afraid, Krale always fears that Tiburon will someday figure out how to break the rings' spell."

I had a sudden bit of insight. "And if Tiburon breaks the rings' spell," I said, "he could escape the tower."

"Aye."

"But it seems unlikely that Tiburon will ever get the rings back. Not if Krale has them or keeps them hidden."

"Aye, but unlikely things happen, now don't they? And the thing is, the rings speak to Tiburon, they always have, ever since he forged them long ago. So, while Krale can hide them, Tiburon—when his mind is firm—can sometimes see or feel them." *That must be what happened! With the Lightkeep there to support his mind, Tiburon was able to see where the rings were hidden. Now that I have the rings, I might be able to help Tiburon escape. Although I'm not sure how that helps me and Linnia...Or even if I want the old Guard to be free.*

Enestria came close to where I sat and stared into my eyes. It was unnerving. Finally, she spoke.

"If," she said pointedly, "someone was to find the rings—especially someone with the ability to solve puzzles—that person would want to guard the rings closely. Hide them carefully. Krale would be furious to know they were gone, since they hold the key to Tiburon's escape." Then she closed her eyes, revealing delicate patterns inked on her lids. She breathed deeply, then stepped back toward the table.

"I'm not sure I want to help Tiburon escape," I said slowly. "I'm not sure what he would do, or if he might be dangerous."

"Dangerous?" she scoffed, "Tiburon? No, escape would mean only one thing to the old man."

I waited.

"Death," she finally said, shaking her head as if I were hopelessly slow. "He wants to die, but he needs to escape the tower first."

"Enestria," I asked slowly, "how in the realm do you know all this?"

She turned her back to me. Silently, she unfolded and then re-folded the towel on the top of the pile. I stared at the tattoos that covered the back of her scalp and thought about how painful they must have been to get. I was about to apologize for being intrusive, when she spoke. Her back stayed turned and her voice was low and rough.

"I know many things about Krale that I wish I didn't know. The bastard."

"Enestria, I'm sorry–"

"I'll be back later with your breakfast," she interrupted. Then she walked quickly from the table back to the door, one hand stroking the leather of her bandolier. Had I been in her path, I had no doubt she would have knocked me aside.

Chapter 26: Linnia and Tiburon

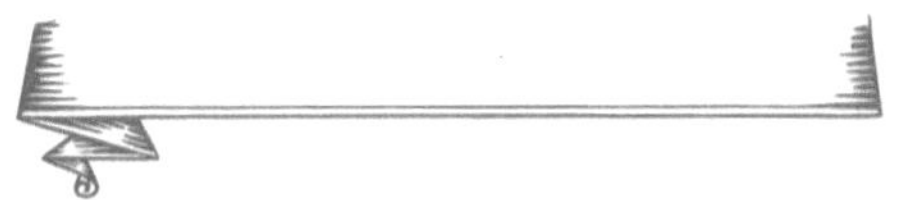

Elden leaned over the old-fashioned stove, carefully scooping eggs from the boiling water with a wooden spoon and placing them gently into a pan of cold water. Linnia had seen Errituo, the cook at the Peace's guesthouse, do this several times before. But while the elderly cook moved quickly–almost tempting an egg to escape her spoon and leap to the counter or floor–Elden was slow and methodical. Each egg joined its neighbors in the pan as if destined for one spot and only that spot.

Linnia hoisted herself onto a tall stool and waited for Elden to finish. When the last egg was settled, the big man turned to Linnia and smiled. She smiled back. She was glad to see him.

"Is Enestria still upstairs with Marolaine?"

Elden nodded and pushed a basket of fresh rolls across the counter to Linnia. The girl had already eaten breakfast, but she grabbed a roll eagerly and looked around for the butter crock. Elden smiled again and pointed toward the sideboard. He cleaned while she spread yellow butter thickly over the roll, then took an appreciative bite.

"Thanks, Elden, this is just what I needed. Mmm!" Brushing a crumb from the front of her tunic, she continued. "I was hoping to find you and Enestria and ask if it would be alright if I visited Tiburon. And if one of you would unlock the tower for me."

Elden raised his eyebrows. He'd taken a ham from the icebox and begun to cut thick slices to fry up with eggs and onions for lunch.

"I'm not sure, really," Linnia replied in response to his question. "I just feel like I'd like to talk to him. Maybe it's just curiosity, but I'd like to know more about the past. It might help us—me–understand what's going on now with Krale."

Elden's gaze shifted to the kitchen door at Linnia's back, and Linnia sensed that Enestria had returned. She turned around to see the small woman standing a few feet away, looking aggrieved.

"What?" asked Linnia. "Do you think I shouldn't talk to him? Do you think it's a bad idea?"

"Huh! Since when do you ask anyone's permission for anything?"

"Enestria, is everything alright?"

"Fine, girl, fine. I had a conversation with Marolaine just now, and it...well, it brought back memories, that's all. I don't much care for some of the memories I have." She spoke roughly, discouraging further questions.

Linnia could relate to bad memories and not wanting to talk about them. She nodded curtly and changed the subject.

"If you don't mind me visiting Tiburon, would you help me make a tray? I thought I'd take him some tea and maybe a roll or a biscuit." She eyed the basket on the counter. "I thought some food might help focus his mind and make him more likely to answer my questions."

Enestria smiled at the girl's honesty and began to assemble a tray.

LINNIA HAD PREPARED herself for the smell when Elden opened the door, and she was glad she had. She didn't want to hurt her chances of getting Tiburon to talk by insulting his dignity. The old man seemed tired as he beckoned her to enter, neither glad to see her nor not. Linnia thanked Elden, then entered the room with determination. She greeted Tiburon, reminded him who she was–he seemed indifferent–then set the tray on the table beside him and took the second chair in front of the fire.

When Tiburon reached for a biscuit, the orange cat jumped from his lap and began to sniff Linnia's pant leg. She watched him, then reached into her pocket and drew out a slice of overripe pear. She had asked Enestria for a scrap of chicken, but Elen had given her the pear instead. Enestria had only laughed and said she trusted Elden's judgment when it came to cats.

Now, it seemed that the big man had been right. The cat drew back his lips–rather like a dog–and took the pear daintily from her fingers. He fixed her with a stare from his one good eye, then turned and walked to the hearth, where he curled up and began to eat the soft fruit. Looking up, Linnia realized the old man was watching the cat with a fond expression. She gave a brief smile and wiped her hands on the napkin Enestria had placed on the tray.

In truth, Linnia had no reason to like Tiburon, and she didn't. But she knew her own advantage, and she'd woken that morning with a desire to know more about the history of this place and the people who lived here.

The old man surprised her with a weak chuckle. "You're like me," he said, his voice scratchy, as if he hadn't spoken in years.

"Oh," said Linnia, "how so?"

"We both like the cat."

"Oh."

In the silence that followed, Linnia wondered what she'd been expecting. Tiburon looked like a decrepit old man, but he was also–or had been–a formidable mage and a man who'd wielded much influence over others. Had she thought he might recognize some similar power within her? She cleared the thought from her mind and turned slightly toward Tiburon.

"How long have you had him? The cat."

Tiburon looked confused. "The cat? Oh, yes, you're right about that. How many...so few...how many..." He shook his head.

Linnia groaned inwardly. Patience wasn't her strength, but it was called for here. She reached into the deep pocket of her tunic and pulled out a tablet and pencil. She'd found the tablet of paper in the back of the wardrobe in the room she was occupying. It reminded her of a child's school tablet, with each blank page full of promise.

She opened it to the first page and quickly began to sketch. After a minute, she held up the paper so Tiburon could see.

"It's my cat!" he said with delight, reaching toward the paper with his right hand. Linnia tore the sheet from the book and handed it to him. He studied it carefully, holding it first close and then at arm's length. He glanced between the sketch and the actual cat as if astounded by what he saw.

"Have you had him long?" Linnia asked.

"Oh, close to twenty years now," Tiburon replied promptly. "Krale found him in the woods, just a stray kitten, and brought him back here. I think Krale wanted a mouser, but Cat has never killed a mouse that I know. He's peculiar that way. He eats chicken and such, of course, but his favorite treat is fruit."

Linnia nodded, feeling pleased that her sketch had unleashed this verbosity.

"And how long have you yourself lived here in the mansion?"

"Oh, well..." His enthusiasm dimmed visibly, leaving his face gray and still again. Linnia feared he wouldn't continue, but after a sip of tea, Tiburon said, "I came here almost one hundred years ago, after the Battle of the Peace, as it's called by many. I needed a place to be alone."

He stopped speaking and his right hand reached under his left sleeve and began to stroke the disfigured stump of his arm. Linnia remembered the image the Lightkeep had created of a young man, Tiburon's son. Dase had said he died at the Battle.

"But that must mean you're at least 140 years old now," she said. "How is that possible?"

"Magic. Magic of a terrible kind." He shrugged his thin shoulders and began to scratch aggressively at the skin of his arm. Linnia averted her eyes, but not before seeing flakes of skin drift toward the floor.

"Was Krale with you from the start?" She'd learned enough from Marolaine and others to have a strong suspicion that Krale had been involved in Orme's death last fall. And maybe also the deaths of her own sister and mother. She felt the tightness in her chest that could proceed either tears or anger.

"Oh, no. The boys came to me many years later, after I had studied alone for a long time, and traveled some as well. They were not much older than you are now when we first formed the Council..." His eyes became unfocused, and Linnia feared he was falling asleep.

She looked pointedly at the cat, who stared back from his place by the fire. Then, slowly, the old tom lifted one front paw and slowly licked the pink pads. Having established his autonomy, the cat uncurled, walked to Tiburon's chair, then jumped heavily into the old man's lap. Tiburon reacted with a gasp, then straightened, pulled his right hand away from his mangled arm, and began to stroke the cat's fur.

Linnia picked up her questioning, like her aunt catching a dropped ball of yarn before it could roll away.

"How old is Krale?"

"How old? Well, I don't know, child. He and his friends came to me more than forty years ago now. I brought them to me..." He made a strangled sound, and–young though Linnia was–she recognized despair.

She forged ahead anyway.

"Do you know what Krale has been doing all these years? Do you know that he's been hurting people?" Her tone was harder suddenly, and she felt the tightness in her chest deciding it was anger rather than sadness. Her sadness was private, after all, not something to show to this old man. The man who had, perhaps, been partly to blame for the loss of Prin and Mother.

"Oh, child...no, oh no..." Tiburon began to move his head forward and back, rocking his frail upper body as if trying to soothe away a bad dream. As if wishing there was someone in the world who cared enough to hold him, brush his hair back, and whisper that it would all be alright.

Linnia opened her tablet again and began to sketch. Her jaw was clenched, and a line showed between her brows. The pencil moved relentlessly over the paper, and the old man followed her hands with his eyes. He appealed–silently–for her to stop, but she had the cruelty of youth and loss, and so she continued.

After a few minutes, she removed the paper and held it up. Tiburon's lip quivered, and tears welled in his faded eyes. As Linnia watched, they spilled over, filling and flooding the channels that lined his cheeks.

"Beck," he whispered.

Tiburon couldn't help it. He saw the anger in Linnia's face, and some undamaged part of him knew why she was angry. Knew that he himself was to blame for what he'd started all those years ago, when he decided to break his vows and turn against the Lightkeep.

But he reached out anyway. His wrinkled hand, marked by the splotches of age and shaking with eagerness, reached out for the picture of his son. The boy who had died almost a hundred years ago because of the stupidity and arrogance of his father. The boy who had never had the chance to become a man. It felt like it was yesterday, and only Tiburon's desperation to hold the sketch prevented him from collapsing entirely under the weight of his guilt.

But Linnia had suffered too. She held the sketch out of Tiburon's reach. Then, as the cat and the old man watched–one in resignation, the other in pitiful terror–she stood and pushed her chair back. The tablet and pencil fell to the floor, where the pencil rolled slowly until it struck the edge of the hearth. Tiburon paled, and his empty hand dropped into his lap. Linnia didn't look at him as she walked to the fireplace, crumpled the sketch, and threw it straight into the flames.

Chapter 27

I was surprised when Enestria returned about two hours later. I'd assumed she might send Elden with the tray to avoid further interrogation from me. I was sorry to have upset the strange housekeeper, but also energized by the information she'd provided. Still, I had no intention of pushing her further, at least for now.

Before I could offer an apology or introduce a neutral subject, however, Enestria greeted me and moved purposefully toward the table. I followed, glad I'd thought to clear it of the towels and linens she'd delivered earlier.

"I brought something different for you and the girl," she said as she lifted the cover from a dish on the tray. The aroma that filled the room brought me instantly back to Erritus's kitchen at the Peace. Griddle cakes with melted butter and a pitcher of warm berry syrup. *I'm ridiculous, thinking about food at a time like this. Still, it smells amazing. I wonder if this special meal is because Linnia is here. Or maybe there's some other reason...*

I immediately feared that I'd struck on the reason.

"Is he here? Is Krale here?" I asked. I had to know.

Enestria looked away, then nodded her head slowly. With her eyes downcast, I saw the tattoos on her eyelids again. "He arrived this morning, after I talked to you. The bastard," she added quietly. "He heard about the girl yesterday and came as fast as he could."

"I don't understand what he wants from her." I felt a knot in my stomach; my hunger was gone.

"He wants to control her. She's a girl, but she has much power in her, much love and also much destruction. If he could force her to his side now, while she's young, he thinks he'll have an unstoppable weapon at his command. For whatever he has in his crazy mind." She looked like she wanted to spit.

"He has some control over Lorn, I think." I said slowly. "Some kind of magical control that he doesn't have with Valek."

"Aye, he does. Some evil magic that binds with the blood."

"Do you think that's what he plans for Linnia?" The thought made me sick.

"He's insane, Krale, so I don't know what he plans. It won't work though. Lorn is a simpler mind–not simple minded, I don't mean that. But easier to control. I think he's the only one Krale ever succeeded with, and even there the hold is weak. Nay, a blood bind would never work with Linnia. She has too much spirit and Krale knows it."

"We have to protect her, Enestria, we have to. Can you open the front door? Is there any way out?"

"I have no magic, if that's what you mean," said Enestria. "And no weapons. But the wrist keys can be used together–it makes them stronger. So, if Krale's distracted or weakened, Elden and I might have a chance to get the entryway door open."

"Where are the guards?"

"Lorn is with Krale, and Valek is patrolling outside. I'm told that Krale sent for more men, but I don't know if that's true, or when they might get here if it is." She rubbed her hands over the intricate designs that covered her scalp.

"I need to leave this room to find a weapon, Enestria. I want to search the storage room downstairs. Can you–"

We were interrupted by a knock on the door. It sounded polite and measured, but I knew it could be Krale, and a chill touched my skin. They say that there's relief when one finally faces the thing one's been dreading, but I felt no relief, only fear.

There was fear on Enestria's face as well, and I wondered again why she worked here, and what hold Krale had over her. *I can't count on her help now. She won't stand with me against Krale. I can only hope she keeps her word and opens the front door if she and Elden have the chance.* I met Enestria's eyes and nodded. I hoped she would understand that I wasn't expecting anything from her when Krale entered the room. And it was true; the last thing I wanted was to put someone else in danger.

The dark mage Krale was tall and clean-shaven. His face was lined, but it was difficult to guess his age; Dase had said he was older than he looked. He wore the tailored black suit I remembered from our meeting at the Chancellor's office, with the gathered pouch secured across his chest on a leather strap. I wondered what it held.

Krale's hands were clasped behind his back, and they remained there as he stepped, expressionless, into my room. Not that I was expecting a forearm-grip or even the chest-touch that was the greeting of strangers. Still, no greeting at all felt odd. As if by doing nothing, Krale had seized control of the conversation before it even began.

I was dressed in a tunic, vest, and pants, but I wished mightily for my familiar Guard's uniform. Or the weight of a weapon at my side. *That's not to be, though. And Master Bowden would surely tell me to deal with the situation at hand, not the situation I was wishing for in my head.*

I stood near the table, with Enestria to my side. She had picked up the breakfast tray–the food uneaten–and I felt her tension. Krale glanced at her, and she hurried toward the open door, nearly colliding with Lorn, who hesitated in the doorway. His face was still disguised by magic, but there was no mistaking his anxiety.

Krale turned toward his guard and muttered, "Close the door and get in here, you fool." Lorn obeyed, and the three of us faced each other, standing awkwardly in the middle of the nearly-bare room like uncertain pupils on the first day of school. Krale's eyes circled the space, landing on the window with its view of the lake. After a moment he drew a breath and turned his attention to me.

I forced myself to meet his dark, hooded eyes. I willed my hands still at my sides, my posture straight. Whatever might happen here, I was a Guardian of the Peace, a soldier under the command of Captain Matteo, whom I liked and admired and tried to emulate. And like most soldiers–most people in fact–I didn't respond well to intimidation.

"I'm Marolaine, Senior Guard of the Guardians' Peace," I said formally. *Thank the Lights, my voice is steady. I need to find a way to take control of this interaction. I've certainly dealt with bullies before. Maybe not bullies with magic this powerful, but still...*

"Yes, I know who you are, Guardian. And I am Mage Krale, the owner of this home and property, and the head of the Council of the Realm Defenders." Now that the silence was broken, Krale had apparently decided to match my formal tone. "I would welcome you to my home, although I suspect you find my hospitality unsatisfactory. To be frank, I've received information from my guards about your recent conduct." *No surprise there. But this confirms that he has some way–some magical way–of communicating with Valek and Lorn when they're not in his presence.*

"I've had little interaction with Lorn, but I've found Valek to be cruel and heavy handed," I said, "since we're being frank." I tried to catch Lorn's eye, but he stood with eyes downcast. His right hand shook slightly where it rested on the pommel of his sheathed sword.

"Ah. You know the names of my guards," said Krale. "I wonder what else you know. Shall we sit down together and discuss this further?" He gestured to the table and chairs near the window, keeping his eyes on my face.

"*I* wonder," I said pointedly, ignoring the invitation, "why I'm being held here against my will and when I'll be allowed to leave." I shifted my weight. It was awkward standing, but sitting would be worse: a mockery of the social niceties and an indefensible position should I need to run or fight.

"I'd prefer a civilized conversation, since you are a guest in my home," Krale replied tightly. "But if you insist on standing, so be it."

"You haven't answered my question."

Krale's right hand began to stroke the pouch that hung at his hip. I had a sudden memory of how he had cast the swirling sphere of black smoke in the Chancellor's office. *I must keep my courage and make good decisions. For Linnia's sake and my own.*

"You're direct, Guardian, and so I shall be too," he said. "I want the Sword, and I think you can help me locate it, if you choose to be reasonable. I need to know where it is and how to access it. I know that you and Dr. Li found it in one of the libraries. And I know that you have connections with the Lightkeep." His lip curled on this last word.

"Why do you want the Sword?"

"You know already that I'm the leader of the Council. I'm also an accomplished scholar, and I've worked tirelessly to advance our cause and to draw worthy individuals to our ranks. We have a mandate to move forward with the mission of the original Defenders, those who fought to return power and control of various knowledge and artifacts to their rightful human stewards." His voice rose as he continued. "So much valuable human knowledge has been seized by those unworthy...creatures. But soon our knowledge will be reclaimed from these oppressors, no matter the cost. I've dedicated myself to this cause, even if–"

Krale stopped abruptly. He smoothed his jacket and wiped his forehead, where a sheen of sweat had appeared.

"You want the Sword," I pressed, hoping to keep him off-balance, "so you can destroy the Lightkeep. So you can seize their knowledge for yourself. So you will have an excuse to exert power over others. You seek the same power you claim to oppose."

His fingers clenched around the pouch. *Should I really be provoking this man? I wish I had someone here I could trust.*

"You are incorrect," he said tightly, "I'm trying to be reasonable, as I've encouraged you to be. I would prefer us to resolve this issue amicably, rather than through less pleasant avenues." His eyes were cold, and I felt the sting of bile at the back of my throat.

"You're threatening me."

"No, Guardian, again you are incorrect. I'm imploring you not to force my hand to violence. I have enough people already who fail to understand my arguments, who fail to recognize the importance of the current moment, whose lack of intelligence and insight makes them unworthy of an association with the Council." A vein twitched at his temple, and I could see the rise and fall of his chest.

"I can't give you the Sword," I said quietly, hoping to calm his agitation. It was to my advantage to keep Krale off balance, but I also needed to keep control of the conversation. "I don't have it, and in any case, I believe it belongs in safe keeping. It was never intended to be used to enforce an ideology."

"You really think that's what I'm trying to do?" he hissed, taking a step closer.

I took an involuntary step back.

"I thought you might be persuaded," he continued. "But I can see I misjudged you. You're as ignorant and short-sighted as all the rest, and as self-righteous. But never fear, I'm used to a lonely path. I'll continue to walk it as long as necessary to achieve justice and the triumph of my cause. I won't stop until my ends have been gained, by whatever means I must." *Lights, he's a fanatic.*

"Since I can't help you," I said, "I ask that you release me and the girl Linnia, immediately."

"Oh, the girl," he said, and an unsettling look crossed his face. "The girl is an unexpected gift. I've tried to reach her before, but now you've drawn her to my very doorstep. I suppose I should thank you for that, at the least."

"She doesn't know anything about the Sword," I lied quickly.

"That remains to be seen." His eyes had lost their hard focus and the look on his face was dreamy. And all the more frightening. "She might and she might not. But either way, she's more valuable to me than a thousand of you." He shook his head in disgust.

"You won't hurt her?" I hated the pleading note in my voice, and I knew Linnia wouldn't have liked it either.

"Hurt her? Of course not. She's the future of the Council, whether she knows it now or not. In fact–since you've been so intractable–I think I shall go talk with the young lady now. But you and I will have another meeting soon, Lady Guardian, never fear. You may yet come to see reason, or at least to act in the interest of your own life."

Krale was preparing to leave, and all I could think of was Linnia. I decided–without much time to reflect–that as soon as he turned his back, I'd attempt to strike him from behind and get past him any way I could. I wasn't overly worried about Lorn. The older guard had looked decidedly ill throughout my conversation with Krale. He might not even try to obstruct me, but if he did, I was confident I could overpower him. I would do what I had to.

Krale started to turn, then lashed around like the crack of a whip, taking me by surprise. As in the Chancellor's office, his hands cradled a seething ball of darkness. He caressed the darkness, and then thrust it toward me with a cry. I tried to step aside, but the spell came too quickly. It caught the side of my body and spun me around. I dropped to my knees. It was several moments before I could move or breathe properly again, and by that time Krale and Lorn were gone, leaving me imprisoned again behind a locked door.

Chapter 28

There's nothing worse than being trapped in a room you can't leave. Unless, perhaps, it's being trapped in a room you can't leave and knowing that an insane dark mage is roaming the halls outside your door, possibly threatening the life of a young woman for whom you feel a sisterly love and responsibility.

I seethed with impatience and annoyance with myself for being in this situation. After Krale left, I spent the first half hour pacing between the door and the window. At the window, despite knowing it was futile, I tried to lift the sash, break the glass, or at least look out and see something useful I might do. I stood on a chair for a different view. I pounded my fists against the glass hoping to attract attention.

At the door, I tried the knob, then ran my hands around the frame, imagining I might somehow trigger a break in the magic that sealed me inside. I banged on the door with my fists and called for someone to let me out. I lay down and tried to peer between the bottom of the door and the sill. I pressed the faint circular mark on my palm to the wood, the frame, and the lock.

Back at the window, I scanned the grounds and the lakeshore, hoping for some sign of Hollon or Laeglin. Linnia had said they were camped in the woods, and I longed for some way to communicate with them, or, barring that, to at least know they remained close.

When I grew tired of pacing, I disciplined myself enough to complete several sets of drills: first stretching, then balance, and finally meditation. Nothing settled my mind, and I returned to the door, placing my ear against the thick wood in hopes of hearing something. Nothing.

I decided to examine the rings.

There hadn't been much opportunity to do so since I'd discovered the rings in the library last night. Before bed, I'd hidden them in the wardrobe. But after Enestria's warning this morning, I'd decided that was too obvious, and I moved them inside the mattress box on the opposite end of the bed. I retrieved the rings now, looking around as I did, as if someone might enter the room and catch me, linens askew and arm-deep in the wooden slats of the bed frame.

I sat down at the table and set the rings in front of me. For the first time–thanks to Enestria's comments–I saw them not simply as rings, but as a puzzle. A puzzle representing Tiburon and the three circles of power that bound him: the tower, the mansion, and Krale himself. A puzzle that–if solved–might have the power to free the old man.

The puzzle comprised four rings, all of similar but slightly different sizes. Each ring was forged from a different metal. The smallest appeared bronze and the largest a pale metal with a dull sheen that I couldn't name. The two in between were silver and gold.

Each ring appeared smooth and seamless. They interlocked with one another at more than one point, so that–rather than forming a chain–they formed a sort of flexible circle. The smaller rings could be twisted so they fit through the larger rings, changing the shape of the whole but not its interconnectedness.

The solution to the wooden sphere had taken several attempts, but I'd visualized it quickly once I held the polished pieces in my hands. The tangram, too, had made sense to me, presenting its multiple solutions to my mind quite easily. The rings were different though. Something in their motion, their connections, made me feel that they were meant to stay together. As if any "solution" that separated them would place them in disharmony. *Does this possibly mean that I shouldn't try to solve the puzzle? Maybe because it's wrong to free Tiburon, even if freeing him only means hastening his death?*

I sat at the table and held the rings as I looked at the lake. I let the rings slide over and around each other in any way they preferred. They flowed like thick water in my hand, and I made no attempt to analyze their configuration or to visualize their coupling or uncoupling. The shimmer mark on my palm felt warm, although the rings themselves remained cool and aloof.

I don't know how long I sat, entranced by the rings I was ignoring. But I was startled when the knob of my door rattled. I only had time to slip the ring puzzle into the side fold of my brassiere before the door to my room was thrown back with such force that it struck the wall. I jumped to my feet as Krale stormed in. Lorn trailed his master.

"Where are they? I'll kill you!" Krale's face was alive with fury and flecks of saliva clung to his lip. He stopped in front of me.

"I don't know what you mean," I replied, trying to appear calm.

"Don't lie to me," Krale hissed. "Valek told me everything, so don't you dare lie to me. Tell me where they are, and tell me now if you value your life." Krale's hands clenched at his sides and his chest heaved. He reached into the pouch at his waist, and through the fabric I watched his fingers groping, searching. I reached into the pocket of my tunic and shaped my fingers around my own weapon: a ridiculously inadequate shard of pottery. *As needs must.*

And then there was a change in the mage. Krale stopped moving his hand. He closed his eyes and stood still, breathing deeply. When he opened his eyes, reason—or perhaps just some twisted strategy of his own—had returned. He had mastered his anger.

His voice was now unnaturally slow and calm. For some reason, I thought of Erritus's kitchen helper, Kip, lugging a sack of potatoes up from the basement, the sack lumpy and bulging and threatening to give way to its shifting load.

"I apologize, Lady Guardian," said Krale tightly, "I have misplaced an item of value, and I assumed, based on certain information, that you might have it. I may have overreacted, being not myself following my conversation with the young lady." *Linnia. Well, that makes sense. If anyone could drive a dark mage to outrage, it would be Linnia. I wonder if he's talking about the rings?*

"You spoke with Linnia," I said cautiously, not wanting to provoke another outburst.

"Yes." The single word was nearly strangled with frustration.

"What did you want from her?"

"I asked her to consider her future," he replied. "A future of power and influence by my side, in fact. I invited her to stay with me here for a time, to study my books and to learn about the history and mission of the Council, with me as her mentor. In short, I suggested a rational and mutually advantageous path forward." He paused and his lip twitched. "But she refused. Without consideration or courtesy, she threw away all that I offered as if it were nothing but some worthless garbage." His voice had risen, and his eyes looked wild again.

"I'm sure she didn't mean to be rude," I said, hoping to placate him, while knowing full well that Linnia had probably meant exactly that. I needed to calm him though, to gain the advantage of time if I possibly could.

"I asked her where the rings were, but she said she didn't know what I was talking about. I know she talked to Tiburon though, I know you both did. The old man is against me, he always has been. I'll kill you, I swear I will, if you do anything to interfere with me. Anything to get in the way of my plans. I want the Sword. I've devoted myself to the study of history and the world. I'm an educated man. The old man deserves what he gets. I need the rings and...and..." Krale was rambling now, and Lorn glanced at him in alarm.

My attention snagged on two words: the rings. *So, I was right.* I was aware of their smooth coolness against the side of my breast. My heartbeat quickened, somewhere between excitement and panic. I suddenly imagined the rings would accidentally fall to the floor, separate into four, and roll away from me. I imagined they would grow larger and larger as they rolled, smashing through walls and windows, picking up speed as they raced toward the shores of the lake. Once there, they would slow and sway, finally toppling sideways into the dark water and disappearing forever. I felt sick and had to restrain the impulse to squeeze my arms protectively around my chest.

Krale didn't notice my struggle because of his own. He grasped his head with both hands, running his hands through his dark hair and rocking his upper body back and forth. He was again caught in the grip of emotion.

With his arms raised, I could see the tops of Krale's forearms above the cuffs of his jacket. His left inner arm was disfigured by a large lump of ridged flesh, the skin a deep purplish red like an angry scar. My mind flashed to Tiburon's amputated left forearm.

I had no time to muse though, because Krale straightened, and I felt a sharp push against my mind. My attention snapped back.

The push was like the sensation I'd felt in town last fall when Andris and I were attacked in the street. Except now I knew what to do, thanks to the training I'd received from the Seer Gyra. I threw up my mental shields, and Krale shrieked. Lorn drew his sword and took a step closer to Krale, looking afraid.

"Hold her, you fool," Krale screamed at his guard. "I'm going to kill her, but first she's going to tell me where the unholy Lightkeep have hidden the Sword."

Lorn took an uncertain step toward me, but stopped as Krale fell to one knee, holding his head.

"Sir?"

"Wait." Krale got slowly to his feet. His voice was choked but calmer. "Just wait." He turned to me, his face tight with strain. This cascade of emotions appeared to be exhausting him. He looked like a man on the verge of apoplexy.

"I am a scholar and a gentleman," he said finally, as if speaking to an audience. "I am a respected person, a person of science and ideas. I have no wish for bloodshed unless you force me to it. One last time, one time more, I will ask you to tell me what I want to know. If you do, I'll release you, and I won't harm the girl."

"You'll let Linnia go?" I knew his control had broken, and I couldn't trust anything he said or did. Still, time was always an asset, and I had few enough of those. I would try to keep him talking while I thought about what I'd learned.

"No," he growled, "I won't let her go because she belongs here with me. In time she'll come to see that. Through reason or through force–that will be up to her. But either way, the girl is mine now. I've waited years for this, but I won't wait any longer."

Lorn lowered his sword and looked at Krale for the first time. There was a new stubbornness in the lift of his chin, although there was still fear in his eyes. "Don't hurt the girl," the guard said. "You've got no right to hurt her or to keep her."

Krale stared at Lorn in disbelief. Then he laughed unpleasantly and turned away from the older man as if he were of no account at all. Lorn tightened his sword grip. *I'm not sure why, but Lorn seems to have gotten some courage to oppose Krale. Will he help me defend Linnia now?*

At that moment, what might have happened was overthrown and forever erased but what did happen. As is always occurring in this world, and perhaps in other worlds as well.

From the foyer downstairs we heard crashing furniture and men's shouts. It sounded like a fight.

Krale stepped into the hallway, with Lorn and I close behind. The sounds of fighting were louder now. Valek swore viciously in the foyer below and glass broke. Over the melee, I heard a man's voice call my name, then Linnia's. *Laeglin.*

Krale turned and shoved Lorn toward the staircase. "Get down there and do your job," the mage snarled. But Lorn was looking past him, looking toward the other end of the hallway, past my room. I turned too.

Linnia stood in the hall. She was wearing rolled-up trousers, a long tunic, and a knitted shawl draped around her shoulders. Her hair was held back with a ribbon, and her blue eyes were wide. She looked child-like, unlike the confident young woman I'd grown accustomed to over the past months.

"Get down there and help Valek!" Krale screamed again at Lorn. "We're under attack!"

I didn't want to leave Linnia, but I also saw that this was my opportunity. Krale had lost control, Lorn—for some reason—was not obeying his master, and Laeglin was downstairs. I assumed this meant Enestria and Elden had opened the front door.

I took a step toward the stairs, but even with his thoughts scattered, Krale was powerful. He pushed me back with an unseen force. As I stumbled and tried to regain my balance, he reached behind his back and pulled a knife from its sheath. In an instance I felt the blade at my throat.

Heat radiated from Krale's body, and his breath was hot and stale on my face. His eyes gleamed. I shifted slightly and the knife bit my skin. A drop of blood rolled down my neck, like the tickle of a summer fly.

"I'll kill you. I should have killed you right away." His voice was low, a growl. I stood very still, barely daring to breathe. I knew that nothing was beyond him, and even with help so close, I knew Linnia and I were in danger.

I couldn't turn my head, but I sensed the movement from the side of my vision. Linnia was walking toward us down the hall.

"Leave Marolaine alone," she said calmly. "I can see you're upset, Krale, but let's not make this worse than it already is. Put down the knife, and you and I can talk some more." Her voice was soothing, her movements slow and controlled. *Lights! Linnia is being diplomatic. Will wonders never cease?*

Krale wasn't deceived though. With a bellow, he pushed me hard against the wall, dropping the knife as he did. He lunged toward Linnia. She was quick on her feet, sidestepping his first attempt. But Krale had the tenacity of madness and he lunged again, managing to pin her arms and get a hand to her throat. She bit his hand, and he yelled.

Lorn broke his stupor and ran at Krale, hitting the mage in the side and back as Krale grappled with the resourceful young woman. There was momentary chaos. Then Krale did several things in quick succession.

He used spell-force to throw Lorn back. The guard's head struck the wall with a crack, and he fell unconscious, his head to one side and a fine line of blood leaking from his nose. Lorn's enveilment vanished, and I saw his features as I'd first known them.

He reached out to my mind, only this time with more anger, more clawing desperation. I hurriedly pitched my mental shields–hoping Linnia was doing the same–but a disabling pain washed over me, and I fell to the floor with a cry.

He created a shield around himself and Linnia. The air sizzled with the metallic smell of magic. Linnia looked at Lorn and her lips moved, forming a word I could not hear before she turned to face Krale's attack.

Krale's mind attack left me stunned. He had turned his attention away from me after the initial blow, but the reverberations continued to pass through me in waves. It was as if my mental shields were armor with a thousand perforations. Each tiny hole allowed a sliver of his power to penetrate and pierce my brain. I curled into a ball and tried not to move; no other action was possible.

After seconds that seemed like hours, I became aware that something small and cold was touching the back of my hand. I opened my eyes cautiously and saw the orange cat just inches from my face. He was pressing his dry, cold nose to my hand, nudging me in a dog-like way. I groaned, and he cocked his square head and stared at me with his one clear eye. I lifted my own head from the floor and felt a wave of dizziness. I waited, but not for long. I knew—even the cat knew—that I needed to help Lorn and Linnia.

I crawled slowly to where Krale had dropped his belt knife. It was small, but it felt wonderful to have a real weapon in my hands again. My head ached and my limbs trembled, but I made my way to where Lorn lay. The old cat padded after me.

Lorn was breathing, but his life signs were weak. I'd get help for him as soon as I could, but there was nothing I could do immediately. I turned my attention to the shielded confrontation taking place between Krale and Linnia.

I'd seen this shield before, when Krale possessed Orme back at the Peace, then battled with Master Bowden for the Sword. That fight had been a fight that a soldier would recognize: a vicious exchange of blows, kicks, gouges, and knife strikes. Wrestling, attacking, lunging, and blocking until both men were exhausted. And then the final knife thrust that had ended Orme's life. *Stop. Don't think about that now.*

What was happening here between Krale and Linnia was quite different. Krale's eyes were closed, but his lips moved. Sweat beaded his forehead. He'd discarded his cloak and it lay pooled on the floor. Linnia stood an arm's length away. Her eyes blazed blue, and her hands were fisted tightly at her sides. She shifted her weight from side to side, all while keeping her eyes fixed on the unmoving form of the mage. Blood trickled from her nostril.

Knowing it was futile, I moved forward anyway, knife out, only to be repulsed by the wards Krale had erected around them. My heart was beating fast, and I was nauseous. *I can't let myself vomit. And I don't have the luxury of waiting for the effects of Krale's magic to wear off. I need to help Linnia now. I don't think Krale wants to kill her–she's valuable to him alive. But who knows what he might do in this crazed state?*

I took a deep breath and focused on clearing my head. I thought about calling for the Lightkeep, but remembering their previous visit, I quickly dismissed this possibility. Reflections wouldn't help; I needed to take action myself, and I could. Because in theory, I knew how to break the shield. I'd seen Linnia do it once before by using her ceramic bird.

"Linnia!" I rasped, waving my hand and trying to get her attention. "Do you have your bird?" She didn't seem to hear me. Linnia usually kept her bird in her pocket, but even if she had it with her now, there was no way I could reach it through the shield.

I can break the shield myself, but first I'll need to get the second bird from the storeroom. I remember where it is, but I'll have to go downstairs to find it. And that means I'll have to leave Linnia...oh, I don't want to leave her...

I turned to where the cat sat, still by Lorn's side and not far from the shield. "You'll watch them while I'm gone?" I asked with a catch in my voice, feeling oddly unembarrassed to be talking to a cat. I didn't expect a reply, and I didn't get one. The orange tom gave me a tolerant look and began to lick his front paw, stretching the toes until they splayed like an open hand. I hadn't known many cats, but I decided to take this as a yes.

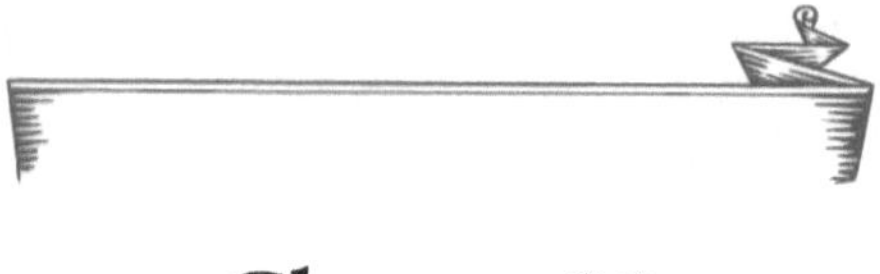

Chapter 29

Laeglin was coming up the stairs. His short sword was drawn, and his face was intent. His lower lip was badly split, and his chin was smeared with blood, as if he had wiped the wound with the back of his hand.

When he saw me, we both stopped, then continued—down and up—until we met in the middle of the staircase. There was fighting above and below, but for just a moment our eyes locked on each other. I reached for his free left hand with my right. Our fingers held, his sticky and mine cold.

"Marolaine." He smiled softly, relief showing on his face. Something inside me loosened. We leaned together until our foreheads pressed. I felt his warmth, and I sighed.

Then taking a breath, I straightened. "Krale has Linnia locked in a shield, like he did with Orme," I said, gesturing toward the second floor. "I'm going to look for the bird."

Laeglin nodded; he understood.

"Hollon and the quiet man are dealing with the guard," said Laeglin, gesturing downstairs with the tip of his sword. "Oh, yeah, and there's some other guy, although he seems like no trouble." *Barret.*

"Help Linnia if you can until I get there."

"I will."

"And be careful. Krale is powerful. Dangerous."

"I will."

IN THE FOYER BELOW, Hollon was tying up Valek, assisted by Elden who held Valek's arms behind his back. The tall guard swore and struggled, but he was no match for Elden's strength or Hollon's determination. Laeglin's brother glanced in my direction and gave me a nod of greeting. He'd grown a beard since I'd seen him last, and I wondered briefly how Laeglin had stayed clean-shaven while camping in the woods for the last week. I raised my eyebrows at Hollon in a question. *Are you all set here?* He nodded again and resumed his knots, deftly avoiding Valek's attempt to kick him.

Nearby, Enestria stood near a seated Barret. The man I'd known as Stelan was slumped in a chair, staring into his lap and showing no signs of resistance. His hair was flat on one side, as if he'd just gotten out of bed. Enestria held a kitchen knife in her left hand. Her right index finger was hooked into one of the small pockets on her leather bandolier, so that her hand hung in front of her chest. It looked both casual and intimidating. Her face was blank.

I hurried to the storage room. I had no lamp this time, and the room was cluttered and deeply shadowed. The bird had been on a shelf with other pieces of glass and ceramic. I moved toward it quickly; there was no need for stealth or secrecy now. My mind was bent on finding the bird and using it–as Linnia had–to break Krale's shield. Every second that she spent inside that shield–locked in mental confrontation with Krale–was too long.

My heart pounded. I stood before the shelf that I remembered, but I didn't see the bird. The bowl with the red velvet was empty. I peered closer. I moved my hands over the shelf, moving items around and feeling the panic rise in my throat. I needed the bird. I had no other option for helping Linnia. *Where is it? It was here, I know it was. Did someone else take it?*

I wanted to scream in frustration. Instead, I forced myself to breathe slowly. I stood quietly and thought about the possibilities. The bird was not on the shelf; that was clear. That left only two options: the bird was someplace else in the storage room, or the bird was not in the storage room at all. I couldn't contemplate the second option, because if the bird wasn't in this room, it could be anywhere, and I'd have little chance of finding it in time.

I looked around. It was hard to see in the dusty dim. I listened. As a Guard, I was trained to use all my senses, yet still I was surprised when I heard the noise.

It was faint and it took me a moment to localize it. I moved cautiously through the crowded aisles, coming at last to the back of the room and the source of the sound.

On the back wall stood the wooden cabinet I'd seen the first time I'd explored the storage room. In front of the cabinet, a bizarre struggle was in progress.

The ceramic bird hovered, as if arrested in mid-flight. Its wings beat erratically, producing the gravelly swishing sound that had caught my ear. I found myself certain that the bird had roused from the velvet-lined bowl for a purpose, although this fanciful explanation was unlike me.

If there had been a purpose, the bird could not complete it now. The bird was trapped, entangled in strands of black smoke that twisted around its legs, infiltrated its feathers, and clamped shut its beak. The spell-smoke swirled, and as I watched, it seemed to pull the bird nearer to the cabinet.

I knew what the cabinet held, but my mind couldn't fathom an explanation for what I was seeing. I decided not to try.

The spell-smoke reminded me of the invasive vines that had taken over my mother's rose garden one summer when I was a child. That had been a summer long ago, before everything changed. My mother had loved her gardens then, and she'd battled the vines all season, refusing to relinquish her roses to the predator.

I pulled Krale's knife from my belt and stepped forward. The bird vibrated and shifted position. It looked like it was turning toward me, as if glad to finally get some help. *Ridiculous, Marolaine, it's a glass figure. Now focus.* The black tendrils shifted too, massing on the side of the bird closest to me and tightening their snare around the bird's legs and wings. The most distal fingers of smoke waved in my directions. I pulled back to avoid contact, then–when the tendrils retracted–I moved the knife forward and slashed through the smoke. A stinging sensation weakened the muscles of my hands as Krale's blade sliced into Krale's magic. I gripped the handle tighter. I needed that bird.

My first knife strokes were tentative, but when I suffered no worse than stinging hands, I grew bolder. Soon, I was battling the smoke with full effort, while the bird beat its wings and tried to break free. Still, after a few moments I could see that the spell-smoke was continuing to draw its victim closer to the cabinet. I was losing.

What had Mother done? At first, she'd cut and pulled, trying to disentangle her roses from the thorny vines. But eventually, she'd gotten her sharpest spade and begun to dig. "You need to get to the root of a problem like this," she'd said. "It's too strong and too stubborn to simply be clipped or pulled away like a common weed."

What is the root of this spell? I know it's Krale's magic, but it also seems tied to the cabinet somehow, maybe connected to all the bits of hair and bone and skin in those vials? The spell seems to have almost a mind of its own, and it's clearly pulling the bird toward the cabinet. I need to do something soon–time is running out for me to get back upstairs and break the shield.

I thought only long enough to know that I was out of my depth. I was a soldier, not a scholar of magic, and not a person with any magical abilities. I didn't understand what I was seeing, and there wasn't time for me to figure it out. Action was needed, and Linnia's life was in the balance.

Avoiding the swirling mass of darkness that surrounded the beleaguered bird, I pulled open the cabinet door. The labeled vials were undisturbed, but the cabinet was filled with spell-smoke and the acrid stench of magic. Striking the smoke with Krale's knife was having no effect. I set it down. I needed to try something else.

I looked around. There were many options in the crowded storeroom. Moving quickly, I chose a set of rusted fire tongs from a nearby rack. Taking a breath, I swung them at the cabinet shelf, clearing all the glass vials in two swings. Most of the samples broke as they hit the floor; those that didn't, I smashed with the tongs, careful to avoid contact with any of the contents.

An inhuman sound rose around me, like the scream of something that was never meant to scream. The smoke in the cabinet started to coalesce into a darkening ball, pulling the tendrils away from the bird as the ball grew. With a shake of its wings, the bird broke free and began to fly toward the exit. I slammed the cabinet door. I couldn't see the spell-smoke, but I had no doubt it was still there.

Some instinct made me press my Lightholder mark against the cabinet. The scream intensified, then faded. I didn't wait. I ran toward the door.

When I was almost there, I spotted the bird—now a static piece of pretty ceramic again—resting on a shelf that held an assortment of paperweights, picture frames, and ornate jewelry cases. I picked it up and tucked it into my pocket. As I ran out of the storage room, I passed Hollon coming in. I didn't stop.

"WHAT'S HAPPENING?" I called to Laeglin as I reached the top of the stairs. Linnia and Krale were still locked in their mental duel, although Linnia was now on the floor, half sprawled. Krale had removed his jacket and–for some reason–his shoes and socks.

Lorn was still near the wall, but arranged more comfortably, lying on his back with his jacket folded under his head. Laeglin must have done what he could.

Laeglin stood on guard at the edge of the shield, his short sword held ready. The orange cat was nowhere in sight.

"I haven't been able to do much," Laeglin said with frustration. "I think she's weakening. They both are, but the shield is still up. I couldn't break it."

I drew the ceramic bird from my pocket, cool and inanimate. I didn't want to damage it by throwing it, so I approached the shield, holding the bird in my outstretched hand. The shield shimmered and pulsed against me. Without speaking, Laeglin positioned himself behind me to push and brace. I moved forward until the bird contacted the shield, then slowly penetrated the barrier.

My hand and arm were cold and numb, but I kept my grip and forced the bird slowly forward through the wall of magic. Finally, with a small pop, the pressure released and the shield broke. I nearly fell forward, Laeglin's hands on my back.

"I'll get Linnia!" I called to Laeglin. He moved around me, putting himself between Krale and the girl. As I pulled Linnia toward the wall, Laeglin rushed the mage. I heard a terrible laugh, but my eyes were on Linnia as I cradled her head and checked her life signs. A weight lifted when I felt her pulse and saw the movement of her chest.

She opened her eyes, so blue. Something in her gaze embraced me and thanked me and loved me as much as I loved her. Tears filled my eyes.

She turned her head so she could see Lorn. "Is he...?" she croaked weakly.

"He's alive," I said, a bit surprised by her concern for a guard she barely knew. I wiped my eyes. "But he's badly hurt."

Linnia shook her head, then closed her eyes and settled her head back in my lap. I thought she was asleep, but then she whispered, "Pa."

KRALE HAD TAKEN AN unfamiliar weapon from his pouch. It was a braided cord, with a shiny, black stone at each end. He gripped the short cord so that a stone emerged from each side of his right fist. The two men moved around each other, waiting for an advantage. Krale stayed out of reach of Laeglin's sword, while darting in with his hand weapon at any opportunity.

I wondered if Krale was using any mental attack against Laeglin. I didn't think so, but it was hard to tell. *Maybe he's too exhausted after his fight with Linnia? Or maybe in some perverse way Krale wants to fight hand to hand?*

Laeglin was stronger and younger, but Krale had the recklessness of age beyond reason. The mage merely laughed when Laeglin's blade sliced his side. He seemed to have little humanity left, and no caution. He threw himself at Laeglin, and each time the stones touched Laeglin's skin, there was the hiss and smell of magic. Each brush of the stones caused Laeglin a momentary paralysis, as if drawing away a bit of his life.

I settled Linnia on the floor and jumped to my feet. Krale had gotten a hand on Laeglin's neck, forcing the Guardian down. Krale's other hand gripped the stones. Somehow, the mage had kicked Laeglin's sword out of reach. Laeglin grasped Krale's wrist and struggled to keep the stones away from his face. Krale began to giggle, his face red and distorted with rage and pleasure.

I stepped to Krale's left side–away from the stones–and struck him sharply across the ear with my flat hand. While he was distracted by the pain, I grabbed his fingers and bent them forcefully back, breaking his grip on Laeglin's throat. Then, before he could recover, I gouged the tips of my fingers as hard as I could into the grotesque mass of swollen skin on his left forearm, the site–I thought–of an attempted blood-bind.

Krale screamed as blood and gore oozed from under my fingernails. He dropped the stones, which I kicked away. I tightened my grip, forcing Krale to kneel.

Laeglin was regaining movement when we heard feet pounding up the stairs. Hollon appeared on the landing, breathing hard and holding a sheathed Guardian sword. I recognized it immediately but wasn't sure why he had it. It didn't look like mine or Laeglin's, and it was covered in dust.

"Hello, Marolaine," Hollon said politely, stepping around the blood on the floor. "I know you're quite a hand fighter, but still, it doesn't seem right to see you without a weapon. Would you like this one?" He held the sword forward, hilt first, then inclined his head toward Krale. "I take it this is the mage who's caused all the trouble?"

I was deciding what to do when Krale fell limp, dropping away from my gory grip. I wiped my hand on my pants and looked at the sword that Hollon held out.

"No," I said. Krale was deeply unconscious, crumpled on the floor. His bare feet made him vulnerable in a way I hadn't expected. For days I had planned to kill him, but I wouldn't kill him like this.

Hollon gave a small shrug that reminded me of Linnia. He turned to his brother and held out the sword. "This is yours anyway," said Hollon. "I found it in the storeroom, just as I hoped. I can only say how sorry I am for what I did."

Laeglin nodded and took the sword, buckling it to his own belt without a word. For once, Laeglin's handsome face was perfectly unreadable.

Chapter 30

The rain had returned, and it streaked the windows as we contemplated the aftermath of Krale's attacks.

Lorn had not regained consciousness. He lay quietly in his own room, which turned out to be on the first-floor hallway that I'd never entered. Linnia was tired and subdued, but once she'd slept and eaten, she came to Lorn's room and sat cross-legged in a chair a distance from his bed. Enestria brought her a blanket and a pot of tea, but no one tried to talk to her. I'd heard the word Linnia had spoken, and I'd seen the recognition in her eyes. But I still couldn't imagine the story that had brought the estranged father and daughter together in this place; maybe I'd never know.

Krale was also unconscious, muttering and thrashing in the bed where he lay with his hands and feet bound. The wound on his arm was a festering mess, although Enestria had reluctantly bandaged both it and the knife cut along his side. The mage looked both frightening and pathetic, with his hair tangled and his feet still bare.

Hollon and Elden stood guard. We had no real plan for countering Krale's magic, should he awake and try to use it. We had to content ourselves with restraining his body and hoping he would either stay unconscious or be too weak for spells. Hollon had expected me to kill Krale, but now that my decision was made, he and Elden seemed content to follow it. I didn't regret my choice, but I had to admit it would be much easier for everyone if the mage had died.

Valek was dead. Apparently, after binding Valek's hands and feet, Hollon had asked Elden to guard Valek while he searched the storeroom for the Guardian sword. When Hollon returned to the foyer, Valek was dead on the ground. His hands were untied and there was a small silver pin embedded in his neck. Enestria stood beside the tall guard's body, wiping her hands. The small woman told me that she had no weapons, but this had proven untrue. The events leading to Valek's death were unclear and were likely to remain that way. All Enestria would say was that the bastard had tried to hurt Elden.

Barret was gone. As best anyone could gather, Ren Dalesin's son had simply walked out of the mansion once Krale's control was diminished and Enestria was occupied with Valek. He'd seen his chance and taken it. I thought wryly about our last conversation. Barret had said that he was growing weary of the mansion and was thinking it best to leave soon. Well, this day had certainly proven him right.

HOLLON, LAEGLIN, AND I talked, but we were unsure how to proceed. The men had seen a letter post in a nearby town, and we were anxious to contact the Peace. We'd all feel more secure with a healer and some additional soldiers on hand, just in case any of Krale's reinforcements arrived. I also wanted to send word as quickly as we could to the Chancellor, letting her know that her son was alive and expected to recover.

But the immediate situation was uncertain. We had several sick or magic-captive people in our care, and it seemed likely that either Krale or Lorn or both could die of their wounds at any time. The connections—the blood-binds—that existed between Lorn and Krale and between Krale and Tiburon made the situation more complicated. It seemed logical to have another conversation with the old man.

ELDEN WAS SITTING AT the kitchen worktable with two bowls in front of him. The bowl on his left held the twirling peels of shiny green apples. The bowl on his right held neatly peeled and trimmed slices of the same apples. A few feet away, on the side counter, two pastry-lined pie plates waited under clean dish towels. *Life goes on, as it always does.*

Elden looked up when I entered. He nodded. The cat was with me, twisting around my legs as I walked and making a general nuisance of himself. He made a beeline for Elden's chair, a rumble of pleasure starting in his throat. Elden smiled and leaned down to rub the cat's bony skull. The cat closed his eyes, thrusting his head forward and purring louder.

I sat down at the table. The kitchen was quiet, but it had the yeasty smell of Enestria's recent industry. She was upstairs now, cleaning Linnia's room, but somehow, she'd found time to set bread dough to rising in the battered copper bowl near the cookstove.

Elden returned to his peeling as the cat settled on his feet. The paring knife was like a child's toy in his huge, calloused hand, but he wielded it deftly. I'd seen Erritus peel apples, and she'd first quartered them, then used her small knife to make two angled cuts that removed the core and seeds. Only then did she peel.

Elden had a different technique, and I watched in fascination as he moved the paring knife in concentric circles down the face of the apple. Following the knife like a flat, green tail came an unbroken spiral of apple peel. Once the entire apple was peeled, Elden used a larger knife to slice straight down, making four cuts that left behind a narrow, squared-off core.

"Can I help?"

Without taking his eyes from the apple in his hand, Elden slid the cutting board toward me. I took the peeled and cored apple and hesitantly began to slice it, trying my best to copy the slices already in the bowl. I glanced sideways at Elden, but unlike Erritus, he didn't appear inclined to supervise my work.

"I'm sorry about what happened with Valek today." *Although I don't actually know what that was.*

There was silence as he peeled, and I sliced.

"How's Enestria?" I asked.

Elden tipped his head from side to side as if to say, "so-so."

"I'd like to see Tiburon again. I know that Krale's spells no longer bar the doors, but I think I'll still need a wrist key to enter the tower. Will you help me?"

Elden had finished the last apple. He held the spiral of peel in his hand and traced it with one thick finger. Then he broke off a piece and dropped it on the floor. To my surprise, the cat opened his eyes, speared the peel niftily with a claw, and began to chew on it. I smiled, and when I looked up, Elden was smiling too.

He met my eyes and nodded.

THE DECREPIT SENIOR Guard sat in his usual chair. I'd planned to come alone, but I was comforted when Elden, after opening the tower door, walked to a chair by the far window and sat down. I took the companion chair in front of the fireplace, and for some time Tiburon and I sat in silence, watching the flames and listening to the rain patter the exterior stones. The cat had followed me in, and now curled in Tiburon's lap.

"I know what you've come to tell me," the old man said slowly. There was a wheeze in his voice, a faint whistle at the ends of his words.

He continued, dreamily, as if talking to himself. "I've been bound to Krale for so long. At first, he was in my power, and then for many years, I was in his. So much time has passed, and for so little good. Ah, well. His mind is truly broken now. He's passed beyond reason, and no cure will heal him."

"He will die then?" I asked.

Tiburon began to stroke the stump of his left arm, letting his gnarled fingers play over the limb. I hoped he wouldn't begin to pick at his skin. I avoided looking at him directly, but tried to convey, still, my attention to our conversation. I was grateful that his mind seemed clear today, even without the Lightkeep to strengthen him.

"No, child," he replied. "For he cannot die while I live. Long ago I was the master, and in some ways—the ways of magic and blood—my hold over him cannot be broken in life."

"Then he will linger in his current state?" I asked. This seemed awful. And Lights, I couldn't help but think, the logistics...

"Miss Marolaine." His tone was ruminative. "Many's the many." A faint smile raised the corners of his mouth and creased his cheeks. I thought he might be slipping away from me, but he shifted in the chair, causing the cat to open one eye in mild protest.

Tiburon continued. "It's my time to go. Long past time that I leave this realm and put an end to the trouble I started one hundred years ago."

"What will allow you to..." I paused. "To die?"

"I need help to break the spell that holds me in this tower. I need the rings, and I need a Seer or a Lightkeep."

WITHIN MOMENTS OF MY call, both Dase and Kies had returned to the tower. They looked serious. "We heeded your call, Lightholder, as we must," Dase said, speaking her words—as usual—into both the air and my mind simultaneously. "But as you know, we can stay for only a limited time, and take on only those tasks that you yourself cannot perform."

"Are you here again as reflections?" I asked.

"No, my dear, this time we've come in our Lightkeep forms. The poison that pervades this place has ebbed, although it isn't gone. We sensed that our forms would be needed for the tasks that await us. I assume you called us because something has changed."

"Yes," I replied. "Krale is unconscious, nearly dead. But I understand that Krale cannot die while Tiburon lives."

"That's true," said Dase. "And the Senior Guardian wishes to die." Dase tilted her head toward Tiburon. Her words were a statement not a question, and no one responded. Elden rose from his seat by the window and came to stand behind the old man's chair. He placed one large hand on Tiburon's shoulder. Tiburon touched Elden's hand with his clawed fingers, and a tear rolled down the old man's cheek. The room was silent except for the popping of logs in the fireplace.

A few moments passed, then Tiburon wiped his eyes. Responding to a shift in the old man's position, the cat jumped to the floor. Tiburon braced his right hand against the chair and pushed himself slowly to his feet. The smell of his body and clothing was strong, and I felt a wave of pity, despite everything I knew he was responsible for. Elden moved to place a hand under Tiburon's elbow.

Tiburon faced the Lightkeep, with Elden by his side. I stayed seated in my chair.

"Once more, Madam and Sir Light," said Tiburon formally, "I offer my apologies for my past wrongs, and for the wrongs that have been done by those who came after me. Your presence here is more grace than I deserve."

"All humans deserve grace," said Dase quietly. "This realm is a shifting pool of feelings and thoughts and actions, some for good and some for ill, but never doubt that all are a part of the Light."

She moved closer to Kies until their two hovering forms lost individual cohesion and became one shape of light, with the semblance of two focus areas. My eyes—and my limited human mind—still saw them as the motherly Dase and the grumpy Kies, but on some plane I knew they were not that at all. I felt a sense of peace deeper than any I'd ever known, and my consciousness drifted.

I stood on the shore of the lake. Only the lake was not dark, but light. Its surface rippled with waves that moved in all directions, creating a directionless blur of motion. The shore was carpeted in round, flat stones, and between the stones—filling the gaps—were beads of amber and blue. As I watched, the beads began to shimmer and pulse. They lifted from the ground, and each bead assumed the shape of a Lightkeep. The Lightkeep surrounded me, and I lost awareness of my body. I could no longer feel my feet against the stones, or the air on my face. I felt sure that if I were to step forward, to let my skin contact the surface of the lake, I would float away and never return. But if I stepped back...

My thoughts became my own again and I returned to awareness, sucking in a breath. Tiburon was back in his chair. Elden was kneeling, adding a log to the fire and extinguishing an errant spark with the press of a thick fingertip. The cat had taken a seat on the warm stones of the hearth and was watching the flames. Had only minutes passed? I felt disoriented.

Dase moved to my side. "You're alright, my dear," she said soothingly. "You drifted, but only for a moment. You're still the Lightholder, which means you have a sensitivity to shifts in the Light, even if you don't usually notice. Kies and I should have warned you before we reached out to the Assembly that way. We're sorry."

"I don't—"

"You don't need to understand," said Dase. "At least not now. Now we need to help Tiburon find his way."

She moved away from me and back to Tiburon. "In the name of the Light, I ask: Guardian Tiburon, are you prepared to leave this realm behind?"

"Yes." Tiburon's answer was a sigh, a weariness.

"Furthermore," Dase continued, "are you prepared to take Krale with you? I sense there is nothing within him that belongs here in the human realm. He was a proud but fearful boy, an angry young man, and now for many years a man and a mage filled with prejudice and hate. I can only hope that he hasn't influenced too many others, and that his legacy won't be more darkness." She sighed. "He has exceeded his time."

"Yes."

A thought struck me. "Wait," I said, "What about Lorn? Will he die too?"

"That's interesting," said Dase. "I believe Mr. Lorn is connected to Krale through a blood-bind, but the magic is incomplete, distorted. It could be broken, or it could be enhanced. Either decision would affect his fate."

"And if you break the magic, Lorn will live?" I thought about Linnia, sitting silently near her father's bed. I didn't think it was our place to decide how that story should end.

Kies spoke now for the first time. "I could draw out his darkness," he said gruffly, "but I don't know if he would live or die. Depends how much within him is dark."

Dase gave him an approving nod. "Yes, Kies, that's a valuable suggestion and a generous offer. Once that's attended to, we'll return here and release Guardian Tiburon from this tower. Let's proceed, and let's move quickly."

I'D HEARD ABOUT LIGHTKEEPS' ability to draw forth human darkness. It was how they battled opponents, at those rare and unwelcome times when Lightkeep were forced to fight. I knew that the process could leave the human dead if the darkness was too pervasive. But sometimes it offered a new life, a better life in which the positive elements of the person's being had a chance to assert. It could literally be the grace that Dase had spoken of. And for Linnia's sake, I hoped this might be true for Lorn.

Like many things momentous in concept, Kies's task was soon completed, and with far less fanfare than I'd expected. Linnia stayed by her father's side, and I held her hand as we watched. There wasn't much to see though, and Lorn had looked the same before and after: a worn, middle-aged man asleep in a bed.

It was hard to gauge Linnia's emotions, and we hadn't spoken about the events of the morning. I recognized her closed expression and knew she needed time. I wished Master Bowden was here, but comforted myself by knowing that we could soon return to the Peace, where Linnia would have the support of both her aunt and her champion.

Chapter 31

The room was full when Dase and Kies broke the tower spell. Enestria and Elden had come from the kitchen. Linnia had left Lorn–still asleep–and arrived with Laeglin. Only Hollon was missing, staying on duty to guard Krale.

As when Kies drew away Lorn's darkness, the breaking of the spell was underwhelming. In fact, if Dase hadn't announced that it was done, I would not have known.

I stood to the side, holding hands with Linnia and Laeglin. We watched in silence as Tiburon stood, then bowed stiffly to the Lightkeep. Without speaking, the old man shuffled toward the small bathroom at the end of the room. Elden followed.

Enestria inclined her tattooed head toward Dase and Kies, then silently left the room, leaving the door open behind her. I sat down heavily in the companion chair. Linnia moved to the hearth and dropped down gracefully, cross-legged. The cat settled in the girl's lap, making a rough chirping sound that I'd never heard from him. Laeglin moved to the side of my chair and stood with one hand on my shoulder. His thumb rubbed absently at my collarbone. We waited.

Elden emerged first, followed by Tiburon. The change in the old man was shocking. His hair was cut to his shoulders, damp and combed back. His beard was entirely gone, revealing the tender, nicked skin of his wrinkled cheeks and neck. In place of the robe, he was wearing a faded Guardian uniform. The red jacket had an old-fashioned cut, and both the jacket and pants gaped as if they'd once belonged to a much larger man. The uniform boots must have been lost, because Tiburon's feet were shod only in woolen socks.

Still, there was a dignity in the old soldier that was impossible to miss. Laeglin dropped his hand from my shoulder and stood to attention as Tiburon passed. Tiburon nodded to the younger man.

I felt something different though, and I stayed in my chair. Linnia, too, seemed unmoved.

"I'll need the ring," said Tiburon, speaking to Elden. The cat left Linnia and came to sit at Tiburon's feet.

The large man gestured to me, and all heads turned in my direction.

"Yes," I said slowly, "I have them." I suddenly felt the four-ring puzzle where it pressed flat against the side of my breast, still held in place by the fold of the brassiere.

"Good," said Tiburon, "that's very good." He paused, now—at the end of his long life—the center of attention again. "I found the rings and gave them to Elden once, as I'd given him other puzzles over the years. He's a good man and a smart man, but I wasn't sure he could master the rings." Tiburon smiled fondly at Elden, and the quiet man smiled back, shaking his head ruefully.

Tiburon continued. "Then Krale took the rings again and hid them. For years I thought they were lost to me, although I caught glimpses of them sometimes. Glimpses in my mind."

"Well, Marolaine has them now," Dase said firmly, "so all is as it needs to be."

There was an expectant quiet in the room. Dase and Kies moved away from the fireplace, leaving the rest of us in a rough circle. I reached under the neckline of my tunic and drew out the four rings, feeling their smoothness, their symmetry, their connection.

For a moment I held the puzzle in my closed hand. When I opened my fingers, I stared at the rings. It was plain that the second ring–the gold ring–was the one Tiburon needed. *Somehow, I need to separate Tiburon's ring from the other three–the three that have bound him.*

I allowed my vision to blur, and as it did, I glimpsed both the joining and the un-joining of the rings. As if both processes were one and the same. Inevitable. I looked away from my open palm, focusing on the movement of the flames in the hearth. I allowed my hands to move together, and when I looked down, the second ring was separate from the other three. I replaced the three-ring puzzle under my tunic. Without thinking, I slipped the gold ring onto my own finger, then curled my hand around it protectively. It seemed like the right thing to do, although I had no reason for it. I turned back toward the group.

Laeglin's eyes were on me, and I knew he'd been looking at the ring. The tops of his cheeks were flushed, and I felt a matching warmth in my own face.

THE WALK FROM THE TOWER to the lake was too much for Tiburon, and halfway there Elden had picked the old man up and carried him. Now, on the shore, Elden lay him down gently on the smooth, round, gray stones. *Belva's stones.*

The rain had stopped, and the sun shone. Linnia and I sat on the still-damp ground to Tiburon's right, away from his mangled arm. Laeglin had returned to help his brother, in case anything unexpected happened with Krale when Tiburon died. Dase and Kies had said they were not needed for this final passing, although they would return if called. It was just the four of us now.

Elden helped arrange Tiburon's clothing, smoothing the pants, straightening the buttons, and finally removing the socks so that Tiburon's narrow, white, vein-etched feet could dig into the shore. The sun was warm, and the waves that ruffled the distant lake had returned to this shore as well. The old man looked at the sky and smiled.

I looked up too and was surprised to see birds overhead. For a moment–my mind no doubt affected by the strangeness of the day–I thought the sky was filled with Linnia's ceramic birds. Logic re-asserted itself though, and I knew these were seagulls, silhouetted against the descending sun. Belva had talked about them: their crooked wings, their raucous cries, their distinct personalities. I hoped that wherever she was, Belva was enjoying herself.

Tiburon turned to Elden. His bony fingers sought Elden's hand. "I'm ready now," Tiburon said. "Will you please take care of my cat?"

Elden nodded. Then he turned to me, and I came forward to kneel at Tiburon's side. I slid the ring off my finger and held it out to Elden. He shook his head and looked toward Tiburon, who now lay with his eyes closed, the sun making his eyelids glow pink. *So, I'm the one who must help the old man into death. Very well.*

I took a breath. Linnia scooted to my side. She put one arm around my waist, while with the other she touched Tiburon's cheek. Her words were a whisper, but we all heard: "I forgive you for what you started." Tiburon's eyes flicked open and met hers for an instant, before closing again. He nodded, and his thin lips twitched upward.

I eased the gold ring onto Tiburon's finger. Elden leaned forward and placed his large hand on Tiburon's shrunken chest. The big man's voice was low and quiet when he spoke. "Find peace, my friend."

HOLLON ARRIVED AT THE lakeshore a short time later, to find us sitting in a silent row: the large, quiet man; the lady Guardian, now without uniform or weapons; and the young woman whose power could be a new future. We had all removed our shoes and were feeling the stones' warmth under our feet as the seagulls reeled and laughed overhead.

"Sorry to interrupt," said Hollon. We turned but no one rose. "I just wanted to let you know that Krale is dead. I assume he died when the old man did..." Hollon stopped and looked around. I knew he must be wondering where Tiburon's body was, but I was too exhausted to explain.

"Thanks, Hollon," I said.

"And Lorn?" Linnia's voice was small.

"Sorry, love, no change there."

Linnia shrugged, unreadable.

Hollon shifted his feet. It was uncomfortable to stand when others were sitting. "Well," he said, "I'll head back to the house then. Laeglin and I are...well, we're taking care of things there. There's no hurry for you to get back." He nodded awkwardly and moved away, back up the shore.

We sat for another hour, watching the sun sink into the water, leaving behind just purple and orange streaks as the air cooled. I thought about what it meant for my family to have the threat of Krale lifted from their lives. I wondered if Krale had been an isolated point of anger and bigotry, or if there were others like him, maybe others who were worse. I thought about seeing my sisters, my brother-in-law, and my baby nephew at their house in town. I thought about Linnia and Lorn, and the journey ahead if daughter and father chose to be a family again. I thought about my mother and the time I'd wasted being angry with her when I might have focused on the good. I thought of my life at the Peace and all that it had given me. I thought about my friends. I thought about Laeglin and our future. I thought about my future.

I don't know, of course, what Linnia and Elden thought about as the day faded into night. I do know that somewhere along the way, Linnia lay her head in my lap and slept.

Chapter 32

The following morning was busy for everyone. Even as a child, I preferred to do the worst first, so I was glad when Elden and Hollon offered to join me at daybreak to begin the burials for Krale and Valek. None of us were sure of the legalities, but Krale's body had started to decay as soon as he died, and we were all anxious to complete this task.

While we worked, Laeglin took over the kitchen, freeing Enestria and Linnia to clean and attend to Lorn and Stelan. Lorn was still asleep, but Enestria said his color had improved, and we took this as a hopeful sign. Stelan was awake, emerging from the spell that had restrained him for the past few weeks. Linnia reported to me that the Chancellor's son was cute, for an older man. I refrained from saying he was barely thirty.

At mid-morning, we all met for a breakfast of cheese, bread, pickles, and hard-cooked eggs. Then I wrote letters to the Peace and the Chancellor, while Laeglin and Enestria washed dishes. Linnia and Hollon prepared for a ride to the nearest letter post. As Lorn had told me in the library, the mansion's stables held Valek's horse and two others. Linnia had been satisfied with their care, despite the crumbling state of the stable building itself. Apparently Lorn—and Elden in his absence—shared Linnia's appreciation for horses.

I hadn't seen Laeglin for most of the morning, and I happily accepted his suggestion that we take a walk along the lake once the chores were done and Linnia and Hollon were off on their errand.

The lake had formed the background to my days at the mansion, but it had always been a dark background, a brooding presence. I wanted to explore the wooded side of the lake, away from the path Valek had used when he brought me here. It was an unusually mild day, and sunshine, birdsong, and waves all seemed like a lake as it should be.

We walked quietly at first, our hands brushing together but our thoughts separate. The shore was covered in flat stones, and as we rounded the bend out of sight of the mansion, it became littered with driftwood, larger boulders, and occasional downed trees. It felt wonderful to use my muscles again, climbing over trunks and jumping between rocks to avoid pockets of water. The wind blew my hair across my face, and the sun was warm. We might have been just two young people enjoying a hike on a spring day.

Halfway back we stopped and sat on a weathered bench set back from the water. Our fingers intertwined on the wood between us, and I found myself aware of Laeglin's closeness as I hadn't been during our walk.

"How are you?" he asked quietly.

I'd always found this a hard question, in the way it both invited and resisted honesty.

I shrugged. "I'm not sure what to say, really. I'm glad that Krale is dead, but also that I didn't have to kill him, if that's what you mean. I'm glad he and Valek are no longer a threat to my family."

"I'm sure you're looking forward to seeing them. Your family."

I nodded. "Yes. I'd like to meet the new baby, and I want to thank Obrin for the bracelet." I fingered the amber beads around my wrist. "He might not have known, but he gave me the means to break some of the darkness here. I'm looking forward to seeing them all, and I'm hoping Captain Matteo will give me a few extra days before I return to duty."

"I'm sure he will."

"How about you?" I asked. "Will you take any time off?" I was thinking about Hollon but wasn't sure how to raise the subject.

"Probably not. I've been busy at the Apprentices' Academy, you know, since Master Bowden was hurt. I've taken on some of his classes, working with the boys, and he's been mentoring me. I really like it."

"I've heard that you're doing a great job," I said warmly. "And Master Bowden would never give you those responsibilities if he didn't think you were ready. I'm so proud of you." Laeglin smiled and squeezed my fingers.

"I hope maybe you'll help me with the girls' class," he said, "once everything settles down. So far, it's just Linnia and her friend Wyst, but a couple of the boys in the Academy have sisters who might be interested. Master Bowden thinks it could really grow."

I was quiet. Laeglin shifted to face me on the bench. "You're so amazing," he said, brushing hair out of my eyes and leaning closer. "I missed you while you were in town, and I'm sorry it took us so long to get here and help you."

My eyes traced the cut on his lower lip.

When I stayed quiet, Laeglin touched my arm. "What's on your mind, Mar?"

"I don't know," I said slowly. "Being away, everything that's happened. I plan to go back—of course I do—but everything just feels different now. I know that sounds silly."

"No, it's not silly, it's normal. After everything you've been through, it's normal to feel unsettled. It's probably true for Linnia, too," said Laeglin, "now that she's found her father again. Of course, there's no way to know what he'll be like when he wakes up. Assuming he ever does."

"Matron always said Lorn was no good. Back when he was married to Matron's sister, when they were young. I've been thinking that Lorn might even have been the reason Krale knew about Linnia and her sister Prin in the first place."

"I wondered about that too. And if Lorn did tell Krale about his daughters, could Linnia ever forgive him for that betrayal?"

"I don't know. I truly don't."

"Then again," Laeglin continued, "Lorn might be different now, after what Kies did. I'm not sure how it works or what Lorn will remember. Matron might even feel responsible for him, for Linnia's sake. Do you think he might come back to the Peace to recover?"

"I hadn't thought about that," I said. "That would sure be complicated. I don't even know how Linnia feels about him, or if she would want that."

"Yeah." We were both quiet, and I guessed we were thinking about how complicated the past could be. How it twines around the present, like an old cat weaving around your legs. Hard to dislodge and threatening to trip you up at each step.

"Did you know I offered Linnia the second bird?" I asked. "The one I found in the storage room."

"No, but I wondered what you'd do with it. Doesn't seem to be much point in taking it back to Nod now. Although it might be valuable, or even powerful, if you can believe Nod. What did Linnia say?"

"She said she didn't want it. She said that a dyad pair only has one token, and that her own bird–the original bird–will always be the token she shared with her sister. She was pretty adamant about it."

"So, what will you do with it?"

"I'm really not sure." We fell silent again and I listened to waves lapping the shore. The air smelled like water.

Laeglin broke the silence with a change of subject. "I wonder what Elden and Enestria will do next. Stelan will go back to town soon, and the rest of us back to the Peace, but I don't know if they have any place to go."

"Enestria told me that the mansion was owned by Tiburon. And since he has no living descendants to inherit it, I'd imagine it might be tied up in bureaucracy for quite a while."

"Is Chancellor Axelle the administrator here in Lakelands?"

"Hmm. I don't know. But even if she isn't, she might be able to help. It would be nice if Elden and Enestria could stay on if they wanted to. Maybe serve as caretakers for a while, until everyone figures out what to do with this place."

"Watch out," said Laeglin with a smile, "If the Chancellor and Prefect Tal get to scheming, this estate could end up as the Peace's new annex." He stretched his legs out in front of him.

"What do you mean?"

"You know I've been serving as Tal's assistant since last fall"—I nodded–"well, there's nothing official, but Tal and the rest of the leaders' group have been talking about finding a second location. It seems we're outgrowing the Peace's library and archive spaces, plus Bowden and the Captain would like some new training facilities."

"I didn't know that."

"You've been busy."

Shaking my head with a smile, I stood up and walked to the edge of the water. I scanned the ground until I found a hand-sized flat stone. I'd seen Hollon do this yesterday. I slung the stone side-arm, but it sliced into the water and went immediately under with a slurping sound. Laeglin laughed and joined me, picking up his own stone. Like his brother, he threw it so that it skimmed over the surface, jumping effortlessly again and again until it finally disappeared in a circle of ripples.

"No fair!" I said, laughing. "Let me try again!"

We skipped stones for a few minutes, then I sat down on the beach, enjoying the sun on my head and contemplating taking my shoes off. Laeglin came and sat beside me, and we stared out across the lake together.

Laeglin scooted closer and put his arm around me. I felt his warmth and leaned my head against his shoulder. When I looked up, his eyes were on my face. I turned toward him, and he lowered his head to kiss me, first gently then with more energy. I could feel the roughness of his split lip, but it didn't distract me for long. I'd missed our closeness and the way being together could temporarily erase all cares.

When we pulled apart, Laeglin held my gaze. "What about us, Marolaine?" His voice was quiet, and I could hear the hesitation. "Maybe this isn't the right time, with everything that's happened, but I can't stop thinking about you and wondering what our future might be. If we have a future together."

I dropped my eyes from his and turned toward the lake. I felt a slight shift in his body, but I knew he was waiting for my answer, giving me time. This was one of those moments that mattered, and I felt desperately afraid that I would say the wrong thing.

I now knew without question that I loved Laeglin. This past week had shown me that. I'd never said those words aloud, and part of me knew that they were all that he needed to hear. But I hesitated. Those words–while true–were only part of the answer to the question Laeglin was asking, and I didn't want to give him only part of an answer.

I picked up a stone at random–smooth and warm from the sun–and tossed it lightly. It hit the surface of the water with a flat plunk. I pressed my knee against his. *Is there any such thing as a marveling that can help you find the right words at the right time?*

"I've been thinking a lot about that too," I said slowly. "I–"

My words were interrupted by the sound of a female voice calling my name. Laeglin and I turned toward the mansion and saw Linnia approaching, waving her hand.

"I'm sorry to bother you," she said when she got closer, "but, Marolaine, Kies arrived unexpectedly and said he needed to talk to you. He seemed grumpier than usual, so I offered to come and find you."

"What does he want? Is everything alright at the Peace?"

"I think so, but I'm really not sure. You know how Kies is. I didn't want to interrupt you, but I thought you might want to talk to him."

Laeglin and I had both gotten to our feet as Linnia approached, but I felt the weight of our unfinished conversation in the air between us. I reached for his hand, and we walked with Linnia back to the mansion, our fingers entwined.

Chapter 33

I found Hollon in the stables, inside the stall with the gray mare. He was brushing the horse with a flat, round comb and whistling under his breath. Although the stables were old, the stall itself was clean, with fresh straw on the floor and a warm animal smell. The waning sun shone through a window, catching dust in its slant and bringing a glow to the dim space.

Along the wall beyond the stall, barn swallow droppings marked the spots where mud nests clung to a rafter above. I wondered if the steely blue birds were back yet from their winter migrations. I thought about seeing swallows when I walked past the old granary in town with my father, and I felt peaceful.

"Sorry to disturb you," I said when Hollon turned around. "Linnia said you might still be out here. How was your afternoon?"

We chatted for a few minutes about his ride with Linnia to post the letters, then Hollon offered me the comb and showed me how to stroke in the direction of the horse's hair. At first, I was tentative, but after a few minutes, I began to enjoy the rhythm. The horse shifted her weight lazily from one back foot to the other, while Hollon leaned against the wall beside me. If a kiss was one way to escape the world, it seemed that I had just found another.

"I had a message from Kies this afternoon," I said into the easy silence, "right after Laeglin and I got back from the lake. That's why I wanted to talk to you, in fact. Kies is one of the Lightkeep who were here yesterday." I ran the comb along the horse's back, then reduced the pressure as I moved the comb over the horse's hip. Hollon had instructed me to be gentle over bony areas, and to avoid the horse's face and legs altogether.

"Laeglin tried to explain the Lightkeep to me one night while we were camping," said Hollon, "but I don't think I got it. Mystical creatures who balance the light and dark of the world? Oh, and who also take care of old books and sometimes fight?" He raised his eyebrows. His eyes were shadowed in the dim light, but I could see the quirk of his lips.

"I know," I smiled. "It sounds strange when you say it like that. I've been around the Lightkeep for years at the Peace, and even though I'm sworn to their protection, they're still a mystery to me too."

"Kies seems to like you."

"Well, maybe in his own way he does. I hope so, anyway, because I like him."

"What was the message about?"

"It was brief, but Kies said he wants me to carry out an errand for him. He wants me to deliver a letter of sorts to a woman who lives on the coast. It's more than a letter really, it's a message that must remain fully secret, even from me. It's a long story...But anyway, I need to travel to a small village south of Burns. It's called Ajorica. Have you heard of it?"

"Yeah, I have. I know some people in that area. I moved around over the years, and I spent some time along the coast when I was younger."

"Oh. Well, maybe that's why Dase suggested that you should come with me."

"Me?"

"Yes." We were both silent. The horse turned her head to see why I'd stopped combing. Her velvet-soft lips explored my hand, and

I was sorry not to have an apple to offer. I stroked her neck and returned to combing.

"And when a Lightkeep suggests something," I continued, "there's usually a good reason to do it, even if we humans don't know it right away. So, what do you think, Hollon, do you want to come with me? I think it'll take about a week to get there, and I'm not sure how long I'll stay. I won't leave for Ajorica right away though. I'm planning to spend a few days in Clanstin with my family first. That would give you time to make any plans you need to. If you decide to come."

"I wouldn't need much time. And I'd like to see the coast again and talk to one or two people I should have talked to years ago." I was used to Hollon's reserve, and I didn't ask for details. There'd be plenty of time if we had weeks to spend together.

"But Marolaine," he continued, "I'm not sure why you'd want to travel with me instead of Laeglin. Or one of your other capable and respectable friends. In fact, if I were you, I'd take that woman with the head tattoos. Now there's someone who'd be useful in a tight spot." He made a low whistling sound, and I laughed.

I turned, and he gave me his crooked half-smile. He looked tired despite the smile, and I wondered about the toll these past days had taken on him. *And now I'm asking him this favor. Just when he and Laeglin might be starting to become friends again.*

"And we both know," he added, "that I'm not great company. So frankly, I don't know what recommends me, other than your friend, the Lightkeep."

"Well, I do trust Dase. Plus, I like you and I think we'd get along," I said, moving to lean against the worn stone wall beside him and nudging his shoulder, "and it will be safer for me to travel with someone. That's just sensible. As for Laeglin, I know he'd come if I asked, it's just that..." I trailed off.

Hollon shifted but didn't look at me. "It sounds complicated, and I'm not one to pry," he said quietly. "You can tell me another time."

"Thanks." I felt miserably conflicted. I loved Laeglin, and yet our lives seemed to be heading in different directions. This time away, at the request of a Lightkeep whom I was sworn to serve, seemed like an opportunity to make decisions about my future that I just couldn't make back at the Peace.

"I'm willing to join you," said Hollon, "but I'm not sure how Laeglin will feel about it. He's my brother, and I think I should talk to him before we make any decisions."

"That's alright, Hollon, I need to talk to him too. I'll do it tonight."

SUPPER THAT EVENING was late but festive, and I credited Linnia. She had returned from the letter post with her humor restored. Or at least it seemed that way. We are all, of course, capable of deception, but I hoped her good spirits were genuine.

Linnia and Enestria found a beautiful linen tablecloth and matching napkins, and they worked together to set the battered kitchen table as if for a feast. There was a coziness to the warm kitchen that we all felt, and a camaraderie to preparing and serving a meal together. Laeglin was a good cook, and he and Elden had an easy companionship as they peeled vegetables, boiled stock, and shaped dinner rolls into knots. Elden had baked the apple pies last night, and they sat on the sideboard, ready for dessert.

Linnia wanted the ladies to dress for supper, but that proved hard to manage. Enestria refused outright, earning herself a rough but affectionate shove from Linnia. Enestria did bring forth an embroidered scarf though, which Linnia happily draped around her own shoulders. Linnia decided that I should wear my hair down–which I never did–and I should put hers up. However, after many complicated instructions involving braids and twists, she finally gave up on me in exasperation.

"It's like you're not a proper woman at all," she said, rolling her eyes playfully.

"On behalf of all men," Hollon called gallantly, from across the room, "I must disagree." He had been reserved all evening, although he'd brought in firewood and helped Stelan, the Chancellor's son, settle in a chair by the cookstove. I hoped he wasn't regretting his willingness to travel to Ajorica with me.

"Well thank you, Hollon," I said, blushing and fumbling to get a different grip on the comb.

To my surprise, Elden stepped forward and gently removed the comb from my hand. Linnia raised her eyebrows but sat still while the large man stood behind her chair, deftly parting and twisting and curling. It turned out that he was good not only at peeling apples, but also at styling the hair of irritating adolescent girls. Who knew?

While the rolls baked and everyone except Enestria and Linnia sipped brandy, I drew Laeglin aside.

"I wanted to talk to you privately," I said, taking his hand and leading him into the foyer, "but it's been a busy afternoon. I...well..." *Lights, this never seems to get any easier.*

"You sound worried, Mar. What's on your mind?" Laeglin leaned against the wall, facing me. His body was relaxed, but his gaze was attentive. I felt awkward and had to resist the urge to shuffle my feet or give way to some other childish fidget. *It would be easier if we were sitting down. Is it too late to ask him to sit?*

"I didn't expect this," I said slowly, "but it turns out I'm not going to return to the Peace right away. Kies has a message–kind of a Lightkeep letter I guess you could say–that he wants delivered to Sola Pellaqua. She's staying with friends out near the coast. The message needs to be delivered in person, and Kies has asked me to take it there. I don't fully understand it myself..." I trailed off, feeling like I was babbling.

"This was what Kies wanted to talk to you about, when Linnia called us back from the lake?" Laeglin asked.

"Yes," I said. "I'm sorry I didn't have a chance before now to tell you. Everything with the Lightkeep is a little unconventional." I offered a tentative smile, and to my relief, Laeglin reached out and took my hand.

"Well," he said, "it's sudden, but I don't think Kies would ask you unless it was important. Especially now, after everything you've been through here." Laeglin turned my hand palm-up and kissed the pale circular mark in its center. His lips filled my palm with soft warmth and a shiver went through me.

"I'm not sure about the errand," he continued, "but I understand why they trust you to do it, especially if it's important. And it's not just because you're the Lightholder. People count on you, Marolaine. You know that, don't you?"

It felt strange to hear those words: they made me embarrassed, and proud, and unsure, all at once. I dropped my eyes.

Laeglin squeezed my hand. "And don't worry," he said, "you might not feel like taking a trip when there's so much to do, but I'm sure Captain Matteo will make arrangements for the time."

Relief filled me, then quickly drained away as I realized that he didn't understand. *He thinks I don't want to go, but he also thinks I'm asking him to come with me.*

Uncertainty entered his eyes at the same moment I began to fumble with an explanation. "I'm sorry, Laeglin. I would naturally ask you to come with me, but Kies said that Dase suggested I should travel with Hollon. Apparently, your brother knows that part of the realm and wants to visit some people he knows near Ajorica. We talked about it just before supper and he's willing to come, as long as..." I paused. *Hollon won't come unless Laeglin agrees, although I know he didn't quite want to say that to me. Kind of annoying, but also sweet, I suppose.*

I continued. "Hollon wanted to ask you himself, but I told him I'd talk to you tonight."

I put my hand on Laeglin's cheek, feeling the prickles of evening stubble.

"I want to make sure I understand this..." He stopped, not meeting my gaze. I lowered my hand. "Have you decided...Marolaine, it's your own choice, of course it is. But if you're leaving the Peace, or leaving me, you can say that. We're friends, and we always have been. You should just tell me the truth." His voice was thick, and my eyes and nose prickled in response.

"I'm honestly not sure, Laeglin. If not for Kies, I planned to return to the Peace in a few days, after I visited my sisters. I truly did. But now, well, this seems like an opportunity to travel and to think about what I want to do next. I've never even seen the coast. I've never been anywhere other than Clanstin and the Peace. And to be honest, I've heard a lot about Sola. I met her briefly when she was here, but I'm looking forward to getting to know her better while I'm there." I squeezed my arms around my chest and waited. A minute passed.

"I'm sure you'll like her," Laeglin offered finally. There was another long pause and we listened to the sounds of the others, laughing and clattering in the kitchen behind us.

Laeglin took a breath. I dropped my arms to my sides, although I missed their comfort immediately.

"Marolaine," he said slowly, "I think you know this already, but my life is at the Peace. I feel like I've found my place there, and I have a lot to learn and do if I'm planning to become an instructor." His eyes were locked on mine, dark and steady.

"I know—"

"Wait, Mar. Please, let me finish."

I nodded. I felt oddly calm.

"What I mean is that I've found the life and the work that makes me fulfilled, at least for now. I get to spend my days with people I like and respect. I might even have a chance to make amends with Hollon. I love you, and I'd be the happiest man alive if you wanted to stay with me at the Peace. But I don't think that's your path. Or at least, I don't think you know what your path is yet."

"I love you, too." I spoke quietly.

"I know you do. We've been friends for a long time, which is why I want to be honest with you. I think you should go to Ajorica. By yourself, or with my brother, whatever you want. And you should meet Sola Pellaqua, and see the ocean, and have a great time, and think about what you really want to do. Not what you wanted when you were twelve. Not what you think other people want from you. But what you truly want for yourself."

This was a long speech, and Laeglin suddenly looked tired. I stepped forward and put my arms around him. We stood in silence, and I could feel the beating of his heart and his breath against my skin.

"I don't want to lose you," I said in a muffled voice.

"You won't lose me. Impossible."

"Oh, Laeglin..."

"Life is long, Marolaine. I'll miss you—you know that— but I think it's a good idea to take the opportunities that come along. It's one of the few things I can honestly say I learned from my father." We parted slightly, and he leaned down and kissed me gently.

"Oh," he said, "And I meant to give you this when we were down by the shore today." He reached into his pocket. I remembered the way he'd looked at the ring on my finger when we were in the tower with Tiburon. I felt a pinch of alarm, even though I understood that he had just given me my freedom.

Instead of a ring, Laeglin pulled a stone from his pocket. It was a flat, gray lake stone with a notch that made it look like a heart. It was streaked with quartz. In fact, it was Belva's stone, the stone that had been in my pocket on my last night at Belva's house! I hadn't seen it since arriving at the mansion, and now this handsome man with the steady eyes was holding it out to me. My chest felt tight.

"I found it on the shore," Laeglin explained. "On the first night, when Hollon and I came close to the mansion to check the windows and doors. I don't know why, but it caught my eye when we were walking back to our camp. I picked it up because I thought you might like it."

The stone was warm from his hand as I slipped it back into my pocket.

Epilogue: Two months later

Hollon found Master Supervisor Bowden in one of the small training rooms in the Guards' complex. The room was recently swept, and bare except for two chairs and a water pitcher in the corner, a stack of folded mats, and the rays of sun that entered through a single clerestory window high on the wall. Master Bowden sat in one of the chairs. His training clothes were plain, but something in his manner marked him as a Senior Guard.

The younger man was nervous. He'd known he would be, and so he'd rehearsed what he would say. After introducing himself and greeting Bowden, Hollon launched into his speech. Bowden listened without comment. When Hollon finished, the older man invited him to sit and poured him a glass of water.

"Thank you, Hollon, for explaining what happened back then," said Bowden, "and for your apology. I'd guessed at some of it, but at the time I chose not to pry into the matter more than was necessary. Laeglin was young, but he wanted to keep the details to himself, and I respected that. He was loyal to you."

Hollon understood that this was not a reprimand, but he still felt wary. He nodded. "Yes," he said, "he was always a good brother. Better than I deserved."

"Have you seen him since you returned from the coast?"

"We met last night in town for a drink. I told him I'd be coming here today to talk to you." Hollon took a gulp of the water. Suddenly–and for no reason that he could explain– he badly wanted this upright, compassionate soldier to understand. "I'm sorry," Hollon continued, "I wanted to make things right, as best I could. I should have done it years ago—I only hope my stupidity hasn't caused too much trouble for Laeglin."

Bowden chuckled, and some of Hollon's tension eased. "Well, as they say," said Bowden, "you can't expect old heads on young shoulders. I've worked with young men long enough to know the truth of that."

There was a pause, and then Bowden added, "I lost my own brother a long time ago, during the siege of Burns. I think of him often, and I miss the friendship we might have had if we'd been able to grow old together. I'm glad to know that you and Laeglin are finding your way again, Hollon. And I'll do what I can to help."

"Laeglin is already grateful to you," Hollon said, his voice stiff with emotions held back. "He feels you gave him a break when you didn't need to."

"Yes, I know he thinks that," said Bowden slowly. "Though, to be honest with you, I hope in time he'll let go of the obligation he feels toward me. He's becoming a fine teacher in his own right, and an asset to the Academy—has he mentioned it?"

"Yeah," said Hollon, "but just a little. He said he's starting to teach some of the apprentices at the school. He thought he'd be no good, but I'm not surprised that he is."

"Who's no good?"

The interruption came from the doorway, and the two men turned to see Linnia. She was dressed in training clothes, and her hair was pulled back tightly. A worn set of sparring leathers hung around her neck on a strap.

"I'm here for my lesson with Master Bowden," she said to Hollon. "I wasn't expecting to see you. Does this mean Marolaine is back?" She sounded excited.

"Yes, she is," smiled Hollon. "We got to Clanstin two days ago, and she's there now. It was quite a trip and I'm sure she'll have a lot to tell you about. Oh, and it's nice to see you too, Linnia."

"You know I'm only kidding," laughed Linnia, coming into the room and wrapping her thin arms around Hollon's waist. "I'm happy to see you, you know I am. Marolaine has written me a few letters, but I didn't know you were on your way back." She paused, and a new expression crossed her face. "She's been writing to Laeglin, too, while she was away."

Hollon nodded and glanced at Master Bowden, who was smiling faintly. "Yes, I believe she has," said Hollon with amusement, "although Marolaine would be the first to say she's not much of a letter writer."

"She doesn't give herself enough credit," said Linnia with a shrug. "So, Hollon, how long will you stay?"

"I've got permission for one night in Matron Rosevale's guest house."

"You mean Auntie knew you were coming, and she didn't tell me?" Linnia gave a mock pout. She was at the age when some girls are already women, some are still girls, but most are caught between.

"So, I guess you'll meet Lorn while you're here?" she continued with a shift in her tone. "You remember that he came here after the mansion, to recover for a while since he had no place else to go."

"Yes," said Hollon, "And I heard from Laeglin that Lorn was doing better. That's good news. I'd be glad to meet him."

Hollon wasn't sure how much had been shared with Linnia, since he'd been away himself. But last night Laeglin had given him a letter from Matron Rosevale, asking if Hollon would be willing to have Linnia's father accompany him when Hollon returned to town. Apparently Lorn's strength was still limited, and Hollon could help with travel bags and logistics. Something in Matron's careful words had made Hollon wonder if the man also suffered from fear. It wouldn't be surprising after what he'd been through with Krale.

Hollon knew what it was to have no money and no friend to ask for help or company. He didn't mind carrying a few bags, and he'd said yes when he saw Matron this morning.

No doubt Linnia would hear of this plan soon enough, if she didn't already know. "Actually," Hollon said, "Your father plans to travel back to town with me when I leave tomorrow. Matron arranged for him to rent a room, and he's going to meet Dr. Li. Apparently your aunt thinks they might be of some mutual benefit to each other." He raised his eyebrows, letting Linnia know this was not a plan of his making.

Linnia was quiet. In repose, her features had an adult seriousness. Both men saw the woman she was becoming, a person of strength to match her spirit.

Hollon glanced at Bowden, looking for a cue. Master Bowden was easy to talk to, but he wasn't a man who spoke just to fill other men's spaces. The Senior Guard contemplated the patterns of sunlight that fell to the floor and thought about his brother, the brave boy of a past that was gone. Hollon took another sip of water as Linnia remained standing, silent.

"Well," Linnia said finally, "I heard Dr. Li has a cute little dog now. Maybe I'll get a chance to see her the next time I visit town." With that, she unfolded a mat from the stack, spread it on the floor, and seated herself in a patch of light.

The End

Don't miss out!

Visit the website below and you can sign up to receive emails whenever Sunny R. Winstead publishes a new book. There's no charge and no obligation.

https://books2read.com/r/B-A-JDGCB-BUPAD

BOOKS 2 READ

Connecting independent readers to independent writers.

About the Author

Sunny Winstead is an occupational therapy professor, mother, and wife. She is the author of one previous novel in the Realm of Light series, The Lady Guardian. Sunny lives with her family in New York and "commutes" remotely to her job in Boston.

Read more at https://sunnyrwinstead.carrd.co/.